Praise for *Four Hands* and Paco Ignacio Taibo II

"An intellectual with a love for humanity, popular culture, good jokes, and the romantic history of the left. . . . Mr. Taibo's novel soars, in its best moments, with conviction, fraternal love, and the old-fashioned lyrical idealism of lost leftist causes."

—*The New York Times Book Review*

"A political thriller that sometimes resembles a crazy mosaic fashioned out of the shards of shattered novels—E. L. Doctorow's *Ragtime*, Robert Stone's *Dog Soldiers*, and, above all, the half-plausible, half-paranoid works of Richard Condon. . . . A marvelous story."

—*Los Angeles Times*

"The novel . . . resembles Joseph Heller's *Catch-22*. Taibo mercilessly lampoons American imperialism, with all its dirty tricks; the comedic pace rarely slows. . . . All the while the work sustains diverse, bizarre, and ultimately believable characters."

—*Kirkus Reviews*

"A virtuoso blend of satiric comedy, international intrigue, and revisionist history . . . one of Latin America's most entertaining authors."

—*San Antonio Express-News*

"A hilariously disorienting tale. . . . Taibo's cleverly fractured yet unmistakably pointed plot . . . ranges all over the map, and we follow, curious and entertained."

—*Booklist*

"Taibo's prose is rich in metaphor, and his confident, insightful storytelling makes the individual pieces of his novel intriguing. . . . Dail's translation does fine justice to the author's colorful, virtuosic narrative."

—*Publishers Weekly*

"Audacious. . . . Taibo takes as his models this time E. L. Doctorow and especially John Dos Passos."

—*New York Newsday*

FOUR

PACO IGNACIO TAIBO II

HANDS

TRANSLATED BY LAURA C. DAIL

PICADOR USA ❧ NEW YORK

DESIGN BY JUDITH A. STAGNITTO

Library of Congress Cataloging-in-Publication Data

Taibo, Paco Ignacio.
    [Cuatro manos. English]
    Four hands / Paco Ignacio Taibo II; translated by Laura C. Dail.
       p.   cm.
    ISBN 0-312-13079-1
    I. Title.
    PQ7298.3.A58C8313   1995
    863—dc20   95-2838
                                                CIP

First Picador USA Edition: July 1995

10 9 8 7 6 5 4 3 2 1

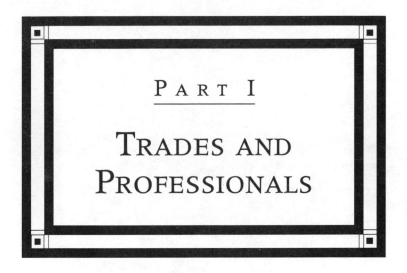

PART I

TRADES AND PROFESSIONALS

STAN IN PARRAL

July 19, 1923, around five-thirty in the afternoon, a man made his way across the international bridge that separated El Paso (Texas) from Juárez (Chihuahua). It was hot. Four carts transporting barbed wire into Mexico had filled the air with dust. From his office, the Mexican customs officer absently contemplated the skinny man, dressed in gray, wearing a black derby and carrying a shabby leather bag, who was approaching him. He didn't find the man important in the least and went back to submerge himself in the book of poems by Rubén Darío that he was reading conscientiously. He was trying to memorize a poem so that he could recite it later, sprawled out on cushions with a French whore he frequented who liked such things.

The gawky man, who seemed to be walking on clouds of cotton, reached the Mexican customs officer's desk and deposited his bag on the counter gently, as if not wanting to get mixed up in anyone's life, perhaps not even his own. The customs officer lifted his head, filled with images of acanthus flowers and brilliantly feathered birds, and carefully observed the gringo. He recognized the face. Someone who crossed the border frequently? A merchant? No, that wasn't it. An extremely pale face, ears wide apart, a mouth that begged a smile that never came, small flustered eyes. It all made you want to protect him, made you want to invite him to recite poetry in a duet with you.

The skinny gringo paid no attention to the Mexican official who was sizing him up. The official switched to his professional mode and opened the man's bag: eight bottles of Dutch gin meticulously packed, nothing else. Not even a pair of socks or underwear. This crazy low-life gringo was planning to piss himself away. He ought to send the no-good back to his own turf. But he couldn't quite work up a nationalist rage. The gringo was a lovelorn guy just like himself, he decided, another fool driven crazy by his old lady. And he felt a vast, bursting solidarity growing inside him. He closed the bag and made his white chalk mark, the signal to let the traveler pass freely.

Suitcase in hand, the gringo entered Mexico, without having uttered a single word. The customs official saw him fading away through the dusty streets of Juárez, and as the Mexican went back to immerse himself in his book, he remembered why the face of the skinny, big-eared man was familiar. Even his name popped into his head: Stan Laurel, the guy in the movies that played the Trinidad Theatre, the comedian. The customs man followed Stan with his eyes and lost him around a corner.

Stan roamed around the city erratically, until he stumbled upon the entrance to the train station.

"Where to?" the ticket seller asked.

"South, anywhere."

"Just south, pal?"

Stan shrugged.

"You like Parral, buddy?"

Stan shrugged again.

"The train for Parral leaves at eight tonight and arrives at seven in the morning. It's a freight with two passenger cars."

An instant later, suitcase in hand, Stan plopped onto a green metal bench outside the Juárez train station, and he sat there, looking at the storage bins and the street vendors, and occasionally looking into himself.

He came up with several quite evident truths. Things with Mae couldn't continue this way. They were destroying each other. Doing it calmly, as though in this business of mutual destruction neither one was in the slightest hurry. They hurt each other and poked each other's open wounds with anything—a toothpick, a fork, a kitchen knife—depending on the time and their moods; there were moments now when they didn't do it furiously, but with simple curiosity, as if testing the limits of suffering, the limits of boredom. Mae had her reasons. She thought he was throwing her overboard, casting her aside to pursue his career. Twenty-five films playing the same role in a single year. After they'd spent so many mornings waking up, fleeing from hotel clerks demanding payment, stomachs as empty as the theaters where they played, sad drunken binges. And now each to his and her own luck. But that wasn't it. John was right. She was a character actress, not a comedian, and he couldn't keep pulling her down his path, she had to find her own or they were both going to drown, end up back on the same vaudeville tours in the lost towns of the Midwest.

Stan cries. He doesn't know whether it's the dust in the air or Mae Dahlberg, this woman with whom he is and is not in love, the singer, dancer, circus trapeze artist, the Australian he married four years ago in New York.

On July 20, 1923, at seven-thirty in the morning, Stan Laurel crossed Juárez Plaza in Parral and entered the Neptune Hotel. For two pesos he got a room that normally went for 1.20. He went in: a bed with a metal headboard, a tiny desk against the window, a striped rug on the floor. He put his bag on the desk and opened it.

The sun streamed through the window. He took out the bottles of Bols and arranged them in a straight line. He opened the first one. Below the window a man kept wiping sweat from his face with a red rag. It was a strange gesture, more a signal. Stan lifted the bottle to his lips and in a single swig drank a quarter of its contents. He tossed his head, cleared his throat. The sun glinting off metal a hundred yards away distracted him. He looked carefully. Gabino Barreda Street, which ran in front of the hotel, ended with two houses set against the river. The reflection had come from there. A gun? Several guns. There were armed men in the windows of the houses. What was going on?

A Dodge car with seven men passed the front door of the hotel. The nine soldiers under cover behind the doors and windows of Numbers 7 and 9, Gabino Barreda Street, saw the signal by the man with the red rag. They were armed with 30-30 and 30-40 rifles, Winchester automatics and .45 pistols. Once the car was twenty yards from the pair of houses, doors and windows swung open and a shower of bullets began to rain down. The first discharge of explosives destroyed the windshield and instantly killed Rosalio, who'd been hanging on to the outside of the car, about to jump. He fell to the road. The shots flung Colonel Trillo, who was sitting by the driver, against the window. His body contorted horribly, his hands reached for the floor. The soldiers kept firing. The driver, wounded by multiple bullets, shot out of the car like a shuttlecock and the Dodge exploded against a tree a few yards from the houses where the gunfire originated.

When the soldiers' rifles were empty, they continued firing with pistols. The response from the backseat of the car was timid. One of the men shooting from the houses fell dead, sliding out a window. Two passengers ran out of the car, trying to flee under a hailstorm of bullets. They were both wounded; one would die a week later, the other would lose his arm.

In less than a minute, two hundred bullets had been fired at the Dodge car with Chihuahua plates. Suddenly, silence. Nobody moved inside the car. Three of the soldiers approached and fired their automatics over the inert bodies. The assassins slowly unmasked, got their horses out of the stalls and mounted. A man approached them and shelled out three hundred pesos a head. They left Parral at a trot, peacefully.

From the window Stan watched them leave, his eyes wide open and red. He couldn't move. One of his hands tried to grasp the neck of the bottle.

A boy ran toward the car and looked at the corpses.

"They killed Pancho Villa!" he screamed.

The scream broke Stan's trance and he managed to lift the gin to his lips. He emptied the bottle. It was 8:02 in the morning, July 20, 1923.

JOURNALISTS' STORIES

(G R E G   S P E A K S)

Wen I saw Julio from a distance, I knew he was trying to trick the customs official. He put on the pale face of a Buster Keaton, not the innocent look of a Stan Laurel. Julio had a way of affecting expressions typical of the actors in Hal Roach comedies. He had been seen with that imperturbable, distant Keaton look of innocence on a multitude of borders. I put my glasses back on and the reality of the Pan Am waiting room in the Los Angeles airport took form around me. The customs official, a hefty Asian man, was asking Julio the usual questions. Any fruit? Food? To which old Fatso answered with all his cynical confidence. Finally he smiled when the Jap waved him along.

"You crazy, stupid tub," I said to myself, "I love you."

His English was as primitive as ever. It was as though he'd learned it using a method designed by Tarzan with the assistance of Eric von Stroheim.

My ribs almost broke in Julio's brutal embrace.

In this country where privacy, fear of germs and the attitude that the body is private property make everyone avoid personal contact, where people touch each other as little as possible, old Fats went all out, offering a profusion of affection: handshakes, wet kisses and embraces all over the place; we were creating a spectacle with our bear hugs, interrupting the flow of executives with briefcases. Our last hug had been three months before, behind a Red Cross ambulance in Santiago, Chile, and I had smiled at him through the blood and two broken teeth while he sheltered me with his body from a cloud of tear gas. The truth is we had both cried; Fats because he's a crybaby in any emotional situation that permits or justifies it; and I, more frugal with my tears, because my throat was full of the fresh taste of tear gas.

"You're fat, Julio," I said, not in Santiago, but much later, in the Los Angeles airport, in April.

"I've been eating like crazy for two weeks and drinking Mexican beer like it was holy water. What do you want? As my General Zapata said, the belly belongs to him who works it."

"Julio Fernández, my brother," I said in Spanish.

"Your *big* brother, like Orwell's," he said, smiling.

"Let's get out of here, this place looks like an airport," I said.

Fats clinked the bottles in his handbag against each other, and, like drunken sailors, since Julio was all over me like an octopus, we left, weaving through the halls.

The two of us could put names and dates to dozens of airports: Boyeros, Linate, Benito Juárez, Marco Polo, Schiphol, Ranon, Eceiza, Barajas, Fiumicino, Sandino, La Guardia. We could match each of them to their cities. The tumultuous demonstrations passing in front of rifles whose barrels burst with red carnations; the roasted fish on the shore of the beach, the hoarse voices of the last stragglers leaving discotheques, music mixed with the sound of the Number 105 buses; the solitary brothel in the middle of nowhere even though the maps said it was the jungle of Honduras; the rickety jeeps, the photo lab in the bathroom of the third floor of a hotel, cockroaches crawling over the negatives; the planes that creaked when they ran into a tailwind. Landscapes of the religion of the *scoop,* the exclusive; the faces of the truth and the truth that made faces as one drummed one's fingers on the typewriter, creating immortals, freezing in time the stories arduously chased down alleys, into living rooms and plazas. The airports could have seemed the same, but one knew they were all different.

An hour later, when we stopped at the front door of my house in Studio City, Julio said:

"I like these houses because they're all alike, you can get drunk and it doesn't matter, you'll always make it back to your own house. I bet they all not only have the TV in the same place, and the same book on the table, and the same toothpaste, but they even have the same wife in the bed."

I forgave him his simplicity. Julio always becomes a little elementary when he arrives in a new city. It's his defensive way of dealing with change. And I forgave him all over again when he pulled out an absolutely, authentically Spanish Serrano ham. My adoring face must have been extremely obvious since he said:

"You must be the only Jew in the world who gets this face of ecstasy before a Serrano ham."

"I have something for you, too. It's somewhere over here." When I showed him the two dozen videotapes, Julio almost died of happiness. I left him rummaging through them, giving me time to ponder the Serrano ham. Later I opened his suitcase; bottles of wine, books and tin cans of Austrian pork sausage and beans began to spill out. Fats was touching his videocassettes the way he would have touched a virgin bride. I was hugging my ham. My neighbors would have been shocked. They're from a generation that forbids so many emotions at one time.

"Shit, you're a genius, where did you get these? Where did you get these gems?" Julio asked, tearing at the growing bald spot that ended in a halo of long hair hanging below the nape of his neck.

"Blackhawk Films, a distributor of old Hal Roach material. It's in this little Iowa town, Davenport."

Fats was so moved that even when I got a corkscrew and the only two clean glasses in the house, he still didn't let go of the tapes. Sixty-six of the best Stan Laurel and Oliver Hardy films, copied straight from the originals. Half an hour later he was still holding the tapes to his chest, he didn't let go even when I showed him the copy of *Rolling Stone* where our last story had just appeared.

T H R E E

ACCESS TO THE SD
IS . . .

. . . extremely complicated. It has nothing to do with an excessive concern for security. Alex wouldn't permit that, that would take away the snobby assurance, the intellectual wit the boys need. It's complicated because the essential nature of life goes along making complications and the SD doesn't try to line them up or resolve them; instead it makes them even more muddled. Nothing subtle about it, just a game.

In '77, some repairs forced a temporary closing of the central hall, and access to the SD, quite accidentally, became through the library, which necessitated a strange detour. Lorelei discovered that it could be even more complicated if you went through the janitor's closet. Because of misfortunes of planning by the Armenian architect who had designed the building ninety years earlier, in order to save space this had a double door. So you had to come in by way of the hat boutique on Madison Avenue, pass through the ladies' room, cross through the double-door closet, and take the service elevator up.

In '79, Dr. Washington B. Douglas added a new complication to the affair, using the fire escape on the second floor to enter the boss's office. Alex, playing along in the game, placed his desk under the window, requiring everyone who entered to climb over the boss's working surface, jump elegantly down and then cross his office to the door that led to the conference room, known as "the toilet."

In '80, Sharon, who held her doctorate in journalism from Columbia, but had written only one article in her entire life, gave Alex a doormat to cover his desk. That way those who entered could wipe their feet before jumping off.

Alex, obviously playful, but also practical, didn't use the desk for work. He kept it for its function as an obstruction in this strange, labyrinthine obstacle course by which one gained access to the SD. For work, Alex used a corner of his office where he had placed a chair surrounded by two small angled tables, the kind that always have big lamps on top. He didn't have many papers. The walls of the room, however, were draped with scraps of paper. Messages, notes scribbled on yellow pads, memoranda pierced by thumbtacks. In '82, Mario Estrada found a note from Alex that was six years old, cryptically reminding the reader to heed Malraux's maxim to remember every day that heroes exist only in books. In the margin, the word "Philippines" was underlined in red.

But the SD has more than just complicated access and decorative rhetoric on the walls. It also enjoys the virtue of nonexistence. It has no archives, no sign on the door, no receptionist to help you find someone, no telephone listing in Manhattan, no social security number, no letterhead.

Instead, it jealously preserves the memories of its employees' trips, because one of the many unwritten rules Alex has established states that each time you travel, you must send a signal, obviously not a letter since the SD doesn't exist and has no address, though they could use a post office box, but yes, for example, an Australian beer label, a condom with letters from the Cyrillic alphabet, a stamp from the Bavarian Alps, a tram ticket from Jalapa, an unpaid bill from a child-care center in Rangoon, a napkin from a Japanese restaurant, a Polaroid photo taken in Chalatenango. All this material had accumulated on the walls next to the messages, memoranda and reminders. In the beginning it was all confined to Alex's office, later it crept into the "toilet" and onto the wooden walls between the cubicles.

Among its peculiarities, the SD has no schedule. People who work there arrive whenever they want and leave when they feel like it. The only formal connections they have are the assignments on green paper from Alex—assignments that indicate some kind of work, specific tasks, lines of investigation. Infrequently do they have so ritual an event as a meeting. Alex usually calls meetings two or three days ahead of time and it's not clear whether they're obligatory or not, though it's rare that someone misses one.

It is not clear how they make money or how much. When a meeting adopts one person's ideas or point of view, his or her monthly salary envelope will arrive with more money in it than usual. But it will never have been clear how much more it will be or why. Nobody knows who establishes their salaries. It might be Alex himself, and this could be why he keeps the tiny notebook he whips out halfway through the meetings and in which no one can guess what he's writing; maybe he simply connects his method of fixing the salaries to the horse races in Yonkers and a randomly programmed computer.

It is not especially clear who maintains the SD either. One time someone suggested their paychecks came directly from the National Security Council. But if that's the case, they arrive in a very strange way: white envelopes with a figure penciled on them. After removing the money, one had to sign and return the envelope to Leila (Alex's secretary? Lover? Aunt? Psychiatrist? Cook?).

In April of 1989, seventeen people worked in the SD, not counting Alex. Each one had a private phone, a cubicle and computer access to the various information networks and banks of public and private data. Each phone is a world and responds to the cover that its SD user and employee created with Alex just after he or she was hired. They all know that if the cover accidentally blows, they'll be fired automatically. Aram is thus "Lingrave's Wooden Toys" and Julio is "Pacific Insurance: Complaints Department," and Martin Greenberg is "Greenberg Consulting Services." And when they don't personally pick up their phones, the answering machines recite the litany. Nobody uses or answers any other phone, nobody touches anyone else's correspondence, nobody takes books or papers from anyone else's cubicle. Nobody invites anyone out to eat. Nobody is sure whether Eve is Eve all the time or only when she's in the SD.

Alex seems to be Alex.

It's a game designed for closed, limited spaces, a game that doesn't carry on outside the office building, located above the hat boutique at Madison Avenue and Forty-sixth Street, in the center of Manhattan, the heart of New York, where they say the worms that poisoned Manhattan live.

Alex thinks that someday a bureaucratic backlash will kill the SD, but their own bureaucracy will forget to inform him and they'll go on playing. Alex's psychiatrist, whom Alex lies to with absolute regularity about his job and working life (including having invented a family in crisis who shares his destiny and about whom he feeds precise information to his shrink), thinks his patient, Alex, is just inches from clinical paranoid schizophrenia. If the psychiatrist continues to question this diagnosis, Alex himself doesn't have a shadow of a doubt; he's completely convinced of his absolute insanity. But as long as they'll let him, he'll keep running the SD, owner and master, omnipotent czar, ruler of strange destinies. And it doesn't bother him to play God in an office that one enters through a hat boutique, a ladies' room, a cleaning closet, a service elevator, a fire escape stairwell, a window and the boss's desk. Actually, he loves it. This is his idea of heavenly bureaucracy.

PANCHO VILLA'S HEAD

Arthur Stanley Jefferson (known after 1920 as Stan Laurel, at the suggestion of Mae Dahlberg, who considered "Stan Jefferson" a dangerous name of thirteen letters) was an Englishman who believed that after Paradise, and in his worst drunken stupors even Paradise took second place, was the cinema.

Stan was the rightful heir of a father, a "strictly business" kind of man called A.J., who had acted, written scripts and sketches, and worked as a theater producer, comedian, director and set designer throughout England, and of a mother named Madge, a dramatic actress of tear-jerking melodramas. Stan had the blood of a dancer, a comedian. He knew his blood only flowed when he was onstage; real life existed only with a set behind him, and a stage under his feet.

One time, Stan told a journalist interested in tracking the past that had inundated his character with magic:

"I was born a comedian. I can't remember a single moment of my infancy in which I wasn't acting. Pa and Ma were always moving and I went through public schools mitigating my loneliness by turning my schoolmates into an audience for my clown acts. This has got to be an inherited talent. My heroes were always comedians, clowns, music hall actors. I was an abominable student, but I had a good time. At sixteen, I made my professional debut."

In 1910, together with Charlie Chaplin and the Karno Troupe, he made a trip to the United States. In 1912, he toured again, but when Chaplin went under contract to Mack Sennett, the group disintegrated and Stan entered the difficult business of vaudeville. For ten years he toured towns, villages, cities, foul theaters, second- and third- rate hotels, rooming houses with half board. He married the Australian Mae Dahlberg and transformed himself into Stan Laurel. After 1917 he started acting in movies and in 1923 he began to triumph as a comedian with producer Hal Roach. Around the end of 1926, he reencountered a comedic actor with whom he had worked in 1917.

Oliver Nowell Hardy, known as Ollie, a pauperized son of an aristocratic Georgia family, was fighting to make a career for himself in film and comedy to see whether once and for all he could eat well. (One time Oliver fled a military academy because they didn't feed him sufficiently, and he refused to return until his mother gave him twenty pastries, which he ate in one sitting.)

Forty-five Minutes from Hollywood was the title of the film they made together. Oliver portrayed a hotel detective, most of the time wrapped up in a towel and stumbling around in the bathroom, trying to avoid his wife and make it out the door. Stan appeared in only one scene, playing an unemployed actor, "too hungry to sleep and too exhausted to stand up."

By the end of the filming, both characters, who had known each other through sharing the miseries of the itinerant and uncertain world of comedians and film actors (in 1917 they had worked together on another movie, and previously Oliver had acted in one that Stan directed), discovered they had something else in common. They both liked to sit in places like hotel lobbies, cafés with ample, large windows, hospital waiting rooms, and there they would study people, observing their gestures and attitudes. This was the best possible acting school.

During the last months of 1926 and the first of 1927, Oliver and Stan collaborated in seven other Hal Roach comedies, until finding, in a two-reel film directed by Yates, the style that would never abandon them. The movie was called *Hats Off.*

Accompanied by pianola music, the film began with a sign on the screen in black that said: "The story of two guys who think the world owes them a living. With thirty-five years of back pay!" The picture went on to tell the story of a couple of door-to-door salesmen selling a machine that washed dishes; the two climbed up and down stairs without a single success. The story culminated in an absurd street fight in which they hurled each other's hats to the ground, bringing in dozens of onlookers and passersby. In that final scene, sitting on the ground in the middle of the street, Stan with his sad face and Oliver with his expression of reproach exchanged hats. That was the birth of the glory.

Stan did not set foot in Mexico in the years that followed Pancho Villa's death. Even though the image of the running boy who announced the *caudillo*'s death went through his head often and he frequently associated Pancho Villa with Dutch gin binges, he was never again inspired to take that southern route. Mexico was a long way from Hollywood. Nevertheless, in February of 1926, a year before Stan and Oliver found the formula that would make them famous, Pancho Villa strangely reentered Stan's life.

On the night of the fifth or sixth of February, 1926, unknown intruders entered the pantheon in Parral, profaning the tomb of the *caudillo* of the Agrarian Revolution of the North, slashed off the head of the cadaver and stole it. The affair caused rivers of ink to run in the North American press, since the United States continued to feed the myth of the fierce bandit who had dared in 1916 to attack the town of Columbus, in New Mexico, accomplishing the only foreign invasion in the history of modern North America. The Los Angeles papers devoted a large space to Villa and the pursuit of him. Mexican rumors rapidly crossed the border, placing the missing head one day in the hands of the widow of a rich rancher whom Villa had assassinated; another day a circus had it and was touring Texas exhibiting the remains; then it was in the hands of a group of fugitive lunatics from a mental asylum in Chihuahua; after that it was the illicit property of an Oklahoma spinster who had been in love with the Mexican military genius and who had commissioned a band of professional thieves from San Francisco to steal it.

Stan carefully followed the information in *The Herald* for several weeks, scratching his head before each new fact with that peculiar gesture the cinema would convert into a monument of indecision and worry. Although he began a warm and loving relationship with Oliver when they made the first film in what would become the "Laurel and Hardy" series, he would never tell him the details of his escapade south of the border the day Pancho Villa died, let alone his bizarre interest in the missing head.

JOURNALISTS' STORIES

(J U L I O   S P E A K S)

W hen I was sixteen, I wanted to be a basketball player, but everyone else kept growing . . ." I said to Greg, and waited for his reaction. The jerk looked at me over the top of his glasses and continued to clean the body of his camera with a tiny brush equipped with an electric charge to throw out the dust. Later he gave me a smile. It seemed my declaration merited nothing more. But I went on.

"I abandoned the grade-school team the day I discovered that no matter how long I hung from my feet in the closet I would never be taller than one point eighty-two meters. My mother thought I was so desperate that at dinner she tried to divert me by ceremoniously handing me my grandfather's journal," I persisted.

Greg remained immersed in his camera, as if the fact that my life had been prescribed in my grandfather's journal before I lived it meant jack shit to him. He had placed the dismantled pieces of his camera on the table on a strip of garnet-colored flannel. I don't know which I liked better, watching him toil with the meticulousness of a medieval artisan, or seeing the color and texture of the flannel. One day I was going to steal a piece and make myself a scarf.

"How tall is one point eighty-two?"

"In feet?"

"Of course."

"What kind of dumb-ass question is that?"

Greg shrugged.

"About six feet, something like five-eleven."

I let fifteen minutes of silence go by and returned to my story.

"At dawn the next morning, when I finished reading the journal, basketball meant shit to me. I cared one huge zero that everyone else was still growing. All that my life would be was down there in my grandfather's stories. There lay the keys to everything that had to be done in the coming centuries. All I had to do was adapt myself, interpret correctly, make the necessary adjustments of time to what my grandfather had written. Have you ever read books with subplots you had to uncover and relate to someone's life? Have you ever worked a crossword puzzle?"

Greg didn't bother to respond. One time, when we spent five days locked up in a jail in Asunción, he let me speak for six hours without answering. One of two things: either he didn't give a fuck about my story, or he didn't want to ruin it by interrupting. There is no doubt that Greg was a magnificent listener. Such a good listener that he turned his back on me and started rummaging through a plastic box full of subcompartments, containing tiny screws of all different sizes.

"I don't know how the sun comes up in this shithole of a city, but back then in Mexico, the sun really came up, not like it does now when it looks like the yolk of a fried egg in the middle of the shitty fog. And there you have me with the journal in my hand, smack in the midst of a mystical experience, saying, 'Fuck basketball! Long live journalism!' "

Greg turned and again looked at me over his glasses. His smile gave him a picaresque look; it was taunting. I wanted nothing to do with him and set about trying to find a bottle of Rioja wine that I remembered leaving behind the armchair.

"Do you have a good picture of your grandfather? A good one, not a close-up."

How had he guessed? I poked around in my wallet and pulled out the folded picture, a copy of a copy: Grandfather standing near the sea, in a three-piece suit and hat, a thick mustache and the look of a dreamer, a little lost. I handed it to him.

"*He* never stood a chance of being a basketball player. He's about my size. Really tiny, your grandfather," Greg said, contemplating the photo attentively. After a few minutes he looked at me again and asked, "What was the journal like? That's the only thing I don't know, because you've already told me this story twice."

Since I had found the rest of the bottle of wine, I didn't bother to answer. He would just have to imagine my journal, the little runt.

SIX

ALEX'S FIRST
"THINKING . . .

. . . Group" had a complicated pool in 1965. You had to put in eleven dollars and jot down the country where Che Guevara was. (If someone else had already picked the country you wanted to choose, you had to specify a region of that country.) That was to win the whole pot. Then you guessed what was going to happen there. The group regulars almost always (four out of five) bet on Latin America, with its variations: the Dominican Republic, Peru, Venezuela and Argentina. The irregulars, less wrapped up in the tangle of disinformation, ventured a bit further. One of them suggested on a coffee-stained card that Ernesto Che Guevara could be found somewhere in Black Africa, and offered the options of Mozambique or Rhodesia (when they made him choose one or the other, he opted for the former); the other went further and suggested that the guerrilla warfare that would shake Franco's Spain was being prepared in France in the Pyrenees. Alex didn't choose any of these options.

The solid information, which Alex had at his disposal and which he offered to the participants as the first step of the game (he gave them only this; they could generate speculative information themselves that was much sounder than what came from the Agency's official analysts) could all fit in one dossier of seven sheets with ample margins and abundant blank spaces at the tops and bottoms of the pages.

The pot got up to eighty-eight dollars, which Alex kept in a little box and which years later he spent on the New York Lottery (losing it all, of course); but none of that took on great importance. The SD still didn't exist, but Alex was nevertheless Alex, and even though he was only twenty-six, he had just been recruited for the very prosaic work of assistant analyst at Langley. His task was to review the press of leftist parties in the Cone of South America: Chile, Argentina, Uruguay and Paraguay. The Paraguayans gave him the least work, the Argentines the most. The Argentines seemed to believe that whatever was not written down would remain off history's record.

The eight members of the "thinking group" who played the pool constituted a totally informal structure: five people from the information apparatus and three external consultants with whom Alex had working relationships. It was a game, highly marginal, very simple.

The fact that Alex spent the money that he had made from the pool by correctly answering the question about where Che Guevara was in 1965 was not extremely significant, because when Che reappeared in Bolivia at the beginning of '67, none of the players could claim the pot, since Bolivia was not one of the countries on the list.

Thanks to the frequent ricochet-like movement in the world of North American professional intelligence, one of the players who rose to a high position years later remembered the story and traced the information in the data banks that Alex had provided in 1965. He carefully reviewed it; later he found Alex and asked him how he knew that in April of 1965 Che Guevara was in Léopoldville, the Congo. Alex shrugged. He knew even then that in those offices and interminable halls full of rumors and whispers, where ingenuity was scarce, nobody seemed to respect logic, mostly since official logic failed with such regularity. After shrugging his shoulders, Alex therefore limited himself to a smile, knowing full well that what they loved at Langley those days was intuition.

JOURNALISTS' STORIES

(G R E G   S P E A K S)

I had everything written down
in the same notebook I'd been keeping for six years. Julio, on the
other hand, showed up with the same disaster of a haphazard
collection: checks, the same notes scribbled on tourist cards, papers stapled to published articles, and the same defective memory
as always. It didn't bother me in the slightest. Julio must have
thought it did, what with my obsession for order. What Julio
doesn't know is that my obsessions are absolutely democratic and
private, and I don't try to impose them on anyone. At any rate, just
for appearances, I complained about the shit he was putting all
over the table; I used my best Madrid accent to curse the whore of
a mother who gave him birth, and I threatened to get a new
partner, Swiss and intelligent.

Julio expects a mixture of astonishment, frustrated paternal
relationships, commiseration and dazzle from the world. I confine
myself to offering him a measured solidarity. For partnerships to
function, someone has to be the pragmatist. One real character,
someone not out of the movies, one person free from illusions, a
man who doesn't buy into dreams and doesn't like clowns, magicians or children's carnivals.

"What happens in these meetings is you start to represent the
well-to-do-society," Julio said very seriously, searching for a check
crinkled up inside his passport.

"And you represent the junk sellers of a Moroccan market in
Casablanca. The worst traditions of the third world, wouldn't you
say?"

It irks Julio that my Spanish improves noticeably when we
argue. He loses one of his few advantages. He doesn't count on the

proverbial mimetic capacity of a Los Angeles Jew raised in an orphanage for Catholic boys, later living in a black neighborhood, and finally going to a high school that for some strange reason was full of Koreans.

"I sold the Beirut report to *Interviu* in Spain, the interview with the guys from the Frente Patriotico to *Pagina 12* in Buenos Aires and *La Jornada* in Mexico. Those two still haven't paid, I've got two checks from the German Agency, and one big one for the Armenian photos that *Der Spiegel* bought. The photos were also placed in a Polish magazine that paid sixty dollars, according to a letter from Ana. They sent me the royalties from *Bajando la Frontera* in Portugal, but that's nothing, pennies. And a two-thousand-dollar bonus from *Herederos* in Spain, the people from Ediciónes B. I sold the Jim Thompson biography to Jucar in Spain, they paid me a thousand dollars and nine hundred for the translation so I should have about . . . wait, this check from Mexico, from *Herederos,* and sixty thousand pesos from the article on kids in Disneyland that Mexico's *Encuentro* magazine published . . . ," he went on, sounding proud, shuffling his scraps of paper. After a while he pulled two or three more out of someplace.

"I withdraw half of what I said, Mister Fernández," I told him.

"About the Moroccan junk market?"

"No, that would be from the worst side of you, brother. Here you represent your highest commercial side. How did you do it?"

Julio rubbed his hands together. "Moving around like a Trojan in the desert. Not bad for four months, eh?"

"I think I've got more money here than you do, because converting Mexican pesos to dollars . . . I've got a cashier's check from the Canadian agency, a check for six thousand pounds from the Brits for the book, and all the money for the last three articles in *Mother Jones, Playboy* and *The Village Voice.*"

"Add it up, kiddo," Julio said, uncorking the last bottle of Rioja.

"Eleven thousand, seven hundred dollars after the reserve for taxes."

"I've got eight thousand dollars and four thousand bolivars, whatever that shit is," he said. "And you got fucked again. Now you see why it's better to be a Mexican writer, we don't pay taxes down there."

I wrote him a check for the balance in his favor, as usual. The

English-speaking market paid better than the rest of the world together, and this made Julio move about like a whirling dervish. Little by little he was abandoning the strange prejudices he had had when we first met, which had made him think that an honest journalist couldn't accept a check in marks from a yellow and conservative German magazine, or couldn't eat caviar at a reception at the Russian Embassy, or that avoiding corruption had anything to do with living anemically but purely.

Very ceremoniously he laid out my 2,000 bolivars.

"How are your debts?" he asked me.

"So-so."

"You could come live a few months in Mexico, it's always cheaper there and you'd stay at my house," Fats offered.

We both knew I'd say no. If I accepted, we'd end up worse than a married couple and our excellent working relationship, which had endured a good half dozen storms a year, would go to hell. We spent too many hours together as it was.

"Much Mexican kitchen boy in that country," I teased in broken Spanish, shaking my head at his invitation.

"No, I like the United States, too, the pisser is all the idiot gringos hanging around all over the place."

"Go figure, brother, each to his own."

Julio took this as philosophy. He had finished offering me his house and his money. We both knew it. I lit up one of the filtered cigars old Fats had brought me huge quantities of. I savored it.

"Oh, bloody hell, I've got a voucher for fourteen hundred Cuban pesos to spend in Cuba, from the series they published in the magazine, *Enigma,* the one about Mengele that they're making into a book."

"What's that worth?"

"Three weeks in Varadero. For two, a week and a half. Hotel and food."

"And the plane fare?"

"No, that we'd have to split. The Cubans modernized, they pay authors' royalties, but not plane fare, *compadre.*"

"How much is it from Mexico?"

"About three hundred bucks, round trip. I left all the articles on the Frente with ALL; they said they could gather them into a pamphlet of reports. If it comes out, we could wait and have a vacation in Havana at the end of the year."

I sat there thinking about what my grandmother Karen would

say about a vacation in Havana. After all, her poker club friends from Gardenia and her three brothers had voted for Reagan in '80 and '84. The truth is, if she could leave her grandson in a shelter, she could well let him travel to Cuba, the bitch. It would be my eleventh trip to the island, a fact that would make the Florida immigration people look at my passport the way they'd look at Laika, the dog's, but for the first time I wouldn't be going for work reasons.

"We could probably get two or three good interviews and an article out of the vacation," Julio encouraged me.

"I would only go to Havana to drink *mojitos* and sit awhile resting in front of the reservoir at Hemingway's house in San Francisco de Paula, nothing more, brother."

"And listen to boleros on the terrace of the St. John Hotel, and play nine-piece dominoes with your big G-2 friends from *Moncada* magazine."

Julio poured the wine into both cups. I got up to turn off the television, whose dull noise was accompanying our talk, and I took the opportunity to walk into the kitchen. The floor was cold. I took out two cans of smoked salmon and a box of crackers. As I recalled, the G-2 friends from *Moncada* were friends of both of ours, and I knew they weren't from G-2, they were journalists who every once in a while took to wearing olive-green uniforms. But Julio couldn't let that jab by a North American pass, even when the North American was his best friend. . . . My feet were cold, the world was big and old Fats had certainly had myriad predisposed neuroses. He'd be surprised. I had a ton of my own neuroses in my notebook of orderly notes. The world was big and for the moment I had no fears. No more than necessary. When night came we could go out for a few cognacs at Sidney's Bar in La Brea, and later head for the movies; the problem would be convincing Julio that Oliver Stone's latest film was better than Harry Langdon's first.

EIGHT

ELENA JORDAN'S
REJECTED THESIS
PROPOSAL

H e who can contemplate the gi-
gantic cave murals in the mountains of San Borja, San Juan, San
Francisco and Guadalupe in the Baja California desert knows he
has glimpsed a fragment of another world. Those figures of men
painted on the rocks, in dark red colors, knights superimposed on
reindeer and stags that cover the immense stone walls of the caves,
astonishingly preserved, do not have a place in Mexico's history.
Figures painted six or seven yards from the floor, of men six to six
and a half feet tall, raised arms, are stylized characters from a
dance to which we are not invited.

This barely explored world of Mexican cave paintings cannot
be integrated with the vestiges of other prehispanic worlds that, for
our information, were interpreted during colonial times by the
ecclesiastic communities' intellectual elite (Hambleton-Von Bor-
stel, Fourth week, Historical Studies, BCS).

The tribes who fundamentally interacted with the Spaniards
upon their arrival on the Baja California peninsula apparently in
no way carried traces of those primitive peoples. Neither the
guaycuras, nor the *cochimi,* nor the *pericues,* could give the Spaniards more than incoherent information about the "big men who
painted the rock walls," and even that was more legendary than
not.

The length of Baja California's colonization, which lasted two
centuries (Leon Portilla, First week, Historical Studies, BCS), the

isolation of the colonial enclaves and missionaries appear to have been factors in the disappearance of any traces of this hunting tribe who left hundreds of signs of its pictorial skills.

This is the official history held to this day.

Let's incorporate a new element:

In a region that currently hosts some of Baja California's most important painted caves, the remains should also be found of the St. Isabel mission, known to historians as "the lost mission," whose ruins have disappeared, and according to documented sources should be situated between the Calamuyue and the San Borge missions (Jordan, p. 188).

Tracking the Jesuit chronicles and the Viceroyalty's registries about this lost mission, I found in the Nation's General Archives, Viceroyalty Department, Inquisition Section, a bound manuscript of indigenous narrations transcribed by the Jesuit Father Francisco Osorio. In his last pages, a document is found that makes reference not only to the lost Mission of St. Isabel, but also to the indigenous tribes' predecessors, whom the Spaniards met. In Cota's words (p. 16) those tribes "died of fear at the toll of a bell." The document consists of seven pages, with some portions deteriorated or impossible to transcribe. It is a confessional letter (I lament the similarities with Daniel Chavarrias' novel, *The Sixth Island,* but as you will see, reality veers from the fiction and surpasses it), written in Spanish and dated during the first years of the eighteenth century. References to participation in the Diego de Vargas expedition allow absolute precision in determining the dates and situate the document loosely in the years subsequent to Vargas' attempt to push the Northern borders up to New Mexico, which cost the narrator his arm in 1692.

It says the following, according to my poor transcription adapted to Spanish which I have learned by ear (and I only got a B in paleography):

> Having come to these lands in search of death by weariness or loneliness in the desert, I was a Godless man after having lost Governor Vargas' military campaign where I lost my own arm in combat with the Indians, and had seen all that my eyes could see. It remains only for me to tell the story of how and why I became someone else and leave it in the desert's arena, in case someone equally as fortunate wanted to follow my example.

I had stumbled upon the San Francisco mission, and after I had shared Father Benito's meager food, he informed me of the traces of enormous paintings which the Indians had made long ago. He told me of their proximity to the mission, and offered to guide me to the paintings accompanied by the natives the next day. These natives said they did not belong to the marvelous Indian painters' heritage. They lived peacefully in the mission, members since ancient times of a tribe of different beliefs and Gods than the Indian painters' tribe, and now in the bosom of the Church thanks to the Jesuits.

In the following days, I visited the Caves, overwhelmed by the grandeur and the mystery of those wonderful murals and their appeal—not to the simple excuse of Faith, which the missionary used in order to deny what was revealed before his eyes, but to reason: the desire of the dancing men and women who at times were superimposed upon the animal figures to be one with these magnificent creatures with antlers and horns or, to the contrary, the desire of the beasts to be men and women.

For hours I wandered in those parts, consumed by astonishment and glimpsing a greatness there far beyond the perceptions of the soldier's life that I'd led since infancy. Friar Benito would tell me, as we sat in the heat of the hearth, that according to legend, the Indians who had painted the caves, or their direct descendants, were still alive in those lands, but were invisible to other mortals.

One day later, before sunrise, I took the desert route alone, believing in the legend with blind faith, because I had nothing better to believe.

A few steps in front of the cave, I threw my scarce belongings on the ground and stripped as naked as a son just born of his mother. My nakedness, my scars, my mutilated arm, my graying beard were exposed to the sun. If the Indians of the caves wished to be invisible to others, only my absolute and naked visibility, without the trappings and shams of clothing, could invite them to an encounter. Unable to hide anything, not even my most intimate spaces, nor my flustered soul, I prepared myself to wait for them.

Two days and one night passed in the desert's solitude.

My body was yielding to exhaustion, pain, sleeplessness, and madness came from my feet, walking, and my head, overheated. I didn't falter, for death did not frighten me and when one announces to his bruised remains that life can go, that he has granted his permission, life clings on in rebellion.

As night fell the second day, the Godless Indians emerged from the rocks and shrubs and welcomed me.

I rely on this brief excerpt, whose editing and punctuation I have altered as little as possible, limiting myself to fill two small gaps of six and three words each. And to this astonishing information, one can add some of the legendary stories transmitted by the cultured natives in the Jesuit missions who say "the invisible people," "the big men" lived crazily following some insane reasoning, and practiced free sex in their ceremonies, later returning to normalcy, and they did not have chiefs, nor did they engage in war, nor did they have Gods or permanent homes (Cabrera, 147, 190–198, 212).

Foucault would say: "Affirmed insanity in the end has its way."

The precise history of a lateral chapter. Modern knowledge of Baja California's rock caves, or rather the dissemination of that knowledge, is due to, among others, the North American mystery writer Erle Stanley Gardner, author of the literary brainstorms featuring Perry Mason, who visited the region as a tourist.

So we find ourselves before a sui generis point of departure. It is established by a field experience that the author of this thesis proposal had.

As a result of the remodeling of the Interior Circuit's works, in the access zone to Chapultepec Park and the entrance to the Calzada de Tacubaya, the old park where they used to skate and ride bicycles, one can see, fragmented into several pieces, diminutive gardens surrounded by panoramic bridges, fast roads, cloverleaf junctions and unlevel crossings. Due to their inconvenient access, these small abandoned gardens have become meeting points on Saturday and Sunday mornings for ethnic groups from the Mexican provinces.

With surprising precision, as if in response to the hugeness of the city, Amealco maids meet in an eighteen-square-yard triangle of field, dozens of bricklayers from Huajapan de León in another, twenty-five Zacatecan bakers in the one beyond, half a dozen traveling salesmen from Santiago, Nayarit in the last, and so on. Throughout the week, the city throws them into areas far removed from each other and their economic status impedes intercommunication. Life separates them for five or six days and sometimes two or three weeks, but the existence of the fixed redoubt, the meeting place, allows them to always find each other in this place, an extension of their native origin. There life is reorganized around affinity and nostalgia, and friendship becomes a stronghold in the strangeness of their surroundings, urban areas recovered and transmitted into reconquered spaces. Fragments of a Chiapas town, a small agrarian villager community, an imagined Michoacano lake, all in the middle of a city with twenty million inhabitants.

The essential nature of these incrusted city presences is their invisibility. In a survey by the author (April 12–18) of 372 motorists who regularly drive through the region, the existence of a strange phenomenon has been established. These "tribal, urban" groups are invisible to them. They are not perceived, they do not exist.

According to what has been captured in these outlines that led to a thesis proposal, this would be a work about mimicry, but above all it would be a work about the invisibleness of "the others" in the Sartre sense of the term (Sartre, Works II, 118). The work's hypothesis is the following: Identify the geographical space of the most invisible invisible groups. Attempt to verify whether they have produced the migratory phenomena of native Baja Californians from the mountain regions to Mexico City and in what positions the immigrants have essentially stationed themselves. Attempt to distinguish the old invisibles from the new ones. Seek out the definitive reason for their invisibility.

I hope such an unorthodox project as this will at least enjoy the benefit of an impartial evaluation and an objective study and that the author is permitted to proceed with the investigation limiting herself to (pre) judgments on the subsequent appraisal of the results. Basic bibliography attached.

Elena Jordan, Mexico City, April 1988

NINE

THE DAY THE . . .

. . . Beatles broke up, Alex found himself absolutely outside the course of history. On April 10, 1970, while information that the British group was falling apart jumped out of newspaper teletypes all over the world, Alex was recovering from a drunken binge of three days and four nights, which had left him just centimeters from death by shock produced by too much alcohol. And this was no metaphor. Alex had been at death's door in Acapulco and that may be why he was able to remain unmoved by the dissolution of the questionably immortal boys from Liverpool.

Paul McCartney said that he was preparing to record a series of songs with a new group and Alex was attempting to pull his head out of an ocean of vomit. Later, he would try to remember those three days and four nights. Right now he limited himself to stopping the ground from moving and shutting down access to biliary vomiting. In his room at the Hotel Tortuga, he tried to let the sun sweat the alcohol out of his body. He thought that if he remained still, with all the lights turned on, the full sun pouring through the terrace window, the air conditioner turned off, four aspirins in his stomach, he could manage to get his cerebellum to sweat.

Paul was going his own way. John Lennon had announced the end of the Pink Spring and the birth of the "John and Yoko Mobile Political Plastic Ono Band Fun Show." Ringo promised an exhibit of his sculptures and George Harrison informed the world press that he and his wife would retire to transcendental meditation.

Alex simply wanted to return to the other reality, even though that too was absolutely hazy, authentically imperfect, formed essentially of an amalgam of troubled dreams and real nightmares.

He had started drinking Tuesday night for work reasons and because he wasn't particularly fond of the two Mexican cops he had to deal with. They were a couple of surly types, slippery, with whom it was very difficult to determine where black humor began and where insinuation ended, their language teeming with half-spoken words and cutoff phrases that could lead anywhere.

Alex had spent some time demonstrating to them that pain does not exist, that it is found only in the mind of the one experiencing it. It was one of the usual routines that gave him a small advantage over the vandals he sometimes had to deal with. Smiling, he started burning his forearm repeatedly with a cigarette. One of the guys tried to imitate him and burned the palm of his hand with the flame of his gold-plated lighter. Later, one of the cops felt uncomfortable, dislocated the jaw and kicked out an eye of a merchant selling coral necklaces who had approached them with his wares. The other guy had been drinking in silence, barely altering his immobile face in hours. Alex had tried to play with them, to find their weaknesses, confront them, manipulate them, wrap them up in a torrent of words, show them the possibilities of insanity. Suddenly he had realized that he'd lost control of the game and that these guys could kill him just to see his expression at the final moment. That's why he began to drink, nabbing every cup that passed by, and letting the other two men take the initiative.

He remembered pieces. One of the cops wept with his face hidden on the table while he told about how he had beaten his sister to death, the other described each step in preparing par-boiled shrimp, with a wealth of details. One went into a seedy cabaret and concentrated knowledgeably on searching out transvestites, dodging tables and drunks to catch up with them and make them take off their clothes in the middle of the floor by threatening them with a pistol. One held Alex while he threw up, missing a marvelous sunrise over Revolcadero Beach. Later he stuffed the barrel of his .45 down Alex's mouth to help him continue to throw up. But it wasn't these gestures of violence, it was the double-edged words, the domination through games of fear and ambiguity that Alex recognized: "Yes, I do love you, but I don't love you," and "I respect you one flying fuck, but maybe you suddenly shit bricks and I break your fucking rib," and later "I cry because you forgive me and then I yank out your fingernails because no son-of-a-bitch gringo has ever seen me cry."

Lying on the bed of the presidential suite in the Hotel Tortuga, trying to make the heat detoxicate him, he was impossibly far from the switch that would shut off the background music playing one of the Beatles' songs in homage to their breakup. He couldn't hear, let alone understand "Listen, do you want to know a secret." The music hid in the room and those who played the song would never again sing it together.

When he tried to steady his vision by fixing on an ashtray on the bedside table, to get hold of something, anything, before the nausea destroyed it, he couldn't do it, but he thought he had never been so close to the truth, and at the same time he felt incapable of knowing what this profound truth was about, or how he could hold on to this mystery that he could almost touch with his hands. He couldn't even remember how he had gotten to his room, or why he owed his life to the fortuitous fact that the mother of one of the secret Mexican police agents had been born on the same day that the Beatles decided to separate, though with a fifty-nine-year difference.

He knew he was alive thanks to this coincidence, and it didn't bother him too much to have verged on death, but it did bother him to have discovered that his insanity had limits, it had anchors in reality, it was susceptible to fear. Attempting to recover the use of his body through sweat, trying to think again, Alex decided that the operation he had come to set up in Mexico would go on, but in it, not only did the schoolteacher turned guerrilla fighter have to die, but so would the two "nice" cops, Judiciales, with whom he'd been drinking the last three nights. It was there that Alex discovered that the best antidote to fear is power.

JOURNALISTS' STORIES

(J U L I O   S P E A K S)

Greg had gone to the supermarket. It was one of the old guy's moments of pleasure: he could fill three carts with ridiculous food and exotic crap that would probably go on to live an eternity in the pantry. I had already seen him act out this ritual a couple of times, and the truth is, it bored me. I belonged to the generation of immediate consumption, lifesaving consumption: "Never buy tomorrow's can of sardines, for tomorrow does not exist." One shouldn't expect security out of life. If you truly wanted security, you could spend the rest of your days locked up in a room. Greg was such a gringo about some things, it was surprising that he was so little gringo about others. He lived tied to things that make you believe you can control the future. He had true reverence for objects. That's why he bought three boxes of Japanese colored pens and he had two dozen flashlights stashed somewhere in case the others burned out. That's why there were three different kinds of pasta in his house, and he was sure to bring home another new kind now, that's why he had two TVs in his home, not because I would eventually visit. Greg participated in the ritual of consumption because having things, being able to buy things, constitutes ninety percent of the framework of every North American's subconscious. And frameworks are made from things as diverse and varied as a can of Dutch cheese, seven pairs of different-colored tennis socks made in Hong Kong, a subscription to *The New York Times Book Review,* a box of Swiss condoms, seven spiral notebooks with tiny graph paper with "six subjects and three pockets" from a Boston manufacturer, a collection of little tin trucks, six monstrous boxes of bran to avoid constipation, a can of seasoning for spaghetti Bolognese, two German staplers and seven different kinds of vitamin C. Because Greg was also, obviously, a hypochondriac. With the money he'd spent on potassium pills and analgesics, he could have founded a new religion.

At any rate, I did not go to the grocery store because I had one of the best Laurel and Hardy films in front of me and because I was turning thirty-six, and I was not going to spend my birthday in a grocery store, but rather smoking a filterless Montecristo and watching *The Laurel and Hardy Murder Case,* which had already passed through my hands in Mexico under the title *Night of Goblins.* It was one of the masterpieces of the indisputable kings. Produced in 1930, the film tells how they find themselves involved with an inheritance from an obscure and now dead uncle of Stan's who seems to have kicked the bucket from unnatural causes. I adored the pair, running through the house in those marvelous long nightshirts. I was just getting to the third scene of the story when Greg appeared with five grocery bags, one of them at least his size.

"Gordito," "Little Fatso," he said to me in his best Mexican accent. "I brought you two dozen Sinaloan shrimps."

"That's why they don't sell those giant shrimps in Sinaloa anymore. They bring all those motherfuckers to California."

"No more anti-imperialist nationalism today, brother, do you or don't you want to enjoy the advantages of being in the imperialist capital?"

"Before I answer I want to know who's cooking."

"Me," said Greg.

"Okay. I'm in," I said.

A dog barked in the street; it was hot in the house, but not too hot. I was such a wickedly happy man that I smiled. We were approaching my favorite way to turn thirty-six.

After dinner, Greg ceremoniously sang "Happy Birthday" to me, I pulled a bottle of Lepanto cognac out of my magic bag, and he put on his favorite records, some recently released remakes of Bob Dylan, the most nauseating sixties nostalgia.

"What have you got there?" I asked my associate. "Are we going to work?"

"On your birthday?"

"You're right, we'll start tomorrow. I'm sure we'll work better tomorrow than today; some Greek god might punish us for working on my birthday."

Greg started unpacking his groceries. I approached to see

whether I could get something. There was a new pen he didn't have, one of the seven notebooks, a can of Indian Ocean tuna. I was like a third-world pariah. I had no problem whatsoever in attacking the U.S. Empire's leftovers.

E L E V E N

THE SD's FIRST
OPERATION . . .

. . . came about in '75, even though the SD didn't really start to take form until the end of '74, in the foul-smelling years of the Ford Administration, with the later-President Bush running the CIA, when the word espionage seemed synonymous with tuberculosis over breakfasts in five-star Washington hotels.

The old story of the betting pool and the riddle of the Congo had gotten Alex an audience with high-level interlocutors, but it didn't yield more than the first step in that marshland of permanent bureaucratic war. Alex didn't want that. He had his own ideas. He was the sole proprietor, the singular owner of a proposition still to unfold that struck him as diabolically attractive. The logic of his project was what impassioned him. With the volumes of information managed in modern intelligence operations, frequently a piece of data wouldn't find its path to the appropriate analyst for weeks and that piece of data would cross with dozens of others, or mix with hundreds of papers that told the same story in another way, or other, different stories, creating an absolute mess. And this happened in both camps, if camps really existed, something Alex wasn't sure about even after five years of prowling around this world.

That's why Alex's idea was interesting. In the beginning, it would be enough to saturate the enemy machinery with abundant disinformation and then offer the poor misguided a providential exit. This was a different kind of game, but it couldn't be played too often. It must be saved for essential operations worth the high cost of revealing the player's style. Alex proposed creating the SD to test his proposal, converting it into a governing theory whose use should be apportioned prudently, at the risk of perverting it and rendering it ineffective.

In Langley's labyrinths, where the Minotaur waits in hiding down every hall and a dinner invitation sounds at times like a call to attend the Borgia banquets, where the only practiced variation on boxing is a Taiwanese version that protects the ribs of the boxer from the jabs of his colleagues, they knew little about the multiple lateral moves Alex had to carry out in order to get the funds and the authorization to start up the SD. With no special thanks to sexual gymnastics with the bosses' wives, without great skill in the manipulation of high-ranking officers or of the other eighty percent of personnel at his own level, without the glamour of some, the frankness of others or the charisma of practically anyone, Alex had to be extraordinarily convincing or extraordinarily capable to find the knots and contradictions that would turn a decision into an order. The future of the SD would be contingent upon its first results.

Sometimes they met in the men's room of Macy's in New York, and other times in the cubicle of a member of the Princeton University Department of Sociology. The initial group could not therefore exceed four and clearly could not include a woman when they met at Macy's or enlist anyone who didn't look academic at the Princeton meetings, or they risked losing their offices.

The members of the original SD didn't even know they belonged to an organization with a strange name, and the officials who had authorized its existence didn't have the slightest idea that the operative unit they had approved was known by Alex as the Shit Department (SD). And with such a euphonious name it would pass on into the clandestine history, the unspoken record, of the North American security apparatus.

For the members of the recently created SD, attending weekly meetings in which they were asked opinions and assigned reviews of strange letters and reports was not part of an operation. Alex had arranged for the operation to circulate through natural and official Agency channels, though its logistical work seemed to remain within the SD. In reality, nothing existed, it was all in his head. The SD was a consulting group, a group of suggestions, elaboration of material, whose members, with the exception of Alex, did not have the slightest idea what use their ideas and texts would have. It was all a game. But only one player was playing. So Alex initiated a tradition of compartmentalization, not for security reasons, but rather by exclusive virtue of his own tendency toward paranoia. The SD's first game was not, therefore, just a manipulation of the group itself. In the initial weeks, the SD, which was not called the SD, was Alex's property and Alex was the property of a CIA assistant director of operations (or at least that's what the poor man believed).

The SD's first operation was based on a proposal of Alex's that could be summarized as a simple concept, and was formulated for the assistant DO as follows: "Fill up their yard with shit, then send someone who providentially offers to clean it up. They'll thank you. Use their own sickness against them, sit back, and let them drown in inertia."

It was a complicated operation whose only function was to test the theory and leave it in place for future use.

Alex offered three possible settings to his boss: Guatemala, El Salvador or Argentina. These had the virtue that their political situations were unlimited, and that they were on the periphery of the grand intelligence confrontations. The games played there could remain hidden from Soviet observation, which at the end of the day was the sole mortal obsession capable of enraging the Agency. Alex never knew what type of debates they had at the top, but they authorized his group to carry out the plan in one of those Latin American locales.

One cold afternoon in January of '75, Alex called a meeting of what would be the first group of the SD, and established the operation's objectives:

"Now we are going to kill a poet," he said. Nobody thought to ask why or how poets were assassinated. Nobody asked where and to what end. Nobody got maudlin pointing out that poets were substantially more immortal than other mortals, or that it was a sin to kill a poet in practically all known religions.

In the subsequent two weeks, the SD was activated and began developing strange and apparently unconnected routines. Various Spanish-speakers appeared in the ranks of the small group: an expert in contemporary Latin American poetry, a cryptographer, two text analysts quite well versed in Central American guerrilla warfare, an anesthetist recently graduated from New York University and a transvestite from New Orleans whom the Agency occasionally used for his skills in the art of disguise. They were never together, they never met one another; there still weren't any common offices for the operation. Alex was the link that united the chain, Alex was the boss and the office.

Four months later, Alex presented the report on the operation's results to his superiors. It consisted of a couple of leaflets clandestinely distributed by the ERP, the People's Revolutionary Army, in the streets of San Salvador, two pictures of a cadaver and an extensive packet of articles from a multitude of Latin American magazines reporting the death of Roque Dalton, poet and guerrilla leader. Alex did not attach a report on the SD's actions, and one of the Agency colleagues who later on studied the case dared to suggest that Alex and his boys had had nothing to do with the affair. Alex never bothered to refute the rumor; to the contrary, he propagated it: he preferred to see himself wrapped in a halo of uncertainty rather than one of certitude.

The Ejército Revolucionario de Pueblo, the People's Revolutionary Army, affirmed in the leaflet that Dalton had been shot "because, while a militant member of the ERP, he was collaborating with the secret apparatus of the enemy." This version was not accepted even by the genuine bases of the guerrilla organization, producing an important split. Dalton was forty years old, known not only as a novelist and poet, author of several brilliant essays on the history of El Salvador, winner of the Casa de Las Americas poetry prize, but appreciated also for his tenacity, his moral fortitude, his tremendous human passion, the transparency of his public life.

In '73, after the electoral fraud of El Salvador's government, Dalton had abandoned his long exile and left an unfinished novel to join the armed fight as a member of the ERP. In Mexico, Havana, Buenos Aires and Lima, his death provoked a grief-stricken condemnation of the scoundrels who, in the name of the purity of the Revolution, had assassinated him. In the prologue of his book of poems, published one year after his death, an anonymous anthologist summarized the general thought of those who had known Roque Dalton: "A terrible illness runs through our ranks, an illness that makes its victims incapable of appreciating the personal, political and cultural life of a poet, and capable of slander to resolve political discrepancies. To be able to kill him, they had to forget those afternoons in his house of exile in

Havana when he played Mexican ballads on his guitar; they had to forget the pages in his novel, *Poor Poet That I Was;* they had to forget his marvelous escapes from Salvadoran jails; they had to forget every line of *Taberna,* the most lucid portrayal of Prague in the sixties; they had to forget his picaresque look, his anguished conflict between continuing the work of the intellectual left or joining the armed fight. And they had to forget the man, or perhaps they simply didn't know him, because they think the idea of the Revolution is created in manuals and not in poems. Only barbarian thought, only the most primitive and tribal religious mentality can think that someone who wrote these lines could be a CIA agent: 'Beloved philosophers / beloved progressive sociologists / beloved social psychologists / don't get so fucked up over alienation / here, where we're most fucked up / is the nation most alienated.' "

Another schism divided the Salvadoran guerrillas and the left lost its most lucid militant. Alex included this prologue in his report.

T W E L V E

JOURNALISTS' STORIES

(G R E G   S P E A K S)

Sleet fell over Montreal at dusk. The city was somewhere else. From the window of the waiting room all we could see was a layer of grayish snow and a couple of power shovels clearing off the runway. The flight was thirty minutes late and Julio had gone into a store determined to inspect, piece by piece, the hideous Eskimo crafts on sale: little carved seals, leather hats, moccasins, abominable wooden figurines. This much I had to grant old Fats, his extraordinary capacity to find useless things to do, his inability to sit still.

I had my own recourses when faced with the necessary delays, those dead times that comprised fifty percent of our profession. Mine were Buddhist: contemplation, deep thought, reducing my heartbeat, exploring the inner world, concentrating on a cigarette ad to the point where I could decompose the tip of the ashes into its black and red points. Fats could recite the complete poetry of Miguel Hernández. I was not gifted with such cultural dexterity. It's true, at times I was able to make my mind photographic and memorize a complete document with just one quick glance, but that memory was of short duration and a couple of hours later the neurons reorganized themselves to reoccupy the useless space.

We had an exclusive interview with Otelo Saraiva de Carvalho, obtained from the officials in the Portuguese jail where he was being held. A singular interview, because he told us the rest of the revolution with the added perspective of ten years, but we were scared some colleague would scoop it so we didn't send it by the telex offered to us in Lisbon. We thought we'd spend a couple of days in Los Angeles polishing it to submit to *Rolling Stone*'s editorial board, but the flight connections turned out to be absurd. Fats had compiled more interesting material, which we could use to fill a good historical piece on the Revolution of the Carnations of April for which Madrid's *Historia 16* had already offered by phone. I thought we could make a bilingual version in one fell swoop and sell it to *Radical History*. What's more, we had an article with color photos that might work for *National Geographic,* about the firefighters of a small village in the south of Portugal who dedicated two days a year to training the entire population, simulating fires where they burned down old houses. Inflammatory firefighters who loved pouring the gas and throwing the match.

It was raining that day in Montreal's airport and suddenly Fats appeared with a bottle of Spanish cognac taken from his marvelous bag and proposed that we screw journalism once and for all and dedicate ourselves to writing a novel, or to living. This was a crisis that occurred regularly, and halfway through the bottle of cognac it had already disappeared. A crisis that was based on the horrors of a profession in which one is constantly an observer. A profession in which one tells the stories that others, normal people, people with passions are living. The cognac assuaged Fats's anguish and I set about telling him that we had a better passion, the passion to report. Sometimes it was he who had to convince me, he who had to review page by page the manual of journalistic ethics and professional motives that was never written but that every member of the tribe, as Leguineche the Spaniard would say, kept annotated in idle corners of his or her mind.

I remember all this now, a year later, in Los Angeles, far from the snow in Montreal, because Fats took a bottle of Spanish cognac from his bag, and I feared he wanted to convince me that the moment had arrived for us to write a novel.

"What happened with that Philippine girlfriend you had in Mexico the last time I saw you?" I asked, to derail the thought.

"She wasn't Philippine and she wasn't my girlfriend. She was the wife of the cultural attaché from Peru's embassy and she was with me because she'd lost her contact lenses and was absolutely blind drunk. If your memory functions so poorly it's because that day you were with an Ethiopian novelist who had yet to publish his first book, and who I suspect was neither Ethiopian nor a novelist, but rather the doorman of the Peruvian Embassy who had snuck into the party to down a dozen canapés and a bottle of old wine, and to whom someone had entrusted the job of watching over the cultural attaché's wife."

"The Filipina?"

"That's right, the Filipina who wasn't Philippine."

"Well then what was the Ethiopian who wasn't Ethiopian doing with me?"

"You were holding him up so he wouldn't fall, because at every diplomatic reception, the kind and solitary Mormon in you comes out and you spend the majority of the night taking care of drunks."

"You can certainly bear witness to that. More than ever at that party in Warsaw when you threw up on the Romanian general. What was his name?"

"I always thought that was an Egyptian whore you were trying to persuade to go to bed with you for free," Fats said, pounding the bottle on the table, thereby terminating the conversation. We had escaped the danger. Now we could talk business.

"Let's see where the fuck we can spend the next few weeks."

"You first," I said to Julio, uncorking the bottle.

I walked toward the record player and turned it off. I picked up my little notebook on the way and put on my glasses.

THIRTEEN

THE ROLE OF GOD . . .

. . . had its most accurate equiva-
lent in earthly matters within what has come to be known as labors
of intoxication, which are nothing more than sophisticated proce-
dures of disinformation induced to make others believe what one
wishes them to believe; in sum, the fine art of espionage work. The
classics on the subject believe that the vital core of espionage
consists of knowing things about your enemies that they don't
know you know. They are wrong. The greatest games, the major
leagues of espionage, are found in intoxication. That the others
know what you want them to know, whether it's true or false, that
they act according to the information you furnish, that their ties to
reality be mediated by the dark lenses you put on them.

Alex believed that God had dedicated himself to the topic
when he dictated the Bible, and the clearest proof was in the
apocryphal description of Paradise. Alex believed God was a top-
rate disinformer.

The SD's second operation emerged from a cryptic note from
the director of operations of the CIA, placed in the margin of a
document classified with the maximum level of security used in
those days: "Top secret, for your eyes only," which circulated
among seventeen people including a cousin of the president of the
United States who was touring the Oval Office and who saw the
document for just a moment while his cousin went to take a piss.
It was an appraisal of the contradictions at the executive level in
the Movimiento de las Fuerzas Armadas Portuguéses, or Movement of the Portuguese Armed Forces. The DO's note said, "Use
them." Alex received the document, an authorization to resusci-
tate the SD, a budget and three months' pay.

Instead of traveling to Lisbon, he memorized the document,
caught a flight to New York and took a walk through Manhattan.

The trek convinced him of the certainty of his profound antiecological convictions. He swore that he would never again work at Langley, where he hated the woods and the little birds that came up to the office windows and were treated as second-ranking officials of the KGB. He preferred New York, though not for the usual reasons. Manhattan did not have the magic that the inhabitants of the island claimed for their territory and that the tourists accepted as real. Alex saw it as the greatest hotbed of abnormal people in the history of humanity. Spending just a few hours on its streets put him in direct contact with so many demented vibrations, he felt spiritually fortified for the next ten weeks.

He studied the alcoholic old ladies dressed like Uncle Sam who promised universal salvation and played the pedal organ, and the skinny black guys consumed by syphilis who with sleepy eyes sold shabby pornographic magazines. He directed his view carefully to the paranoid midlevel executives of publicity firms, and understood completely the Lebanese and Cuban shopkeepers who looked at him with the eyes of a dying bird as he passed their Fifth Avenue store windows. He loved them, oh god, how he loved them all! He adored the Chinese patriarchs sitting on the fire escape stairwell above Grand and Canal, numbed either by their age or by opium, and he loved a group of Jamaicans who operated in the Hudson Street park zone, selling hard kiddie porn. He especially loved a redheaded adolescent who tortured cats and two Vietnam vets who drank 90-proof grain alcohol with Canada Dry and flashed their scars to scare the women who were going to the deli on Eleventh Avenue near the river. Alex was a Manhattan professional who smelled the icy Atlantic winds and the hot shit of the Fifth Avenue mounted policemen's horses with equal delight. Oh how he hated them all!

Operation "Horrifying Bossanova" (the code name belonged to him, of course) began when he rented a room in the Wentworth Hotel on Forty-sixth Street between Fifth and Sixth and lay down to think with the television blaring so that the noises of hotel life wouldn't distract him. The first conclusion was that the information about the Portuguese wasn't worth shit. The type of report corresponded to the variations in style among CIA analysts, who, during that era, tended to copy their intelligence reports from the theses of the Jesuit Loyola University's graduate students, and tended to emphasize certain figures, evaluating them according to secondhand sources. A few rumors and some solid information that could be gleaned from even a light reading of *The Republic* and *Das Kapital* formed a database by which to arrive at a truth, which had been preestablished by the creator of the report, the same truth already suggested in the original ideas by the chief of the station in Portugal, to whom without doubt it had been suggested by one of his stupidest aides. The information was thus always confirming what one wanted to be known and said, and was absolutely devoid of contradictions.

Alex advocated information rich in contradictions. Years later, this would come into style in top-secret reports, but not because the analysts suddenly became intelligent, but rather because contradictory information didn't commit the informers to specific actions and it was more useful to paralyze decision-making and thus hinder their putting their feet in their mouths. The CIA should have learned in the seventies that those who err the least are those who do the least. Alex was a believer in sticking everyone in the ass and then in the ears, but if he wanted to escape Langley and be able to drink coffee every day in a Greek coffee shop in Manhattan, and play God in the minds of others (and he didn't give a shit who the others were as long as our guys allowed it, paid him his check and gave him sufficient trucks, locomotives, freight trains, gondolas and a caboose for his little electric train), he had to launch a spectacular game with comforting results. Some imbecile with a position no lower than secretary of state had to smile on the results of operation "Horrifying Bossanova," officially called "Lace."

He returned to Langley with a heavy heart, but he needed their technology. There the wizards had computers and a pair of galley slaves to translate the Portuguese, plus a telephone that didn't require coin after coin and satellite communication with Lisbon. From Virginia, after a few brief moments, he departed for Washington, where he caught a TAP flight to Lisbon.

On December third of '75, Alex returned to New York from Lisbon on a Pan Am flight just hours before Otelo Saraiva de Carvalho and the military officers of COPCON, the extreme left of the Movimiento de las Fuerzas Armadas, had been arrested, accused of implication in the preparation of a military coup. Back at Langley, rumors awaited him, attributing the work of poisoning the interior of the MFA to the chief of the CIA department in Lisbon and a veteran from Chile. Not only did Alex not contest the rumors, but he publicly stated them on various occasions. His report included only a few little-known dates regarding the events; it provided no information about the internal work of the SD. Everyone was convinced that this had been his affair.

A couple of years later, the Australian analyst Wilfred Burchett wrote in a book dedicated to the Portuguese Revolution: "It was difficult to establish whether the paratroopers were manipulated to give the rightist officials a pretext to start up a meticulously planned counter-attack. It was also difficult to know the extent of the CIA's intervention." Alex cut the page from the book and hung it on one of the walls of his new office with a thumbtack. Later, he forgot about it.

F O U R T E E N

THE STORY OF GRANDFATHER'S NOTEBOOK

(F R E E   V E R S I O N)

At eleven years old, Tomás Fernández was a boy obsessed by addition and subtraction. He was also a miner with four years of experience working twelve-hour days, six days a week. They had just promoted him to miner's assistant. The three previous years he had been just one more little boy working outside the mine picking up slags, the remains of the industrial exploitation later sold to the retail trade to heat ovens and kitchens. Tomás was also one of those rare financial geniuses whom the Spanish working class would produce, and whom the tortuous travels of his social class over the next twenty years would oblige to use his brilliance in the most unusual ways.

Tomás Fernández, unlike all the other masterful alchemists

produced by the twentieth century, never got rich; he didn't even make other people rich. When he died, run over by a car in 1947, his children inherited a second-class hotel/restaurant specializing in grilled shrimp in the city of La Paz, on the Gulf of California in Mexican Baja California, on the Sea of Cortés. He also left the notebook which years later would transform the life of his grandson Julio from future basketball player to future journalist.

Tomás taught himself to add as a boy in Spain, using scraps of coal on the asphalt of a dance floor, creating his own numerical system with a base of five. Several years later, when, working as a guard at the Santa Barbara mine, he tried to show it to a miners' union schoolteacher, the teacher told him he was crazy and Tomás had to learn addition all over again starting with zero, like everybody else, with a base of ten. At seventeen, now knowing how to sign his first and last name, and the fastest multiplier of all the miners in the Nalón River valley in Asturias, the most important coal region in Northern Spain, he married. That same year, he took part in a general strike, spent three months in jail, and read the two-volume, tiny-lettered Aurora Publishing edition of *Les Misérables* by Victor Hugo six times; he read Zola's *Germinal* once and Fauré's *Twelve Proofs of the Nonexistence of God* six times. He left jail convinced that they had to bring more teachers to the miners' valley, that they had to better organize the general strikes, and that there had to be something beyond eleven-digit division.

In 1918, an Asturian coal miner worked a twelve-hour day in terrible mine conditions, had a life expectancy of forty-five years—the most probable cause of death being silicosis or tuberculosis—had one chance in seven of incurring a serious accident, and was proud to sing among the best popular choirs in the world, play with the best bagpipers in the world and belong to the best union in the world. Tomás joined the union at the age of nine because "if a nine-year-old can work, a nine-year-old can vote to strike, just like anyone" (so read the Resolution of the Asturian Miners' Syndicate of the Sobrescorbio Mine, into which he was admitted).

Tomás was born with the century, and this bothered him solely because he was almost sure he wouldn't see the year 2000, the date by which with all certainty man would have reached the moon and socialism would prevail throughout the planet with the exceptions of Russia, because it had already advanced and embraced communism, and France, because it would retreat to feudalism. On the other hand, he liked it because he never had to ask himself what year it was, he had only to remember his age. He measured a little over five feet and was convinced he hadn't grown taller because he was malnourished as a child. He didn't remember his mother or father, who had drowned in the Bay of Biscay returning from their honeymoon in Santander, taken eight years late; he had only a vague recollection of his siblings because they'd been picked up by an uncle from León and he never saw them again. He had two families: his wife, Elisa, and the union. He was teaching Elisa, the daughter of illiterate miners, to read. In the union, he was learning commercial accounting, analyzing the mining laws written during the first months of Primo de Rivera's dictatorship, and studying all the reports on the mining industry from the Ministry of Public Works and the Economy.

In 1925, as he was leaving a union meeting in the town of Moreda, the scabs at the Marqués de Comillas's mines fired a shot at him. Tomás, who was also armed, answered the aggression and fired back toward the flashes a couple of times. He shot one of his aggressors in the eye, resulting in a medal for the scab and seven months in jail for Tomás. The union paid his wife his full salary while he was in the Modelo de Oviedo prison, but upon his release, he found himself on the employers' blacklists and couldn't get work for three months.

In early 1926, the miners' union sent him to the San Vicente mine, a small mine abandoned by its manager after a strike that lasted two years, and which remained in the hands of its twenty-four workers, who handed over its administration to the union. The mine had no great economic importance; the seam of coal was not especially rich. It was technically in shambles. It was far from the central highway, it did not have credit at its disposal, its market was in perpetual danger of strangulation because the metallurgical industries of Mieres and La Felguera were under the same owner-ship as the principal mines. Even so, everyone knew Tomás would win the battle. Even Tomás, who was never renowned for his optimism and who smoked like a chimney, a sign of his anxiety, the day they offered him the management of San Vicente knew that he would win. The union was motivated by honor and class pride to demonstrate that a mine managed by workers could be more productive, richer and more secure and pay higher salaries than any mine run by the employers.

Until the beginning of the Republic, in April of '31, the As-turian workers' movement remained dormant; even the socialists who ran the miners' union dedicated themselves to an agenda of organization and social peace, trying to maintain the gains already won and directing their greatest efforts to the development of a series of social works like union buildings, libraries, culture, education and residential and commercial co-ops that would keep them on the sidelines in the harshest confrontations with the dictatorship. Tomás was not exactly in agreement with this agenda, which he believed alienated them from socialism and the worldwide revolution, but the administration of the mine kept him busy and almost unknowingly he became just another functionary of the social peace that proliferated in the union. The blood ran slowly through his veins, but that did not deter him from stockpiling an abundant quantity of dynamite beyond the necessary amount for the commercial exploitation of his mine ("in case one day they had to use it"), or from obsessively studying algebra and geometry in the precious free time left to him.

The mine became the most profitable in the region, paying the highest salaries by far and curiously boasting the best technical operating methods. Tomás had little to do with that, outside of having carefully chosen the engineer who oversaw it. Tomás knew little and wanted to know even less about the technical aspects of the mine; his was the administration and the business.

The day the Republic arrived, Tomás drank a dozen bottles of cider, got out the dynamite just in case, and bought a nine-millimeter Star, which he learned to use on the patio in his house. His wife would watch him firing in the family vegetable garden while she picked lettuce heads or improved the fertilizer on a patch of brussels sprouts. He was firing shots when his first child was born.

The Republic signaled, among many other things for the Asturian miners, a period of deployment of the union's forces, a series of tremendous confrontations with the owners and a growing share of the power exercised over society. The miners' union decided to publish a newspaper and Tomás was named publisher. He left his village house and moved to Oviedo, a small city of bureaucrats and public civil servants, which as the capital of the region became the necessary headquarters of the paper.

From the beginning, Tomás took charge of the layout of his paper, modeling it not after the ephemeral partisan papers, but after the great Spanish newspapers. For two months, the tiny miner dressed up in a borrowed three-piece suit and toured the printing plants of Madrid's major newspapers. He visited the offices of *El Sol* and *El Socialista*. He entered the rightist papers' offices, like *ABC*, sheltered by his union identity; he walked the streets with the distributors, visited *Bilbao*, observed the network of *El Liberal*, hand-sold papers on the streets of Seville and Vigo, studied the accounting of some and the printers of others. He visited the paper plants and German companies who sold linotypes, he analyzed the English Harris and the French rotary presses, he read a thousand and one papers and later met with Asturian socialist management and the miners' union representatives, reporting that he needed one director and he would handle the rest. Over the next four years and until the *Avance* newspaper was burned by the military and Tomás was exiled to France, he didn't eat one dinner at home and never missed one fresh page off the first printing in 1,094 editions.

Tomás made *Avance* a paper of fine technical quality, with an excellent distribution network, printed with a rapid rotary which rarely leaked, well organized with excellent informative services. In its first years, the paper never ran a deficit. His skills as a wizard of organization and finance demonstrated as always his exceptional caliber.

When the right won the elections in late 1933, Spanish socialism took the offensive. They were black times in Europe; fascism had devoured Germany and Italy; in February of '34 Austria fell and ultraright mobilization swept the entire continent. In Asturias, *Avance* supported workers' alliances and political insurrection; since the paper was at the service of these ends, censorship fell upon it—the arrests of journalists, the seizure of editions, the pages mutilated by judicial order, the editions that couldn't leave the warehouse due to their prohibited articles, and police attacks on the editorial offices and presses. In eight months the paper incurred four substantial fines; a hundred editions were seized, its circulation prohibited, its director thrown into jail three times, the presses attacked twice.

That's when Tomás's head began to kick in. He created parallel distribution networks. The mines stopped production if the paper wasn't on sale at the start of the workday. Public collections financed the fines; informal groups delivered the bundles to the paper sellers. Clandestine groups placed them in the public transportation system and the people distributed them at no cost. The red unions financed the lost editions. Unknown to the authorities, they changed the closing hours, they sped up printings; they snuck the papers directly out of the warehouses and from one house to another with the aid of the neighbors. And the paper continued to be published with absolute regularity. Emergency situations required urgent technical resolutions, and there Tomás discovered the keys to traditional organization mixed with the organization of popular resistance.

Around August, the union placed him at the head of a new project to purchase arms for the future insurrection. Tomás tackled the problem with his usual seriousness and, to throw the police off his trail, launched an operation so complicated that even years later it was never cleared up.

He bought arms in Cádiz to be resold in Ethiopia; but since these shipments ran up against a League of Nations embargo, he created a distracting operation over the first, phantasmal operation. The stealthiness of the merchants helped conceal the truth. In reality, instead of departing for Africa, the mysterious dispatch circumnavigated Spain in search of the Asturian coasts in a union-owned ship rebaptized with the name of the green stone of good luck: *Turquoise*.

The defeat of the revolution after sixteen days of combat (in which Tomás took over the problem of transporting the insurrectional miner troops) obliged Tomás to go into exile in France, where the organization assigned him a new financial operation. During the October movement, the revolutionaries had attacked the Banco de España, as well as a series of smaller banks and mining company offices. Tomás was entrusted with recovering that money, dispersed during the flight between hundreds of activists, buried in the mountains, in the hands of prisoners' relatives, under the power of fugitives still hidden in certain parts of Spain. He managed to regain eighty-nine percent of the money and figured out where another nine percent could be found: in the hands of a man who had fled to Argentina and in those of the police and the civil guard who had seized three deposits. The missing two percent infuriated him for several months. He always said socialists today just aren't what they used to be. The money recovered was used to help the workers' widows and to refinance the paper's machinery, destroyed in a fire set by the military.

After the electoral victory in '36, *Avance* was published again, though just for a short time because a few months later war erupted. Tomás was vice minister of finance in the Republican government of Asturias, the region isolated from the Francoism that had dominated Galicia and part of the Basque country. Once again his talents came to light. Not only was he capable of organizing the wartime economy, he also learned to execute several international operations worthy of Houdini, in spite of the farcical nonintervention embargo.

His method of calculating worked well, but he had to abandon all forms of financial orthodoxy. The Loyalists had to maintain the army of workers with arms, food, munitions and clothing. This was the moral point of the story; he therefore used what he had learned.

In September of '36, he bought 8,000 boots for the left foot, industrial rejects from Belgium. He insured them at Lloyd's of London for six times their value, registering them simply as "boots." He sank the shipment in the Bay of Biscay, bought Czechoslovakian submachine guns for Portugal with the insurance money, falsely converted them to scrap metal in a ghost operation in France and bought them from the French, who were committed to blocking the flow of arms to Spain, but who had no problem sending "scrap metal." As he disliked using intermediaries, he promptly created his own export company in Toulouse, whose principal front was a ninety-year-old gypsy who'd been recruited by the network of the crazy reds.

By the beginning of 1937, he had already learned more about illegal international transactions and organized a complete maneuver with the speculation of gold obtained from churches and the Asturian bourgeoisie. He cheated Dutch entrepreneurs and pirates of the Belgian war industry, he swindled Panamanian shipowners and Greek bankers. He bought cannons, waterproof jackets, thousands of guns and even an airplane. He chartered nonexistent freighters that changed flags and names, he hijacked them himself, he seized shipments, sold the same loads of coal to different buyers six times in one week. He pretended to be Greek. He stole Cuban cigars and Portuguese carrots, he exchanged them for Ford trucks and had them converted to armored vehicles in Asturias. A couple of weeks before the end of the war he was trying to organize a massive counterfeit of the Venezuelan lottery to sell it in Francoist territory by way of a band of Portuguese racketeers.

Elisa died during a bombing. His grief became some undefinable thing inside that he could not address. In '39, holding his six-year-old son and four-year-old daughter by the hand, Tomás crossed the border to France at Le Perthus and had to surrender his revolver. Carrying a diplomat's passport, he was not committed to one of the concentration camps and could hide in Normandy. When the Nazis declared war on France a few months later, again, he took his children by the hand and traveled to Paris. There, at the entrance to a Parisian subway, he met Longoria. What he was unable to do during the Spanish Civil War for lack of time, he did in German-occupied France with his friend, Longoria, an astonishing thirty-nine-year-old anarchist who had falsified the date on his birth certificate to enter adult movies when he was thirteen and who had participated in the defense of Madrid.

The "Sacramento Network" was formed by two men and two kids who helped by drying the falsified lottery tickets in the bathroom. Tomás learned to sleep standing up, leaning against a wall with one ear glued to the door, while Longoria's small press manufactured tickets. In one year, avoiding the hunt for them organized by the Paris gestapo, they carried out the most extravagant and imaginative operations. From supplying food to the resistance troops of the Loire, packed with Spanish veterans, to falsifying tickets for the soccer game between Paris and the German armed forces, tripling the number of tickets the field could hold and forcing the Germans to suspend the game. From poisoning two trucks of champagne headed for the Luftwaffe airfields outside Paris to controlling the production of the cosmetic firm of Guerlain and using its resources to create an escape network for English pilots shot down over Andorra. During the three years of their adventures, Tomás dreamed of publishing a paper.

In May of '42, the Germans managed to infiltrate the network at its lowest echelons and it collapsed. Tomás and Longoria had two minutes to embrace each other in a small forest outside Lyon. They never saw each other again. With a false passport and two children by the hand, Tomás crossed Spain and Portugal, pretending to be a Greek Jew, and set out for America. He slept for hours on the ship. He ate briefly, watched the children play on deck and slept again. Sometimes he woke up and before the children made him dress for breakfast he'd go up on deck to contemplate the flight of the seagulls. He had the unpleasant sensation that his life was over. The ship was headed for San Francisco via Panama. Tomás disembarked in the Mexican fishing port of Mazatlán, where there was a small colony of Spanish refugees. He was exhausted, mentally in ruins. He discovered that he'd forgotten how to do square roots, and a Republican doctor who auscultated him found pernicious anemia.

He couldn't tolerate the debates of exiles for more than a week and with the money he'd made in France, trading fake Toulouse-Lautrec paintings to German officials for gold, which he considered a personal reserve, he bought a small hotel in a shy, silent town on the Sea of Cortés, the port of La Paz.

There he prepared to wait, raising his two children, while he considered how to publish a paper in hundreds of thousands of copies and with several airplanes bombard them over Francoist Spain.

He was forty-two years old, just like the century.

F I F T E E N

STAN IN LA PAZ

In August of 1942, at the culmination of filming a disastrous one-hour comedy called *A-Haunting We Will Go,* Stan Laurel rented an old Duesenberg, hired an Irish driver named Larry and asked him to head south of the border. Again, he brought half a dozen bottles of Dutch gin in his suitcase, but this time he had just turned fifty-two and wasn't even sure why he was going to Mexico.

In every ritual behavior there is a small amount of self-deception and a good dose of guilt. Stan did not want to deal with those two obscure spaces in his head. He therefore confined himself to gesturing to the driver, pointing at the freeway toward San Diego. He sank into the backseat of the car and closed his eyes.

He was exhausted. His return to film was a failure, his marriage to Ruth a disaster. She had deteriorated rapidly because of a stupid infection that had spread after a wisdom tooth extraction. He was sick of public appearances; they made him feel like a deceased legend and not an active film actor; he was even sick of his eternal and indissoluble marriage to Oliver and to his characters. He was, in short, quite annoyed with himself. In Tijuana, he signed an autograph for the Mexican customs official, and pointed the driver toward the road to the desert.

The first day they slept in Rosarito, and the second they headed south with the backseat filled with cans of water and gasoline. Stan practiced a few routines as the heat began to numb him, bringing him to a state of absolute bewilderment. One of the routines was a dialogue with a cactus, Stan playing the role of a man lost in the desert. Another was Stan mistakenly drinking the gasoline instead of the water. The others were erotic and he didn't see any way of exploiting them in a film. Several times along the highway they sighted Mexican army squads in all-out anti-Japanese paranoia. The North American tabloids had spread the rumor that the Japanese were staging an invasion against the United States using the desert of Baja California as a trampoline and the idea had caught fire in Mexico.

They arrived at the bay of La Paz three days after having abandoned Los Angeles, which Larry considered a fine record given the state of the roads in the desert zone. Stan didn't appreciate his driver's triumph and simply asked that he stop the car at the edge of a beach. He took off his shoes and socks and walked toward the sea. He stopped a few meters in front of the water. It was warm. Stan stood still as several fish approached and circled his toes.

They ended the afternoon in a small motel at the foot of the city that nibbled away at one corner of the small bay. Stan liked the looks of it. Solid wood chairs, a central patio with a big fountain full of climbing flowers, the smell of the sea, Spanish love songs on an old jukebox and a woman sewing an enormous tablecloth who didn't pay him the slightest attention. Larry dedicated himself to tequila and the Chinese whores and Stan watched the waterfall in the stone fountain and drank his Dutch gin watered down with the lemon water that the hotel owner placed in front of him in an enormous pitcher. The hotel owner was a gray-haired Spaniard of small stature, who sat beside him as evening fell to write in his enormous hardcover accounting book. Stan was convinced that the man was not writing a financial history, but narrating the story of his life.

Stan tried to tell him the anecdote of Pancho Villa's death and the Spaniard listened attentively, though clearly he understood very little since he didn't speak English. In exchange, the man read fragments of the story in his notebook and Stan, fascinated by his voice and gestures, and by the intensity of this character's story, was convinced he was hearing something of great importance. He couldn't penetrate the story beyond the sound of the words, because his Spanish was as nonexistent as the man's English.

Their relationship continued to grow the next day. They discovered their shared capacity to listen to strange stories without understanding and their mutual love of paella. Stan licked his fingers and got up for a third helping under the hotel owner's satisfied smile. He tried to repay the hospitality with something more than money and he acted out a couple of sketches from the Golden Years, the silent years. The man was truly delighted. In turn, he showed Stan a photo album in which he was pictured on towering balconies speaking to insurgent multitudes, in government meetings, with important personages unidentifiable to Stan seated around enormous mahogany tables, on the deck of a boat with an English flag, smiling for the camera, in processions, trenches.

The third day, Stan told the stories of the women he had loved and the mistakes he had made, and he showed photographs of them all. The small Spaniard nodded seriously before each photo and in his gruff voice offered ample opinions on each of the women: he analyzed their clothes, their possible characters and the defects he saw in their suitability to coexist with Stan. He said a good many other things which Stan interpreted as benevolent assessments about the breasts of one, the thighs of another or the excellent size of another's ass. Stan was sure about the "excellent-sized ass" because he asked if the word *culo* the Spaniard had used could be translated as "buttocks" and the man confirmed it. In general, Stan was in absolute agreement. He decided this character knew well of what he spoke. He'd never met anyone who understood him better. Even so, on the fourth day, Stan decided to leave La Paz, with the sensation of having achieved whatever had drawn him from so far. A profound sense of "mission accomplished" filled his soul.

He and the Spaniard left each other with a strong embrace that lasted several seconds; very ceremoniously they exchanged calling cards. On the road north, Stan shed a couple of tears for his friend whom he had not been able to communicate with in words. He was sure that were it not for lack of a shared language, they could have done great things together, gone fishing, written an inspired film, not a comedy, a great melodrama. Moreover, he knew that Tomás Fernández, owner of the Hotel La Fuente in La Paz, Southern Baja California, was the best friend he would ever have.

They would never see each other again. They would, however, have news of each other.

JOURNALISTS' STORIES

(J U L I O   S P E A K S)

Do you want the short story or the long one?" I said.

Greg smiled at me. He knew I would begin with the least important. He is quite unskilled at selling an idea. He flings his best story on the table as if it were an interview with Walt Disney after a press conference. I appreciate good narrations, so I blurted out what he thought was the grand finale. Some people never quite get it. Sometimes what starts out small keeps growing.

"The Sandinistas had a draft list to create international brigades in case the gringos invaded Nicaragua, they even had a group ready for the military aspects of the project."

"Ex-Argentine guerrillas," Greg said.

"Exactly, among others. There was also an old Spanish soldier from the Republican era and two Peruvians from the De la Puente Uceda group and the Miristas of the sixties."

"That's not a big deal," said Greg, rubbing his left wrist with his right hand. It hurt from time to time. He had fractured it badly many years ago in a motorcycle accident, or at least that's what he told me. It hurt when it rained and when we didn't have a story at hand. This was marvelous to have a physical sign of good and bad reports.

"Okay, there it is, if we go to Nicaragua, it might be worth looking around to fish out another story."

"In other words, you have a story that might actually make a trip to Nicaragua interesting."

I smiled. It was not easy to sell a used watch to this guy.

"They caught the guy who killed Benjamin Linder," I said unexpectedly.

"Why haven't they spread the news? Why haven't they said so? Are you sure? Shit, that is big, at least here in the States."

"Because they don't know. He's one of the Contras they were after last week in Operation Hammer. The guy hasn't confessed but I interviewed his brother in Mexico, who says he's ready to talk to a gringo journalist if there's money in it."

"How much?"

"I don't know, a thousand dollars, something like that. I think the Sandinistas would give us all the facilities and you could get some gringo magazine to cough up the money. He's one of the guys who trained in El Aguacate, CIA people, Honduras military people."

"Yeah, I think that can be arranged. Are you sure? Are you absolutely sure, brother? Why didn't you tell me earlier?"

"Nobody's going to find him before we do. The guy's not going to say anything. He's waiting for amnesty. He's a miserable little devil, a first-rate asshole. A sunken son of a bitch."

"And he's going to risk it?"

"That's what his brother says."

"Who's the brother?"

"A brother. Who the hell do you want the brother to be? Since you're a lonely orphan, you don't get this, do you? You know—brothers? Two guys who share a mother and a father, or just a mother."

"Fats, this story stinks. A brother in Mexico who offers you a story this big . . . Wait a minute."

Greg walked out toward the room where we kept our papers. He obviously had a file on Linder. What's more, this wasn't the first time we'd written on the subject. We'd done a small report on the electrical center Linder had been constructing when he was shot, published a year ago in *The Village Voice*.

When he returned he brought a blue folder stuffed with papers, and two German beers. At one point he had told me we'd met Linder. Frankly, I didn't remember it. I had one of those false memories of him that we reporters acquire about stories we tell. My false memory also told me that I'd had coffee with Che, but that was impossible, I'd never seen him. Only in photos, the photos that hound us eternally. I remembered a photo of Linder, bearded, with a pleasant smile that engendered trust. The look of a guy you'd allow to take your fifteen-year-old sister to the movies.

"You talk, I'll connect the story."

Now it was my turn to look for a notebook somewhere in my magic bag. I, too, had done some checking before I could swallow the story.

"His name is Cañedo. He's a young kid, about twenty. Do you remember that group that the Contras kidnapped in seventy-eight or seventy-nine? They were middle-class kids who ducked military service or something like that and who kept getting involved. El Loco Suri reported on it. He was in the Job Five force, with the crazy pigs of El Negro Valdés. That's it, that's the story. They stumbled across Linder and they killed him. . . . This is the man who fired. He shot to scare him, that's what his brother says. They realized later that this involved a gringo and got scared. The Sandinistas have him guarded in an interrogation center in Managua. According to the brother, they don't think he's important."

"And the brother?"

"He sells watches in La Merced market in Mexico City. He struck me as an idiot looking for money. A painter friend, Manuel, took me; he thought I might be interested in the story."

"And if it's all a lie just to rip us off?"

"I don't see how. We're giving the money to the brother in Managua, not the brother in Mexico."

"And didn't he ask you not to say anything to the Sandinistas?"

"Even if he asked, he's fucked. I don't make those kinds of deals. Besides, once it's published it'll go straight to his dick."

Greg organized his notes. Inside the folder, on top of a pile of papers, was the photo of Linder I remembered. Greg had taken it in Managua.

We sat there staring at it.

IT SAID ON THE
WALL . . .

. . ."Alex hates old people and children," on a little card pinned on the bulletin board in his office. It was a new contribution from the SD staff. Next to it were others invoiced earlier: "Alex loves widows, but prefers self-made widows." "Alex says: don't trust your mother, even she could be a CIA agent." "Alex's historical utterance: dwarfs, dogs and babies have ears too." "Alex sucks Mengele; Hitler sucks Alex."

Alex encouraged the creative spirit in his kids, "the shitheads," as he affectionately called them, but today he was in an erratic, uncontrolled mood because he'd had to interview a chief of Guatemala's army near the United Nations, a man he wanted to use in an operation. The man had seemed intelligent but cowardly. Halfway through the conversation Alex had begun burning the palm of his hand with a cigarette and the following dialogue ensued:

"What are you doing, Mr. Smith?"

"Burning my hand, Major Becerra. Have you never had such an experience?"

"No, not on my hand."

"Do you believe in torture?"

"I believe it is useful, at times inevitable."

"And you don't think one should experiment before practicing it on others?"

"No, frankly, no." The chief laughed nervously.

"That seems slightly irresponsible."

"If you lend me your cigarette, I can burn the palm of your other hand. Lamentably, I don't smoke."

The office was practically empty. In one cubicle, Nelson, a black man from Jamaica, toiled away with a bunch of Madrid telephone books. Laura, a little farther away, was on the phone speaking to someone in Polish. The next day the SD would be five years old and Alex wanted to celebrate with champagne and cake.

Alex made a positive balance of the five years of survival. He had managed to bring up his monster son through the tunnel of disasters in the late seventies, in the midst of desertions and congressional campaigns. He had survived the transition from Colby to Casey unscathed. The Reagan Administration was not characterized by its subtlety but indeed by an obsession for action, requiring Alex, from 1980 on, to act more swiftly and more directly than usual, but in exchange for a rougher style they offered him dozens of scenarios and hundreds of possible operations. In those years he managed to convince the entire intimate circle of an exiled Chilean socialist leader that his best friend and confidant was a shameful homosexual, fancied adolescents and traded information to the CIA for money, with which he embittered the complete inner circle of exiled socialists. He equipped an operation that ruined relations between the Czechs and the Yemenites for six months; he forced Sandinista counterintelligence to spend enormous time and resources trailing a phantasmal CIA operation in Costa Rica, induced the Syrian president to surround himself with bodyguards for a year, drove a Welsh labor leader to suicide, served as a "reliable source" to reporters for a Mexican magazine without their knowing it. While the official sector got covered with shit over Irangate, the SD's irregulars played small games that produced results. And that was what mattered.

On the table, there was an injunction from Central ordering his team to pass the annual psychiatric exam. He flung the paper in the trash can. He'd find a way to outwit the bureaucrats. If they were to discover that they had seventeen lunatics on staff in New York, they were capable of dismantling the SD. There is nothing more dangerous, Alex said to himself, than an apparently sane bureaucrat.

"Leila, please bring me the ointment for the burns," he asked his assistant. Later he turned on the transistor radio and started studying the complete works of Stalin on the page, text and volume where he'd left off the day before. He truly sympathized with Iosif Vissarionovich Dzhugashvili. The man had a good-natured face, he even played with hollow language, words that said nothing. Fortunately Alex never got bogged down in his reading because next to his texts he kept two excellent biographies

(Deutscher and Souvarine), and he could enjoy the distance between what was said and what was done. The beauty is that they
never coincide. He had to remember to tell that to his kids. There
was a certain wonderful congruence in the permanent disparity
between what's practiced and what's preached. Stalin could have
been the great director that the CIA, always in the hands of military aficionados, Wall Street shopkeepers, amateur spies with no
creative paranoia, never had.

If the bureaucrats knew that the chief of the SD was studying
Stalin and listening to African-Antillean music, they would demol-
ish his transistor radio. He put his book aside and looked through
the papers in his in-box. He found something attractive, a campaign proposition. This was worth the trouble, and could fit within
the SD's experience. He began to plot, and Stalin suddenly struck
him as an ordinary guy who didn't understand that information
was the key to power, that what one thought, what one knew,
made things happen, created beliefs. And later all this came to be
known as "free will."

E I G H T E E N

BEN ARRIVED IN
NICARAGUA PREPARED
TO LEAVE HIS HEART

(N O T E S   F R O M   G R E G ' S   F O L D E R)

- Nothing special about Linder, just another of the sixty
  thousand North Americans who've visited Nicaragua.
  Perhaps his stubbornness. The intensity with which he
  faced his mission. A mitigated obsession. A love affair with
  a persecuted nation?
- Address the moral debt. Those who come to teach ballet
  and build dams. A kind of answer to the existing moral
  debt. Your country pays the mercenaries' salaries.

- The technical networks created by North American civilians in support of Nicaragua. Aid to construct hospitals, harvest crops, teach literacy. The network that covers the United States. Ruminate over the anecdote just after they killed him when one of the construction brigades was about to leave the Los Angeles airport and the organizer led them to a room and announced: "Hey guys, we have just been informed that Ben Linder has been killed in Nicaragua. . . . We all knew this work could be dangerous, but with this new information I'd like you all to think harder. The plane leaves in ten minutes. . . ." It doesn't matter how many went and how many stayed, what matters is those ten minutes. What goes through the mind of a young North American of the new Pepsi generation in those ten minutes? What ghosts flutter inside around his neurons? Who puts those ghosts there?
- Go through the ads in the liberal and radical papers, the technology ads, community plans, the low-paying job offers for union technicians. The "Study Spanish in Nicaragua," the "Fight the Forces in Nicaragua," "Send one hundred dollars to buy generators that give light to the Corinto hospital," Chinese generators bought in Shanghai. The ads for Medical Aid in the pages of *Mother Jones* requesting antibiotics to avoid the infection of a boy's recently cut umbilical cord, calling for aid to resolve the penicillin blockade under which the Nics suffer. The Groundwork projects to construct cheap housing. All the paraphernalia of the brigades of the moral debt.
- Linder as a clown. Be careful here. He toured the streets of Managua on a unicycle dressed as a clown talking children into getting their vaccinations. Hundreds followed him to his clinic shouting: "No more measles!" His semiprofessional work in the National Circus of Nicaragua. He also juggled. Engineer-clown, explore that.
- Record conversation from '82, tape may cover that. What he said about heroism: "I don't have the stock of a hero. Only idiots are heroes before their time because death is hovering close by, it's just that there are some things that must be done. You must do them."
- He was in Nicaragua since '83, as soon as he graduated in

mechanical engineering. I saw him sitting on a park bench, dirty shirt, not having slept, playing with his calculator.

- The El Cua Project: a small hydroelectric plant that brought light to the zone. El Cua: fewer than three thousand inhabitants, close to San José de Bocay, bordering Honduras, a region especially devastated by the Contra raids on Nicaragua, attacking nonmilitary targets like co-ops, buses, construction sites, to further destabilize the region and later retreat to their sanctuary. According to Linder's declarations, the plant would serve to bring energy to night schools, electrical equipment, to dry coffee, for refrigeration and light in the village.
- Blandón's guitar. The Contras attacked the village and stole the guitar of his friend, Oscar Blandón. Blandón didn't have the money to replace it. Linder sent a request to his contacts in Oregon to send him a new one.
- How did he get wrapped up in such an abnormal project? There were thirteen hundred North American volunteers in Nicaragua when Linder was killed. They all had their personal histories motivating them to swim against the stream.
- How did he integrate into society? He lived outside the village in a little house, owned by Oscar Castro, an old man whose sons had been killed by the Contras. They were very tight friends. The house was painted red and black.
- Linder's political past. Practically nonexistent, ten years earlier, at seventeen, he'd been arrested for protesting the construction of a nuclear plant. Founder of the Committee for Solidarity with El Salvador at the University of Washington. His parents and siblings were much more involved in this kind of action. Did he think engineers had to be the practical type? Is that why he disguised himself as a clown to work with children and why he finished his degree in mechanical engineering?
- The electrical plant had been attacked before in mid-March, the militia drove back the Contras. There were rumors of threats against Linder. Linder spoke with colleagues who suggested he flee the region. He stayed on.
- He was armed. A full debate in the United States over whether it was an AK-47 or not. The argument of the State Department's spokespeople to outline the facts of his

death: if he was armed, he deserved it, we're not responsible. There was debate among the volunteers in regions attacked by the Contras over whether to carry arms or not. Some said not to carry arms was suicide, others said arming themselves attracted the Contras. Still others said the contrary, that Contras attacked defenseless targets. Linder chose to arm himself.

- April 28th, 8:00 a.m., Ben Linder sets out for the plant construction site to measure the flow of water before the rainy season. He is accompanied by a couple of young farmers who have been collaborating on the construction, Pablo Rosales and Sergio Fernández. He puts his AK aside to measure the water. They throw grenades at them, his arms and legs are wounded. They finish off his two friends, one with a machete.

- Burial on the 30th in Matagalpa. Clowns and jugglers in the funeral. We were there. See photos of Ortega and his wife, next to Linder's mother. The tremendous pathos in the father's face. I took a picture of a fifteen-year-old Sandinista armed with a rifle crying outside the village. Julio asked him about the death. He knew him. He gave us a picture of Linder drinking coffee: glasses, goatee, very tan, boots that are too big for him, an enormous smile. Not a very North American face, if there is such a thing. He looked like a young professional Nicaraguan, who was savoring his first coffee of the day and who had just received a long-awaited love letter.

JOURNALISTS' STORIES

(G R E G   S P E A K S)

I am a member of a dozen minorities, I told myself, lighting up a filterless Delicado. I had stuffed my backpack with cigarettes during the plane change in Mexico City, enough for this flight plus the next sixteen thousand parachute flights into nothingness that our work would make us undertake. I belong to a dozen minorities and I have to remind myself of that before every beginning, after every dream, just before every morning, so that I never forget it.

In Lost Angeles I am an honorable member of the smoking minority and in my neighborhood a member of the almost non-existent heterosexuals; I am a gringo in Managua, a Yankee in Chile, a *yuma* in Havana, and a Lakers fan when I visit New York; I am a member of the minority of avid Kafka readers and a member of the super-minority of journalists who prefer an American camera to a Japanese one. When these voluntary fringe conditions slip into some hidden corner of my mind, I remember that I belong to one minority by birth, that of the Jews, those rare people who feel obligated to be in a minority, to feel even as excluded on Broadway as in a synagogue or inside Israel's parliament. . . . Sometimes this is a drag, a boil on the hand, but the majority of the time it's a virtue because it makes one wary, defensive, suspicious, professionally paranoid, all of which sooner or later makes one a member of some kind of group.

Fats refused a cigarette. He didn't smoke when he was working, he said it made him nervous. Fortunately he didn't work very often and he smoked the rest of the time. One time I found his ashes next to the toilet in my house in Los Angeles, a fact which he never cared to explain, even when I delicately asked him: "Were you smoking on the can?"

Julio stirred nervously. We were waiting for our interviewee in one of the courtyards of the Managua jail, and I was thinking about myself, about my obsessive minority status. While they were bringing out the guy I set about finding something that would alter my self-image as a minority member, and I found it. I still belonged to an important majority, followers of Carlos Santana music.

The guy was not impressive, a skinny kid about twenty years old, a budding mustache, rebellious hair trying to escape his head. He wore camouflage fatigues frayed at the knees and had a hole in his sleeve where the bullet that brought about his capture had entered. The Sandinista guard who placed him in front of us let him sit on the walls of a fountain in the middle of the courtyard and left as if he'd left us a pile of trash and he had no reason to stick around and smell it.

"So, do you have the money?"

"Do they let you keep it here?"

"You can leave it with the guard under my name when they come get me. They won't take it."

He looked at us with contempt, as if he were paying us to tell him a story, to entertain him. Fats handed him the envelope. The kid took out the bills and counted them one by one.

"I'm going to be fucked in here when you tell this story. But I don't care, sooner or later they had to find out."

"How did you hook up with the Contras?" Fats asked. By beginning the questioning, he had established the division of labor. He would drive the interrogation, I would devote myself to the photos and occasionally try to surprise the kid, exploit him, throw him off balance. The hit is always harder when it comes unexpectedly. I took a few steps back and began shooting my telephoto, trying to capture his carefree face, a face without malice but full of confidence.

"I got caught near Jinotega, the Fifth Resistance, the Blacks' forces. I was deserting the service."

"And you put yourself in another military service to escape this one?"

The boy shrugged.

"Where did they train you? Who directed the training? How

much did they pay you? Were there North American soldiers at the base? Honduran soldiers? Argentine officers?"

The boy looked at Julio in protest. The thousand dollars was to tell one story, not all his stories. I snapped a photo at that moment, trapping his insolent grin.

"No, they trained Nics exclusively. Sometimes Bermúdez was around. One time there was a gringo, but he was visiting, they called him Possey, he carried arms and stocks. There were no Argentines."

"And the place?"

"Choluteca, previously called B-L5 base before it was armed by the FDN, then everyone called it by its name."

"Whose regional command did you belong to?"

"Jorge Salazar."

"And your task force?"

"The fifth in the beginning; later the Sandinistas turned the fifth into shit near Jinotega, and they made a new one with no name or number."

"How many Nicaragua operations did they run?"

"I don't know. Several, enough."

"You didn't normally work near Ocotal?"

The kid is startled, Julio's hit a nerve. I conceal my excitement. I fall back a few steps to reload the camera and take out the black-bound notebook with yesterday's notes for the interview.

"What, you want the stuff on the gringo or you want something else?" He gives a faint smile.

"Was Bandera your task sergeant when it was the fifth?"

"No, Bandera was from another force, we were led by a man called Gualterio Vargas who was missing two fingers from his left hand."

"But three months before the attack on the El Cua plant, the March attack, you were all headed for Ocotal," Julio insists.

"The truth is I don't remember."

"You were leading the task force when they attacked El Cua in March, weren't you?" I ask him. He turns his head in surprise, two fronts are too much, we want to implicate him, but in what? He's surprised the other things matter. Didn't we want to know about the gringo?

"Well, I wasn't exactly leading it, it's just that they had blasted Gualterio's dick the week before and we didn't have anyone to lead."

"You're the ones who massacred the women in the truck in Ocotal," Fats states.

"No. What truck?"

"Did someone speak to you in Choluteca before you went for El Cua?" I ask.

"Who ordered the attack on the electric plant?" Fats asks.

"The business in Bocay was not a coincidence, they went for the same thing twice. Who was so interested in the electric plant?" I ask.

"I'm not hiding anything. I told you to come. I told you to come to tell you about the gringo."

"Earlier, a little earlier," Fats says intransigently. "Earlier. Seven women in a truck machine-gunned. Who slaughtered them? Who hung the head of one of them on a lamppost after raping her? January twenty-ninth."

"Who was so interested in the El Cua plant?" I ask.

"Which one of you should I answer?"

Fats indicates me with a nod. The guy breathes, he doesn't want to know anything about those broken women. Seven nurses whose decapitated bodies lay across the middle of the highway.

"March was coming and we didn't want to go back. There were thirteen of us left in the task force and we didn't want to know anything else about anything. They offered us a hundred fifty bucks each to attack the plant. They said it was a critical electric plant, a military target—"

"Who said?"

"Rosales, from Tegucigalpa. With a gringo, but the gringo didn't speak this time. Somehow the operation failed. The soldiers saw us and hit us with AK bursts before we even got near."

"What was the gringo like? What was his name?"

"They called him Walter."

"A thirty-year-old blond with a lisp and a scar over his eyebrow?" Fats asks, inventing a character.

"Yes. That's him."

"He doesn't exist, sucker, Fats just invented him," I tell him. My Spanish confuses him again. I must have the classic gringo face, proof against looking like a Contra.

"Well, it seemed like him."

"Like who?" Fats asks.

"Like the person you described."

"No, no he wasn't like that, he was five feet, five inches tall with a graying beard, dark glasses even at night, and he spoke Spanish with an accent which struck you as strange, little snitch, but not a Central American accent. That accent was from Chile. His name wasn't Walter, it was Benjamín. Not Benjamin the gringo way, but our way, with an accent at the end. He smoked dark cigarettes, like short little cigars, Dutch, and went around calling you 'kiddo.' "

The man was upset. His head was racing; we were on his side, but how did we know so much? Fats gave a faint smile. Old Fats had balls, how had he guessed? I had to ask later where he found this magic trick. I deliberately created a pause, to protect Fats's trick, and lit a cigarette.

"Who sent you here? I'm not saying anything. Nothing besides the stuff on the gringo, but that's my only thing. I don't know a thing about you two."

"Calm down, you retard. What did Benjamín tell you when he ordered the attack on the El Cua hydroelectric plant?"

"To kill the gringo."

"How were you going to identify him?" I asked, remembering Linder's sunburned face the last time I saw him alive.

"They gave me a picture to study, then they took it away again. But I didn't recognize him. Pablo recognized him. The gringo had put down his rifle and there he was, doing weird things, near the water."

"So then you wiped him out with a machete blow?"

"For a hundred and fifty dollars you killed him," Fats said, turning his back as if, for him, the interview were over.

"You wiped him out with your machete?" I asked, grabbing the tape recorder from the floor where Julio had placed it and lifting it to the boy's face, who drew back as if it would burn him.

"Yes," he answered.

TWENTY

ELENA JORDAN'S SECOND REJECTED THESIS PROPOSAL

The potential of the North American drug-consuming market, its proximity to Mexico and the tremendous economic turnover generated by narcotics traffic have converted this marginal production activity (marginal in the sense of its illegal status and level of industrialization) into the most important trampoline for an economic blast-off for any Mexican citizen with imagination and balls, when and if he or she has an enterprising mind on the commercial track, even if it is immoral and shows little respect for the law.

According to DEA estimates unofficially gathered in the Mills and Vasconcelos reports (*La Jornada,* February 11, 1988), the volume of dollars picked up by Mexican networks involved in marijuana operations with the United States equals at least the gross annual product of the three most economically important states in the north of the country: Baja California, Nuevo León and Tamaulipas.

This kind of operation, according to the above-cited report, has spawned a new generation of multimillionaires whose economic interests, based in narcotics traffic, have expanded into sectors such as the hotel and tourist industries, cattle raising, modern irrigation farming, commerce, machinery and transportation exports.

Fifty years ago, in the country's northern region, a similar development of new barons occurred, essentially linked to the mining and metallurgical industries (see, for example, Leticia Reina and Sergio Perello: *Millionaires and Fraud in the Construction of Coahuila's Mining Emporiums,* ENAH, 1986; or the extraordinary work on the double-entry bookkeeping of the mining industries in Chihuahua by Enrique Cortazar).

The purpose of this thesis is to compare the biographies of a group of known Mexican drug traffickers who have recently risen to fame (Caro Quintero, Sicilia Falcón, Don Neto, Rolando M. Limas) with some of the robber barons who amassed enormous fortunes under the protection of an alliance with the governments of the Revolution subsequent to the end of the armed period.

Starting from the fashionable concepts of that branch of social anthropology which developed into what we know as "life stories" (Sergio Yanez, p. 132), it is possible to coordinate a series of biographies and trace the parallel significant dates of some with others in search of shared qualities.

The thesis seeks not only to find a similarity in concepts such as risk, opportunity, development of innovative infrastructures, originality, relations with the power sector and contextual utilization of key conditions in the world market, but also to postulate, in appropriate psychosocial and psychological portraits, a criminal sociopathology (Bremer, II 21–27). This thesis furthermore intends to bring the prevailing social morals under analysis and, in a parallel study, provide an analysis of the social schizophrenia that turns some people into industry commanders and others into vulgar criminals.

Following Hans Magnus Enzenberger's line of reasoning (*Politics and Crime,* chapter "The Ballad of Chicago: Model of a Terrorist Society"), one would have to readapt the concept of criminality in accordance with the collective uses of society and its best and most recent needs. This is therefore not about proposing a vision of the drug trafficker as a marginal industrialist, adapted to the peripheries of the system by market mechanisms, but rather about the character of both social indices as variations of social amorality.

The thesis will attempt to put forth a series of parallel spaces, two of which I would like to point out: an attempt to construct a reflective look at the drug trafficker's mythology with the mythology of the robber baron, the classes in which they are produced and the behavioral models they generate. This will follow Alphonse Capone's reasoning when he suggested in one of his last public interviews: "I am a ghost wrought from a million minds," and compare that to Nelson Rockefeller's vision, summed up in his statement: "Millions are made from myths and from other millions."

A second level of investigation was suggested to me by the quotation with which the Valencian author Ferrán Torrent opens his novel, quite in accordance with the philosophies of disillusionment that have proliferated in Europe, and that states: "Society is divided into two classes, those who have money and those who never give up hoping to have it" (Torrent, *Don't Play Games with Me to the Police Inspector*, p. 19). It relates to the concept of permissible risk, an increasingly used category in management handbooks. (Lemus, p. 12, 134–136. Weaber: "The Philosophy of Triumph," Limusa, 1987). This vision invites me to break down in studied processes the legal and illegal aspects continued in each of them.

This is the initial project which, in the case of approval and previous analysis of the eleven cases proposed for your consideration (see Appendix 2), would take the form of a more definitive project.

TWENTY-ONE

STAN RECEIVES A LETTER FROM MEXICO

Midway through filming *The Big Noise,* in 1944, Stan received a letter from Mexico. This was not unusual; thousands of letters from the entire planet escaped the war embargoes and managed to reach Hollywood. But this particular letter had not remained in the hands of one of the producer's secretaries. It was a personal letter. Stan liked the brightly colored stamp, the Mexican eagle biting the serpent's head. He tried to read the elegantly formed, round letters, but he couldn't get beyond *"Querido Stan,"* so he stuffed it in his pocket, then transferred it to a vase in the hall of his house, and there the letter dreamed the dream of abandoned mail for almost two months.

At the end of the filming of the comedy, Stan was very unhappy, and in one of his moments of depression an escape to Mexico crossed his mind. He then remembered the letter and retrieved it from the vase. It wasn't hard to find a translator. One of his maids, Doña Laura, was from Aguascalientes and could read. He thus discovered that his friend, Tomás Fernández, owner of the Hotel La Fuente in La Paz, wished to create a prize for investigative journalism, in which their names would be associated, his own and Stan Laurel's. He also invited him to spend a few days at the beach. Tomás figured he could contribute five or six thousand dollars to the project and asked Stan whether he could be counted on for a few more. At the same time he suggested a series of criteria, to which Stan, in his maid's version, paid little attention, suggesting to Doña Laura that they skip the rest of the letter. A couple of weeks later, Stan brought it up with one of his lawyers and, with a brief note scribbled on the back of the envelope, instructed him to accept and imposed his only conditions, that the journalistic prize be called "Pancho Villa," and that it not be awarded until forty years after being established. Forty years seemed long enough, for no journalist would ask him how this strange affair came about. Later he forgot the matter.

THE MAKING OF A DRUG TRAFFICKER'S LEGEND (I)

A pockmarked guy approached and said to you:

"Are you that man whose name means danger? You're M. Limas, right?" He made it sound like *"Me la limas,"* a vulgar invitation to fellatio. "M. Limas, M. Limas, what a cowardly name."

Right there you killed him with a stab between the ribs, ruining the knife's point, you'd never be able to use it properly again, or maybe you would, maybe better, because that knife with the chipped point would indicate to anyone interested that it had already been used, it had struck bone like a bad bullfighter's sword.

You were a bastard, Rolando, no doubt about it, surviving in hookers' bars where even lottery salesmen wouldn't venture, sleeping in your own vomit one day after another; with a case of syphilis you couldn't shake no matter how many million doses of penicillin you took; because every time you got rid of it, it came back like a gypsy's curse. But all that shit was like a dream, and one day you were in Acapulco selling coke, and the next day you were letting hot cars pass into McAllen, Texas, one day drunk in Matamoros and the next getting wasted with two dirty traitors in TJ. It was like a dream because you knew this was part of the apprenticeship of the big ticket and as soon as you learned everything, you'd start sowing and reaping.

When did the fat cows first let you milk them? When did dear God give the order: "Don't fuck around with this guy anymore; let him become a keeper of the money he deserves after all the shit he's had to swallow"? What started for you when you hooked up so tightly with the gang from Chihuahua and they entrusted you with getting the whores for the harvest of the poppy fields? They'd gathered two hundred farmhands and kept them like slaves in the times before Moses was the prince of Egypt and for two months they retained whores who served as cooks and maids in addition to whores. And you went to the heights of Jalisco to gather old prostitutes and you emptied close to two brothels and stuck the women in a van. It must have started there, because when the military came sweeping through, the only asshole who knew where the airfield and the warehouse were was you, and you sold that to Milton for fifty thousand dollars. From there to reality.

You were the same asshole, Rolando, but in one year you were rolling in cash, and when it came time to crown the Queen of Spring in Ciudad Obregón, you got it in your head that she was your girl and you sent the boys ahead with shotguns to sell tickets at a thousand pesos apiece. They put the girl on top of the counter and said, "Isn't Henrietta gorgeous, and don't you want to buy the tickets, compatriot?" And so the girl won the elections and they were clean elections, vote for vote counted, and not those bullshit elections the PRI holds.

There, those who had to notice you noticed you and they called you. And you, Rolando, did not commit the stupidity of pretending to be a powerful man, dressed in a small phosphorescent red jacket, showing the .45 and with four idiotic thugs protecting you from the dust your boots kicked up. You were going to sell technology, kiddo. You were the never-again-to-the-border boy. You were going to make all the assholes south of Río Bravo cross the line with two hundred grams of coke up their asses, well encased, yes, because you didn't want it to burst from a fart and push them out in front instead of staying at the back. You were going to mastermind operations so grand they'd go crazy in Los Angeles from all the shoddy marijuana jobs you'd give them. You were an asshole who, before being a no-count whorehouse loafer, was a public accountant certified at the University of Mexico. And in a short time you would sit at the table with a banker and a governor.

When do you sleep, Rolando? Because you spend these last years organizing deals and fucking and conducting business here and there and outfitting yourself at gringo stores and hanging out with a grade-school teacher who when not harpooned with heroin teaches you geography and English and whom you occasionally handcuff to the foot of the bed to repeat to you at night where the capital of Malaysia is, how many pesos in a pound sterling or how you pronounce "race horse" in English, because at night you don't sleep, you merely rest. Because you don't sleep. It's been two years since you've slept. And that's the most important thing. On a border lined with assholes who occasionally sleep, there is one asshole, the asshole of assholes, Rolando M. Limas, born in Toluca, who never sleeps.

And it's very scary to do business with an asshole who never shuts his eyes or gets upset, who never loses his cool. An asshole who doesn't know sleep. A son of a bitch who, while others go around with their best faces, wanders around swaddled in his old blanket, like a vampire in the night, his eyes eternally open.

ALEX THOUGHT KLEE . . .

. . .was unpleasantly crazy, but was absolutely sane when it came to tricking others. And Klee was taking advantage of the idiot Americans who, having found culture late, spent the best hours of their lives wearing down the heels of their shoes in museums. It didn't matter that he had died many years ago. He was exploiting the imbeciles; with his suave naïveté, he put them in front of his paintings and extracted sighs of admiration. Two canvases from the latest exhibit at the Metropolitan had particularly offended Alex, one painted between 1921 and 1923 that was called "Woman with Bent Head," because for some strange reason it seemed to revive the image of a woman from the past whom he wanted to forget, but who mysteriously opened the way through the painting to his memories. But an infantile painting of lions that Klee had repeated with variations multiple times bothered him even more. A painting of four stylized, tailless lions and a sun, with a fortress-city in the background. This one annoyed him because the lions were pleasant and decorative; it put them in harmony with the afternoon sun.

Leaving the Met in a wicked mood, he wandered around picking up snippets of conversations. A couple of old men debating fishing rods, two teenagers comparing the finer points of New Jersey hamburgers and Thirty-sixth Street hamburgers. A girl complaining that the rain had screwed up her whole day. Alex knew the day did not belong to this girl with the long braid who spouted nonsense from the first floor window of a Seventy-ninth Street apartment building at anyone who cared to listen. The day was not hers. If it did by some chance belong to anyone, it was Alex's, and he had nothing against rain. Rain was a blessing that kept imbeciles off the street.

Alex had the clear knowledge that he could dominate the city, not totally and not forever, but long enough to stop it in midair, detain it, pass on the cost, establish ownership. Lamentably, when he slept, he lost control; when he got distracted, it likewise slipped away. Running New York was a complicated affair, too many things happened at once.

He passed through Central Park not noticing the marvelous green trees emerging from summer toward autumn. Instead, he carefully watched a group of Sikhs with long beards and turbans eating peanut butter sandwiches on a bench, attracting a horde of ants. The idiots laughed; those assholes didn't know that he possessed the information, including a map on a one-to-twenty-five scale, that would let him enter the Sacred Grounds and gain access, dodging traps and secret corridors, to the Golden Temple of Amritsar. They could cover the Central Park lawns with tiny ants, but from now on a little less arrogance would behoove them. The first chance he got, he would give the map to the Hindu security guards. Let the Sikhs go complain to Paul Klee.

JOURNALISTS' STORIES

(J U L I O   S P E A K S)

Greg was totally drunk in the elevator of Managua's Hotel Intercontinental. Two bottles of Flor de Caña rum had worked the miracle. That and a visit to a hospital with half a dozen kids mutilated by shrapnel when mortars had bombed their village, a peasant farm community nineteen miles from the Honduras border. The children knew the names of the mortars they'd used and the calibers of the projectiles by heart, how much each one cost and which division of "humanitarian aid," authorized by the United States Congress for the Contras, had provided the money to buy them. They'd probably heard it from one of the nurses accompanying a commission of Swiss doctors who had in turn heard it from some Sandinista military official. The kids had told this to Greg, not without pride in their voices. A twelve-year-old girl had explained that they'd been fucked, but that later these kids had nabbed a group of Contras on this side of the border and they'd fucked them back. They had to have been the ones who'd bombed them, she told Greg.

I left him under the shower singing "The Battle Hymn of the Republic," his nose running, letting the rum escape with the hot water and soap suds. We'd discuss our plans later. Greg said he had an excellent idea; I had half a story that if it congealed promised to be extremely important. Maybe we'd both get them done, maybe neither of us would, maybe we'd split up for a while, each to his own turf, to write his own story, and later we'd translate for each other and try to place them somewhere.

At times we got tired of all this.

Managua by night is a nonexistent city. The few landmarks that exist by day disappear completely and one hides in wastelands, in nowhere land, in dark alleys and in esplanades that shouldn't be there. It's a city wrought from disasters. Bombings, earthquakes, broken pipes, floods, fears.

I wanted to live. This comes over me from time to time, and I feel an inevitable desire to hear boleros and drink soft drinks and sharpen my senses and relish seeing, not touching, the women who sit next to me and splash their scents and their million sparkles a minute and the brutally brilliant colors of their skirts. It was one of those nights and I was looking in the direction of the lake for the house of a Mexican film director who was making a short documentary about the war, but deep down I didn't really want to find him. I wanted to sit on a park bench surrounded by posters of Sandino, whom I love a lot because he seemed like some Nicaraguan straight out of the Casasola photos of the Mexican Revolution, and listen to love songs until I cried with sadness, remembering girlfriends with fancy hairdos and blue tulle skirts, girlfriends I never had.

I don't really know how I got back to the hotel. Greg was wrapped in two towels, looking like an extra from *Lawrence of Arabia,* consuming a ton of vitamin C and antacids and potassium salts and fizzy pills, to see whether he could kick his body's depression.

"Let's get out of here, Fats. We're headed for hell's inferno."

"It's called an inferno, asshole, because there's no air-conditioning."

"Where to now?"

"Mexico, Shorty. I've got a story, since we don't have anything else to write. If you're over your hangover, I'll tell you about it."

"To California, Fats. I've got a perfect story. Ideal to show you that good gringos are a joke. My story, which is better than yours, is this: What happened to the Berkeley boys? Where are the kids from Columbia twenty years later? Where are the people who led the student rebellion of the sixties and what are they doing? Where the fuck is sixty-eight? Fuck them all! Do you know what Buffalo Bill said? 'The only good gringo is a dead gringo.' "

"That bit about the only good gringo being a dead gringo was Crazy Horse's, Chief of the Sioux. And don't come at me with this inverted patriotic shit. You know how to find the Mexican in a bus full of Japanese? He's the one with his finger up his ass while the other idiots snap their cameras. Why the fuck do you think it's your fault that the money for those bastards' bombs came from some neighbor of yours in Los Angeles? Your job is to write about it. Take part by writing. Isn't that what we do every day, *compadre?*"

Greg dropped two Alka-Seltzers into a glass and watched them dissolve. Later he polished them off in a single, long swallow. Finally, in his best, recently recovered Spanish, he asked me, "What do you want us to do in Mexico?"

T W E N T Y - F I V E

SKIING

In April of 1947, after two weeks of hospitalization, Tomás Fernández died, accidentally run over by a car. Obviously, he refused the attendance of a priest and established his only contact with the future by submitting his biographical notebook to his son, an agricultural engineer, who kept it in a chest. The funeral was held in La Paz, and by his express wishes his ashes were scattered over the cliffs of Cabo San Lucas into the Sea of Cortés, far from the Bay of Biscay where he'd been born, but a sea just the same, as he said hours before his death.

Stan never heard about the death of his strange friend. Almost eighteen years later, in February 1962, he in turn suffered a heart attack, and though he survived the initial onset, he remained in a very delicate condition.

His final words, or at least those registered by his biographers, were part of a fairly absurd dialogue with the nurse who worked the night shift:

"I'd rather be skiing."

"Do you know how to ski, Mr. Laurel?"

"No, but it would be better than what I'm doing here."

At the time of his death, Stan had a mess of papers, lawsuits against some of his film producers, various muddles from his multiple divorces. Add to this the regular will and testament conflicts. In the middle of that disaster of papers, placed in the hands of a San Francisco law firm, was a paper obscurely outlining the project for the Pancho Villa journalism award.

T W E N T Y - S I X

THE MAKING OF A DRUG
TRAFFICKER'S LEGEND (II)

You were one, you are others, and you're on your way to becoming one of Mexico's black legends. It's been a good long time since you could have washed your hands and devoted yourself to legal business, to robbing within the law; but that doesn't fly with you. You're not going that way. You'd rather make half a million dollars in one week with three truckloads of drugs and burn half of it bribing the world's most sightless people, guys who don't see a truck pass because they're blindfolded with twenty thousand one-dollar bills. You'd rather do that than raise milk cows in Coahuila.

But in order to stay in shape, you have changed. Before, Rolando, you were the man who never slept, now you're the man who's never there, the genuinely invisible little prick, the missing, the man who enters through the door and then isn't inside, the man who never left because he never came. You are like the sixty-ton trucks that cross the border kicking up not one speck of dust because they don't really exist. They say you traded in your face for a new one, you got rid of the scar on your chin that you got from a chipped bottle of Tecate beer in Hermosillo, they say you're not blond at all anymore, that you wear dark glasses that change color according to the neon lights. They say you change your face every week, that you've got a plastic surgeon in the back of your limousine who devotes himself to nothing but regularly redesigning your face.

You've got a beach house in Ensenada, but the furniture is draped with dust sheets. You've got a house in the Mexico City valley, but there's no furniture there at all. They are the houses of someone who doesn't exist. You only have them so that the police who say they're on your trail can look after them. They are paid to look for you, you pay them to take care of the houses you never see. It's a straight, fair deal. They work like hell and get two salaries.

In Toluca, you donated a hospital to the people who lived in the Rosario neighborhood. Let them get sick as the devil. Besides, someone forgot to staff the hospital with doctors. You forgot, too. There, the dogs howl at night and the screwed-up adolescent couples get down and fuck on the cold floor. Not only do you not sleep, or have a face, but you're also the owner of phantasmal hospitals, empty houses.

But you're still the same asshole, Rolando. Because you do see, and you control. Like a buzzard flying across the border, checking every shady deal, every laboratory that stinks of sulfuric acid, every sown field in the middle of the sierra that is suddenly ready to be harvested and sent off in phantom trucks. You're out there, floating like a skydiver over your millions, like a ghost. You're twenty-seven years old and they've already written a Mexican ballad about you that the Mexicali radio stations have banned. But sometimes, in the middle of a hot Tijuana night, a mariachi band appears in the center of a plaza, hired by who knows who, playing "The Ballad of Grass," and without a single word, without even whispers from accomplices, the whole world knows you must be nearby, listening to the ballad, watching for every off-key trumpet note, insomniac, with other people's faces.

THE MEETING WAS
HELD . . .

. . .at midnight, Cinderella's hour. Alex did not wait for everyone to finish taking their seats in the conference room to establish the point of departure:

"Let's establish an axiom: by an occupational idiosyncrasy, journalists do not believe in coincidences. Are we all in agreement?"

He did not obtain great comments. The junior SD members had learned not to try to be witty before their time in conversation with Alex. Someone got up and went to the deteriorating coffeepot, poured four cups and returned to serve them at the table.

"An axiom prior to the last one and that we've discussed many times, the Goebbels axiom: if a lie is repeated with sufficient frequency, it becomes the closest thing to the truth we know. One more, prior to the prior one: credibility of information is identified with the solidity of the source that emits it. If you want someone to believe something, it is essential that the archangel Gabriel whisper it in his ear. Finally, one last factor: if you mix two elements of fear, you create a reaction of hatred. All right then, here you have the essential philosophical elements of our campaign crassly dubbed by one of our cerebral leaders the 'Trojan Horse.' But so as not to be vulgar ourselves, it shall be known by the more sophisticated name 'Operation Dream of Snow White,' because this nation remains in urgent need of heroes and doesn't claim vigorously enough the few it does have, almost all of whom were created by Walt Disney. I need to compose the team and I want to know what each of you is doing and how important it is."

"How important is this issue? I'm involved with the Kabul

thing," said Jason, who by dint of working at it physically resembled his idol, Jason Robards.

"Priority of priorities. This is our biggest gig right now," Alex said, charming them all with one of his marvelous smiles, the kind that days later still floated in the air.

PART II

INTERLACING PLOTS

LEON'S NOVEL

The old man in a French peasant's blue shirt carefully closed the door, placed his wire-framed glasses on the bridge of his nose and made his way toward the desk, absolutely convinced that he was committing an atrocity, that he was breaking the rules, that he was perpetrating an amoral act.

The light entered indirectly and a pair of sparrows perched idly on the windowsill, the old man opened his thick notebook with the stiff black marbled cover that he had asked Sylvia for, and began writing on the first page: "*Words of Glass,* a mystery by Leon Wagner Salazar. Preliminary notes."

The page was blank, he started from zero. He would approach the novel like someone entering a dark tunnel, the end of which is occasionally illuminated by flashes of lightning. Unlike his ultra-meditated writings, this would be a celebration of the cult of improvisation. Writing it would be like reading it, letting it unfold in his hands, before his eyes. There was a plan, though, if these vague ideas could be called a plan: construct a highly detailed outline, then return to the beginning to adjust the defects in the general picture, revise definitely. He began to write with hurried strokes:

1. The novel begins with the sentence "The fever of Summer seemed to dominate everything," and begins in Madrid, Spain, around June 1936, just before the onset of the Civil War. Update my 1916 memories. The economic bonanza of the War must have altered the city's exterior aspect and much of the things I experienced. Consult with someone from Madrid. Set up the pre–Civil War climate, its manifestation in the streets, its daily expression.

The protagonist arrives in Madrid.

My memories: Madrid. The station. It rips me apart. A great number of problematic existences. Chained prisoners, newspaper boys, shoeshiners, tour guides, agents commissioned for who knows what and for everything, beggars. That teeming multitude in Southern Europe's three peninsulas. When, upon arriving in a new city, a multitude of people wrench the luggage from our hands and simultaneously offer to shine our shoes (one "shine" per foot), sell us newspapers, crabs, peanuts, etc. . . . , you can be sure that the city leaves something to be desired from a sanitation point of view, that there is a lot of counterfeit money circulating, that store prices are set without compassion and that the taverns are ridden with insects.

Hotel de Paris, a tavern where they do not speak French. Use mimicry. Emelia, the owner, sets the price with her fingers. When one registers surprise, she reveals her teeth, at which point there is no recourse but to pay.

In the streets, people with felt shoes endure the rain. Street urchins cry their papers and later play heads or tails on the wet pavement.

One afternoon, an unexpected tour guide took me to the highest bridge in Madrid and eulogized its great potential for suicide. (What is the name of that river?)

The Café Universal, overflowing with people. There's a greater variety of types beyond the Pyrenees; from the gypsy thief to the Julius Caesar profile. The first shock upon entering is a deafening cacophony. Everyone speaks loudly, they gesticulate, slap each other on the back, burst into laughter, drink coffee and smoke.

Two kinds of monumental buildings dominate Madrid: churches and banks. Old Spain puts its capital into churches. In the marble recesses, the gold shines for the world to see, as if it were testimony to the good relations between the owners and heaven. But Spain puts the majority of its money into banks, not churches. And in the battle over Spain's soul, the banks erect enormous buildings, temples of overwhelming sumptuousness. Their number is countless and they stand between the churches and the grand cafés.

2. Reflections of that era valid for the protagonist. When sitting in a café, grasping nothing of the rapid Spanish language, one is ideally positioned to study a city, prepared or not for that study.

3. Continue with Madrid: a great city, especially at night. Here one stays out very late, until one or two. The cafés are still full after midnight, the streets splendidly lit. Nocturnal life in Paris is also extremely intense, but only in isolated parts of the city. In Madrid one eats at nine or ten. Theaters open at ten or eleven and end at one in the morning. The pace of life is lazy.

4. The protagonist's first contact with the city envelops him, just as it did me twenty years ago. Fascination with the foreign. The will to see and observe, before acting. Back to the political climate. It has to have profoundly surprised him. The skin-deep violence, the posters, the graffitied walls, the insolence of the Guardia Civil, the threat of the proletariat. The sensation that the wave of the revolution had taken off and destiny could sway it in any direction. The tension should touch all the secondary characters: doorman, waiter, bricklayer, banker, cop.

5. The character's last name is Wolf. North American? He's lost his left arm. For now, I don't have more on him.

6. Madrid again: "I find myself for the first time in this city where I know no one and no one knows me, literally no one. What's more, I don't understand the language."

   He takes a letter or a telegram to the Post Office. Madrileños ironically call it "Our Lady of Communication." He visits the Prado Museum. My impressions from that time. (Reconstruct them from my journal.) Recall in particular the impact the hips of Rubens's feminine figures had on me, the vitality they entail, and the tragic asceticism of El Greco's figures.

7. They've been following Wolf since his arrival in Madrid that morning. Atocha train station. A small, well-dressed man. His clothes contrast with Wolf's, who carelessly wears a dark

blue corduroy jacket. Wolf knows they've been following him all day. It doesn't seem to bother him. In fact, he takes small measures not to lose him. Until this moment, we did not know Wolf was being followed or that he was aware of it. The entire beginning of the story is dedicated to Madrid and the impressions it leaves on the character. The sensation that Wolf feels revitalized by contact with the new city must be insinuated. (I don't know exactly why he feels it.)

8. The *pensión* at night. Wolf lies down. He hides a pistol under his pillow, and another lower-caliber one in one of his boots. It's hot. He dozes. Screams in the street. It's not a fire, just two guys conversing loudly below the window. A priest walks by, smoking a cigar.

The afternoon was getting late. Leon carefully closed his notebook. Not irate, but clearly dissatisfied with the results. He knew it would be like this. He would always be dissatisfied with such an absurdity. But he did like that bit about the priest smoking a cigar. A cigar-smoking priest in his cassock in Madrid at night. Slowly he was forming his character. There were funnier things. The idea that the city brought Wolf back to life was good. Where had he spent the last years? Who was he? Leon hid his notebook in the trunk, with several confidential documents, and opened the manuscript of Stalin's biography, which he was reworking to transform into an article for *Life*. Suddenly he craved hot tea. He left his office and walked toward the kitchen, ruminating.

"Natalia, can you get me some tea?"

"Do you deserve it?" his wife asked, smiling.

"I don't think so. I didn't make much progress on the *Life* article," Leon Davidovich Trotsky said, returning the smile.

MIAMI

The dwarf climbed out of the trunk shaking a pair of maracas, singing like Carmen Miranda. He ran around the room possessed by a malignant fever, an insane rage seeming to have sprung from a strange illness which left him half an hour to live and which obliged him to take advantage of those last thirty minutes to leave testimony of his fundamental stay on the planet. The air-conditioning was on full blast. It was a contradiction, the tropical dwarf singing *"Mama Iñes"* and the polar air freezing Benigno to the bone, and he seemed not to pay much attention to either one.

"Look, sit still, you motherfu—"

"Come dance with me, tight-ass," the dwarf said, ignoring the suspicious look the bodyguard shot at him.

"If you don't calm down I'll lock you up again."

"If you don't let me dance, I'll tell the motel manager that I'm here and you'll have to pay for a double room. Don't be an asshole, Rolando gave you the money for both of us and you're stashing it like a pimp, sneaking me into the hotel in the trunk so no one knows. Let's see, asshole, how're you going to get me out of here? You gonna walk the streets all fucking day with a trunk?"

"If you don't calm down, I'll calm you down, goddamn dwarf," Benigno replied and turned on the TV.

The dwarf concluded that Benigno hadn't decided how to get him out of the room. He thought about it twice and discovered he didn't give a shit how Benigno did it. It wasn't his responsibility. An episode of "Gunsmoke" was on TV, a rerun he'd seen fifteen years ago in Mexico. He abandoned his maracas on one of the pistachio-colored spreads that covered the twin beds and said to his roommate:

"I'm going to tell you how it ends, worthless Benigno. I've already seen it, you shithead."

"The boss sent you because you speak English, you worthless piece of shit. Pick up the phone and rent a car, a large van. For people, you loser, not for dwarfs."

"Listen to me, asshole, don't call me a dwarf to my face. Call me by the name my mother gave me, Marcelino, and if you don't like it, just act like you don't see me."

Marcelino the dwarf walked over to the minibar, kicked it open and took out a Heineken.

"The kind I like, Dutch."

Benigno ignored him. The dwarf was dwarf enough. He was only about three feet tall but he didn't have the deformed face that some dwarfs have. He was simply small, and definitely tacky; he wore a big plaid suit and a salmon-colored shirt with an enormous silvery tie. Benigno was skinny, very dark, and had a permanently contorted face, as if his food had hurt him. His eyes were glazed over and he had a tiny, usually greasy mustache. He carried a holster for his pistol hanging from his armpit over an unwashed pepper-and-salt-colored shirt. In the trunk, one of those enormous old two-doored pieces that you'd see in a chorus girl movie, he kept an iron Colt .45.

The dwarf drank some of his beer with relish, then placed it on the floor in the middle of the hall, secretly hoping that Benigno would trip over it, and went to the phone.

"What time does the boss arrive?"

"What, you don't know?"

"I lost my sense of time locked in that damn trunk."

"This afternoon. We have to be at the airport around five."

Marcelino flipped through the motel directory, found the car rental service and dialed carefully. His English was fairly fluent but even when he deepened his voice, the woman at the agency mistook him for a girl. He ordered the car for three-thirty, hung up and returned to his beer. On the way he retrieved his maracas.

"I'm going to sing one of the songs your mother, who must have a been a great whore, used to sing you. Listen, I learned this in a tavern in Mexicali. It's called 'Mama, I Don't Know What the Negro Wants.' "

"The prick," Benigno responded, moderately interested in what Chester was going to do to the guy who was determined to empty a bottle of whiskey in one long swig.

"That's probably true, but I'm singing it to you anyway."

Benigno looked at him hard. He threatened, "This is the last time I get sent on an assignment with a dwarf."

"A dwarf, but with balls this big," Marcelino said, throwing open his arms toward infinity.

"That's exactly what it takes to put up with you," Benigno fired back, and didn't speak again until three o'clock, when they left for the airport, taking precautions so that the maid would not see the dwarf and make Benigno pay for the double room.

JOURNALISTS' STORIES

(G R E G   S P E A K S)

Not only is Julio capable of deep sleep on airplanes, he also snores. I spend half the flight wondering whether I should pretend I don't know him or should explain to nearby passengers that he's a famous journalist hopelessly suffering from an incurable disease, to evoke their pity. Occasionally I elbow him.

After so many years, I should have a more peaceful relationship with airplanes, but I can't help thinking the ground is six thousand feet below, awaiting our fall. That's why if Julio snores, I just drink. Gin. The ideal drink for airplanes. It dulls the brain, packs it with cotton candy, makes the tongue heavy, leaving a sweet taste you'll remember with horror days later. As the pilot announced we were over Guatemalan territory, I was on my fourth gin on the rocks under the irritated watch of the stewardess, who couldn't give a shit if I got drunk but was running low on the tiny bottles and was annoyed to give them to one single passenger. The gin was aggravating the previous day's Flor de Caña hangover. If this went on, I'd have to choose between Alcoholics Anonymous and marriage.

Julio emitted a strange noise, a walrus's hiccup mixed with an elephant's fart, startling a luxuriant blonde trapped between Fats and the window and wishing she'd stayed in Managua. I opted for compassion.

"Mister Fernández, you have a phone call," I said, shaking him.

Fats opened one eye and smiled. It must have been a good dream, and by the look he gave the blonde she seemed to have been the lascivious main character.

"Was I snoring, chief?"

"Very good."

"That's weird, I don't usually snore during erotic dreams," he said, staring at the blonde.

I thought Julio, too, would someday have to choose—between marriage and Snorers Anonymous.

"Where are we?"

"Over Guatemala."

"How many gins have you had?"

"Four. This is my fourth."

"You're the closest thing I've ever seen to a British old lady in the midst of the Indian Empire's collapse. . . . I like planes. . . . Miss, do you like planes?" he said, looking at our flustered female companion. The woman dissolved into complex and profuse apologies and Fats decided this blonde was created expressly for some of his dreams. Then he turned his back, closed his eyes and went back to sleep. To my astonishment, three minutes later he was snoring. There was nothing I could do but order my fifth gin.

The gin and a collection of Quevedo's poetry I'd bought in a used-book store in Managua accompanied me over the final miles. Quevedo created that precise image, that perfect sonority and exactness of idea that no matter how many articles I wrote in my life, I would never achieve. Journalism lacked that precision. Journalism made a mist of words, it hid truths behind the cult of information. We'd been fooled into thinking that sixty-three percent of the electorate, the nine burned cadavers, the proof of fingerprints, the confidential document, held more truth than sentences like this: "Search in Rome for Rome, oh wanderer! And in Rome itself you will not find it." One could get more drunk on Quevedo than on Mexican Black Bear gin. "Yesterday's gone, tomorrow has not arrived, today is moving without stopping at any point; I am a was and a will be and a tired is."

Julio got off the plane sleepy and began to wake up in the long hall between Gate 14 and passport control. He finished coming to while we waited for our luggage.

"What does *postrer* mean?"

"*Postre?* Dessert."

"No, *postrer.* Sonnet Fifty-two, line seven," I said, showing him the book.

"The last, the *postrero.* What the hell are you doing reading Quevedo? You have to lug around a good dictionary in addition to the book."

"I want to be a cultured Mexican friend to have," I said in deliberately bad Spanish.

"When did you become a Quevedo fan?"

"Shit, Julio, cut with the national anthem bit. Who taught you journalism?"

"John Dos Passos," he said, resigned.

"And Dos Passos was born in Sinaloa, right?"

"He was of Portuguese origin," Fats said, laughing.

Fats's bag and my red suitcase slipped through between the countless others. It was two in the morning; a porter with a trolley yawned, a female customs official with plump legs had dozed off in her chair. Everyone in the Mexico City airport seemed tired.

"Shit! Isn't that Armando?" Julio said suddenly, tugging at my arm.

My eyes followed his hand, pointing to the exit for taxis. He was right. Armando was approaching a cab. A little stooped over, in a gray suit and with two green canvas suitcases in hand.

"Armando!" I yelled. I think he heard me but he didn't turn around and his taxi peeled out from the curb and disappeared into the night.

"Didn't he hear you?"

"I think he did."

"Things with Armando will always be like this. He's worse than a Chinese spy. . . . Was he on our flight? I didn't notice."

"You were asleep the entire time."

"That's why I didn't notice," Fats replied.

THIRTY-ONE

THE FIRST TIME THEY
SAW ARMANDO

Someone was firing M1s from the building ahead, and the two journalists took cover behind a car whose frame was smoldering. The pungent smoke made them cough. The boy who accompanied them, practically a baby, was looking for the sniper. They heard the distant siren of an ambulance. Then nothing. Cities under siege are strangely silent. Suddenly, a short burst of fire shattered the car's metal and the splinters hit the wall behind them, leaving three fist-sized holes.

"Fucking A, what a son of a bitch, that guard," the boy said.

Greg Simon lifted his camera and aimed the telephoto lens at the flat roof of the building. His hands were sweating and it was hard to focus. Nothing. Only TV antennas and a few shirts flapping on the clothesline.

Two pistol shots rang out. The journalists tried to see where they'd come from. They both seemed to have been from the same place, but it's always difficult to fix a shot's origin. Julio and Greg never agreed. The boy's pointing finger alerted them. Suddenly a body in a guard's uniform came into view on the roof. Then, from behind, a man pushed him. The Somoza guard fell to the ground from the third floor, his M1 behind him. The sounds of the two impacts on the asphalt street fused, the dry thud of the body breaking inside and the metallic sound of the gun. A man on the roof saluted them, waving a pistol.

"Look, they've taken away our cover," Julio Fernández said, standing up. Fats did not like to be crouched down. In the distance, two smoke columns indicated the bombed areas. Greg took mental note of the direction of the sound of the other sirens. A new character appeared in the door frame. He was dressed incongruously, in a brown three-piece suit. It was hot.

"Journalists?"

Greg nodded. The boy at his side reinitiated the march after appropriating the dead guard's rifle from the pavement. The soldier's death was one more small story in a day full of stories.

"Let's go, guys."

"Armando, gentlemen," the suited man said, extending his hand in greeting.

Julio shook it affectionately.

"Julio Fernández. Greg Simon, Manuel," Julio said, introducing his colleagues.

"Okay. Let's go," the boy urged them.

"Can I come along? I'm slightly lost. Goddamn this city. There's shooting everywhere," Armando said. The boy smiled, accepting him into the group. They now had one rifle with the butt smashed by the three-story fall and two pistols, and the suited man's was better than Manuel's, a .22-caliber revolver that looked like a toy.

They took off again. Manuel led them with strange confidence, considering this was not his city. They were detained a couple of times. Once they were alerted by two women running by, warning that there was an EEBI truck ahead.

"The assassins are shooting at a bunch of boys!"

A little later a teenage couple in camouflage attached themselves to the group, with only two Molotov cocktails to add to the arsenal. The girl couldn't have been more than thirteen or fourteen. The boy was even younger. They held a whispered conference with Manuel and joined the expedition; Armando was now leading the march. Greg carefully studied the man in the coffee-colored suit. In spite of his strange attire, in Kafkaesque contrast to the tattered Sandinista kids who walked behind him, he had a certain grace of movement, among a forest of houses damaged by shellfire and showing the dark stain of Molotovs he handled his pistol as if he were opening a path. The countryside was unreal. A mattress on the ground, a broken, open cage from which a bird must have escaped, a pile of empty tuna fish cans carefully stacked on a corner, as if creating a strange traffic signal. Greg took several shots using his telephoto lens, directed by Armando, who seemed to have appointed himself their guide through this urban jungle. They stopped.

While Manuel and the young boy stationed themselves on the corner, the girl, with a red and black handkerchief over her face, harangued invisible neighbors. "They're leaving. The insurrection has begun. We've got to erect barricades." Faces began to appear in the windows. Little by little the people peered out the doors.

Manuel led them to see the children who had been killed. It was a pair of adolescents inside a burned car. Both their faces had been blown away.

When they got back to the corner, a barricade made of paving blocks had been piled up against a car and a lamppost. A Sandinista patrol directed by a woman with a rifle was mobilizing the neighborhood.

Julio tried to interview the woman, who shoved him away. "Journalist, if you want an interview, fix my Sony. We must hear Radio Sandino." Julio started tinkering with the little set. Suddenly a lively cha-cha blared out. Julio noted on the top of his notebook page: "Managua, June 10th, second day of the insurrection. 3:00 p.m., El Dorado neighborhood. Cha-cha on the radio."

When he raised his head, Armando had disappeared.

T H I R T Y - T W O

IDEAS FOR A THESIS PROPOSAL ELENA JORDAN NEVER EVEN FLESHED OUT

The purpose of this thesis proposal is to lay the foundation for an investigation into the mutual influence that the country's two essential public languages have upon each other: the language of Mexican movie superstars and the rhetoric of the national government.

It would mean finding the relationship between, for example, Clavillazo's peak, his penetration into popular language in the sixties, and the connection with the speeches, for example, of the Secretary of the Treasury during the presidential administration of Díaz Ordaz. How, for example, to discover the synchronicity between the phraseology of the popular wrestler El Santo in the vampire film series made from XXX through XXX and the political behavior of the State Department. Or the relationship between the Mexican cowboy movies of the forties and the politics of Pemex during the same era.

Beyond the seeming insanity of the proposal, one has to consider the powerful influence of film in forming the collective subconscious of the nation and the permanent necessity of the PRI's rhetoric to speak to the common subconscious to fortify its dominant discourse.

If Mexican film dominated the national cultural scene from XXXX to XXXX and appeared to be the major ideological influence, reproducing itself on television by transmitting characters to the small screen and receiving consecrated figures, it is no less certain that in the residual period of this great expansion, new cinemagraphic experiences inundated Mexican society: vampire film in the . . .

T H I R T Y - T H R E E

JOURNALISTS' STORIES

(J U L I O   S P E A K S)

After Greg stumbled through the door (I had to watch him on airplanes, that volatile taste for gin was beginning to worry me), I flung my bag over the rocking chair in the hall and silently gave thanks for having come home. The blessed homecomings of soldiers.

You only have one home, my mother used to say that my grandfather used to say—my grandfather, the permanent outcast who never found a home, even though he owned several, a stranger to himself, exiled from his own bones. Blessed grandfather.

"Where do I sleep?" Greg asked in a Spanish unaffected by the gin.

"Are you really tired? I recommend the ironing room. There's no telephone, no noise, nothing. You can spend what's left of the night plus all morning snoring."

"What a cynic. Shit. *You* snore, not me."

"Home sweet home," I remarked, letting my pal drag himself down the hall to the little room at the end. Laboratory, ironing room with a small bed, usually full of old books, filing cabinets stuffed with documents, toilet paper reserves for when Mexico City gets hit by catastrophe. . . .

Had I come home? I usually dedicate a few private moments to each return to Mexico. It's a necessary ritual for a journalist who spends half the year waking up in some damn corner of the world asking himself where am I, who am I, what city is this. I was getting old.

"See you tomorrow, old man," Greg howled from the end of the hall, confirming my thought.

"See you tomorrow, *compadre.*"

In the taxi on the way home from the airport, the city had escaped me. I had lost it on the plane. The descent over the colorful small lights, the world's great geometry, the pink and yellow penstrokes, the neon and tungsten lines that meant streets, had all passed right by me. I was definitely old. I had two gray hairs in my beard. It was evidence, I felt sure, and what was worse, it was getting me down, sprinkling me with nostalgia for the city to which I'd returned. As though I were in another city but still my own. The moment when I abandoned journalism and moved to editing the unfinished works of Hegel was approaching. That would be a work to test my potential. Julio, you Australian faggot, wake up.

I got a beer from the refrigerator. At least the strategic reserves were in place, awaiting the return of the shipwrecked. Greg had stopped making noises in the tiny back room. This damned gringo was like a little boy and he'd no doubt fallen asleep by now. It was four in the morning. I walked over to the stereo. I put on an old

Antonio Carlos Jobím record very softly. I let the answering machine play:

"... Fats, this is Luis Escalante's questioning machine, I hope your answering machine doesn't abuse me like last time, cutting out parts of my message. The interview you want with Cuauhtemoc Cárdenas will be at the end of the month which is around the corner, the engineer doesn't want to improvise and he's going on a tour through Puebla, Tlaxcala and Veracruz. No way, you're fucked, tell that to your gringo. . . ." Crash! . . . "When do you get back, big guy? This is Elena. I'll call you later. . . ." Crash! . . . "Fats, this is Marcelo. Did you remember the alkaline battery you were supposed to bring me from Los Angeles? Did you remember the battery? Because if you didn't remember, I'm going to shit on your whore of a mother. It's been two times now, and I'm sure you forgot this time too and I've got this shitty exposure meter strewn all over the house that I can't use. Did you bring it? I'm sure not, I'm sure you forgot. This makes me an asshole, because I already knew I couldn't trust you with anything. Listen, this is Marcelo, about the alkaline battery. . . ." Crash! . . . "Señor Fernández, this is Margarita, attorney Biriukov's secretary, confirming your appointment Thursday, the twenty-second, at seven-thirty. He asked me to inform you that the handwriting matches your grandfather's and that I say how funny. Thank you, I'll reconfirm later. . . ." Crraash! . . . "You didn't pay Comercial Mexicana, asshole. Elena. This is Elena. I don't know how to talk to these stupid answering machines, they make me nervous. Fuck whoever invented the machines and fuck you for using them. This is Elena." . . . Craash! . . . "No, he's not there, he's got the answering machine. . . . Julio? My dad says yes, it is Trotsky's handwriting, you nailed it. What else can I say, boss? It's his, Julio . . . !" Crash! . . . "Julio, you're a faggot. It's Elena on your shitty answering machine. I need you to read what I'm writing. When the hell are you coming back." . . . Crrash! . . .

Wow. So it was true. Bull's-eye. Cosme had hit it. With news like this I couldn't leave Greg alone. I did a little jig on my way down the hall to his room. Greg was awake, with the face of a dead man, staring at the ceiling, totally Buddhist.

"Now what? New ideas, Julio?"

"What would you say, little guy, if I told you that Leon Trotsky wrote a mystery?"

"Christ."

"Well, he wrote a mystery. Christ! Christ! You want to split a beer?"

"I want a whole one."

MEXICALI, THREE DAYS BEFORE THE TRIP TO MIAMI

The milkman literally pissed in his pants when he saw the hand nailed to the door. He didn't have time to think about it, he just threw the bottles to hell and ran. It was the noise of the crashing bottles, not the noise they must have made nailing down the hand, that made Benigno open the door. The dwarf got up after him, rubbing the sleep from his eyes. Marcelino studied the hand carefully. Benigno, more practical, after having correctly deduced what had happened from the shattered milk bottles on the floor, looked up and down the block to see whether the milkman had left some trace and could tell them something.

"What a stupid lazy hand, they cut it with one slash," the dwarf observed.

"It's a message for Rolando. Don't get involved."

"No, it even has a note, all clutched up," the dwarf said, observing the little paper between the severed hand's fingers. "It's a small hand, look, after cutting it, they inserted the little paper and then pierced it, and there it is demurely holding the note."

"Maybe they put the note in before cutting it."

"Don't you understand anything?"

"Could it be El Cuervo's hand?"

"It's got so much hair it could be."

Benigno and the dwarf studied it carefully, then looked at each other.

"Who was on guard last night?" the dwarf asked.

"El Cuervo."

"Then it has to be his. He's lucky it's his, because if it weren't, Rolando would have kicked his balls off for letting them nail a hand to the door. . . . Now what do we do? Wake him up to come see it or take it to bed?"

"I say we take it," Benigno said, and, taking the slashed hand by the fingers, careful not to let the note drop out, he proceeded to pull out the nail.

Rolando had his back to them when Benigno and the dwarf entered bearing the messenger hand. He was wearing a navy blue sweatsuit, as if he might go running, and was on the phone. With a gesture as if to say "I'm leaving it to you," he threw the phone into the dwarf's hands.

"What the hell? Who is this? No, this is Marcelino, Rolando is busy. . . . You talk to me. . . . I'm telling you he's busy, asshole. . . . Two trucks? What time? But if they were bribed. . . . Stupid Aguilar, son of a bitch."

Benigno laid out the hand for Rolando, who looked at it curiously. The dwarf hung up the phone.

"Aguilar and his cops busted into two of our trucks, shooting, in Juárez. Wasn't that asshole on the payroll? Rolando, if that stupid cat is insolent, it's because someone said we're good for shark bait and they believed it. We lost two trucks. Son of a bitch!"

"When are you going to grow, Marcelino? We didn't lose anything. Those trucks don't exist, nor will they ever exist. They're a message, just like this stupid hand. . . . Throw it away, Benigno, it already stinks."

"It has to be El Cuervo's, boss," Benigno said, delicately taking it away. "Have you read the note yet?"

"I'm going running for a while. I'll be back soon. Save the message for me, but throw out the stupid hand, you're not putting it in the refrigerator," Rolando said.

"I'll go with you, boss, wait a second, I just have to put the hand away."

"Two trucks. . . . Marcelino, I want both of Aguilar's hands here tonight. Both, I won't be satisfied with less. One won't mean shit to me. Take care of it. Talk to Jorge in Juárez, tell him I'll pay double. They send me one hand, I go back and ask for both. This way, while we verify who's the dick out there, we get them thinking. That asshole probably has manicured nails . . . ," Rolando said.

The dwarf swallowed his saliva. The message read: "I know who you are, I've been waiting for you." Rolando seemed to have divined the message. Benigno stared at the clawed hand. Rolando smiled at them.

T H I R T Y - F I V E

"MODIFYING THE PAST . . .

. . .is a craft of erratic delicacy. You don't travel backward and change, you don't alter the witness's vision, the page of the book, the photograph. That is Stalinist amateurism, chess for Yagoda mental retards, Beria Ping-Pong, that only works if you have all of history's subjects locked up on the porch of life's school. We're operating in the realm of art, not plumbing. It's more subtle," Alex said, drinking third-rate Alsatian white wine from a paper cup, to the group that had come to be known by the rest of the SD's members as the dwarfs, because of the Operation Snow White thing.

Dwarf Number One, who looked at Alex with a mixture of mortal hatred, envy and a mangled Oedipal complex, was a famished, pale, young Armenian, whose functions had to do with running the computer terminal for the exclusive service of the operation. Dwarf Number Two, Eve, was a cross-eyed woman with huge breasts overflowing a bra several sizes too small, with which she tried to compensate for her crossed eyes in her first visual assault on an opponent; generally she achieved it. She had been named controller by Alex. Dwarf Number Three, Eloise, was a corrupted feminist, who practiced a reverse form of *machismo* outside the office. (One of the grounds for divorce used by her penultimate husband was that she made him wash the dishes by hand even though they had a dishwasher.) She held the title of pinch hitter, whose functions still were not clearly defined and temporarily amounted to only one: listen, know everything, ask everything. The fourth member of the Snow White network, Dwarf Number Four, named Benjamin, was the operative and had not been invited to the meeting.

"The key is to lay things out in such a way that they seem different. You don't play with the past, you play with the traditional interpretation of the past. You therefore play with the way the past is viewed from the present. In other words, you put the past in order. To this end, occasionally you have to embellish the past, but basically what you have to do is offer alternative interpretations," Alex said, drinking his wine.

His dwarfs contemplated him in absolute silence. They hadn't even asked him to share the wine. The issue was obviously important, since before beginning his speech, Alex had taken his phone off the hook, an unusual act on his part; they were alone in the SD. Even the afternoon traffic noises seemed to have been muted.

"First of all, I need a midrange drug dealer, not a rat and not an elephant, something in between; and I don't want just one, I want two or three options, moreover I need him not to exist for two months, so that we can go back during that void and re-create the story we just created for him. I need him in limbo. I need to appropriate his story. His friends, his misfortunes, his houses, his hideouts, things we know he did, things we suspect. I need a bible on this guy. This is your first task, Eve. Yours, Aram, is to start looking for everything about these types in all computers, all data banks, all memories. I don't want just the information, for every byte of information we obtain I want to know who supports it and on what grounds it is based . . ."

"What nationality do you want, Alex? Does he have to have worked in the States, some other country? Age? Sex? Something to orient me," Eve said, scratching her elbow.

"Give us more, Alex. It's hard to play when we're blind-folded," Eloise, his third dwarf, suggested, chewing each word separately in her unmistakable Texas accent.

Eve scratched again.

Alex stared directly into her crossed eyes. The allergy that was making the second dwarf scratch ran dangerously through her neurons; he was catching it. He started to feel a prickling in his thigh, increasingly intense. He restrained himself from scratching. Like a Jesuit in flagellation, he enjoyed the suffering of abstaining. Two beads of sweat broke out on his temple.

"I'd like a Mexican. A young Mexican. But I'll accept anything you pull from Latin America. I want an intelligent guy who's never heard of Klee."

"Of who?" Aram asked.

"It was a joke," Alex said.

"Klee, the painter," Eloise commented, justifying her salary and clearly determined not to let Alex, who'd shown up with a bottle of wine and one single cup half an hour before, totally dominate the situation.

"Okay. Resources A, Priority Number One. Anything you want. And that means anything, kids. . . . Second goal. I need a Bulgarian, Romanian or Czech communist who embodies the following characteristics: he took part in the Resistance as a supporter. He traveled abroad frequently throughout the seventies. He's dabbled in journalism or is a writer. He is publicly renowned for his circumspection and reticence in dealing with Stalin and his boys. He is moderately patriotic. He's got a bad memory. Single or widowed, he cannot be homosexual. He's got dental problems. He speaks English or Spanish. He smokes. He's got a slightly adventurous streak. He likes Cubans and Nicaraguans. He was in Nicaragua after the victory of the Sandinista Revolution. He reads novels, especially adventure stories. He must have, or have had, a high-level post in the party. . . . A guy who has prestige in foreign countries for his critical attitudes, his stubbornness, his 'moral strength.' Isn't that idea fashionable?" Alex stopped himself, consulted his notes for a moment, took another sip of the horrendous wine and refilled his cup. "I'd like him to be familiar with Los Angeles, but I know that's tough. I'd like him to have an old wound, a bone ailment, something wrong with his feet."

"Is it really necessary that he smokes, or has been in Los Angeles, or reads adventure or crime novels? You need all those things?" Eve asked.

"Alex, this is ludicrous. Do you know this guy and just want to make us prove we're as efficient as we say we are?" Eloise asked.

"If you couldn't perform, you wouldn't be here, little dwarf. This is real life. It's Operation Dream of Snow White. It is the most important intelligence game in the world today. It's like David Copperfield's best magic trick," Alex said, later regretting the vulgar comparison.

"If you pour me a cup of that shit you're drinking, I'll find him for you," Aram proposed.

"Get him for me," Alex responded without offering a drop of the brew.

"Anything else, bwana?" Eve asked.

"Yes, a routine assignment. I want everything this country's intelligence knows . . . , bloody hell, what a euphemism, as if this country had intelligence . . . , everything on Carlos Machado."

"Nicaragua's vice minister of the interior. Machadito," Aram said.

"The same. One and the same Machadito. Casey's obsession. That little boy who, when Reagan has nightmares and dreams the Sandinistas are pulling out the hairs on his testicles with tweezers, appears in our ex-president's head leading the operation at the side of the Ortegas and Tomás Borge. Everything on Machado. Everything."

"One Bulgarian, three drug dealers and Machado," Eve said, lighting a cigarette.

"Exactly," Alex confirmed, raising his hand to his eyes to keep from scratching. "Eloise, you'll be the filter for what the others find. The devil's advocate. You decide whether it works or not."

She nodded. Alex gave them a depraved smile. The three dwarfs correctly deduced that the assignment had begun at that instant and that they'd be locked up like slaves in a galley until they produced results.

"Aram, if you find him for me and I later discover a lobster on tomorrow's expense report, I'll ignore it," Alex said and exited through the window. Like an imp, like a wizard, like a vampire going into the New York afternoon in search of jugulars, like an efficient clerk who's completed his day.

After entertaining himself in a Rexall drugstore for a while, buying anti-irritation ointment for his skin, Alex went to the Forty-second Street pier to watch the boats.

It was soothing to watch the freighters being emptied, disemboweled, liberated of their contents. The wind blew from the estuary; his nose was almost frostbitten. When he realized it, the itching had disappeared. Night was falling. He threw his ointment into a trash can. He walked along the piers another couple of hours. The prostitutes who had gathered like vultures on Pier 17 to wait for the sailors of a Turkish ship were dispersing now in tatters, on a parallel course with Alex. As he passed, the whores opened a silent corridor. Whores were doubly dangerous, Alex thought, they not only transmitted venereal diseases as nineteenth-century novels described, but they also had a very peculiar instinct that warned them of risk. In addition to feeling slightly proud, Alex felt detected, understood. He didn't like it. Like all agents with more than fifteen days in the business, Alex had built an altar to the god of anonymity in the depths of his heart. At ten o'clock, he headed toward Thirty-eighth Street, where he ate without much appetite in a Greek restaurant, and later returned to the office to infuse the souls of Snow White's dwarfs with bureaucratic panic.

THIRTY - SIX

JOURNALISTS' STORIES

(GREG SPEAKS)

Fats had about twenty-five "best friends." I guess the day they put him to rest, they'll have a hell of a time choosing the pallbearers. One of his best friends was the one who'd discovered the alleged Leon Trotsky novel: Cosme Ornelas, professional dancer in a folkloric troupe, journalist, night watch-man for many years of the solitary and dilapidated Trotsky Museum on Vienna Street in Coyoacán. Cosme had accepted the job as night watchman for three reasons. One, he needed the miserable salary they offered for guarding the gloomy, rambling house. Two, he thought night shifts would give him the time to write a novel. Three, he thought Trotsky's ghosts would enrich the novel: the table, with the papers placed exactly as they were when Mornard wielded his mountain climber's ax, the tomb, the bookshelves, the dark halls. I'd gathered all this the previous night over beers. Now I opened my eyes and Leon Trotsky's hypothetical crime novel danced in my brain as I woke to gentle clarity.

Fats had kept this story in his head without telling me a thing, and before leaving for Los Angeles had turned in photocopies of the manuscript to one of Trotsky's nephews plus another set to one of the historians who'd worked in Harvard's archives with the Frenchman, Broué. It seemed the handwriting was authentic.

"Are you sure?" I asked as we fought for the bathroom mirror, I to shave and he to brush his teeth.

"They're about to send us the translation. It's not too long. It seems to be some kind of outline for a mystery, a sketch with descriptions of the characters. He was putting the biography of Stalin he was writing in the same time frame, just prior to the murder attempt against his own life in 1941," Julio said fifteen minutes later, while cooking.

"I don't recall his ever mentioning that manuscript," I told Fats half an hour later over *chilaquiles* and orange juice for breakfast. As one will see, our morning conversations are not especially quick.

"Me neither, but I'm not well read. I'm only familiar with the Deutscher biography."

"Okay, what's the plan?" I asked with my mouth full of *chilaquiles.*

"We've got a date with my friend Cosme this afternoon. Then we pick up a copy of the translated manuscript and talk to the guy who knows Trotsky's handwriting to confirm it for us. Can you think of anything else?"

"Photos of the office, of the Coyoacán house. A look at Trotsky's bookshelves to see what crime novels he had. And sit and read awhile in a library with a good Trotsky collection, look at his writings on literature, check out a couple biographies."

Fats agreed.

"You want to come into town with me right now? I made plans to meet Elena at La Ópera," he said, looking out the window.

"Your ex-wife?"

Julio pretended not to hear the question. I pretended the tone of surprise in my question hadn't escaped and meekly offered to do the dishes.

We rode into town on a relatively empty subway. It must have been a new line, which the natives of Mexico City left to the tourists for a week, to test it out. Something like the Florentine method of making the pages taste the food first. As soon as it's clear that the line is safe, they'll start to use it. That's the extent these days of distrust of government urban projects and the way the natives feel about foreigners. I tried to explain this theory to Fats but he had more important things on his mind.

A brilliant sun welcomed us at the subway exit in front of the Palacio de Bellas Artes.

"Do you realize that we have been with the best?" Fats suddenly blurted out.

"Who? Who, my little fat friend? Who are the best?"

"The best journalists of our era. We've been side by side with them. We collaborated with *Crisis* when Galeano was the director and we shared a good many bottles of wine with him in Catalonia, when he was in exile. And you coedited with Hunter Thompson at *Rolling Stone.*"

"Yes, we peed in the same bathroom. He a little before me, he went first, he had the prestige . . ."

"I'm serious. We were with the Frenchman, Pisani, in Nicaragua and Kapuscinski in Bolivia. We even lent him a hand in the interview with Coco Peredo's widow, remember? And in El Salvador we gave the exclusive to Leguineche the Spaniard more than once. . . . We slept in the same room as Wallraff during the Palme affair in Estocolmo. We've traveled a dozen times in the same plane as your pal, Marc Cooper. As a teenager, I frequented the same café as Carlos Monsiváis during his stint as a film critic . . ."

"Don't start working yourself up, Julio; we're better than they are. We're better journalists."

"That may be true, but we're not inspired and they are. They've got a spark that we lack. Weren't you in Saigon the same time as Seymour Hersh?"

"So what. As you would say, who gives a shit? What do you want me to do?"

"We lack literary brilliance. We arrive first, but tell the same story worse. Hemingway used to arrive two days after an event but he always told the story far better than the others who'd beat him."

I tried to ignore him. He was ruining my walk through Mexico City. If there are cities that kill, this one more than any other was one of them. It kills with simultaneous colors and images, noises and lights. Fats insisted on spoiling my view of the colonial gratings, the baroque facades of Madero Street, crammed with people, swarming with small merchants, clerks, vagabonds, rambunctious students, messengers, newspaper boys, bricklayers eating tacos on their breaks, rumba dancers headed for the cabaret, consumers seeking the infinite possibilities of specialized commerce in the center of town, locked in dank, dark stores, where chips were stacked right next to tinfoil twice as thick as normal, special tracks for toy trains, fluorescent colored pencils and canned Chinese food. Here, the old theory that crowds come together for the pleasure of seeing each other is confirmed. More than half of the passersby were smiling. That doesn't usually happen in Los Angeles.

"Don't you feel like you're traveling by donkey, writing by hand while they travel by jet and use a word processor? Don't you think we've got to write other stories?"

"No. *Nyet. Rien.* Nooo. *Nanay."*

"Fine, okay, the same stories, but in another goddamn way."

"Are you suggesting we enroll in some college and take a class in literary style? Somebody fucked mine up in a magazine I worked at years ago. There are ads: Improve your style in three weeks. . . ."

"Didn't you fix the patriarch Burchett's ankle once in Cambodia, after a bad helicopter landing?"

"So what? That makes me a nurse, Fats, not a journalist. You've got a story like this Trotsky one in your hands and instead of dancing in the Zócalo with those dancers, you're bitching at me. . . . Why don't you just stick it up your ass?" I said, using one of the expressions I learned from a Spanish journalist we worked with in Panama, Jorge Martínez Reverte, wondering if I'd pronounced it right.

Fats tore at his hair and dodged a newspaper boy, then renewed his assault, gesticulating wildly. When he was trying to convince someone of something he waved his hands and arms vehemently, he vibrated like a drunken sailor, danced around his victim, imposing his big chest, heaving it forward like a figurehead. I don't know whether he was more dangerous this way or when he turned melancholy, wandering around inside himself.

"When you dream, who do you want to be like?" he asked me.

"Julio Fernández would be good. He eats well, drinks Spanish wine, smokes Cuban cigars, he's got an excellent gringo working partner who's not playing around; he writes half a dozen excellent stories a year. He manages a couple of worldwide exclusives. . . . You know what Tom Wolfe told me the other day? That he'd like to be like you, finding those great stories and not having to write that literary shit he does. . . ."

"When did you see him?"

"The other day in New York."

"You lie like a utilitarian Buddhist," Fats said.

"So what."

"When I dream I want to be like John Reed."

We walked on in silence. It was hot. The sun shone on the cars' fenders.

"When I have nightmares, I'd like to be like Scott Fitzgerald," I said after a while and stepped into the La Ópera canteen. When Fats recovered and followed me in, I, like Scott Fitzgerald, had a two-beer advantage over him. He seemed to be forging new arguments. Fortunately, right on his heels, Elena appeared.

THIRTY - SEVEN

BACK IN MIAMI

Despite the fact that instinct was Rolando's best quality, it was his bodyguard, Benigno, who smelled things going sour. The dwarf was making peanut butter sandwiches at the bar in the motel suite they'd rented for the boss when Benigno spotted a character circling the pool whose face he didn't like.

"You'll see, black man, your own mother couldn't make little sandwiches like these babies."

"Tell Rolando I'm going out, there's a guy down there I don't like one bit."

"This is the United States, asshole, it's normal not to like these guys. They're racist here, asshole, and you react to them."

"There's two of them, and one's got a shotgun, shithead," Benigno said, staring fixedly out the window.

The dwarf dropped the peanut butter knife and ran toward the bedroom. Rolando stopped him at the door and put a finger to his lips to shut him up. Rolando was naked, with a bronzed .45 in his right hand. Marcelino was scared for his boss.

"Lend me your gun, Rolando, you're not going out there. Let me. I'm less of a target."

Benigno had left the room, moving with apelike agility, hugging the wall, the pistol like a prolongation of his hand. The halls were empty.

The back part of the motel was designed like a two-story half-moon around a swimming pool, with an open-air corridor flanked by stairwells at both ends. A dozen rooms per floor. The front was formed by a sprawling parking lot that disappeared in the center, where a circular module contained a hallway with the main offices and a cafeteria, replete with, for who knows what bizarre reasons, cheap imitation-naive paintings with Buddhas and Oriental themes.

Since he couldn't stop Rolando, who was dogging the steps of the gunman with the rifle, the dwarf rushed to the trunk and took out a submachine gun; holding it like a kid with a new toy, he went toward the window overlooking the back corridor. It was raining; tiny drops fell into the pool, like the impacts of toy gun bullets. The dwarf thought he sensed a shadow behind one of the palm trees at the far left of the pool.

Aiming at the shadow and ready to fire off a burst if it moved, the dwarf pricked up his ears. Raindrops on the pool, the sound of a couple of TVs in nearby rooms. Nothing.

Benigno appeared on the patio, his pistol in hand, slithering between the trunks of the palm trees that surrounded the pool. Marcelino the dwarf tried to divide his vision. With one eye he contemplated his partner, with the other the shadow he thought he saw. Suddenly the shadow moved, a man in a Miami Dolphins T-shirt fired at Benigno. The dwarf instantly got off a burst from the submachine gun. Two of the shots drilled the gunman. From ground level, Benigno finished him off as he fell. He advanced toward the dying man and kicked his head. He turned toward the dwarf's window and indicated that all was well. The dwarf smiled.

"Don't move, Marcelino," said the dry voice of Rolando at his back. "You've got a guy aiming at your head three meters behind you, but I'm behind him, and if he doesn't stop tickling the kitten, I'll blow his brains out. Let's see, Marcelino, turn around very

| 113 |

slowly and aim, he won't move because if he does, I'll send him skyward. . . . One, two . . ."

The dwarf turned. It was true, a big guy with a twisted face aimed a pistol at him. Behind him, Rolando aimed at the man with the finger of his left hand. He had stashed the pistol in the towel tied around his waist, covering his genitals. He was smiling broadly. Where had he found the towel?

"Now our friend is going to slowly drop his gun, because if not between you and me we turn him into a dead man. Tell him in English in case the asshole doesn't get it."

"Drop your gun, asshöle," the dwarf said in astonishingly correct, British pronunciation.

"Hablo español, sir," the guy said, dropping his gun.

"Stick him in the trunk, Marcelino. He'll be more crammed than you were but the shithead deserves it," Rolando said, lighting a cigar.

Benigno appeared in the door dragging his leg. The pant leg was torn and blood was spurting out.

"Wrap a towel around it, asshole, what the hell are you thinking, letting yourself get injured?" Rolando asked. "And do it quickly, because we're leaving. This motel you chose is a shithole, I don't like it one bit. I don't like anything about it. The asshole at the front desk sees me running by and asks me in English who knows what bullshit. The asshole doesn't realize I don't speak . . . The pool's covered with leaves . . . The driveling maid sees me nude and does nothing. I had to snatch the towel out of her hand. And I don't even know if it was dirty. No, this place is a shithole, an absolute shithole."

"I KNOW THIS VASILEV. . . .

. . . It's not the first time I've seen him," Alex said, toying with one of the pictures they'd shown him of the Bulgarians he'd required.

"Two years ago, in the Daisy Club." Eve refreshed his memory.

"You couldn't find anything better?"

"He fulfills seven of the premises you established, bwana," Eloise said. "He's got a prosthesis in the knee, the result of a World War One injury, he's frighteningly pro-Cuban, Stalin sent him to the freezer in Siberia."

"Do you know this Bulgarian's history?" Aram interrupted. "He's the guy who put an ad in *The Village Voice,* you know, the typical: Bulgarian lessons, his telephone number, et cetera . . . , and some son of a bitch placed it in the sex ad section. And the poor dick spent a week answering all the freaks in Manhattan who wanted to know what this Bulgarian shit was. And the following week, under threat of a lawsuit, the *Voice* ran his ad in the right section, free, and the guy added 'and no matter what you think, Bulgarian is also a language. . . .' "

No one paid too much attention to Aram's story, and he turned back to the keyboard.

". . . he doesn't smoke, lived in San Francisco for one year . . . ," Eloise continued, counting on the fingers of both hands. "He speaks Spanish."

Alex ruminated for a moment. He didn't like coincidences. He had requested a Bulgarian half in jest, adding inconsequential criteria to the necessary requirements just to disorient his dwarfs. He didn't expect one hundred percent. Forty-five percent of positive responses including the key elements would have sufficed. But he didn't like a guy straight out of the Daisy Club. He didn't like anything added to what he himself had wanted.

The investigation of the Daisy Club had been an old game his team had developed a couple of years ago. An accidental interception of mail in the 1950s revealed a retired Los Angeles actor regularly receiving once a year a pair of postcards from one of four or five different countries, both signed with a daisy. Since this guy had been a "premature antifascist," Hoover's boys had monitored his mail and performed a routine investigation. The results were fruitless. Every Christmas he sent and received two postcards signed with daisies and with some insignificant message like "I hope you're well. Love, Max." Alex had heard of the case in his first years at Langley and accidentally picked it back up two years later when, in the trash that was regularly delivered from the information networks, Max Lewis's name appeared, tied to a trip to Nicaragua. Alex tried to do a computer trace of the Daisy trio and Max, the actor, and there among the characters associated with the club was Stoyan the Bulgarian. Alex discovered that the postcards had created problems for the Bulgarian in '49, the beginning of Stalin's purges in the satellite countries due to the conflict with Tito in Yugoslavia. Alex's fascination grew when he obtained information about the third member, a man who'd reached epic stature in Donovan's OSS era, a Spaniard named Longoria. The trace on Max's correspondence yielded a very brief story: two postcards sent and two received. Not much more. If he hadn't had other open cases that tapped all his curiosity reserves and required the concentration of his manias, Alex would have tried to ascertain the old story hidden in the daisies. It sounded like a waltz of loves and lost revolutions, played by three hands, probably originating in 1930s Europe. A lot of romanticism, French wine . . . argh. He regretted it. Especially now that the Bulgarian was back in his life.

"Give me someone else, I don't like this one," he told Eve.

"Let's see, let's try this one, Micha Gravov, widower, head of the party in—"

Alex interrupted with an abrupt gesture and lit a cigarette.

"Drop the Bulgarian thing for now. I'm not sure I'm still interested," Alex said. His head was filling with infantile drawings of daisies.

Each had his own daisy. Max, the North American film actor, drew them with eight petals with a blackened center and a short stem, and he integrated them into the text; there were more than one dancing among the words. The texts always included phrases like "Today is still forever," and things like that, trapped in a jungle of daisies. The Bulgarian drew them with long stems, almost floating at the end of the postcard. The Spaniard made them straight, stiff, in perspective. That shithead was affecting them. Alex was the type who read the last page of a mystery once he got to the middle, or who called a TV station to find out how a soap opera, in its fifty-sixth episode, would end.

In the end, wasn't this the entire history of modern espionage? Century after century, professionals of power hired professionals of information, who hired professionals of curiosity, who hired legalized criminals to keep the game in play.

"Coffee all the way around!" Alex barked. "But not the usual trash, first-rate Colombian coffee, in real mugs, not those disgusting paper cups that leak. Order in, Eve!"

"Boss, are we back to the Glory Days?"

"No, Aram, I simply want my Mexican drug dealer, and I want the best. And it seems quite obvious that you all are not sufficiently motivated."

Snow White's little dwarfs adored their boss for a few moments. Then they hated him again. That morning in New York, it was very cold; the glass on the windows overlooking Madison Avenue was steamy. Eve started tracing on them. Daisies.

T H I R T Y - N I N E

LEON'S NOVEL

Halfway through the morning, after feeding the rabbits and conversing with Van about the conflicts between French factions, the old man slipped away to his office and, contrary to custom, closed the door.

He put aside some copies of *The Militant* that Hank had left on top of the desk and took out his black marbled hardcover notebook. He should be writing in English, English was the language of mysteries, but this would only increase the difficulty of the already inherently difficult task. He started taking notes where he'd left off the day before. A couple of interesting ideas had come to him overnight.

From the window, he contemplated the blue sky of Coyoacán and the prickly pears sketched in his interior frontierland. He wrote:

9. Wolf visits an orphanage in the suburbs of Madrid, he is worried about a twelve-year-old girl. It is a secular institution, directed by an old professor of the Ferrer Guardia Rationalist school. The Republic's contradictions and miseries are reflected in it: lack of resources, pedagogical experiments, clean, but frayed and threadbare uniforms on the live-in kids. Here, Wolf discussed what he already knew, Maria Roja, the girl, was kidnapped two years before, at gunpoint, by three strangers, two men and a woman, who took her away in a car. Madrid's press covered the sensational story copiously. That kind of crime isn't normal in Madrid. Instead, there is a plethora of murders of passion, political crimes, prostitutes' revenges, racketeers' exploits. Maria's abduction was extraordinary. In the conversation, the name of a reporter who covered the case for *La Libertad* comes up. The old man is intrigued by Wolf's concern. Wolf answers vaguely that he met the father in Boston, in a nursing home. On the patio, the Institute's orphans play Revolution. Wolf stares at one whose arm is paralyzed. He identifies.

10. Wolf, still being followed by his faithful and mysterious escort, interviews López, the reporter from *La Libertad,* a vile character, heavy smoker, extremely myopic. López talks to him about the kidnapping case that took place two years ago. The neighbors had called the cops, who chased the car, firing at it. Futilely. One of the three kidnappers was identified later. He was in the Modelo jail for having stabbed his wife's lover to death. But they never got anything on him for the kidnapping. López had tried in vain. What is Wolf's interest in the affair? Wolf: I met Maria's father in a Boston nursing home. López: And why would they kidnap her? A girl from an orphanage. . . . Who was the father? What link could the father

have with the kidnappers? Wolf: I don't have the foggiest idea. The father confined himself to telling me the story when we met. I left the hospital. Two years later, coming to Spain, I thought I'd look into it. I started with the orphanage because that's all I remembered. López: The girl had been left there when she was three years old, abandoned at the doorstep. I didn't even know she had a father. What was his name? Wolf: He was Czech, last name Climnet. A French name, curiously. A journalist, like you. López: And can we contact this man? Wolf: He died when we were in the nursing home. López: The unusual thing about the case is that an orphaned girl would be kidnapped at gunpoint; that's what makes it interesting. If it had been the daughter of some duke or millionaire. . . . Very strange, very strange. Throughout the conversation, it becomes clear that each man knows the other is hiding something. López asks what brings Wolf to Spain, Wolf professes to be selling agricultural equipment. López invites him to lunch the next day.

11. After complicated negotiations and maintaining the story of the father he'd met in a nursing home in Boston where the man was undergoing treatment for serious tuberculosis and he for the loss of his arm, Wolf manages to get an interview with the man in jail, who turns out to be Andalusian. The conversation is slightly evasive, the Andalusian seems disposed to discuss any topic other than the strange incident two years ago. In the end, a small hole is opened. Yes, he drove the car, he was identified because he didn't wear a mask. The man and woman hired him. They drugged the girl and took her to Barcelona, they paid him generously. Where did you meet them? In a bar in Madrid through friends. Names? I tell sins, not sinners. And aren't you, who seem to be a man, ashamed to go around abducting little girls? The truth is yes, killing someone face to face is fine, robbing a bank, fine, smuggling contraband, fine, but kidnapping a girl is really low. Wolf: I met the girl's father on his deathbed, he asked me to figure out something about his daughter. Andalusian: it's been two years, I don't know what to tell you. Barcelona. I let them off in the Ensanche, the new development on Provenza Street, near the Paseo de Gracia. Wolf: And in the few days you were with them, they never said a word about why they wanted to kidnap the girl? Andalusian: No, they never said anything about the

girl, they were careful not to talk in front of me. Wolf: What was the couple like? Andalusian: They were strange, North Americans, like you, Brits maybe. He was for sure, she had darker skin, but they spoke English to each other.

They leave each other. The Andalusian asks that if Wolf recovers the child, not to forget to tell him. He'd appreciate it enormously, it's a thorn pierced in his soul (textually).

12. Once Wolf loses his tail in the labyrinth of alleys that surrounds the Plaza Mayor, he makes his way to a nearby *mesón*. He interviews a pale man, lying down, in a dark room. Their conversation is very short, very dry. Wolf: I need photos of the girl. Other: Did you find something? Wolf tells him he's on a trail that leads to Barcelona. But remember, he came to Spain on other matters, that only due to his old debt to this man is he willing to get involved in such a mess. The man picks up a picture of Maria. Wolf tells him he's being followed. They agree to communicate via the prostitute's telephone in the front room.

13. Wolf reflects on the shipwreck. He capsized once on the coast off southern Chile. The loneliness, fear, isolation. But there are material shipwrecks and moral shipwrecks. The loss of boat, mates, the solid deck of the ship under your feet, sense of direction, place in history. The man he just saw is a shipwreck. He has no boat, no journey. No mates.

14. The novel abuses seriousness, but only in the poorest sense of that word. A serious novel must be irreverent, must awaken comedy in the new life, because the new man wants to laugh, but he won't discard love, because he loves more and better than we do; and he won't forsake melodrama, because these are dramatic times and every one of us has clear ideas about the fragility of life and personal death.

15. Back in his hotel, Wolf meets with two director/members of a lumber cooperative. They discuss the deal, equipment delivery, they determine dates and even . . .

Leon left his novel like a person descending from a cloud; someone was knocking insistently at the door. *Life* magazine was on the phone. He closed the notebook and hid it under his notes for *Stalin.* He knew what the magazine editors were going to say, he was late delivering the article for the anniversary of Lenin's death. Financial difficulties plagued him in those last months. The

Nazis' rise to power in Germany had cut access to the royalties he usually earned. He owed Doubleday in the United States for unrecovered advances. He'd already spent the advance for the book on Stalin, as yet unfinished. He'd donated part of his archives to Harvard at no fee, buried in interminable negotiations. And now he owed *Life* two articles. He smiled to find himself thinking like that. These were the domestic minutiae of a professional revolutionary who now, fallen prey to senile insanity, was writing a mystery.

F O R T Y

JOURNALISTS' STORIES

(J U L I O   S P E A K S)

After I had managed to keep her at the marvelous distance of the telephone for one year, Elena came back into my life just as Greg was refusing for the tenth time to sit down and seriously discuss the mess of a career we'd wound up in. That saved him. Elena is usually like the bell that announces the final round, she arrives suddenly, always in time to ruin the moment.

She'd gone downhill. She was a little less thin. A few tension wrinkles surrounded her eyes. Her face didn't smile the way it used to; she seemed to have become friendly (clear sign she was tired). I said to myself: "You are not in love with this woman, and don't even think about falling in love with her again, because you already know precisely what can happen if you do." That was too long a sentence to place on the permanent alert system. I tried a shorter one as Elena got on her tiptoes to kiss me. "You cannot live with this woman. Asshole if you forget it."

"You're more beautiful every day. The divorce did wonders for you," I said.

"Little Fats, control yourself, I wouldn't marry you again for anything."

"How are you, Elena?" Greg said, very ceremoniously putting down his beer and holding out a hand. Elena pushed away a ringlet of hair that had fallen over her eyes and kissed him on the cheek, ignoring the outstretched hand.

You cannot live with this woman. Asshole if you forget it.

"Greg, you deserve that kiss and much more. If you've been able to tolerate Julio two years longer than I could, you deserve an altar in Mexico's main church, Basílica de Guadalupe."

"I think it's easier to write together than eat breakfast together. Julio tolerates me, which is work enough," said the very decent gringo. He deserved a kiss on the cheek from me.

Elena hopped onto a stool and drank a third of my beer in her first swig. Two or three of the canteen's regular alcoholics watched her like sharks. Elena pretended not to notice.

"What have you got, boys?"

"A gem. We found a manuscript by Leon Trotsky. A mystery novel. It was buried under his papers in Mexico."

"A what?"

"A mystery novel," Greg confirmed.

"That was the only thing lacking to make you both Trotsky-ites."

"Trotskyite police," I clarified. "It could be a new division of the Fourth International, those who exclusively recover the journalistic essays and the mystery novels of Trotsky."

Smiling, Elena finished my beer. *You cannot live with this woman. Asshole if you forget it.* Elena crossed her legs on the stool. Her black leather skirt stretched tighter.

"Fats, forgive me for being so prosaic, but you forgot to pay Comercial Mexicana, and the damn store is after me."

"You've got a hell of a nerve. Why should I pay that thing? That was for rocking chairs that you bought, that you liked, that I never gave a shit about and that you took when we divorced. Now, explain to me, why should I pay for them?"

"Because you bought them for me. I only signed the receipt, but you bought them for me, and now they're after me to pay them."

"I don't exactly recall having bought them."

"Well I do," she replied, satisfied with herself. "Fats, don't be annoying, pay for the damn chairs, you earn a fortune now that they publish your articles all over the stupid world. Pay, then come over to the house, you've got to read some of the stuff I've been writing."

Greg had made himself scarce when the conversation had taken a domestic turn, and was chatting with the Mexican novelist, Gerardo de la Torre, who wanted a few of the articles we'd published in Canada for the cultural supplement of a publication he coedited.

"Give me three or four days, because we're locking ourselves up to write this story. Then we'll get together so I can read your stuff."

"And so you can pay for the damned rocking chairs."

"I'll pay but you have to return them to me."

"But you don't even like them."

"No, but I'll give them to someone."

"Give them to me," Elena said, blowing away a lock of hair that had fallen over her eyes.

"Okay, I'll give them to you."

"Okay, so now pay for them."

"You finished with business yet?" Greg asked. "We've got a date with your friend the graphologist."

Elena jumped off the stool, giving off an atmosphere as she spun around that brought tears to my eyes.

"What's wrong, Julio, are you crying?"

"I got smoke in my eyes."

"By the way, the other day I ran into that pal of yours, that Panamanian who came to the house for lunch once, that guy named Armando."

"Armando's in Mexico?" Greg asked.

"He sent his regards."

"How long ago did you see him?" I asked. But it was late, and as always with Elena, half of the questions were left unanswered.

FORTY-ONE

THE SECOND TIME THEY SAW ARMANDO

Armando would not have become a shared enigma in the life of the two journalists had his first apparitions not always been under unusual circumstances and his disappearances even more like something in a movie. This inspired Julio to start using the phrase "more mysterious than that stupid Armando," and Greg to refer to anyone's disappearance as an "Armandoism." There was more to the story. Both, without much discussion, guessed that Armando worked for the services. They weren't sure which services, but he was definitely a Cuba or a Nicaragua man. Armando, with his very formal attire and his untraceable Central American accent, who sometimes passed for a Panamanian, other times a Costa Rican and at times a Martian, had become a minor enigma in the constellation of mysteries Julio and Greg shared.

The second time they met up with Armando, Julio had an unconscious Greg under the arms and was hauling him down the middle of the street. The North American had been knocked in the head with a stone while taking photos in front of the U.S. Embassy in Tegucigalpa. He was bleeding very indecorously. The protesting rioters, a mixture of Honduran students genuinely pissed off with the Roman Empire politics of the Yankees in their country and a mob of thugs mobilized by the narco-military sector, had enjoyed burning cars and hurling rocks in front of the marines who were guarding the interior patio of the Embassy.

The air smelled like fire, Molotov cocktails were flying and there were burning tires everywhere. Julio tugged at Greg's sweater, trying to get him into the doorway of a lingerie boutique, when Armando stopped his taxi a few yards in front of the journalists.

"Good evening, friend. I believe it would behoove you to step into the car. The army is going to intervene in ten minutes."

Julio stared at this character. He wore a white smoking jacket. He'd grown a long, thick mustache since the day he had opened a path for them in the insurgent streets of Managua.

"Armando?"

"What a good memory, Señor Fernández. . . . Allow me to help you."

Armando stepped out of the car and together they both began tugging at Greg, who was showing signs of coming to. Once inside the car, Armando told the driver to go on.

"And why are you all dressed up?" Julio asked.

"It's the best way to walk the streets in times of uprisings. Besides, I had a social engagement, my friend. I was killing time before dinner and waiting to see if I'd have the good fortune to be able to watch this embassy burn."

"What's your opinion of all this, friend?" Julio asked.

"Contradictions between the official and nonofficial drug dealers. The CIA runs drug trafficking here in Honduras, very linked to the sale of arms to the Contras, but a few members of the military wanted to be independent and the State Department sent a message to the gentlemen of the Honduran government, to make it clear that as long as the United States pays the equivalent of sixteen percent of their Honduran gross national product in fees to keep this country on its feet, they can behave as if they own it," Armando said. He took out a box of superfine, filtered *partagas*, tobacco made in Havana for export. Julio Fernández swooped down on one, lit it and savored the cigarette. They were almost as good as the Cuban/Spanish Davidovs he usually bought in the Madrid airport.

"And what are you doing in Honduras? The last time we saw you in Managua you disappeared suddenly. . . ." The glow of the fires cast a strange light on Armando's face, mephistophelian. Julio contemplated the phenomenon curiously.

"The damned pictures! Did you develop the pictures yet, Fats?" Greg asked, opening his eyes.

"Mister Simon, how nice to see you," Armando said very ceremoniously.

"Stupid gringo, I'm never going to bring you to another protest," Fernández said, drying the blood on Greg's face.

"Shall I take you to your hotel?" Armando asked.

"The military was on the verge of intervening and you were
staining my shirt with your blood," Julio told Greg.

"Let's go back," Greg said.

Armando consulted the Mexican journalist with a look. He
agreed. Armando shrugged and asked the driver to stop for a
moment, then turn around. When the car stopped, Armando agilely stepped out, and with a short military salute disappeared into
a night of fire, absurdly dressed in his white smoking jacket under
which he carried, and couldn't hide from Julio Fernández's keen
eye, in spite of the excellent tucks of an excellent tailor, a .45
automatic in an arm holster.

ALEX'S PSYCHIATRIST . . .

. . . was quite content with the
progress Alex had made in the relationship with the nymphomaniacal wife his patient had invented. To keep from smiling
excessively halfway through the session, Alex narrated a conflict
with his youngest son, likewise fictitious, culminating with his
father giving the nonexistent seven-year-old scion a swift kick in
the balls. According to the version he was elaborating for the
psychiatrist's benefit, Alex spent the night in the hospital, the
infant suffering a terrible orchitis, an inflammation of the testicles,
from which he had certainly not recovered and which had probably rendered him impotent for life. This horrible situation had
made Alex tremendously remorseful, not to mention giving him a
hefty dose of sexual disgust toward his wife, who had decided that
very morning, just a few hours before their session, to take her
revenge by sleeping with the doorman in the middle of the living
room and asking Alex to come out and watch, but of course Alex

had locked himself in his room with the TV blaring to drown out his wife's erotic gasps.

The psychiatrist was astonished and couldn't seem to choose between liberating Alex from the guilt of his (nonexistent) son's inflamed testicles and helping him create a few psychological defenses against the insanity of his (nonexistent) nymphomaniacal wife.

Alex left the Rockefeller Center office quite content. The session cost him $300 but it was indubitably worth it. He walked slowly south, choosing an erratic route that would end at the SD. Suddenly he took a right onto Broadway at Forty-sixth Street. He passed a seedy hotel where a group of Pakistani youths played with a pair of knives. Not only did Alex not quicken his pace, he even stopped and looked on smiling. The spectacle of that extremely skinny, gawky man, wearing nothing over a long-sleeved white shirt and holding a sheepskin jacket in his hands that cold afternoon, smiling as he watched them over wire-framed glasses, disconcerted them. They left the hotel door and went walking toward Sixth Avenue, grumbling morosely. A few meters away, one of them, braver than the others, yelled "faggot" in Pashto. Without losing his smile, Alex replied, in flawless Urdu: "Your mother's a cow."

Alex headed for southern Manhattan, accelerating his pace. Practically ignoring the Christmas spirit, the blood-red lights of the stores, the smell of pretzels and shish kebab permeating the air, the casual offers of gold watches, the bells of sleighs full of cotton.

The Shit Department was strangely empty, though the lights of the "toilet" were on. Alex went to his office. Benjamin was stretched out in the darkness on a tiny rug, asleep on the boss's floor. Alex squinted to make out his face. He could see only the brilliant teeth and shark's smile that shone a few centimeters above the white collar of his black shirt.

"What is all this shit, Alex?" Operation Snow White's operative asked.

"It is the most amusing operation. You'll have to feel your way, organize as you go along. It's going to be the most amusing job of your life. You'll lament just one thing, that for a couple of months you'll have to be a blind black man. Worse than Ray Charles. Putty in my hands. You'll dance to the music I play. You'll have to do a host of strange things without knowing why. You'll set the stage not knowing what play we're putting on."

"Dammit, Alex, I hate this."

"Don't lie, Benjamin. You've always loved surprises. You adore surprises. What's more, on this one you'll be able to shine using your skills as a butcher. And there's more you're going to love. . . . Take note. First, I want you to cut off a man's hand and nail it to his boss's door. . . . Together, I want to launch a series of actions to make the boss flee, disappear, feel for the first time in a long time that he's in uncharted territory and has to take flight. Finally, I want this guy in front of me saying: 'Father, I'm ready to follow God's will.' What makes it amusing is that this is not an easy fellow, he's one of the hardest characters in the circus."

"Where is this guy?"

"South of the border. He's a Mexican drug dealer called Rolando M. Limas. You'll adore him. They say that when he wants to improve himself, he ties an English professor to the foot of his bed to give him lessons during the night. The guy doesn't sleep. This is heaven!"

"Exactly what do you want from him, Alex?" Benjamin asked, getting up from the floor and stretching. He was more than six feet tall. A thin, agile man, fitted with a suit cut by a tailor who obviously knew his craft.

"I want you to make him jump. Make him leave Mexico. Fence him in, cut off his support. Make him come to the States, disconnect him from his networks. And one day, you'll put him in front of me, in New York."

"And this by when?"

"You've got two months to do it. But there's more. He's got to feel the hits, but not know where they're coming from, he can only guess, but even then, he must be wrong. He's gotta grope around. I want you to disorient him, soften him up for me. Wrap him up for me with a big red Christmas bow."

"What do we have on him?"

"Everything. Come here, I'll show you his file."

FORTY-THREE

THE MAKING OF A DRUG
TRAFFICKER'S LEGEND
(III)

They say that after the skirmish with the trucks, you disappeared, you cleared out and headed north to have a word with the big shots, and come face to face with them, make their palms sweat when they see the biggest dick of all on the border. But we know here that that's not the truth, because your next ballad is heard in Ciudad Juárez and Reynosa; and the other day the bells rang out from the Cathedral of Hermosillo because someone had left a million pesos on the sacristy for the priest.

Not only are you an insomniac, not only invisible—now you're also immune. They say in Juárez that you were driving the third truck, the one that passed in front of Aguilar's police rats, who sold you out and later sold themselves to someone else, and that the bullets didn't hit you. You were the goddamned, bullet-proof truck driver, who kicked up no dust as you passed, who ran over ghostlike dogs that never barked before they died. A truck with a foghorn.

They say that before Aguilar lost both his hands with two sharp knife slashes, you fired a .45 at his stomach and the last shot at his face, which is how ghosts are killed, eight in the belly, one in the face, and you just laughed at the asshole. Now he walks around with no hands and you've probably changed your face again and only the whores in the shittiest brothels of Enseneda would recognize you, because they smell you.

Now you're the one who screws whores but never contracts AIDS, the one who stuffs five lines of coke up his nose and feels nothing, the asshole who comes in challenging the bigger assholes in the Caballo bar in Ciudad Obregón and the El Lobo de Mexicali canteen, and you look at them and say you'll pay their weight in gold if they kill you, and right there, their asses tighten up, and they look to see if you're missing a hand (because they say someone nailed your hand to a door), or if there's a trace of an old scar that your face surgeon didn't remove, because you like the way it shines, or if you're called Rolando M. Limas. And even if they're not sure, no one would dare ask you for ID. All the assholes writhe in fear and you leave the canteen in search of something else.

And dogs run from you and miserable little chickens move aside and even fearless cats run down dark alleys when you come. And the traitors do the same when your trucks cross the border again.

A few bastards say you're bored with living so you want them to kill you, but no one dares oblige you.

What's sure is that you went north to organize the business with your gringo pricks. To teach, educate, instruct the fairheaded men to throw out the first and second joints of pot and have balls; so they, too, learn how not to sleep at night, how to have a different face every day, how to repel bullets.

F O R T Y - F O U R

LEON'S NOVEL

He considered the novel a trifle, but curiously, during the three days he was unable to work on it, he felt empty, restless. Two macabre days of conversations with the Rosmers about the death of Liova, and his free time spent working on the Stalin manuscript. Two days in which his marbled notebook called to him from its hiding place: "Come, Leon

Davidovich, come write. Forget about death. Come dream frivolous dreams." He began to understand the tricks of literature. The terrible, hellish vocation of the genre. Many times in his life he'd written feverishly. Many times a text had called him with this kind of invitation into the abyss, the kind of invitation that a deep chasm exercises over the person who peers into it, but almost never had the sensation been associated with such tremendous curiosity as well, and curiosity was what this story held over him.

He awoke before almost anyone in the house and walked to the studio in his slippers. He tripped over Seva's toys and almost fell down the stairs. He recovered from the mishap, and locked himself in and opened the pages of his marbled notebook. He decided that the time had come for an abrupt turning point in his story.

He began to write:

16. Wolf walks through the solitary streets of Madrid. It is night, dogs howl at the moon. He is trapped in a skirmish between young socialist redshirts and Falangist blueshirts. In the frame of a doorway, he provisionally treats a young socialist wounded in the arm. It is understood that he knows a little medicine.

17. After leaving the injured socialist, he enters a nightclub, drinks cognacs liberally while he listens to a black guy playing jazz, a young, black saxophonist, very thin. At the end of the act, the black man walks toward his table, they exchange a cryptic dialogue about a woman named Melisa, whom we assume neither has seen in quite a while. The black man asks how Wolf's investigations are going, Wolf replies they're progressing slowly, but he thinks he's on to something. The black says he thinks he's on to something, too. They leave it that they'll meet the next day.

18. When Wolf gets to his *pensión,* a couple of civil police are waiting for him. They arrest him, accusing him of arms sales. He tries to demand explanations, they do not respond. They drive him to the Modelo de Madrid jail.

19. My memories of the Modelo de Madrid jail (transposed to Wolf's point of view): Jail, old friend, is basically always the same. A soldier with a fixed bayonet, his legs crossed, reads a newspaper under a lantern. They open the gate and we enter. It had been a long time since I'd felt the walls, the corridors,

the jail stench. The assistant guard to the warden, without a tie, is waiting. The cop explains that I'm a gentleman; but the assistant already knows he should treat me delicately. The frisking in the center of the star of the jail, the intersection of five galleries, each with four floors. Hanging iron ladders. Special, prison-like, nocturnal silence, pregnant with dense emanations and nightmares. Meager electric lamps in the corridors. All familiar. The same everywhere. From the central rotunda I glanced at one of the galleries. The assistant's head appeared in the inspection room window and he amiably gestured for me to take off my hat. I marched through corridors and staircases behind the warden. The clank of a steel-lined door opening. A solitary cell with a pathetic bed inspiring little confidence. The warden departs, leaving me alone. I lie down on the bed with my coat buttoned to the neck. I crack up. I didn't expect to find myself in the Madrid jail so soon.

20. The tragedy of the exclusive passions of an individual is too insipid for our time.

21. In the cell, Wolf reflects on jails. How many has he known? Are some better than others? Jails are linked in his memory to impossible revolutions. Could this be another one? Madrid has a special vibration. Wolf couldn't be mistaken, he has felt this sensation, these urban exhalations many times before in his life. He falls asleep.

22. The solitary man who lives in the *pensión* next to the Plaza Mayor is a morphine addict. He gets hold of the drug through his prostitute neighbor. He took a liking to opium in China. Now he's afraid. In his nightmares he speaks Russian.

23. A woman named Melisa is carrying out pre-suicide rituals. She's going to poison herself with arsenic dissolved in a glass of wine. Through the window she hears some *pasadobles* played in a nearby cabaret. On her table she has a portrait of Wolf, dressed in a brown leather pilot's jacket. She turns away so the portrait doesn't see her.

A gentle knock at the door startled the old man. Trotsky hastily closed his notebook and covered it with other papers on the desk. He took off his glasses and rubbed his eyes. Natalia entered the room. The old man wondered whether Melisa would take the poison or not; he put his glasses back on and grumbled affectionately at his old companion.

JOURNALISTS' STORIES

(G R E G   S P E A K S)

The pollution in Mexico City makes my nose itchy and dry. Fats attributes it to my usual hypochondriac reactions, but he is plagued by colds, the strangest skin rashes and the most reactionary sudden exhaustions. You've got to be a hell of a patriot in the face of undeniable truths to ignore that this city is falling victim to poisonous fumes. We'd been working all day editing the Trotsky story, and we took turns—he closing the office window and I opening it. As always, we worked with four hands, taking turns at the keyboard, in an awful but bilingual rough draft that we would later turn into two versions of the article, one Spanish, the other English. In this first session we were arguing the setting and structure and giving form to the story as we filled ashtrays. Every once in a while, we discovered a lateral theme and one of us abandoned the central project and went to the side typewriter to flesh out a box parallel to the article. We'd transcribe a fragment of an interview from the tapes, cite an exact quote from one of the conversations, flesh out a description. Later we ripped the results apart and mounted them. The style led with sufficient ease to the final version. One of us wrote the kicker and the other translated the second copy to his language. We'd done it many times over the last years.

This time it was my turn to finalize the rough draft of some twelve pages, in which we'd introduced fragments of Trotsky's unfinished novel, descriptions of his life in mid-1939, before the murder attempts, the old man's financial situation, a few quotations from his essays on art and literature and the opinion of the two experts who affirmed that the handwriting was inarguably Leon's. We gave credit to Julio's friend as the sui generis future novelist and night watchman who'd found the manuscript. Fats had gone into the bathroom to rinse the photos of Trotsky's office, of the pages of the marbled notebook and the pile of other material in which it had been found. In the packet there was a Polaroid photo of the two of us next to the tomb with the manuscript in our hands. We'd left the color film with a photographer, but Fats had taken personal charge of developing the black and white film while he whistled Vivaldi's *Four Seasons*. It was a good story. It would bring in a ton of money.

"Do you think he could have written a half-decent mystery with the material he had?" Julio asked, coming out of the bathroom with a wet photo between his fingers.

"I don't know."

"Do you like it?"

"I don't know that either. I think it must have been a game, a refuge in the face of so much pressure. A month after he wrote this, the attempts on his life started. They had just killed his son; Rakovsky, his best friend, had abandoned the dissidence club. I don't know. They say he wrote a few love poems to Frida Kahlo."

"I prefer him as a journalist."

"Friend, if you leave that window alone that you're about to open," I said to Fats that afternoon as I took off my glasses, "I'll make a confession. . . . Journalism is the highest literature."

"No, I already I knew that. What happens is there's a conspiracy that tries to hide it," he said and took up whistling Vivaldi again en route to the bathroom.

FORTY-SIX

HOW ABOUT A
BULGARIAN LIKE THIS?
(I)

Stoyan Vasilev was born at age nineteen. He had no past prior to 1926. No native city, no infancy, no parents, no career, no loves, no passions before 1926. In one of the archives of the Control Commission of the Bulgarian Communist Party Central Committee, Stoyan might have ceased to be a nineteen-year-old man and some bureaucrat would have meticulously noted his birth, the place, date, his parents' names and a few other unadorned facts, the kind with which encyclopedias make biographical entries. This simple data would surely be accompanied by one essential fact, the answer to why Stoyan Vasilev had no past. But if that were true, this would not have transpired. There were times in Bulgaria when it was dangerous not to have a past, just as there were other times when it was dangerous to have one. Stoyan survived them all. And it wasn't always easy.

This was not to say Stoyan Vasilev didn't have a history in general. History was something he had in abundance at his eighty-one years of age. Nor is it to say he had an aversion to the past as it's now fashionable to say; nor that he liked living in the past. None of that. Stoyan was quite clear about it: the past was a form of the blurry present that cohabited with the nonblurry present in which one normally lived. It was an alternate space, a continuous and, fortunately, changeable presence. The past was Elisa dancing a solitary tango in an empty bar on the left bank of the Seine while he was buying bread in the center of Sofia thirty-one years later.

The past was the combination of a poker game with Baker; when he had three kings in his hand and an afternoon in which he drank his second cup of one hundred percent Cuban roasted pea-bean coffee at a reception in Sofia's Cuban Embassy, on Metodi Popov Street, fifty years later. The past was the possibility of immense and infinite combinations of cities, eras, faces, sensations that accidentally flowed from other times to deposit themselves in our own. Pity those who have no past. It was almost as dangerous as being a Godless Catholic.

Stoyan Vasilev, however, was missing a piece of his past. Better said, and one has to be very precise in these matters, would be that the question of whether he had it or not was exclusively his own affair; the fact is that nobody knew it (again barring the possibility that he was registered in the aforementioned archive).

The rest of his past, which at eighty-one he seemed to greatly enjoy, was not exactly a public matter either. What's more, we could say it formed a biography-proof puzzle. The course of his life had carried him from name to name, war to war, fear to fear.

Stoyan had been in the right places at the wrong times. This from the traditional historical point of view. Though lately Stoyan practiced a different approach to history. And from the point of view of small histories, he felt he'd been in them all. If one measures the importance of a man by the number of confidential documents he has read that are never to be made public, by the multiple variations of millions of hotel rooms, *pensións,* clandestine houses, rooms of friends' children he's slept in; by the women he's loved who never loved him back; by the books read in jails, by the number of hours of fear and glory he has lived, Stoyan Vasilev was frankly an important character in this twentieth century, which he had lived almost in its entirety, length- and width-wise.

For example, Stoyan could say he'd sipped tea with P'eng P'ai in Hai Lu-feng, coffee with Che Guevara in the Sofia airport and red wine with Durruti in front of the Casa de Campo in Madrid during the Spanish Civil War. He could also boast that Stalin had once told him: "I don't like the way you think, Stoyan. You always approach things from the wrong angle," and he had survived to remember it. But along with this he also remembered how the water descends in a small torrent along the Metlikovitsa when it rains, and how a Stern submachine gun sounds when the firing pin doesn't connect with its cartridge. Simple things such as these, along with the terrible sensation produced by reading the last pages of Fucik's book knowing the ending in advance, or having to write the prologue to the Bulgarian edition of Che's diary in Bolivia when what he should have done was be there to take care of the little black-bound notebook in his backpack just after Commander Ramón wrote it. There were also the Hamburg afternoons in the midst of the feverish insanity of the port on a day of full operation, with sirens screaming and the bridge cranes swaying and the stormy ocean knocking the wooden docks; and not to be forgotten the goodbyes at the foot of a plane to a friend you know with absolute certainty you will never see again, and goodbyes, therefore, although falsely tender, are forever. Stories that were sometimes bitter, sometimes wonderful. Stories that always had two sides, like those reversible jackets in style in the sixties. In that sense, Stoyan was very wary of his memories and didn't grant them more importance than they had in the instant they came to his head.

Unlike the majority of his peers, Stoyan did not attribute a chronological order to his memories, no temporal sequence. The military training camps of Chinese peasants organized during the peak of the Hai Lu-feng Red Guards in 1923, with their three-yard-long spears adorned with colored bows, could well come after the terrifying afternoons in Madrid beneath the bombs in '37 and a little before the Montenegro Insurrection of '41, and substantially later than his exile in the mountain region of Tŭrnovo in '52, in the course of revisited memories. Only those who hadn't lived it would be interested in putting it in order. For Stoyan, they were fragments of memories that at times he wished to evoke, at times he couldn't forget, at times he lost in an obscure drawer of the mind, at times he shouldn't remember, at times he didn't have to condemn to amnesia, at times should never have happened, at times were impossible to forget when they were still crying. . . .

If someone, obviously against Stoyan's will, were to receive a Guggenheim grant and a dozen years to work in the New York Public Library and were to schematically organize an outline of this character's biography, in addition to the strange information gathered and hidden there, she or he would have found the following surprising data:

1. A young student, Stoyan joins the Bulgarian Communist Party in 1926. It is the period just after the onslaught of the White Terror when in very few months, the government had

detained 1,500 revolutionaries and executed 124 of them, and the BCP had gone underground. The era of secrecy and uncertainty in the city, of the decay of the organizations of the masses and of the clandestine contacts that never came about, the electoral reorganization under the cover of the phantom Labor Party and the reorganization of the press. The era in which communists died young and informers earned more for their services than ever. There is an article published in March of '58 in the party magazine, *Novo Breme,* signed by Stoyan himself, which speaks of the occurrences between 1926 and 1927, in those difficult times for the capital. His name also appears in passing in Rothschild's classic text, *The Communist Party of Bulgaria,* the extension of his Oxford doctoral thesis.

2. At the funeral of Fridman, executed during the White Terror, Stoyan Vasilev the student plays the funeral march on the piano during a brief ceremony to which only family members are invited. A fifteen-line account of the funeral is published in the Sofia press and is reprinted in *Imprecor.*

3. One Stoyan Vasilev is the translator of the novel *Under the Yoke,* the classic work of Bulgarian Ivan Vazov, into English and Spanish, which can be verified on the copyright pages of the Argentinian Claridad edition and the North American edition by Little, Brown and Co. in Boston. In the translator's prologue to the North American edition, there are subtle references that situate Stoyan in New York City in 1931.

4. A person by that name, Bulgarian passport number MH 6292, spends sixteen days in the Castillo de Principe prison in Havana for illegal entry into the country on an undetermined date. On March 11, 1934, he is deported on the *Covadonga,* which should dock in the Spanish city of Vigo. According to the ship's logbook, Vasilev disappeared hours before the steamer docked in Cádiz on April 6th. There are brief references to the affair in *El Diario de Cádiz* the previous week, in which Vasilev is treated as a "mysterious character said to have smuggled American money."

5. An actor named Stoy Vasilev works with Alan Ladd and Max Lewis on the film *The Glass Key* for Metro-Goldwyn-Mayer. He plays the role of a Detroit gangster's hired gunman. He can be recognized, always smoking, in various photographs that appeared in the *Hollywood Reporter, The Los Angeles Times,*

and some national publications that cover film and can be compared to the passport photograph mentioned above that was published, for lack of a better one, in the above-mentioned Cádiz paper.

6. The Bulgarian police authorize a search and capture order for the communist fugitive Stoyan Vasilev, who has shot at two gendarmes who were trying to block a protest meeting outside a Sofia textile factory, the Aztek Company. The occurrence took place on June 16th of '35 and was reprinted in a few lines by the *New York Times* correspondent in Belgrade who fished it out while scanning the Bulgarian papers along with a few more reports on the tension in Sofia's textile factories.

7. According to the Madrid paper, *As,* someone with the name Stoyan wins the third stage of the cycling tour in Flanders the same day with a lead of sixty-seven miles. He dies after crossing the finish line.

8. The same Stoyan Vasilev participates in the recruitment and organization of the Bulgarian group that takes part in the formation of the International Brigades that will fight in the Spanish Civil War. He organizes a group of workers in Sofia's wood factories and a few student officers from the BCP. The group meets in France before entering Spain, where the Balkanites who participate in the Brigades have a coordinating office at 54 Mathurin-Moreau Street, Nineteenth Arrondissement, in Paris. There are ample references in the classic works on the Brigades by Castells, Koltzor and Longo.

9. The same documents bear witness to Stoyan's operation during the Spanish War in the Battle of Guadalajara as a captain in the Garibaldi Battalion of the Twelfth International Brigade, March 1937.

10. In Hemingway's story "Under the Hill," collected in the *Fifth Column* anthology, the North American author speaks of a Bulgarian friend of Hans Beimler whom he describes in the following manner: "of medium stature, very robust, with the hands of a pianist, I never found out whether he was serious or not. Pursed lips, but big sparkling eyes, unruly, kinky straw-colored hair, with a slight limp." Some of the elements coincide with the description the Bulgarian police has in its archives and which was divulged in a 1946 publication of the foreign-language editions of the BCP's propaganda office ti-

tled "Founders of Our Nation: Bulgarian Communists in the Monarchy's Police Archives."

11. There is a photo published in *Izvestia* on May 2, 1939, that shows him on the platform of Red Square during the May 1st procession in the Soviet capital. He is six places from Stalin counting left to right. The caption below the photograph lists the names of many of the presidium's members, but not his, even though he is unmistakable in the photo.

12. In the two histories written by Milovan Djilas, in which an account of the 1941 Montenegro Insurrection appears, a noteworthy mention is made of the IC's envoy, the Bulgarian Vasilev, familiar to many officers of the Yugoslavian Communist Party with whom he forged intimate friendships during the war in Spain. The descriptions of Vasilev (they offer only his last name, not his first), to whom they attribute a noteworthy role in the failed insurrection, coincide closely with the character. It is not clear why he was in Yugoslavia at the time.

13. A Bulgarian soccer player signs for the Liverpool Club of the English first division. Throughout the season, he would not play a single game for the title team. In a note published in the *Times* June 16, 1942, his teammate, fullback Kerry, praised Vasilev, remarking that it was difficult for him to recover from a knee injury.

14. In July of 1943, the cattle dealer Stoyan Vasilev simultaneously becomes a father and a widower upon the birth of a daughter in the central hospital of Sofia, according to the medical assistant's own records. The mother who died in childbirth due to a septicemia is named Ana Martínez, from Logroño, Spain. The girl is baptized Maria.

15. Stoyan Vasilev's name is mentioned twice in the history of the BCP edited in Sofia in 1969 (though he is not mentioned in the 1958 or '64 editions) in connection with guerrilla activity against the monarchs and Nazi soldiers. In widely circulated books like *Murgash* by the Dzhurov couple and *In the Name of the People* by Ulov, there are extensive references made to Vasilev's activity as second in command of the guerrilla detail active in the first operative zone during this period.

16. According to an accusation published by the Fourth International in Paris on November 25, 1952, Stoyan Vasilev, "Veteran of the International Brigades during the Spanish War and

one of the directing officers of the Bulgarian communist guerrillas against the Nazis," is one of the 154 soldiers detained immediately after the purges effected in the bosom of the BCP whose fundamental act is the detention of former General Secretary Traicho Kostov. Stoyan's name, however, does not appear on the lists of defendants.

17. In the June 5, 1961, edition of the Havana daily, *Revolución,* it is reported that one Stoyan Vasilev is part of the Bulgarian delegation to meet in Havana with Fidel Castro. In the next day's edition, under the headline "Two Generations of Guerrilla Fighters Collaborate in the Construction of a School," the following text is published: "At age fifty-five, Vasilev was not afraid of the shovel and participated in a day of volunteer work with the Minister of Industry, Ernesto Che Guevara, in the construction of a school on the corner of 13th and 4th in El Vedado." Under the text, there is a photograph where one can see Che and Vasilev loading a wheelbarrow and shoveling, both sweaty. The Argentinian-Cuban, naked from the waist up, and the Bulgarian in a T-shirt with a bandanna tied around his head.

18. Various reports signed by Stoyan Vasilev appear in Bulgarian magazines of wide circulation between 1961 and 1967. All of them on international issues. Basically they are investigative reports and works of a correspondent or special envoy. They cover events like the Congolese Insurrection, elections in Venezuela, daily life in Portugal under the Salazar dictatorship, the death of Ben Barka, etc. . . . Some of these articles are reproduced in those of the West's publications sold by the Sofia Press Agency. He wins several international awards for journalism. His most important articles are collected in two small volumes under the common title *Interminable Bengal Lights,* published in Bulgarian, Russian, Spanish and English. He is a jury member for the journalism award of the Casa de las Americas. He wins the French magazine *Miroir de l' Histoire*'s award for historical reporting. He publishes a book in England on the Philby case. He is president of the Press's Foreign Correspondents Association in Caracas. There is abundant documentation, photographs, travel records and other material over these years, that allows precise tracking of his work. An anthology of journalistic work is published by Columbia University's information science department in 1966.

He wins a FELAP scholarship for historical reporting on the International Brigades, lives in San Francisco, Vienna, East Berlin and Madrid for six months of research.

19. The prologue of the Bulgarian edition of Che Guevara's diary in Bolivia, edited in early 1969, is signed by Stoyan Vasilev.

Faced with this information, all that is clear is that much is lacking, too much to tie it all together. And whatever the case may be, Stoyan Vasilev was not a normal, ordinary guy.

F O R T Y - S E V E N

SNOW WHITE HAD SEVEN DWARFS . . .

. . .and each had his own name. "Let's see," Alex said sweetly. "Obviously, Benjamin is *Grumpy.* Eve is . . . *Sneezy,* because of her idiotic allergies." The indicated blew a kiss to Alex off the palm of her hand. "Aram is *Happy* and Eloise is *Dopey.* So that leaves . . . *Doc, Bashful* and *Sleepy.* The third has already been assigned, better to leave it at that for now. So we have two more roles to hand out. *Doc* . . . Obviously, we need a doctor."

Alex was not joking. An anecdote widely circulated in the SD referred to a time when Alex had hired, by way of an intermediary, one of the great English spy novelists, to brief him on the proper language in which to offer the Argentinian military a double agent. Eve and Eloise were now convinced that the count-off of Snow White's seven dwarfs had introduced into the fantastic script of the story unrolling in Alex's head an unexpected doctor. Alex would wait until later before disclosing why he wanted him and when he would enter the scene.

"Do you remember Doctor Mapleton, the psychiatrist?" Alex noted the doctor's name on a green memo pad so that the next day Leila could summon him to the SD.

The meeting had begun at ten in the morning on a Sunday, and Alex had been torturing them with a rock version of Tchaikovsky's 1812 overture playing over and over again for an hour and a half on the portable record player. Aram was desperate. His second son had just been born and he wanted to go to the hospital to look at him awhile before holing up at home to watch the Jets, who'd made the NFL playoffs. Alex had forced them to go over Rolando M. Limas's biography again and again to try to find holes. Everything was more complicated when you didn't know what you were looking for. A hole, by Alexian definition, was a blank space in time. But there were holes and holes. Until now, they'd been able to work on public holes, or at least relatively public. They'd created silent holes in the report, gathering information from the DEA, the Mexican police, two dozen informers from the world of border drug trafficking, half a dozen local journalists collaborating with the Mexican secretary of the interior, who in turn leaked it to the CIA office in Mexico City. There was too much, and it was unclear. Rolando (they were beginning to love him, indeed they'd tacked a large picture of him to one of the walls in Alex's office, with two candles lit below, a kind of secular altar) was not the type who took highly to public life, nor was it easy to get at his closest advisers. And M. Limas was not the only one giving them problems. After the search, they'd submitted the preliminary version of Eve's biography of Machado for criticism, exposing new spaces to investigate, new lines of interrogation, dozens of questions. Finally, Alex cast off the insanity of Snow White's seven dwarfs.

"All right, we'll drop our chain of command for the moment. Let's return to the Bulgarian. I think Stoyan Vasilev interests me after all. Is he too old to fly?"

"He was in Havana a year ago working in Che's widow's archives," Aram said.

"Okay, let's dust off the material we've got on him. It's easy to place him as renowned journalist, but I get the impression that the file suggests he's an agent for Bulgarian counterespionage. If that's true, then we're fucked. I need a guy who makes decisions individually, for moral reasons and from a personal perspective, not collectively and definitely not utilitarian."

"He seems like a lone wolf," Eve said.

"Would you bet your ass on that?" Alex asked. Eve shut up. "Let's look at this again, from the beginning."

"I don't think Bulgarian security would have ever recruited a guy who spent seven years in jail under Stalin," Eloise said.

The 1812 overture began again on the record player. Aram cursed Snow White–Alex in the three languages he knew.

FORTY-EIGHT

ONE MORE REJECTED THESIS PROPOSAL BY ELENA JORDAN

Several years ago, it was said that the dog found stretched out in the sun in front of the door of the Carolino building, headquarters of Puebla's Public University, wore a collar which clearly read "Rosa Luxemburg Cell, paid up on his dues." Had he not worn the collar, it is quite probable that the dog would have had to take his sun elsewhere.

A well-known Mexican writer told the press (*Jornada,* April 16, 1988) that he'd clandestinely read Engels in 1966, "A Paper on the Work of Transforming Man into Monkey" hidden in a newspaper, while today they taught the text in grade school to his daughter. He said that this disturbed him. Not because Marxism had achieved the right of legal circulation in our society, but because it had become something to be read in order to pass a course.

Among the National University's political science students, a well-known anecdote recounts that in the convocations of the great electricians' protests in '72, a militant got Professor Veranza's answer; he told him he didn't think he'd attend, arguing that someone who'd read *Das Kapital* at twenty-one and had studied it conscientiously could not go out and expose his head to the blows of soldiers. In fact, Professor Veranza injured his head months later, when he fell down drunk at the door of the Kuku bar.

In the Business School of Sinaloa's Public University, there are two courses in Marxism called "Historical Materialism" I and II, one course in Marxist philosophy, two courses in social history, one course in "National Problems," and two courses in Marxist political economy. A survey carried out by Liberato Teran in 1984 (UAS, "The Comparative Political Behaviors of Graduates: A Sample"), however, reveals that, on average, upon entering professional life, graduates follow the exact same rules and political conduct they followed in 1972, before the introduction of these courses. Indeed, in Teran's own words, "these assholes get more reactionary every day."

Anecdotes such as these could fill two hundred pages, and they are a mere sample of a phenomenon widely extended throughout the country: the appearance of a university Marxism, with a primitive edge that has become functional in Mexican academic society, and that is linked to the mechanisms of professional promotion, social ascension in the University pyramid, formal qualification that permits passing courses and a depressing obligation for the student.

The purpose of this investigation is to carry out a concrete sampling of this body of anecdotes and to organize it, in response to the far-reaching and normal question: what's it for? Through exhaustive research, the aim is to analyze this kitchen rhetoric Marxism and observe its functions on various levels, to wit:

The management of Marxist philosophy in the merciless Mexican academic war. If you've read Althuser, what possible chance do you have of becoming a department head? If you frequently quote Lukács, and publish an incomprehensible article in a school journal, how many promotion points do you earn, and just how many pesos per month does it mean to your salary? What extra possibilities to join the PRI in a midlevel post, does having taken five classes on *Das Kapital* at the Acatlán ENEP University earn you?

Through such a path, known to rhetorics as the "reduction to simple reality," we'll show the real functions of this Neanderthal Marxism and its big brother, Academic Marxism, also known as Marx-business. Some of the suggested inquiries are as follows:

a) who the hell invented and propagated, and with what insane intentions, the concept of "theoretical work"?
b) how many students of "Historical Materialism" I and II in the IPN's Business School have brought more than one can of beans to a workers' strike in a solitary act of humility?
c) how many cases of abuse toward minors (popularly called children) have been perpetrated by Professors of Historical Materialism, and is this higher than the average of the Teachers' Association for Higher Learning?
e) how many police agents appointed by the Secretary of the Interior whose work has been made public passed the course on the political value of Hegel's thought taught in the Philosophy Department of the University of Guadalajara, with a B or above?
f) what overlap exists between lottery winners or sports bookies and those who took Dialectical Materialism in the CCH?

The first phase of investigation would be to complete a list of some one hundred questions such as those listed above, and through direct questioning and group polls, obtain the answers.

Copilco, September '88
Elena Jordan

P.S. In light of the previous results of my thesis proposals, the applicant requests that in the case of rejection the HH board not take more than one week to respond (as opposed to two months in the last case). Thank you in advance.

FORTY-NINE

HOW ABOUT A
BULGARIAN LIKE THIS?
(II)

With his eighty-one years of age, Stoyan Vasilev believed that public biographies do not exist. To be public, they would cease to be biographies (recapitulation of all one's own acts, and therefore private). For biographies to exist, one could only penetrate to the social level and thus include stories of others, not personal stories. With the usual manipulations, biographies become dead portraits destined for the attic collections of a grandparent's memories.

Stoyan Vasilev passionately hated the authors of the genre: Emil Ludwig, Harold Lamb and Gerard Walter, and he only timidly respected the heretics of the biography business like Hans Magnus Enzenberger or La Fallaci. It was probably a strong reaction to so many years of seeing photos of Stalin, The Father, the greatest creator of autobiographies produced in the history of humanity, smiling at him from the walls.

So many years of contemplating that face that was always hiding the veiled threat: "I'll cut your balls off," "I'll eat your wad," "I'll come after you even in your dreams," would make anyone antibiography.

This strange obsession had extended to his relationship with anyone suspected of contributing elements to his own, future biography. This made him deceive his fellow reporters, lie to historians, trick customs officers, hurl lies at census surveyors and falsify official documents. Even now, in these times when biographies had ceased to be double-edged swords that sometimes served to cut bread and other times to sink into your own heart.

The origin of his antibiography obsession, undoubtedly very connected to his concept of the past, was probably in the Stalinist purges in the late forties and fifties, the last three bloody years before Stalin's death, when terror fell upon the recently formed socialist states of the Balkans. Echoes from the Rajk case descended upon Bulgaria in late '49, finding a propitious vacuum created by the disappearance by natural death of the great figure of Bulgarian communism, Georgi Dimitrov. The climate of Cold War, the Stalinist insanity of one-person power and the pyramid of loyal servants fit poorly into a generation of clandestine militants, guerrilla soldiers, fighters from the Spanish War. The conflicts with Tito and the sense that Stalinism was losing its imperial control over Eastern Europe produced the judgment against Rajk in Hungary. Months after the machinations of false accusations, Beria's KGB perpetrators of legal fraud mobilized in Hungary. The figure elected as the heart of the process was the old troop leader, Traicho Kostov.

Stoyan saw the new wave of arrests coming. He smelled it in the tenuous tone of the messages one could read between the lines of *Pravda*. He sensed it among his colleagues, but he was too busy with the Cold War, the night trips across the Turkish border and the hunt for saboteurs sent by the British SIS, to sit around and wait for it. Nevertheless, he was not surprised when they arrested him. He was too exhausted to be surprised. He'd been pushing his physical limitations for months and moreover he was one of those who knew that the revolution, while absolutely necessary, had been poisoned from the start. He was not one of those blind, deaf and mute imbeciles of such stubborn orthodoxy, doglike loyalty and bureaucratic insanity who inundated the party. He had been in Spain, he'd been in Moscow in '39 and he knew. Like many, he knew things he wished he didn't. But that still didn't make him hesitate for an instant when the war against the Nazis or the great mobilization that led to the revolution of '44 began. Knowing that destiny is a fire that will consume one in its flame doesn't mean just allowing it to do so. Was he a fatalist in '49? If he was, he was a fatalist bursting with energy. And so, the arrival of two men one night at his house in the suburbs of Plovdiv, the country's third city, in the southeast, just over sixty miles from the Turkish border and thirty miles over the mountains from the Greek border, did not surprise him. He had lived the past days waiting for the last great purge, the one that would finish off the last communists, the generation of the internationals and guerrillas, those who still had thoughts of their own, though they were thoughts increasingly buried in the depths of their souls; those who would be vindicated many years later, those who would remain in popular history, oral history, myth.

Stoyan confronted his interrogators without the doubts that hounded his detained colleagues, trapped in the labyrinth and trying to flee while screaming that somewhere there'd been a mistake, a terrible misunderstanding.

And when his interrogators tried to distort the past, to turn him into an English spy, an infiltrated Nazi, a disguised Trotskyite, Stoyan began his own career as an autobiographer. The logic of the process, as he discovered years later reading Eugen Löbl and Artur London (whom he'd known well in Spain), two of the few survivors of the Czech tribunals, consisted in maintaining that the accused felt a nonexistent and highly abstract guilt. The path was to review one's biography again and again until little by little it began to change. Converting oneself into a catalog of voluntary crimes against the sacred cause of the working class. Confess to a small one under pressure, one that didn't happen but was plausible, a mistake that could be classified as an "objectively counterrevolutionary" act, and they will later create a chain of them. They will distort and reconstruct it. And the pressure will mount: hunger, exhaustion, threats against one's children, forged proof of your guilt, torture, fear, isolation and above all, the terrible sense that it is your own people, not your enemies, who want your head. When you confess to an unreal sin, out of exhaustion, boredom, desperation, it becomes an inarguable piece of your biography, and the biography becomes a chain full of steel links weighing upon your back. The nightmares creep in, in which you are someone else, someone who is stoking the witch hunt's bonfire.

Before others could invent his history, Stoyan began to modify it himself, voluntarily. He found it entertaining. He toyed with insanity, went crazy, returned to sanity, and vacillated between both unstable conditions, creating biographies for other "I"s. He ended up winning the game, as is always the case against an absolutist machinery, by bloody accident. It might have had to do with Traicho Kostov's attitude during the show trial, which, unlike the other Stalinist setups, was broken by the accused's refusal to accept the guilt and his rejection of the charges of having committed treason against his colleagues in prison twenty years before, of having been a British agent or having sought to form a Titoist center inside the party. Kostov's refusal to accept those charges upset and broke the gears of the show trials. Perhaps that's why the pressure on Stoyan let up after five months of detention and he was offered the silence of solitary confinement. After a year he began to receive books, a radio borrowed for two hours a night to hear a concert, paper to write on, and the quality of his food improved slightly. Even so, during his interrogation he did not know what was happening in the outside world, nor would he for eleven years. And that is why his responses merit inclusion in the anthology of the few failed interrogations of the Stalinist trials.

"Comrade Vasilev, where were you born?"

"I am not authorized to disclose that information. Unless you can show me the card of Comrade Chervenkov, secretary general, the card of the Bulgarian Workers' Party, I cannot offer that information."

"Why can't you offer that information?"

"When did you join the party?"

"That is not relevant, we are talking about you, Vasilev, not me."

"When did you join the party? And I warn you that if I don't get an answer, this interrogation is over."

"Okay, 1945. Why?"

"Because I joined in 1926, which gives me the absolute right to demand, Comrade Interrogator, that you not address me familiarly."

"Agreed, Comrade Vasilev, sir. When and where were you born, sir?"

"In 1939, Stalin asked me personally in Moscow please not to divulge that information to anyone. Do you all remember the story of the Man in the Iron Mask? Well then, for the same reasons, Stalin earnestly asked me not to speak of this. If you doubt me, ask him."

"Vasilev, you were not in Moscow in 1939."

"I don't see how you can say such a foolish thing, you're the one who was not in Moscow then, I am absolutely positive we did not see each other in those days."

The distance between the person who had at one time been real and the multiple he had invented began to fade. It wasn't that hard. He'd been so many people. . . . When he docked in Shanghai, he was a Bulgarian industrialist in search of low-priced Chinese silk. In France, he was a drunken chemical engineer trying to improve the formula for the Bulgarian imitation of French champagne by bodily testing. In Germany, he was an insomniac painter by night and a bank's mailman by day. Generally, he'd been himself only in the Chinese and Bulgarian mountain ranges. And even then, who was he?

At times, he remembered a poem by an Italian named Luzi he'd read in a novel by Bilenchi. He didn't even know Luzi's first name. Of the poem, there were three lines he could not forget: "The girls leaning out the windows / Their gazes set far away / Never cease to await the future."

With a piece of coal that a guard who'd fought beside him in the war, and who was replaced a few days later, lent him, he painted a barred window on one of the cell walls. Staring at it, he imagined the sunsets.

During his first year of absolute isolation, without books, without cell windows, without paper or pencil, he rebuilt known literature. At times he recalled Emilio Salgari's complete novel *Good-bye to Mompracem,* the most tragic of the Adventures of the Tigers of Malaysia. He told it to himself, changing it, improving it, adding subplots, perfecting the character descriptions: What mysterious origin brought Yanez de Gomara to this corner of the world? Was there another woman in Sandokan's past besides Labuan's pearl? What economic interests did the English have in the Malaysian archipelago? Salgari would have thanked him. He frequently supplemented the pirates' adventures with his old readings in *Imprecor* of the work of Eugen Varga, the Hungarian economist, and tried to figure out the mechanisms of English colonialism on the Sunda archipelago. Other times he applied his reading of the Vienna School psychologists to the subservient and loyal mind of Kammamuri. Upon finishing Salgari, he moved on to the novels of Karl May and then attacked the North American prairie.

When that didn't suffice, he remembered his daughter, Maria. At times, he confused her in his memory with Shirley Temple, whom he'd seen in two or three films.

The interrogators never used violence. Only psychological pressure, hunger, exhaustion. Probably drugs occasionally, though he couldn't be sure of that. Months went by, under clouds he couldn't see, since his cell had no windows.

One day he explained the following theory to one of his interrogators:

"A fascist thrust has hit Bulgaria. You all are monarchic fascists. You have restored Czar Michael. You try to make me believe
you are communists (he interjected "I've fucked you" in Spanish).
There is no such thing. Long live Stalin, long live the dictatorship
of the proletariat. You can shoot me whenever you feel like it.
From this moment on, I'm confining myself to reciting the few
Aesop's fables I know by heart. The first: A greedy frog . . ."

F I F T Y

"I CAN WORK AROUND
THE FACTS . . .

. . . or the holes," Alex said. "This
is a ballet of shadows, the movements count as much as the empty
spaces the bodies leave behind. I can work with both. Machado,
for example, was in Mexico April eleventh through thirteenth, he
lost an afternoon. He probably visited old friends. That doesn't
count. That's not a hole in the precise sense of the word. On the
other hand, it does serve me to know that on April twelfth he had
coffee with a Mexican anthropologist, one Elena Jordan. His relationship to the dead also interests me. The dead are devilishly
useful. They do not adapt themselves to denials. The dead are
malleable, they are perfectly disposed for a retelling. Their biographies easily admit rewriting. People with secrets are useful to me.
If I know someone's secrets, they are more mine than his own.
What's useful to me are the hours of sleep, moments walking in
solitude, unconfessed loves, private perversions, unspeakable
tastes, obsessions. Listen up, ladies and gentlemen, I'm interested
in obsessions, strange tastes, phobias. Those are the real holes. Get
it, slaves? Eve, get Jason and Doctor Strangelove to work with you

on this kind of hole. Keep feeding the machine. Until it spits information out of sheer saturation. I want everything."

Alex turned halfway around. The meeting had ended. Right there, nothing more. He lit a cigarette and realized there was another one smoldering in the ashtray. He put them both out.

FIFTY-ONE

How About a Bulgarian Like This? (III)

Stoyan dreamed about Maria. He knew his daughter, Maria, was waiting for him somewhere. For the last thirty-five years of his life, he'd dreamed punctually night after night about Maria. In whatever corner of the world he found himself, he dreamed about Maria, a girl with blond ringlets, a turned-up nose, showing him her rag doll. He couldn't imagine that in 1988 Maria would be a forty-five-year-old woman. In his dreams she was the only Maria he'd ever known, a six-and-a-half-year-old girl showing him her rag doll so that he would fix the tattered ear about to fall off.

At night he dreamed of Maria. During the day, he daydreamed about Latin America. One day he'd be able to tie the two obsessions together. Maria would wait for him somewhere in Latin America and he would go find her. It would be very hot, they'd sit outside, he would order a *mojito* and buy the girl a pineapple juice. As this long-awaited event unfolded, Stoyan walked every morning to Exarj Yossif Street, where Sofia's fire department was located; he entered his office, turned on the tiny gas furnace, resolved his small tasks in twenty minutes and dedicated the rest of the morning to writing.

In the first minutes of the morning he wrote press reports of fires, gas explosions, children trapped in floods, birds that caused short circuits, issues of industrial security, experiments with non-flammable insulation, and once a week, he made up a wall newspaper (he did only seventy-five percent; the rest was filled by corps volunteers) for Sofia's firefighters. Later the fun began. From a huge metal filing cabinet he took out several files full of heterogeneous work of his own and decided what he would spend that morning on. It might be the notes from the historical report he was researching on the Montenegro Insurrection; it might be transcribing the tapes of that long interview with Camilo Cienfuegos that he wanted to make into a book, thirty years after the guerrilla soldier's death; it might be the file he was creating on the National Front and the resurgence of fascism in Great Britain; it might be the report he was making taking stock of the violence on Europe's soccer fields; since he'd been clipping so much material on the subject, the entire world's magazines fell into his hands. It might be his notes on the children of the Sandinista Revolution, about which he'd already written a couple of short articles, but still had dozens of pages of notes, photographs and various long interviews with some of the kids he'd met. It might be the investigation of Olaf Palme's death, though he couldn't go much further with that until the Bulgarian News Agency or the Swiss Social Democratic Foundation approved the project and paid his way. Or it might be the memoir of a Bulgarian in the Spanish War on which he'd been working, trying to turn a dozen testimonies, including his own, into a collage of one single voice that would synthesize them all.

His afternoons were spent writing letters. He corresponded with a hundred friends and colleagues around the world. With them he exchanged information, memories, newspaper articles, books, recipes, facts about missing war criminals, difficult-to-find folkloric musical scores, addresses of lost people, documents.

Mornings and afternoons gently slipped away from Stoyan Vasilev. He knew, though, that this peace would not be permanent, but only a way station between the real heat of summer and the icy storms of winter. So Stoyan pretended to work and at times really did work, while he waited for a reason to live again.

When was the last time? Any one of the last times when the risks were greater than the rewards, the odds stacked up against one, the razor's edge stretched out over the one who danced? One lived for others. It wasn't that he found journalism incompatible.

Journalism was the great late discovery of his life, something that he'd begun to practice in his early sixties after abandoning the exile he'd been serving in an agricultural co-op that grew flowers. Journalism wasn't bad. Telling stories. Telling other people's stories. Living in pursuit of facts, of dates, and at the same time hunting for his own sensations to put on paper so as to cut the distance between himself and those who were living.

Stoyan had always been many things at the same time. Even now when he seemed to be a placid old man with strikingly white hair and every right to retire, he worked in the Sofia fire department and filled his spare time with freelance journalism. Articles, reports, chronicles, interviews that went on to blanket the world. Even now, he fooled everyone, including himself; because what he really was, despite appearances, was an old man with strikingly white hair, a lover of cognac, who vainly pretended to wait for reunion with a lost daughter while he pallidly prepared to return to real life. And even this version was incomplete if you knew about the nonexistent, hidden hours in which he worked on the "Madrid Project."

F I F T Y - T W O

BACK IN MIAMI

We can do something, Mendoza," Rolando suggested. "We cut off the entire artillery, we divide up a few good kitchen knives, then we turn off the lights in the room. And in a while, whoever walks out gets the business and, what the fuck, runs it however he wants. What do you think?"

The Colombian stared at him with his eyes half closed. He always looked as if he were dozing off.

"I don't have anything to do with what's happening to you, Rolando. I told you a hundred times. It's true the men who went to your hotel were mine, but somebody bought them. I hope they have to eat a pile of shit. I didn't send them. I've got more than I want, I'm not interested in dabbling along the border; no way, I want the border calm, full of good friends like you."

Rolando stood up and started walking around the table. Marcelino the dwarf and Benigno were playing volleyball in the garden with the Colombian's hit men. Marcelino was cheating on the scoreboard. A group of dark, scintillating girls wearing only their bikini tops lay in the sun on beach mats. Not a bad idea, leaving them without their bikini bottoms. Never in his life had he so yearned to take off someone's top.

"If it's not you, then who?"

"No one, my brother, I can't imagine who."

"Was the guy who paid Aguilar to attack the truck yours?"

"Yes," the Colombian confirmed, spitting out bits of his red paper from his filterless cigarette.

"Were the guys who came to the hotel to take out my heart yours?"

"They were."

"Well, then?"

"Someone's fucking with both of us. If you figure it out, Rolando, I want to know, too. . . . What's more, to show you my good faith, I'll pay for those trucks, to repay you for the wrong, since it was my guy who fucked up the operation."

"Don't even think about it, Mendoza. Money's not the problem."

"Let me do this small favor."

"No way. You just clean out your henhouse."

"Consider it done."

"And those girls?" Rolando asked just to say something, signaling with his head the girls in their bikini tops.

"Nothing, a couple of my kids I don't keep in line," said the Colombian, readopting his sleepy appearance.

Rolando picked up the cup of coffee that had been in front of him since the beginning of the meeting, which he hadn't touched, and took a sip. It was excellent but cold. If Mendoza went on like this, pretty soon he'd be begging outside a church door: gunmen who can be bought off, prostitute daughters. . . .

A servant entered the room and whispered a few words in Mendoza's ears. Later he brought him a note. Mendoza dismissed him with a nod after asking for more hot coffee.

"It's for you, Rolando," he said, handing him the note. "The guy you brought me knows only one thing, this telephone number in New York. They had to report what they did with you there."

Rolando took the note and approached a white phone.

"What do I dial first?"

"Two one two," Mendoza answered. "But don't bother. Reynal already called it. The answering machine just says you've got a dinner date the day after tomorrow on Fifth Avenue with a Mister Smith. . . ."

"No way," Rolando said. He started to dial. He wanted to hear it for himself. He wanted to hear the voice of the man with whom he would be dining.

FIFTY-THREE

LONGORIA'S SOLITUDE

Premature babies born at very low weights sometimes forget to breathe. This is why in the incubation center, nurses often tie a thread from their own hands to the newborn's and every so often give it a yank to remind her or him that life goes on. Of all the jobs that Longoria had had in his life, he felt particularly satisfied by two: the falsification of half a million pesetas with which he'd financed one of the failed attacks against Spanish dictator Generalissimo Franco, and the nocturnal hours he'd spent in the incubation center at the Sanatorio Español, pulling the little thread, while the nurse on duty took a coffee break in the delivery room.

Theoretically, Saturnino Longoria could not have been there, because he had died in 1962 at the hands of a couple of hit men, a cross-eyed Moroccan and a toothless Corsican, in Aubervilliers, a proletariat suburb outside Paris. In fact, he'd died once before that in an airplane crash returning from London in 1946 to win the Distinguished Service Cross for his service during World War II, having saved sixty-one English pilots who'd been shot down in

France. As he never married or bore any children, no descendants had the chance to dwell on the strange deeds of their father or admiringly tell him he had seven lives. Longoria didn't believe in the seven lives, he was aware only that he had three lives and he'd already lost two. One of them in that airplane which he was not on, though his name appeared on the list of passengers, the second when all but one of the Moroccan's bullets hit the bulletproof plaits under his vest.

Saturnino Longoria had watched his own funeral twice, from a prudent distance, crying a little, as one should while watching funerals, someone else's or one's own. They were funerals as they should be; one was absolutely majestic—in Paris, in the midst of a rainstorm, with the procession marching on foot behind the hearse, the adorned black horses, the Seine appearing in the distance along the bending turns that led to the Père Lachaise Cemetery, and the tomb of the last members of the Paris Commune. The other one had been much more frugal, very British; the only hint of color had been furnished by the Scottish pipers, who, in the absence of Asturian pipers, marched at the front of the procession through the streets of London one misty autumn afternoon.

Wonderful funerals. He almost didn't deserve them. He knew that the third one would not pass before his eyes, mostly because the definitive moment was approaching, now that he was eighty-one. At any rate, he hadn't met anyone else who had contemplated two of his own funerals. Nor had he met anyone who could make better hundred-franc bills. One thing and the other had become deliciously inseparable. A good counterfeiter could define the supreme moment of his glory when he counterfeited his own death twice.

Longoria approached one of the cribs where a baby girl slept (he knew because she had a pink bow around her ankle with her name, Marina), and he smiled at her. He didn't feel old. He didn't feel young either. He was in a special situation wherein events would dictate who he would be, how he would behave, how he would live out his final years, how he would either create a legendary ending or disappear into the silence of nothingness. The baby gasped a little; Longoria gently rocked the incubator. The girl began to breathe to the rhythm of the rocking and quieted down. She had a wonderful nose, a perfect little ball. Longoria gave her his best smile.

You had to be essentially stupid to think that life ended at eighty, Longoria said to himself. Just as you had to be an absolute idiot to think life didn't begin with the first sob. He had two choices: fuck the state, wherever he found it, or be a poet. He wasn't sure the latter warranted the trouble of cultivating it. He loved the former. He'd practiced it for sixty-seven years with reliably good luck.

FIFTY-FOUR

JOURNALISTS' STORIES (JULIO SPEAKS)

Goddammit, I'm totally in love with this stinking lunatic!" I said to Greg, throwing Elena's rejected thesis proposals across the table.

"Remember . . . ," the little guy said.

"It's a phrase, asshole. You practice the same art. How many women have you been hopelessly in love with over the last years? The Chilean. Melisa. Remember? When you wanted to make love to her after a week of apocalyptic petting and dinner dates and bouquets of white roses and she started to scream?"

"No comment."

"Who else? The freckled Californian. The *Newsweek* photographer. She pursued you in Los Angeles and you didn't pay the slightest attention. But when you saw the pictures she took in El Salvador, you courted her and then she ignored you. . . ."

"No comment."

"And that Australian who made you crazy until you realized she was originally an Englishman who'd undergone a sex change."

"Even less comment, partner. And stop beating up on this poor lovelorn gringo. What's up with Elena?"

"No comment," I answered, because if I was right, he was more right. I was the only asshole who'd married the same woman twice with the same results.

"There aren't any true passions anymore," Greg said. " 'They are impressions of love in my grief / No one called those God, which is insanity / They are more an executioner in his torment.' We're a couple of utilitarians."

"What a joke, we're the ultimate romantics. These days it isn't even fashionable to fall in love. A beer with your *huevos rancheros, compadre?*" I asked.

"Just one, tomorrow's got to be efficient. I'm going to telex the article to *McLean's* and *Newsweek*. Fred said yes on the phone yesterday. He didn't balk at the money. Who should we send it to in Germany?"

"I feel like a daiquiri, not a beer. This Trotsky thing is going to be huge," I told Greg as I flipped the tortillas in the frying pan.

"Remember how to make daiquiris according to Armando?" my partner and chum answered.

F I F T Y - F I V E

THE NEXT TIMES THEY STUMBLED ACROSS ARMANDO

They were in Panama, walking along a commercial avenue trying to buy a mini tape recorder. They wanted an interview with Spadáfora, the vice minister of health, who'd fought with the Sandinistas, but the obstacles kept piling up on both sides. Someone seemed to be playing them like a Ping-Pong ball. Armando suddenly appeared with the contact for the interview in the palm of his hand. Spadáfora died weeks later, decapitated. Theirs was the last public interview with the man.

They were in Lima on an assignment for *Playboy,* an interview with Alan García. The presidential guard put them on a plane en route to Cuzco, where the president would grant them an interview in his free time during a tour. Armando sat in the back of the tiny airplane. They couldn't talk to him, he was absolutely, totally, deeply asleep.

They were in Mexico City, at a reception the Cuban Embassy was giving for Gabriel García Márquez in its Polanco building. Armando stood next to the bartender, showing the ambassador how daiquiris were better if you added the sugar last. Greg caught him unaware and proposed an interview. Armando's answer was a broad smile, revealing his full dental structure, and he disappeared down the hall.

They were in New York, negotiating an agreement with *The Village Voice* to publish a series of articles on the last cowboys, the survivors of Colonel Donovan's OSS after World War II. It was late December. Julio swore he'd seen Armando dressed up as Santa Claus outside the UN. Greg believed him. He'd believe anything about Armando.

They were in Madrid, in the editorial office of *Diario 16,* negotiating the price of several works published in the previous month's edition of *Aguilar.* On the director's desk, Greg found a UPI radiophoto from Manila; it was that famous picture showing the closet full of Imelda Marcos's shoes. Greg studied it carefully and showed it to Julio. "Who is that in the right-hand corner holding a pair of boots?"

F I F T Y - S I X

LEON'S NOVEL

The pressure was mounting, and all the old man cared about was knowing where the stories of Melisa in New York and the dreams of the morphine addict with Russian nightmares came together.

As he petted one of his favorite rabbits, Leon Davidovich Trotsky knew his mystery novel was doomed by something utterly abstract, but also real, like the course of history; like the course of his personal history. Nevertheless, he carefully closed the cage and slipped away to his office. On top of the desk he had a day's worth of correspondence and the damned *Life* article still unedited. On the side were several files with the outlines of the first seven chapters of Stalin's biography. He could count on fifteen minutes before the conversation he'd promised Rosmer on the Polish affair. Hurriedly he opened his notebook and wrote:

24. Without great explanation, Wolf is set free the next morning. He walks from the jail to the *pensión*, washes and keeps the lunch date promised to the reporter from *La Libertad*. The reporter doesn't show.
25. Wolf takes the night train to Barcelona . . .

Trotsky interrupted his writing. Why would Wolf go to Barcelona? To track down the missing girl? To organize the final details of the arms shipment? Who was Wolf? How the hell was he going to connect this story with the suicidal woman? Trotsky glanced up. Rosmer was watching him benevolently. He closed the notebook and put it away.

At daybreak, he rose from his bed and wandered through the halls of the big rambling house in Coyoacán. He returned to his office and got out the notebook. He'd spent six days with the mystery novel in his hands and it seemed to be going nowhere. He could start all over again. This time Wolf would arrive in Shanghai and he'd be Polish instead of North American. It would begin with the character contemplating the sentence: "In the beginning there was action, and words followed as its phonetic shadow."

He had to drop the story. He was in the midst of a war, and in the midst of war, one does not fall in love or set about writing a mystery novel, the old man said to himself, pacing around his desk. The sun was rising. Resolutely he took the notebook and stuffed it in an envelope, on which he wrote: "Manuscript by Leon Wagner. Of no interest." He signed and dated it, shoving it in between a pile of papers, of rejected articles from young colleagues all over the world, torn-up magazines, friends' manuscripts already published. . . .

He swore never to return to the notebook. Trotsky was just such a man; with sudden, abrupt decisions, terrible coldness, indifference, ferocious discipline, he renounced so many things. The notebook remained forever abandoned.

THEY ORDERED TWO DOUBLE HAMBURGERS . . .

. . . with cheese and tomatoes and a couple of extra-large Cokes. With the food on a hideous plastic tray they headed for one of the empty corners of Blimpie's. Through the windows they watched early-rising runners in pastel-colored jogging suits and people with briefcases and *The New York Times* tucked under their arms.

Alex stared at Rolando, lit a cigarette, and, after blowing the smoke up at the high yellow ceiling, he started to burn his left hand, carefully applying the ember to his palm.

"What are you smoking, Mister Smith?" the Mexican drug dealer asked.

"Mapletons, why?"

"It works better with Canadian Gitanes, the tobacco is packed tighter, the ember is more consistent," Rolando said, and, taking out a pack from his jacket pocket, he lit one with a gold lighter, and applied it to the back of his hand.

Alex gave him an affectionate smile. Rolando gave him one back. For a few moments they studied each other unhampered by words. The skinny gringo looked as if he'd been artificially stretched by weights that his mother put on night after night, hanging him by his feet from the railing of his bed; the small Mexican had deep-set eyes shining behind his crooked nose and villainous mustache.

"We're going to understand each other," Alex stated.

For an instant both attacked their hamburgers in silence, not dropping eye contact. A group of break-dancers started their act outside the restaurant. Neither one paid them the slightest attention. Finally Rolando spoke:

"I suspect we will. We'll do good business, boy."

PART III

DEVELOPMENTS

HOUDINI SPEAKS OF THE
HEADLESS WOMAN

It's nothing more than that, simply a woman without a head, wearing a diaphanous tunic and sandals."

"Well then?"

"That's all. A woman with no head haunts me in my dreams."

"And who is this headless woman? Who do you think it could be, Mr. Houdini?"

"My mother, I suppose it's my mother."

"Clearly."

"No, there's nothing clear about it. I wake up startled, I'm obsessed by the image. This is not a normal case. I am not an office man or a firefighter. I live by virtue of my concentration and this profoundly disturbs me while I work."

"You mean to say you not only dream about her, but also daydream of her in your working moments?"

"Very vivid images that strike me suddenly. I'm telling you it's terribly upsetting, especially when you are in chains and inside a tank of water, with an oxygen reserve of some fifteen seconds. I can assure you, very upsetting."

"Has your mother died?"

"A dozen years ago."

"And what do you propose we do with this story? We can try to interpret the dream, search the subconscious for the origins of this obsession; perhaps we can look for a substitute so it no longer makes you anxious. If we arrive at a rational explanation, you can probably liberate yourself from the dream. . . . Is there anything else I should know?" asked Lucius Kellerman, M.D., specialist in psychiatry.

Houdini, né Ehrich Weiss, escape artist and shining champion of rationality and of the science against trickery, author of the most spectacular acts of illusion the world has ever known, stared intensely at the doctor.

"What do you mean?"

"What does the headless woman do? Does she beckon you with her hands? Approach you? Where is the head? Does she have some other distinctive sign that allows you to recognize her as your mother? Where does it all take place? Some special place? Where is your father in the meantime?"

"My father was a rabbi, Dr. Kellerman, he was not fond of walking the streets with headless women."

"The streets?"

"Yes, it all takes place on a street. It is definitely New York City. It has to be two or three years ago, 1922 or twenty-three, because there's a Leger Circus sign posted on the corner, a brand-new sign. I go up to the sign, she appears at my side and takes me by the hand. I discover it is my mother because of the old sandals I gave her; I look: she has no head. Lately, I don't even look up, I already know she doesn't have a head. Frankly, it's annoying. Have you ever seen your mother without a head, Doctor?"

"No, not lately. Cigarette?"

"No thank you. But you can smoke. It doesn't bother me."

Kellerman lit a very aromatic Virginia short cigar, and blew the smoke toward the ceiling with true pleasure. He debated two contradictory impulses. Treating such a case would allow him to climb the ranks to glory, publications in scientific journals, invitations to university conferences. On the other hand, he truly adored this small great character who sat before him. Were he not a psychiatrist, he'd have liked to be Houdini's disciple, not just because among the most impressive live acts he'd seen in his life was the "Escape from the Chinese Torture Chamber," but also because he admired the campaign Houdini had launched against the false prophets, the occultists, metaphysical magicians, the charlatans of crystal balls and Ouija boards. It was, like the great war of modern psychiatry, a war for science.

"Are you familiar with hypnotism, Houdini? May I call you that?"

"Of course, Kellerman. And yes, I am quite familiar with it."

"Do you have any particular resistance to it?"

"No, on the contrary, according to what I was able to find out when I was on a tour a few years ago. But I have to be careful about that type of experience for very obvious reasons. A posthypnotic suggestion could wind up killing me."

"Good, I propose a deal. I hypnotize you and substitute your headless mother with your headless father. Would this upset you to the same extent? I'll also try to soften the image."

"No, I don't suppose that would trouble me as much. My father didn't have too much of a head, as far as I can recall."

"Good, if it works, you have to promise to tell me the details of the escape from 'The Cylindrical Cross.' "

"It's a deal, Doctor."

"I feel supremely proud. You can have a seat in this chair, your back toward the window, and concentrate closely on this manometer. Watch the movement, follow it with your eyes."

"I feel profoundly pleased that you feel proud, Doctor. . . ."

FIFTY-NINE

LONGORIA'S WALKS

Longoria walked along calmly through the interior gardens toward the gerontology pavilion, vulgarly known as the deboning home, the elephant cemetery or Ali Baba's cave. It was cold. Mateo was awake, in the wheelchair, sitting in the interior patio, with his gaze lost on a bindweed hedge.

"Son of a great Stalinist bitch. Have you remembered anything else yet? You know what I told you. You'll go straight to hell and Andrés Nin and Machkno will be waiting for you at the gate."

"Don't fuck with me, Longoria. Leave me alone. Let me think in peace."

"I'll be back in half an hour, you swine, and no nun is going to protect you from me," Longoria said, shaking his fist at Mateo.

"You're taking advantage of the fact that you're three years younger than I am, faggot."

Longoria gave him the finger and turned his back on the other old man. It was a lie; Saturnino was the same eighty-two years old as Mateo, even though one of the times he falsified his papers he'd accidentally changed his age.

He directed his steps to the hospital's exterior gardens. Familiar territory. The gardeners began their day at that hour outside the pavilion of infectious diseases. They were sure to give him half a dozen cut roses from the hedge. Longoria wasn't the secretary and sole member of the Patients' Committee for Solidarity with the Union for nothing, and these were very bleak times for the hospital's manual laborers.

Fifteen minutes later, with two dozen red tulips (the situation didn't allow for more), Longoria headed for the maternity pavilion. He stopped several times on the way through the labyrinthine hospital. Once to sit in for an ancient peasant from Veracruz for a couple of quite animated rounds of dominoes in the cancer pavilion while the title holder went out for a short time to have blood taken for analysis. The session took a little over half an hour and Longoria seized the opportunity to take 3,500 pesos from the players, playing at a hundred pesos per point. The second stop came about when two office workers called him to the basement of the old building, asking him to forge the administrative director's signature, an utterly simple task. Saturnino did not confine himself to the signature, but pulled from his black corduroy jacket the administration seal, a date stamp, and a black inkpad, and gave final form to the document, which marked as paid two oxygen tanks for an indigent comrade. He wondered whether the "indigent comrade" would receive the two tanks or just one, with the other circulating through the wide-open spaces of the black market that Mexico City's Sanatorio Español's enormous administration had created.

It's better than nothing, he told himself, determined to review for himself those obscure entries in the accounting books, taking advantage of his magnificent relationships with the watchmen for whom he had forged copies of the keys to the director of funds' office.

The third holdup was in the asylum, where he reached an agreement with the head chef of the kitchen to load an old Francoist diabetic's menu with sugar. Later, the minor errands of the morning completed, he took the flowers to the maternity ward and very ceremoniously gave them to little Marina's mother, who was decorously feeding her little blond dwarf.

"In the name of the gerontology patients, Señora," he said very properly, making the floral offering.

"Don't be a dick, Longoria, I'm sure you stole them," said the baby's mom, who was married to the consultant of the crumbling union. "Let's see when you can get out of this place and come over to the house for dinner."

"One of these days, my foul-mouthed youngster."

"I get out on Friday and Paco would love to see you. I'll make garlic bass and croquettes to start."

Longoria gave the mother and child a wide smile and disappeared through the interior halls, fearlessly passing through all the doors that read "Do Not Enter, Authorized Personnel Only."

Mateo was waiting for him, though he pretended to gaze off at the polluted horizon, confined by the hospital's protective brick wall, behind which was one of the biggest beer refineries in Latin America.

"Your memory come back?"

"Come on, Saturnino, sit and keep me company. You tell me about the Battle of Guadalajara, and I'll tell you about Kuprin and his friends."

At the end of the morning, Longoria finished writing his report with the details that Mateo had given him. He decided he didn't need to code it or send it indirectly, it was just a series of historical dates in chronological order. He put the material in an envelope, addressed the label to Stoyan Vasilev at the Fire Department of Sofia, People's Republic of Bulgaria, and he fled the hospital to the Polanco province post office. "The Tank" would be most pleased. Especially since he thought Longoria had been dead for twenty-five years. This would be like that "return of the mummy" movie. Suddenly a cloud of worry crossed his face on which not one more wrinkle would fit. Shit, what if Stoyan was the one who died?

NEW YORK

Benigno had to bare his teeth to the doorman to get past him. With his limp, the guy hadn't been able to match the dwarf's speed in fleeing the hotel. After Marcelino had grabbed the blond cigarette lady's behind, he had no choice but to resort to his fierce expression to escape the disturbance the dwarf had created. Now he searched out the pygmy among the hundreds of people swarming around him.

"Down here, asshole," Marcelino said.

"You're a son of a bitch. Why'd you have to grab the señorita's ass?"

"I waited ten minutes in the lobby for you and you didn't show, my black man, and that old girl was wearing a skirt this short, and the kind of fishnet stockings that drive me crazy. And from down here, as you can imagine, you see everything better. We're all human! Dwarf, human being, and my dick was as stiff as the Zocalo's flagpole."

"Now what do we do?" Benigno said. The sea of people heading the opposite way on Fifth Avenue made him desolate. Flustered by those millions of faces, all strangers: noisy Hispanics, photo-snapping Japanese, circumspect rabbis, giant and threatening blacks, Hindu youths with faces that looked as lost as he was, Texas simpletons, fast Chicanos on skates, Frenchified New York women carrying baguettes, with endlessly long legs that defied the air; New York-ified French women with their index fingers on the tops of their noses, thinking. It was too much to see all at once.

"Let's buy shoes. What did Rolando say? That we look like bigger assholes than we are. You just act natural, light of my life. Our boss, patron and God are at work. I think I know, too, who they put on our tail."

Benigno showed his teeth again. He didn't like New York, he didn't like the situation, he didn't like the pain in his leg, and what he liked least, least of all this motherfucking crap, was the partner he'd been assigned: he did not like the dwarf.

"What size do you wear, my king? I bet one foot's bigger than the other," Marcelino said, dancing about. He loved New York. The miraculous skyscrapers that left no shadows, before which everyone was a diminutive passerby. Here, he felt sure he wouldn't have to outfit himself in the kids' department of Macy's; they were sure to have specialized luxury stores for dwarfs. Out of the corner of his eye, he located the punk in a leather jacket who was following them and threw himself into the middle of the crowd's traffic, elbowing a few knees that got in his way. Benigno tried not to let the dwarf escape him in such a huge damned crowd.

S I X T Y - O N E

JOURNALISTS' STORIES

(G R E G   S P E A K S)

Fats had said to me, "You write it, that way it will have that shocked gringo touch, the anguish of the first world. I would make it sound like a Mexican who couldn't give a shit." His logic was absolutely sound. I could insert the necessary quotas of cynicism, but I could also bring to it the vision of a Midwest farmer surprised by an alien story he'd never heard before, and combine it with a little of the sophistication of a Lincoln Center regular. It's that extremely sound combination that produced the "new journalism," Campbell's soup and the demonstrations against the Vietnam War, the cult of the individual's rights and the return to craftsmanlike automobile production.

I tried to put on my best "intelligent-but-hopeless gringo" face to captivate the man running the press conference, to see whether later I could get some facts about who controlled the money. I was one of three North Americans in the room, among many Mexican journalists and various office personnel someone had brought to take care of the details. One of the other two was a CBS reporter without his cameras (the poor guy seemed naked), the other was the *Newsweek* photographer whom I wanted when she didn't want me and vice versa. I don't recall which phase our relationship was in at the time. She smiled first, but I invited her to dinner before she reminded me I owed her one.

Did the UNESCO-Mexican project to restore the colonial city of Zacatecas genuinely interest me? Six pages of notes and a dozen color photos for Pan Am's in-flight magazine in exchange for an advance of $800 was a good deal. If only to escape Fats's novelistic temptations. That's how he saw it, and he had opted out of the expedition, arguing that he had an interview with Cuauhtemoc Cárdenas, the president the Mexicans had chosen in the last elections, who had been robbed of the triumph with the PRI's monumental electoral fraud. Work. Every once in a while we took a break from each other; I suppose this would be one of those many times, and it seemed as if it would be prolonged, because we hadn't set a date, just the usual promises to call if something worth attacking with four hands came up. I thought I'd slip away from Zacatecas up north and write a few tourist articles to see whether we could place them in some travel magazines. Maybe try to do something on border smuggling, viewing it from both angles. Before I left, Fats had promised me two days of exploring in Rosarito and a monumental drinking binge in San Diego with a paralytic colleague from the *Rolling Stone* era, who'd retired when a mine in Guatemala blew his left leg skyward. I could also buy a few pieces of Seri crafts and take them to Los Angeles to resell them to Anne Watson, who had a store on Hollywood Boulevard and whom I owed the favor. I'd make $300 on the operation in addition to sitting and staring at the Sea of Cortés with my Seri friends, telling myself that the twentieth century sucked, just like the nineteenth, the eighteenth and the seventeenth, and that everything was better in the sixteenth.

Courteous applause brought the press conference to an end. I edited my two pages of notes. I didn't need more. Now I had to walk the city thinking through each picture as if I were Robert Capa. Katherine came over.

"Shall we take photos together?"

"No. I'd have to be insane to shoot pictures with you. We'd always have the same angles and yours would always be better. I'd spend our dinner drinking tequila just to cure my inferiority complex."

"If I take your photos, will you write my article?"

"That sounds better already. I propose something else. I take your photos and you write both our reports."

"That sounds like shit."

"Okay, I choose the angles and you shoot."

"Done. I dictate the article and you write it."

"In your style?"

"In *Newsweek*'s."

"Good, that's easier."

We sealed the agreement with a firm handshake.

The sun shone straight down over the ravine on which the city of Zacatecas was set. We strolled through the streets, verifying where the best examples of colonial uproar were and looking for a paved road that slanted enough for us to see the bottom of the hills.

"They told me a story you might like."

"Who?"

"A friend of a friend," Katherine said, making a face. "May I take that photo?"

A woman carrying recently washed clothes on her head. I didn't see the shot. Katherine no doubt already saw it in print.

"Fine, but that one's yours. I don't see it."

Katherine crouched down. The neckline of her thin blouse revealed the tops of her freckled breasts. Instead of falling to the ground drooling with lust, I was shaken by a tremendous attack of tenderness. I lifted my hand to her hair and caressed it.

"Don't bump me, you'll ruin the photo."

"What did the friend of a friend tell you?"

"That the CIA has a way of getting its hands on a big mole higher up in the Sandinista elite."

"Who?"

"Uhm. That's it."

"How?"

"Blackmail."

"How?"

"Drugs."

"Who's on drugs? The Sandinistas? *Flor de caña* rum and

aspirin, I don't think they go beyond that. *Flor de caña* they've got in abundance, I don't think the aspirin would be a problem in spite of the blockade. It's shit, Kath."

"Yeah, right?" the woman said, standing up and shaking the loose dirt off her pants. I focused on her and when she smiled, I snapped. That wasn't part of the agreement.

S I X T Y - T W O

ONE MORE OF ELENA JORDAN'S REJECTED THESIS PROPOSALS

Thirty-seven miles from Tepic, Nayarit, by highway, and opening in the foothills of the Western Sierra Madre, there is a tribe of Cora, consisting of 320 families, whose economic structure is based on subsistence farming, mostly of corn, the production of charcoal and the crafting of dolls sold through a cooperative run by a group of Jesuits in Mexico City. The sexual habits of this community have been studied in depth by a group of anthropologists from the University of Guadalajara. In the material that can be deduced from these field studies, buried in a huge accumulation of information (Field Work Report, Sexuality, Community #322, mimeographed, Department of Anthropology, University of Guadalajara), one finds the following data: Surveyed men responded in the following percentages to the question: "Are the women from the neighboring community more proficient in their sexual practices than our women?" Yes: 89%; No: 7%; Don't know/not relevant: 4%. Surveyed women respond to the question: "Are the men from the neighboring community more proficient in their sexual practices than our men?" Yes: 96%. No: 0%; Don't know/not relevant: 4%.

The purpose of this thesis proposal is to develop an inquiry into the concept: "Members of the tribe next door fuck better than members of our own," understanding the word tribe to mean a community defined geographically, politically, culturally, racially or socially. To establish, therefore, the origin of this widespread thought, its rational validity, its origin.

I hereby renounce any and all scientific foundation to the proposal, limiting myself to pointing out that if anthropology has not applied itself to addressing this type of problem, it is because anthropologists are a bunch of wimps, and understanding that whatever foundation, no matter how many references to Lévi-Strauss, Frazer and the Marquis de Sade, is doomed in advance by the narrow-mindedness of this thesis seminar in which I find myself enrolled.

I point out only that among the communities I propose to interview in order to discover the traces of this tribal thought ("No doubt any son of my neighbor fucks better than my husband,") you will find the superior authorities of the National School of Anthropology and History, the civil servants of the Department of Programming and the Budget, and similar tribal sectors of the national arena, and among the key questions I hope to ask the surveyed men and women, you will find all those relating to frequency of orgasm, their sexual practices, the greater sexual acrobatic skills of those in the neighboring office, the presence of chronic impotence in regular couples, the use of electronic gadgets, etc. . . .

Attentively,
Elena Jordan,
Cuicuilco,
November '88

SIXTY-THREE

ALEX DID NOT
HAVE A HOUSE,
BUT BENJAMIN . . .

. . . lived in a genuine artist's studio in the center of SoHo, in southern Manhattan, that had to cost him a small fortune. To his friends and cotenants, he appeared to be an expert in economic transactions with exotic countries, on the payroll of multinationals who retained him as a part-time consultant. He knew the daily exchange rate of the dirham in London and what Standard Oil shares were selling for on Wall Street; he knew how trustworthy the great Chinese traders were as intermediaries in Thailand, which was the best hotel in Manila and how to manage a business agreement in Buenos Aires involving the old landowners' money. He knew hair-raising stories of the Mexican petroleum syndicate and could recite by heart the Polish customs laws. All this may have sufficed to explain to his girlfriends and neighbors why he had that apartment and why he alternated his meals between the Four Seasons and The Palm, but didn't explain to Alex, no matter how much he twisted the story upside down, where he got the money.

The unofficial version is that he had worked outside the agency in the mid-seventies in a series of not very orthodox operations with Bolivian drug militants. A strange era, because even outside the agency, Benjamin served as their informer, and passed as an informer for the DEA, as a personal informer for the North American ambassador in La Paz, and eventually as a military intelligence informer in Fort Gullick, many of whose students would go on to hold high posts in the Bolivian military and would offer Benjamin more assignments.

Alex could add, though, and the sum of his addition gave only a possible explanation and not the total number of bank accounts Benjamin managed, now that he was active again in the agency as an SD operative. He knew that the slender black man with the jagged little mustache and Lenox suits responded well to the double combination: monthly salary and weekly terror; so he apportioned them to the extent he could, trying at the same time not to make Benjamin excessively nervous because that could lower his usual rate of efficiency.

Alex thought he remembered a story that portrayed Benjamin as a skilled survivor of a Chicago development where when it was cold they threw the youngest brother in the stove to improve the heating, and that's how he was living with his family when the Agency, instead of letting the military send him to eat mud somewhere between Saigon and Hanoi, offered him a position on the Phoenix Project.

In April of 1967, Benjamin disembarked an Air America plane in Da Nang and started to work for the project. His work consisted of creating interrogation centers throughout villages, districts and regions to locate Vietcong activists and execute them. The project demanded he keep a victim count to justify the tremendous investment they'd made in the infrastructure and organization. When the project was suspended, the figures of South Vietnamese deaths reached about 21,000. They weren't talking about casualties in combat but alleged assassinations of Vietcong militants. Benjamin, who worked gathering information and coordinating the relationships between the military and the South Vietnam police, had doubted since then how many of the 21,000 men and women who died had really been communists. Judging from his personal experience, probably less than ten percent. After all this, and not letting the blood of the dead weigh upon his soul (at this point, Benjamin had decided he had no soul, but only the sensibility to listen to a few rock songs), Ben decided not to moralize the affair, to forget the few faces he'd seen, to let others become part of the statistics and never again set foot in East Asia, or even in the Chinatowns of North America's West Coast.

Almost twenty years later, he looked at Alex with the same inscrutable expression with which he'd confronted his prisoners. A face that seemed on the verge of either going into a nervous facial contraction or unfolding into a charming smile, and remained just like that, "on the verge," for what seemed like eternity. Alex gave him a fraternal look, which he hoped would confuse him, and began to bark orders as if Operation Snow White were a book already written and Alex had only to turn the pages.

"I need a man, who is not currently there, to kill another man in a hotel in Mexico City. I need a third man to see all or part of the murder, who fully or partially recognizes the guy, who can directly or indirectly confirm it. I need the man who is currently not there but is alleged to have killed the dead man to incriminate himself with some piece of evidence; I need that piece of evidence not to be overly obvious and not to be available to everyone, but to reach the hands and vision of the witness who discovers it. I need a believable legend about the criminal that is made public but that is easily destroyed by evidence that will be revealed subsequently. I need us, or people that can be politically associated with us, to be culpable, and I also need it to filter out that we don't care if we're blamed; but all this has to be very subtle, because the formal people, the Embassy, the State Department, guys like that will simultaneously issue an adamant denial with absolute vehemence. I need an identical second operation for a second witness in case the first one fails for some reason, and just keep this second operation frozen. What's worse for you, I need every part of this operation to come off, because it's the link in a long chain, and if the chain breaks at this link, the mildest thing that can happen to you is that I hand you over to Colonel Valdivia on his doorstep, wrapped in gauze like a mummy. And you know me well enough to know that if it's the last thing I do on earth, I will do it."

Benjamin laughed openly, then lit a menthol cigarette with a gold Dunhill lighter and said:

"Now, bit by bit, Alex. Tell me your movie bit by bit. And most of all, don't be afraid you'll scare me, and tell me who's going to die. You know I like things to be difficult. Come on, tell me, Alex, who's going to die?"

"A Sandinista commander."

"One of the nine?"

"No, a guerrilla commander."

"Does it have to be in Mexico? I'd rather work in Peru or Venezuela."

"I prefer Mexico. My other dwarfs have been working on this and they've set a good stage here."

"The murder of a Sandinista, not public, a witness who believes the murderer is someone else, or better, suspects it, to whom we will then give evidence to confirm it, a public version, a denial, a leak that we don't care if they say or think we did it. . . ."

"And a few lesser matters. You have to plant a certain document on the dead man, or make it seem like he sent the document just before he was killed so that it reaches the witness just after the crime. And it's extremely important that this run smoothly. I don't want the Mexicans or the Sandinistas to see what we're cooking behind their backs, not even what the witness knows; in other words, we also have to protect him from them."

"And what are you going to do with the murderer who didn't murder anyone, but who the witness has to think was him?"

"That's not a matter for your people, I'm working on that on the side."

"Fine, then step by step. What's the scene?"

"A Mexico City hotel. I don't know yet where the participants of the seminar on cultural and political issues will eat and sleep."

"A lot of security?"

"I'm afraid so, not just the Sandinistas and Mexicans but because of the issues and the guests, very probably Cuban, I suppose there will even be Argentines, slashers from the DINA and some of our idiots, from the traditional sector, ballerinas of analysis. . . . A seminar on 'Literature and Guerrilla Warfare.' "

"There's literature on that too?"

"You've been reading *The Wall Street Journal* too long, Benjamin," Alex said.

SIXTY-FOUR

HOW ABOUT A
BULGARIAN LIKE THIS?
(IV)

Stoyan remembered two things from the defense of Madrid, in November 1936: the shadows of the Moroccan soldiers from the regular division among the trees as they tried to cross the Manzanares river, and the telegraphic and concise notes General Emilio Kléber sent him on the night of November 9th: "Bear right. K.," "Hold up, there's nowhere to go. K.," "Press, I need to see if they fall back. K." Many years later he dreamed about the notes and remembered the dread he felt unfolding the little paper that held the order he would then carry out to the letter.

He had a nebulous idea about the rest of it, false memories that he'd recovered in subsequent years taken from the books he'd read. At times he wanted to separate what he'd lived from what he'd heard, the real from the falsely remembered things that had managed to lodge in his head from a lecture or a conversation. But now, fifty years after combat, it was impossible. He wasn't even sure whether in those days he used a black leather jerkin with crossed cartridge belts and a peaked cap stolen from a cadaver of a Spanish compatriot, or whether that getup was the one planted in his memory by a photograph taken days before in Albacete or twenty-five days after. He could have sworn he'd seen himself next to a machine gun, opening a can of sardines and eating them one by one skewered on his bayonet, the grease trickling down his beard. He was almost certain he could reconstruct a dialogue with

Longoria, the taciturn character who'd maintained the front with a group of soldiers from the anarchic syndicate CNT until the internationals arrived:

"What I want is the Foreign Legion's seal. I'm going to go through every corpse until I find one. I need an official in charge of legion deaths or something like that. Then I'm going to start counterfeiting medals until they go insane. Can you imagine? Little Falangists and daddy's boys and young military dandies killing themselves because they're all lieutenants," Longoria had said.

"With their carelessness, we're going to leave them with no officials and you won't get the chance at your counterfeiting job," Vasilev had answered.

"And they told me Bulgarians didn't believe in God."

"I believe in Chopin."

"That asshole was Polish, you can't fool me."

But the conversation might have developed months later, on the road to Guadalajara. What he knew for certain was that back then he was teaching the Spanish anarchist to whistle the polonaises. That's what they were doing when the armored tanks arrived.

In theory, he shouldn't have forgotten the procession from the Atocha train station that introduced the Eleventh Brigade in Madrid. They marched down Gran Vía in the afternoon at sunset on the eighth. But he was sure that the images that came to his mind were from a movie he'd seen many years later; and what was worse, in the film, the boys marching were from the Twelfth Brigade, not his. How could he have forgotten that? It was the symbolic moment, the summary of four months' work in Bulgaria, in Paris, in the base at Albacete, in the concentration camp in Tarazona, of the last days in Madrid's outskirts, in Vallecas; bitten by anguish upon the news of the crumbling of the front and therefore of the defeat of the Republic at the hands of the Fascists' forces and the militia of Franco and Queip de Llano. Terrifying days waiting for the call to the first line of fire. Never before, never again, was he in such a hurry for a war to begin. Later he would have to impose his will, the consciousness of the necessity of fear. How had he managed to hide in his memory that march of the three battalions of the Eleventh International through the streets of Madrid? The first internationals who would engage in combat, the Germans of the Edgar André Battalion, the Dombrowsky, where among the Polish majority and the two most important minorities of Czechs and Yugoslavs, a handful of Bulgarians marched out.

The chronicles told how the people of Madrid, desperate and on the verge of insanity due to the bombings, hunger and fear that the front would collapse and the nationals would enter, greeted them, mistaking them for Russians. "Here come the Russians," they yelled from their windows. The chronicles told how the troops responded in ten languages and proudly showed their different guns, Mexican, Polish, Belgian and occasionally a magnificent Russian Spitalny machine gun. In unmatching uniforms, with those mortal rusty French helmets that had lost their rubber interior protection, or the berets of the Belgians from the Commune, or the baggy trousers of Edgar André's Germans.

Stoyan thought he remembered that if there was more than enough of something in that march through the city illuminated by the Heinkel bombs, it was not emotion and if there was not enough of something it was a military air, precision of movement from the squads who couldn't keep time. He remembered one time when an Italian member of the Brigades likened that march through Madrid to a trip through "the center of the world," an encounter with the heart of life, a sudden hit in the temple that lodged the final idea of the sense of existence in your head. We'd been born, we'd battled on four continents and in sixty-one countries for years, just to come to the march through the streets of Madrid that afternoon that revived hope. Three hours later the Brigadiers were under fire from the columns of Moroccan GIs from Varela.

Stoyan had fallen in love with Madrid that night, though he wouldn't realize it until twelve days later, when the rest of the Dombrowsky Battalion were pulled from the front line to rebuild their troops. He'd fallen in love with a city in darkness, where one frequently heard the rhythmic *"No pasaran."* "They-shall-not-pass, they-shall-not-pass." It emanated from objects, the moving loudspeakers propped on ramshackle cars, the radio stations, the groups of volunteers advancing toward the combat zone to the east of the city. He'd fallen in love with a city that had rubble strewn across the streets, posters on every wall (paradoxical Cenetista posters warning of the danger of being with prostitutes, nonexistent prostitutes), sandbags at the door of a pharmacy, children who saluted with their fists held high.

Twelve days later, he could see Madrid under the sun, he had coffee at an outdoor café in Cuatro Caminos, he bought a play by the then missing García Lorca to improve his rudimentary Spanish. He was surviving.

But Stoyan Vasilev had reached the deployment zone of the Dombrowsky Battalion that night of November 8th thinking about inevitable death, destiny. Believing that if one considered himself dead, the worst was already over. While the companies dispersed in the zone near the Parque del Oeste of the University District, some of whose buildings were in the hands of the fascists and which Edgar André's Germans would defend meter by meter, the twenty-eight-year-old Bulgarian found himself surrounded by a group of young Poles, Bulgarians and Yugoslavs depending on their timid Spanish to locate the line of fire. That's when Saturnino Longoria appeared, a Greek character though less metaphysical, lean, with wire-framed glasses that made him look like an unemployed librarian, with nothing covering his head and three rifles over his shoulder. At his side was a tall, blond North American loaded with cameras and armed with a huge Colt .45.

"Internationals?"

"Here," answered Stoyan.

"I am Longoria, the liaison, my sons, and I implore you not to forget it, and if anybody shoots at me, you'll wind up on the front lines. Follow me, boys. Don't be in a hurry to die, death is not worth a dime here."

Creeping through the trees, searching for the river as a point of reference, Vasilev's company found the forces who had maintained the front until then, a couple dozen UGT soldiers, already out of ammunition, but with the bayonets and rifles conquered a few months before in the La Montana quarters.

There wasn't time to ask what was ahead. The cries of the legionnaires upon firing, *"Arriba España,"* signaled the end of the dream of political fraternity, of human solidarity, of the glory and love between the internationals and the city for which they could die. The face of war revealed itself. The next day, Madrid's press would dedicate a few lines to that initial shock, "Pozuelo's counterattack," in which Madrid's defenders did not confine themselves solely to heroic resistance, but rather after the battle and after having stopped the enemy, sprang from the trenches in a confusion of cries in ten languages, organizing the first bayonet charge of Babel.

For twelve days the Internationals fought at the side of the Spanish soldiers in a zone just a few square miles wide, with the university district at the center, the Manzanares River, the big, wooded park of the Casa de Campo and the Parque del Oeste as the scenes of combat.

The memory became somewhat nebulous, filled with remote dreamlike sensations, continuous fears, moments of insanity in which a man came from behind a tree and summoned them all to walk between the bullets that couldn't touch him, immortal, husky archangel, who didn't notice that he shouted in Polish to a group of Bulgarians who understood the message of death nonetheless and jumped from behind cement bags to confront the armed tanks with nothing but grenades.

Forests of mist, bayonet charges among the trees searching for a nonexistent enemy, with whom, suddenly conjured up by the witches of fascism, they found themselves face to face.

The breakthrough of the front on the Manzanares on the fifteenth, before the push from the Moors, Kléber's scolding ("We didn't come here to retreat, we came to die, with the great opportunity to answer every strike we've suffered in the last years from fascism, with the opportunity to confront those who have imprisoned us, those who have murdered with impunity, those who have tortured us in prison basements; here, grab your arms. Whoever loses his gun will have to tread into enemy lines, disarmed, to recover it"), the furious battles in front of Velázquez's house, where the painter, in an act of astonishing foresight, had painted the landscapes of the Madrid where we would die; he painted Madrid for every soldier of the third company of the Dombrowsky Battalion, which was decimated there. The landscapes that later you would see in the Museo del Prado and weep.

Battles in dilapidated university buildings in which not a pane of glass remained intact. A short time later, Stanislav Tomaszewicz was reflecting very seriously on his shame at having barricaded himself behind a pile of books on nineteenth-century German logic when three legionnaires tried to kill him in the School of Philosophy. Hegel sheltering us from the bullets. Bound German philosophy; yes, bound, like the distance between life and death. Kléber's pamphlets. The phantasmal visits of Commissar Matuczacz, who would only offer himself as an example, because there were no more words to elicit from those men, no more energy, no greater strength, no greater capacity for combat.

If he concentrated, he could remember Longoria dozing as an armed force advanced across the Segovia bridge toward their trench, and his own inability along with Max's, the North American, who had exchanged his cameras for a dead man's gun, to wake him up. The anguish not from the deadly machine coming toward them, but from not being able to shake the Spaniard, who'd gone four days with no sleep, from his dreams.

If he concentrated, he could remember the disappointment upon seeing Miaja and Rojo, the superior officers of Madrid's defense, who looked like a couple of routine civil servants, honest shopkeepers of a provisions store, accidentally uniformed and placed at the head of an insane assignment. But no, the thought was not his, it was Max's, the North American's, who was extremely gifted at finding the precise presence of the ridiculous in any attempt to turn routine death into a sublime opera.

On the twentieth, the Twelfth International Brigade relieved them. The rest of the Dombrowsky Battalion retreated to a second echelon of Madrid's defense. The fascists had been stopped. Stoyan celebrated publicly in a Spanish Communist Party meeting in the Monumental Cinema and personally in a drinking binge with his two new friends. With the Valdepeñas wine coursing through his bloodstream, there was less guilt in being alive, it seemed less absurd to be celebrating the simple miracle of survival.

And what's more, the fascists had not passed.

S I X T Y - F I V E

ROLANDO HAD A GOOD
MEMORY AND . . .

. . .told incredible stories, filling them with small anecdotes and minor details that made them real; the Japanese watch of the dead man whose mail he had taken; the three flies flying over the table in the Guadalajara taco shop when Medardo asked him to recommend the best florist in the city; the way the German withdrew wads of money from his pockets, as if there were no end to them; the stupefied expression of a boy watching his father bleed to death, the virtues of Mexican barbed wire over North American to tie someone's hands, the necessary investment of an average organization in the purchase of sausages and chorizos to drive the drug-sniffing airport dogs crazy.

And he acted, interpreted, seduced his listeners; he tickled their balls, danced, took out a knife and sharpened it on his skin, drank glass after glass of cured tequila bought expressly for him, charged to the SD, in a Sixth Avenue deli near Central Park, without seeming to diminish a single neuron of his capacity to show the asshole gringos who were his audience what the real world was like.

He was enjoying it.

Eloise worked on the holes, Aram on the official biography, dating and situating every fragment of the story. Eve looked for contradictions. All this, operating on the character who repeated one story six different ways in a single session, changed the names, places, drinks, times, atrocities, each time to fabricate different, more attractive ones. Aram tried to place dates, comparing Rolando's versions with police reports, newspaper articles, witness testimonies, DEA references. Eloise found the hole and stopped the conversation, trying to force Rolando to fill it, waiting for Aram's confirmation, and then flagged or discarded it. Eve interrupted only every once in a while.

"Are you sure, Señor Limas?"

"Well, who knows, maybe so, maybe not, but the surest bet is who knows. The truth is I don't know if I'm sure or not. Because when one stabs some jerk to death, one continues killing him for some time. Many, many years later, one still sees where one placed the knife, how one sought the rib not to obstruct the path to the heart, how the blood spurted out, the face the asshole made; and from there one adorns it, inserting things after the fact that were not there, you know."

"But a while ago you said that you had not killed that judicial cop in Tijuana, that you'd seen them kill him and you'd paid the killer ten thousand pesos."

Rolando withdrew a knife with which he frequently cleaned his nails to the horror of the three analysts, and the blade glimmered in the twinkling lights of the SD's conference room.

"Look," said Rolando, resting the knife on Eve's overflowing breasts. From the first session, Eve had captivated the certified public accountant who dabbled in drug trafficking. "The knife business is bullshit, I already explained it."

"Please put that away. We cannot work like this," Eve said, pointing to the knife; flustered but attempting a smile that looked more like the expression produced by a violent toothache. Rolando returned the smile and used the point of the knife to rip a piece of the blouse.

"Alex, come here," Aram called softly. "Your friend is trying to give Eve a mastectomy."

"None of that, such a flat chest warrants a retelling of my story. The guy arrived, right? A mariachi band was singing '*El Perro Negro,*' the guy from the time he started, saw me drooping . . ."

Alex appeared on the scene, entering the room from his office with a cocked .45 Magnum in his left hand.

"Rolando, if you spoil one of my assistants, I'm going to send the toes on your right foot flying, then I'll put you in a hospital to treat it, and we'll start again," he said in Spanish.

Rolando studied him out of the corner of his eye.

"Alex, if you shoot me, the job is fucked, old guy. I still don't know exactly how it's going to turn out, but at the last minute when everything seems ready and gift-wrapped like a present, I'll fly about and break wind, cowboy, and I'll say, 'All this feeding time is the work of one Alex.' And no, no I won't because, believe me, you're not going to fuck with me from then on, maybe you will, maybe you won't, but nobody, you hear me, asshole? Nobody, nobody ever held a pistol to me to tell me about fucking life."

Rolando spit at the leg of his chair where he sat reclined; he turned around and kept playing with the point of the knife on Eve's blouse, tearing the material without touching her skin, casually scraping and tugging at a button.

Alex advanced with pistol in hand, foaming at the mouth. Pressing the barrel of the gun against Rolando's forehead, Alex grabbed the knife and placed it on paralyzed Eve's chest again. Aram had recoiled, taking cover behind his computer, and Eloise held a useless thick glass ashtray in her hands.

"Look, Rolando Limas, look!" Alex said, and with two cuts finished ripping Eve's blouse and cut the elastic on her bra between the two cups. The analyst's breasts danced, almost completely uncovered. Rolando looked at them with fascination; they were bigger than he had imagined. Aram peered from behind his computer to contemplate Eve's huge rosy breasts, which seconds after Alex's cut still bobbed in motion, perhaps due to the analyst's agitated breathing.

"Señorita, I don't know how you work with this dirtball savage, allow me to lend you my jacket," Rolando said jovially, taking off his black leather coat and covering Eve with it.

HOUDINI TALKS ABOUT
THE FEAR OF INSANITY

The Hippodrome act was excellent, Houdini."

"Thanks, Kellerman, I'm delighted you enjoyed it."

"Enjoyed? Much more than that, it is one of the best vaudeville acts I've seen in my life. Without doubt the best I can remember. The combination is marvelous, escape acts and public exposure of the tricks of the fakes. The way you unmasked the alleged mediums in New York was excellent, ex-cel-lent. How much does an occultist capable of performing a 'supernatural' act that you can't re-create by material means make these days?"

"I offer ten thousand dollars, but the figure increases with money from other scientific institutions."

"There's a certain tension in the whole spectacle. Not because the audience distrusts you or sides with those charlatans—you heard the whistles clearly when they insulted you—but because they're afraid you might not have the material resources to duplicate the tricks with which those quacks 'call the spirits' and fraudulently play with the 'great beyond.' "

"Doctor, I discovered a long time ago that risk is a necessary ingredient of a spectacle. The escape acts I perform are much more impassioned when I run them against time and danger."

Kellerman sighed deeply.

"You are right. I remember when you locked and chained yourself inside a trunk hurled into the Boston Bay. I was there with some colleagues and we enjoyed and suffered every instant of the wait, until you appeared, swimming. . . . Cognac?"

"No thanks, Kellerman. May I lie down?"

"Only if you think you can talk better staring at the ceiling. That's the reason for the couch, my dear friend."

Kellerman poured himself a double and contemplated his patient. Houdini was fifty years old, about to turn fifty-one; he was starting to lose his hair, though he preserved a face that radiated an enormous energy by virtue of his strong, straight nose and the intense, brilliant shine in his eyes.

"It worked in part, Kellerman. . . . I didn't have nightmares for several nights but yesterday she appeared again with my father. He did not have a severed head and he was reproaching her for something. Seeing them both together might be worse."

"I wanted to avoid a traditional job with you, Houdini my friend, but it looks as though we'll have to start from the beginning. . . . Have you had this kind of dream at any other time in your life? Similar sensations, anxiety?"

Houdini half closed his eyes, reclined and began to narrate as though Kellerman were his future biographer:

"The first time I remember anything similar was during a tour through Germany at the end of the first year of the century. Do you want me to tell it in detail?" He did not open his eyes to observe the doctor's vigorous affirmation and went on. "It had been two and a half exhausting months, never before had I been subjected to greater tension. Germany, Kellerman, is an old country that knows much about locks, chains, padlocks, torture chambers, bolts, handcuffs and handlebars. The tour began in Dresden in September, and for the publicity, I visited the central police station and laughed awhile with them. I broke out of every kind of handcuffs they could scrape up to put on me. I asked for an official certificate and they gave it to me. The next day I filled the Central Theater to capacity. I was flustered, surprised. Victory, in sum. My most spectacular feat was breaking loose from chains on my hands and feet, bolts and padlocks that they'd placed on the prisoners of Mathildegasse of which the padlocks alone weighed forty pounds. Next, I went to the Wintergarden in Berlin, where they had to extend my stay. The key to the victory was in the threat and I kept proposing new challenges. But behind my spectacular feats in escaping was the meticulous study of bolts and padlocks. I worked for hours in the Müller concern located on the Mittelstrasse, with all kinds of German locks, studying their mechanisms, practicing with four spindles of steel four fifths of an inch thick. The press said the locks opened at the mere touch of my hands. In Berlin, I escaped naked from a locked room in the police headquarters and from any metal artifice, rope or chain they put around me. Count von Windheim, chief of the German police, was obliged to sign a paper testifying to my acts. It was fame and glory, but I had only just begun. In one of the acts during that memorable tour, a girl brought a bouquet of flowers to me onstage. Her face remained indelibly captured in my memory. She was afraid of me, her cheeks were still stained by the traces of tears. I tried to console her, I explained that God and locks wanted me to be immortal for now. For several weeks, in England, as I practiced my acts, the image of the girl stayed with me. I suppose it was—"

"The consciousness of your mortality."

"Exactly, Kellerman. The girl's blue eyes said, 'Houdini, death awaits you at the first mistake.' "

"Were you dreaming of her when you hung from the tallest buildings in Washington or Baltimore? Those are my first memories of your acts."

"The escape from the straitjacket on the Mumsey Building in Washington? I don't know. I don't recall the girl in those years. I know that I looked down below my body upon a crowd of fifty thousand people as I violently writhed to free myself from the straitjacket, hanging from a crane at the base of the tallest building in the city, and I felt I was liberating myself from myself, when at last I flung the straitjacket from which I'd escaped at the crowd, a hundred and ten feet below. No, it wasn't the girl in those days, it was the absolute certainty that I'd end up in a mental asylum. And even though I knew I could escape from any asylum in the world, because there was no locked room, no isolation chamber, no rope that could detain me, how could I escape from my own insanity? I am a lucid man, Doctor, but like everyone else, I cannot run from myself."

"When did you start thinking about mental asylums?"

"Just after the death of my mother. I had a strange reaction to that situation. Mama died while I was performing in Europe. I know through my brothers and sisters that from her deathbed she tried to leave me a message, but her paralysis impeded it. I was obsessed with that for months. I used to go to her grave and lie down with my ear against the tombstone, waiting for a message, some sign. My marriage to Bess saved me from insanity. No one, however, has saved me from the idea of insanity, of the fear of a mental disorder."

"That's something the majority of quite normal human beings tend to live with, Houdini. A good amount of normalcy implies a great dose of fear of insanity, it's one of our best motivations."

"I am absolutely aware of that, Kellerman. But knowing that does not imply managing to eradicate the fear of insanity."

"Houdini, I would have to confess, I feel the same thing frequently."

"But you don't frequently hang from hundred-yard-high buildings."

SIXTY-SEVEN

LEILA BROUGHT THE RUMOR . . .

. . .at the least opportune moment. They were working eighteen-hour days in the SD, and the initial group had grown. Alex had had to call upon the characters of "Cinderella," "Bambi" and "The Three Little Pigs," just to baptize all the assistants and external consultants. "The toilet" had been filled with diagrams, charts, courses of action, maps of the story's junctures, conditions to be met in each phase of the critical path, countdowns marked with big red circles, nodal points, moments in which the operation could fail. Alex said with delight that it looked like the outline for a poorly designed Maileresque novel. And he was no more irrational than usual. He arrived at five in the morning, read *The New York Times* and the previous day's edition of Managua's *Barricada,* and later studied the walls where his strange work was brewing.

He usually had a session with Leila, his secretary, around eleven. And by dint of five days of repetition, the SD began to settle into the only routine it had known in its fairly long history. During the private session with Leila on the fourteenth, she timidly suggested to Alex that someone at Langley was trying to screw him. The chief of operations had been speaking well of him during a director's meeting, facts about Operation Snow White had appeared in an internal bulletin addressed to the four chiefs of intelligence services, and someone had suggested they increase the SD's and the operation's budgets, in light of the project's significance.

Leila could read the smoke signals. Nor was Alex half-blind in matters of internal bureaucratic warfare. Who was behind all this and why? He reviewed his last meetings with the CIA's powers-that-be, to whom the Shit Department was subordinate: the assistant director of operations (ADO), the chief of the Office of Special Operations (CSO), the chief of the Special Group for Central America (CSGCA). He thought carefully about the competition. There had been a struggle for power between Goldwater's protégés and the group originally formed by Casey, and as if in a bad version of Shakespeare, he had emerged from darkness after his weekly spiritualism session with his boss. But Alex had been careful to stay in the absolute margin of the affair. On the other side, there was new leadership who seemed not to want conflicts with anyone as they slowly created their court of staunch supporters. Then there were the "Libyans," who'd managed to break into Reagan's nightmares and whom Bush had agreeably inherited. The supertechnocrats seemed to want no say in the matter; as long as no one bothered them, they could go on pronouncing the word "satellite," with a tone of disgust, like something obsolete, and dedicate themselves to playing with whatever new technology was placed in their hands. The club of narcotic spies was dropping off; McFarlane's heirs seemed in poor health, including their mental health as well. Then where was it coming from? He scrutinized the last two hundred (high-level–top-secret–for your eyes only) memoranda and advisory materials that had passed through his hands, which he had filed in a trash can, covered with pages of *The Village Voice*'s theater section.

He found nothing. Alex was indubitably insane, but his insanity did not imply an incapacity to survive in the bureaucratic jungle. Two or three times throughout the morning, the dwarfs interrupted him for some piece of advice. He kept ordering them all to hell, one by one, threatened to burn them and their mothers in green firewood and cut the balls off their children with a dull knife, until the rumor finally spread that Alex was not available for meetings and that it could be dangerous to approach the conference room, where Alex had taken a seat with a cold cup of coffee in front of him, lighting one cigarette with the butt of another.

Around four o'clock in the afternoon, Alex grabbed the phone and began to make calls. When he finished half an hour later, he didn't know much, but he was on the way. If someone was toying with Operation Snow White, he or she would find out very quickly what the Witch could do to his or her respective physical condition with a good dose of poison apples.

S I X T Y - E I G H T

JOURNALISTS' STORIES

(J U L I O   S P E A K S)

Solitude's sister is slovenliness, I said to myself, thinking I had to wash some shirts. Lazaro, the doc, had explained to me one time that pneumonia doesn't hurt and that your lungs do not ache; what aches is the diaphragm from so many jolts of coughing. Was this science or the desire to assuage my worries? Love hurt. And I didn't care what the doc said. Love hurt, a pang below the heart twisting in your chest. Loneliness is disaster's cousin, ten dirty shirts, not one even moderately clean, although the navy blue one might iron out okay, cover it with detergent and give it some air. Dousing it with cologne would do. I would look dirty and messy. Dirty, messy and slovenly with love pangs in my chest. As someone says, that's the best Mexican condition to sell a good interview.

It was one of those mornings when I wandered through the house forgetting what I'd decided a few seconds before, moving a chair from its place, gathering the light and electricity bills to throw them on top of the stove; I thought about one thing while I did another, and neither of the two came out. I had shaved twice, once halfway, and I'd mentally answered my correspondence without sitting down to finally write it. I had one of the most common strains of Mexico's ills: anxiety of assholes, mixed with a sore throat and information saturation about corrupt functionaries, ecological crises, public transit assaults, friends' writing blocks, debtors who didn't pay on time and the news of an old girlfriend's suicide. I was saved by the fruit vendor in the portable market who parked in front of my house on Tuesdays and sold me pears very cheap. He gave me a conspiratorial smile while he explained that the worst thing in the world was to sell absolutely unripe fruit under the burning sun, pursued by middlemen from the Merced Market whom he owed and by some neighbors whose window he'd accidentally broken and what's more by the market supervisor who accused him of running around disseminating pro-Cárdenas propaganda.

"And is it true?"

He winked. Inside the plastic bag of pears was a flyer: "Cárdenas won! The people voted!"

"But I don't give it to just anyone. One can tell you're a worthy person," he said.

Smelling like a pimp, having washed my shirt with cologne, I walked away whistling the William Tell overture, better known among common folk as "The Lone Ranger Theme," choking myself with the excellent pears.

El Chaco, the envoy from Madrid's *Diario 16* with whom I had an appointment to sell the Cárdenas interview, was not in the Correspondents' Club, and I walked around slowly sipping a Coke with lemon but without rum, a kid's Cuba libre, a fairly decent substitute for the real thing at this hour of the morning.

I bumped into Tito Bardini, an Argentine-Mex reporter who wrote specials for the *Prensa Latina* and who was drinking a real cuba libre.

"Che, what's up? Where's your miserable little gringo?"

"I think he's in Zacatecas writing trash to make a living."

"I saw the Trotsky piece last week. Tremendous story, Fats. Congratulations, eh. What are you drinking?"

"Thanks, *compadre* . . . just Coke. I'm spending the day taking care of myself. The next jack who tries to sell me the socialist revolution, I'll buy it. To hell with all that. I do hope it comes to pass, because this stupid country is full of false vendors."

Tito laughed, he clinked his glass against mine and drank.

"Do you still believe in those things, Fernández?" said a Spanish news correspondent from *Tiempo* magazine and the Z group. "I marvel at the way you've remained trapped inside the time machine."

He was a fairly sullen character. A native of Navarra. They said he was one of the founders of the ETA and he'd abandoned ship at the first opportunity. A little cynical, and quite ill-humored. On tours, no one wanted to share a room with him, not even to reduce expenses.

"What are you into, Heredia?" I answered him.

"Journalistic objectivity and contraband bottles of Johnnie Walker, and I'm also into buying dollars in Cuba's and Nicaragua's black markets to buy rum cheaper."

"You're a prick."

"I'm a realist, and Mexico is boring me. Who's buying?"

"To each his own, and for you your own, it makes me—," said Tito in his Argentine-Mexican Spanish, taking flight under the pretext of having to send a telex.

Heredia fell into an armchair in front of my table and stared at me. I started making little drawings on the Formica from the sweat of my glass.

"I'm in from Panama and Nicaragua. Machado sent his regards. In fact, I used your name to get an interview about the reinstallation of the Contras. Nothing out of this world."

"Don't fuck around, they'll shut me out as soon as they read it. The pro-Contra shit you write—"

"You still believe in just wars and unjust wars. They're all the same, big guy. They're worthless. Everyone wants to stay on top. Look, the Contras are shit, a mixture of torturers, lottery salesmen, mercenaries, sadists, unemployed, religious lunatics and fans of your countryman Valenzuela who've seen too many Clint Eastwood movies. But the others are crazy fanatics ruining that country with the allure of purity, and they live like kings in the houses where Somoza's people used to live and they waste no time setting up their stores for functionaries while shortages are bloody awful. There's not even toilet paper anymore in that country. For a dollar, they'll throw a woman on top of you, Fats. I was just there. And Managua is full of Cubans, it's annoying."

"Get out of here, and have your mother retrain you. As for me, modern Europeans bore me. The disenchanted bug me. I don't know why the hell they keep sending renegades who can type to Latin America. What fucking fault is it of the Nics that the Revolution fucked you over at age fifteen and your wife left you cuckolded at twenty-one?"

The guy didn't even shy. He confined himself to giving me a half-bitter smile. "The revolution was fucked a good long time before I turned fifteen, what happened was it took me a while to realize it. You're slower, Fernández. You don't see what's in front of you. Nicaragua is a tablecloth where some people eat and the Russians and the North Americans decide the menu and serve the plates. . . . Incidentally, after the interview with Machado, he remarked he hadn't seen you in a while, and I asked him if he had you and your red gringo on the payroll, if you were in the pay of the Ministry of the Interior?"

"And what did he say? He should have stuck a forty-five up your ass like you deserved."

"It made him smile. Not bad, he did you right, he didn't blow your cover. He told me that if it weren't for the rum you occasionally bought him, he didn't see from where. . . . Believe me, he's falling, you're not doing him any kind of favor by supporting him in the media. Let the ball bounce, he'll end up negotiating with the Contras, everybody will calm down and for that they'll kill us one day in some lousy helicopter over four fucking *miskitos* who don't know their own names."

He leaned back against the window, terminating the conversation. The sun hit his face. He brought his glass of ice to his forehead and began to move it very gently, as if massaging himself, letting the ice cubes clink against each other.

I walked away with a foul taste in my mouth. Tito, the Argentine-Mex, was waiting for me at the door.

"Don't waste your time with scum, Fats. Those guys are already way out of it. They live alone, on a planet full of shit."

"No, what gets me is that later they claim they're on the left, that they're anarchists. Anarchists my ass, they're a bunch of Stirnerian faggots. Runts who walk around reading Nietzsche at age forty. Disillusioned my ass. What the hell are those guys disillusioned about if they were never excited? They're a bunch of reactionary, lying wimps."

"Yeah, but they're in style right now. Skepticism is in, *com-*

padre. Plus the pay is better. Look at me, writing free articles for Salpress. With what *Barricada* pays me for a long feature, I can't even buy a pair of sneakers, my brother."

As we talked, we walked toward the street. We walked along Villalongin toward Sullivan Park, bitching about rightist Stalinists and bullshit "modernists."

"Did the ultra-left catch us? And now, why are we so radical?"

"I am because I just got back from writing a report on the young kids in Nicaragua. And you?"

"I am because the next time I see Greg I'm going to persuade him to sit down and write a novel with four hands. A novel about reporters who refuse to go along with the trend, who keep looking for revolutions in any goddamn corner of the world and fall in love with them. A fucking novel, brother. We'll extract music from the typewriter keys."

We stopped in front of the Statue of the Mother. If that is the mother of all Mexicans, we have one of the world's ugliest mothers, I said to myself, contemplating the mass of stone with absolute objectivity.

"In the deep melting pot of the paaatria . . . ," Tito said, starting to sing the Chilean *"Venceremos."* I gave him the refrain:

"You can hear the people cryyy, and a new dawn has beguuun."

HOW ABOUT A
BULGARIAN LIKE THIS?
(V)

Listen, do you think Max is a fag?" Longoria said to Stoyan at the end of March in 1937, a few days after the spectacular victory of the Internationals in Guadalajara.

"Did he say something to you? Come on to you or something?" the Bulgarian answered, lighting a cigarette with great difficulty in the blowing wind.

"No, not to me. Nor do I give a shit. The Greeks were homosexual."

"Which Greeks?"

"The Greeks of the *Iliad* and the *Odyssey,* those Greeks."

Stoyan blew smoke at the sky, as if to say the conversation was over. If Stoyan sometimes sinned by indulging in nostalgia and hid himself in small cities, walked alone every chance he could, drove himself crazy with an inexplicable strange sadness, Longoria was a freak about education, in a very sui generis way. He adored geography and that might have been why he'd joined the Internationals instead of fighting in an anarchist battalion, where he would have been at home; squeezed the economists, studied graphology. He had discovered a Hungarian in the battalion who'd been a currency printer for the Budapest Royal Mint in his youth and he dedicated hours to milking him, exchanging cigarettes for technical information about paper, ink, engraving techniques, trademarks. In his free time, he worked with the artillerymen studying collimation and topography. He had even made friends with Regler, the German from the Garibaldi Battalion, who translated Goethe's poems for him.

If Stoyan was the tormented pathos and consistency in combat, and Saturnino Longoria the obsession with learning and the insanity of the war, Max was the sweetness, the eternal surprise, expressed in his very large blue eyes and in the way he used his camera. Taking half an hour to find the best angle, the image that would capture humanity in the middle of the mud and incessant rain and the faces contorted by fear as the bombs fell. Each time he had to fire a shot, he suffered, he grieved. And yet he was the typical lunatic who would be fixing his bayonet, yelling, on the front lines and later be seen setting a rabbit's leg in a splint instead of throwing it into the common stew. He had come to Spain as a photographer for a New York magazine, though his work in the States had been as an actor, first in theater in Los Angeles and later in film in Hollywood. By the time he was twenty-seven, he'd been in half a dozen movies, and had even costarred in a Western with Alan Ladd as the good guy and him as the second good guy. He lasted three days as a professional photographer in Spain, then his camera was demoted to his second arm and a Belgian rifle became his first, because since the night of November 8th, he was incorporated into the Dombrowsky Battalion, next to Bulgarians, Czechs, Poles and Yugoslavs.

"I don't care if he's gay, what worries me is that that lunatic's a Trotskyite," Stoyan said after a period of silence. He and Longoria were talking alone under a bridge outside of Brihuega. They had volunteered to pillage munitions abandoned by the defeated Italians of the CTV on the highway, and this was their midday cigarette break.

"What the hell difference does that make? It could be because Trotsky is cuter than Stalin."

"Don't joke about this, Longoria."

"Aren't we on the same side? Aren't we all antifascists? You Marxists are royal fuck-ups. You're like the priests of my town arguing about whether the Virgin of Carmen is better than the Virgin of Covadonga. If you, the most loyal servant of the Padrecito Pepe, don't care, who else is going to care? The guys from *Mundo Obrero*, who go around spreading this shit that the Trotskyites are fascist, rabid dogs? The guys from Moscow, who went crazy and go around killing each other with this trial stuff? We're in Spain, my son. Smell the air."

"Without Stalin, we would have sunk a long time ago. You've got to be careful running around proclaiming yourself a Trots-kyite, it can be extremely dangerous."

"I'm not so sure of that. Without Stalin, we'd probably be guerrilla fighters by now. But close to finishing, no way. In the end, what did Stalin give us . . . ?"

"A few tanks, some planes . . ."

"For what . . . what? Now you'll tell me Stalin also sent you to the Internationals."

"There's some truth to that."

"Stalin sent you?"

Stoyan Vasilev, a Bulgarian missing the first nineteen years of his life who'd seen half the world, and who believed Stalin had sent him to transform it, grew pensive.

"After Stalin sent me, I came because I wanted to," he ended up saying.

A week later, Max traveled to Madrid on leave because he wanted to mail off some photos to the magazine that had sent him to Spain. He didn't return.

The Dombrowsky, now part of the Twelfth Brigade and with just eighteen percent of its original forces intact, was in the process of reorganization in Fuencarral after the Battle of Guadalajara. Three hundred fifty new recruits had been incorporated for train-ing, the majority of them Spaniards. Longoria, in his new post of lieutenant, made them dismantle their rifles time and again, dig trenches, fire. Stoyan had been working with the machine-gun company and overseeing the progress of the Spanish classes taken by the Yugoslavs and the Bulgarians. In his free time, which was plentiful, he gathered personal stories from every source. Twenty years of social strife were summed up in the small battalion, in which there remained about two hundred volunteers from the Balkan countries and Eastern Europe. Strikes, military insurrec-tions, millions of days in jail, tortures, persecutions, personal tragedies, fears, chills and fevers, books, clandestine papers.

The days were relatively placid. Max's disappearance was acci-dentally discovered by Longoria on an expedition to get *chorizos* in La Alcarria. A few anarchists from the Cipriano Mera division who knew Max told him they'd seen Max detained in a Madrid bar by an Ortega policeman, a communist colonel from the Ministry of the Interior who was from the Soviet Cheka, the secret police.

Longoria returned to Fuencarral and went out for a walk with Stoyan. Both knew that strange things were occurring. The events in Barcelona and Madrid had left the entire front extremely nervous. The anarchist POUM's dissolution, the mysterious abduction of Andrés Nin, the show trials of Moscow. It all reeked.

"Do you really believe that Nin could be a fascist? Do you really buy the propaganda about the POUM guys?"

"I don't know, I don't know them."

"I do, they're a drag, they believe in St. Marxengels and St. Lenin Trotsk, just like your people, if a little less bureaucratic than your folks. But fascist, no way. They bring the trouble they've got going in the Soviet Union over here and here you behave like slaves. The whole thing's a fraud."

Stoyan didn't say a word, he even silently swallowed the version of events in Barcelona that the brigade's political commissar gave that night, the one that was highly questioned by Longoria and the Garibaldi men. But at dawn, he rode off on his motorcycle to resolve the problems of a few defective parts of the Maxims that had just arrived. Two days later he returned. He had a cut on his face that spread from his right cheekbone almost to the corner of his lips. Longoria was in the outskirts of the camp, reading Malatesta in the branches of an apple tree, while he sank his teeth into the fruit from time to time.

"Come here. We've got to talk, you and I."

The anarchist climbed down from the tree humming "To the Barricades." They wandered through the outskirts of the town, following the course of a stream. The craters left by the bombs made them walk in s's. Max was waiting for them in a ravine. He had the same surprised expression as always, illuminated by his very blue eyes and ungainly air.

"Where did you come from?" Longoria asked, surprised, and he embraced the blond from North America.

"Madrid. Stoyan brought me."

"Where'd you find him?"

"In the back of a truck on a street in the Chamberi section of Madrid, when they were transferring him," answered the Bulgarian, gesturing for the Spanish anarchist to drop the subject.

They walked through a meadow full of wild daisies. Max

picked a flower every once in a while and started making a bouquet. His camera no longer hung around his neck.

"I suspect that the extremists wanted to shoot me, Saturnino, and then this guy appeared, disguised and with pistol in hand. It was a scene I'd already lived many times, in the movies, you know? Helpless hero on the point of being blown away and his friend providentially appears, prepared to unleash a fury."

"I'd shit in the milk they nursed on."

"What's worse is they weren't bad guys, militants from the CP, like you and me," said the North American.

Stoyan let himself collapse among the flowers, ending up half hidden. Only his green peaked cap with the captain's insignia and the three-pointed red star of the Internationals loomed up over the daisies.

"What the hell's going to happen to us if we win the war?" Longoria asked no one.

"First we win it, then we see." Stoyan's voice rose from among the flowers.

"What a shame not to have the camera now. The photo would be titled 'Soldiers Among Daisies.' You, Longoria, with the bayonet between your teeth, and that lazy Bulgarian with the thirty-eight in his hand."

"What are we going to do?" the Spaniard asked.

"A group of British journalists is leaving for France tonight. McDonald, the poet, is going with them. He can take charge of taking Max. I don't think he's safe here. We could leave him with the battalion, but that could be very risky."

"You think they'd shoot him in the back or something?"

"A week ago, I would have told you that was stupid, now I don't know," the Bulgarian answered.

A year later, in June of 1938, as the Dombrowsky prepared for action in the Battle of the Ebro, Stoyan and Longoria received a pair of postcards sent by Max from Los Angeles and signed with a daisy. In response, they sent a postcard with Goya's sketches that they bought in a little store in Lérida.

SEVENTY

THE VERSION OF EMILIO SALGARI'S *GOOD-BYE TO MOMPRACEM* CREATED BY STOYAN VASILEV IN THE PLEVEN PRISON

D^{on't bite, you shrew."}

"Quit playing with that tiger cub already. He'll end up maiming your arm, little brother," said the old man with very white hair who was cooking in a corner of the room, generously splashing port wine on the meat sizzling on a brazier.

"You have your fun, Yanez," answered the man playing with the little tiger, ignoring the beast, even though it had just sunk its teeth deeply into his arm and several drops of blood attested to the bite. "Let me have mine; however barbaric it might strike you, it heals the spleen and the absolute calm that reigns this island and this sea . . . and this entire planet. God is alive! Enough already! We've aged in the worst way, brother, prosperously," Sandokan, that singular character, said, throwing the animal aside and treating his small wound with part of the port wine his blood brother wanted to use for the stew.

Accustomed to these outbursts of innocent insanity, Yanez turned toward the wide-open window in the ship and contemplated the calm blue sea, which seemed now like a giant cemetery of old stories.

"It's been two years since I quit tutoring you, little brother, and we've succumbed to the illnesses of old age, to observing how the world surrounding us has changed, to pleasure cruises to see the fine Hindu railways, and the brothels of Malacca; to playing chess with Van Horn in his bungalow in Celebes. You're right. I just conceded twenty-four hours to Mompracem to relive his glory and propose to us the greatest adventure of all."

When it is spied on the horizon for the first time, it is nothing but a pile of graceful rocks butting the ocean; a protuberance in a coral-red breakwater situated in nobody's nowhere land. The maps don't show the island, not even the best cartographic studies of the British Admiralty. One finds oneself outside the commercial routes and outside the not so commercial routes of the Chinese contraband junkers. They say the islet was discovered around 1715, by accident, by a Portuguese ship carrying a crew depleted by the plague, storms and scurvy; it had even suffered a horrifying experience with cannibalism. Victims of a suicide pact, the last two survivors of that unfortunate adventure died in the region upon which the small fort would later be constructed. Hence the current owners of Mompracem—as that is the name of the island cursed by the British and Dutch colonialist, by the rajas of Borneo and Sarawak, by the Spanish and Portuguese sailing ships, who descend to the Indian Ocean through the northern sea of China—believe the small fort is an amalgam of blood and rocks, making it indestructible.

It probably isn't, but it certainly seems impregnable, even by a force equipped with modern artillery and armored steamships. The reason is its geographical layout. Ships that attempt to bomb the cove must first penetrate through a natural passage in the coral, an utterly impossible task for those without practical experience and familiarity with the region. If by chance they got through, they would come under the direct fire of the batteries placed on the lateral fronts known as "the fingers of the dead man's hands," that in turn seem impossible to conquer without the invader's use of a significant infantry force, which would have to disembark on the posterior coast of the island, encountering the impractical ascent of its great jutting rocks and taking the defenders from behind, a move that seems beyond the capacity of the most accomplished Swiss mountaineer. This strange combination of natural accidents and defensive dispositions, cocreated by nature and by the owners of the island of Mompracem, render it a bastion that can be attacked only in dreams, which easily turn into nightmares. Mompracem has come under enemy fire three times, two of them fruit-lessly, the third successfully, but only due to the treason of one of its defenders, and not for long.

While for some it is a nightmare, because there dwell the fearsome "Tigers of Malaysia," for others the island is a symbol of freedom and independence in lands defeated by the evil of coloni-alism and slavery. Mompracem is the seat of a brotherhood of bloodthirsty and savage pirates, but it is also a rock where no man calls himself a slave, to bondage or to debt; where money does not rule and where property is limited to arms and clothes and corpo-ral adornments that the inhabitants show off. It is said that in its caves, hidden beneath the deepest dungeons of the main fort, known as the "Soul of the Skull," an unspeakable treasure exists whose ownership is collective among the Tigers of Malaysia. A record is kept in a central book, of the loot from pillages and boardings, assigned according to a certain index of justice known as "Abraham's Wood." It establishes the amounts to be awarded to the captain of an expedition, the ship's boatswain, the sea captains, the wounded, the regular soldiers, those who participate in dangerous missions, those who distinguish themselves in com-bat and so on. At the head of this unusual brotherhood of soldiers, as the legitimate rulers of the island and leaders of its men, are Sandokan and Yanez, by right of fury and fire.

Let's return to our two old men, as both Sandokan and Yanez, bordering on sixty, which, considering their hazardous lives, the multiple scars that show up on the body as much as on the soul, and the extent of longevity that pirates in these latitudes reach, could be considered an advanced age.

"Got something on your mind, little brother?" Sandokan asked, his eyes lighting up with a sparkle that he had seemed to have lost.

Yanez smiled and returned to his stew, which at that moment gave off a magnificent aroma. In spite of his many gray hairs, he kept a flexible body and there was a certain grace in his virile movements. He stirred the meat in the sauce and threw it in the little pot of stew, various tubers from Borneo, which he'd boiled earlier. Later, watching Sandokan out of the corner of his eye, he took his wire-framed glasses from the upper pocket of his white silk shirt and from his pants pocket extracted a wrinkled note.

"Would you believe something as absurd as a message in a bottle floating in the ocean?"

"Bah," said Sandokan. "A hidden treasure. When I was a kid I played with throwing bottles into the sea in Sarawak in that kind of game, and I dreamed about the faces of the imbeciles who, if they followed my map, would end up in a Presbyterian mission in Kinabalu. I dreamed that with a little luck, they'd torture the priests to get the treasure out of them, while the priests insisted that the only treasure was their powerful faith in their God." Sandokan walked toward the terrace and spat in the sea. He usually spat when speaking of European gods, a product of phobias acquired during his education by missionaries, the dubious privilege of being the son of a raja under alleged British protection.

If Yanez looked like the result of a mix of a hundred races, dominated by Southern European blood, Sandokan was a pure example of the Malaysian race, with very light olive skin, eyes and hair the black of a crow's wing, medium height, legs slightly bowed from so many years on board a ship, curly beard and mustache sprouting a fair number of gray hairs.

"No, it's not a treasure. It's a love story, little brother. Care to read it?"

"What language is it written in?"

"French, the language of love, of course. And I'll save you your next question. It fell into my hands last month, when Sambliong returned from the expedition we sent him on to follow the trail of our acquaintance Stal Inchu."

Sandokan walked over to the railing and spat in the ocean again, two hundred yards below the terrace, upon hearing the name of the Chinese pimp.

"I'm going to cut off Sambliong's ear. Why didn't he inform me of this? And you, why didn't you say something? You've had this message in your pocket for a month and kept quiet?"

"Forgive our Greatest Tiger, he didn't understand any of the message and thought I could translate it. You know that French is not a language of these coasts. And as for me, I was waiting for the right occasion to tell you about it. And it seems it has arrived. But first let's enjoy this stew."

Ignoring Yanez's advice, Sandokan took down a combat pistol from a weapons collection on the wall, carefully aimed at the pot where the meat and port wine stewed, and destroyed it with one shot.

"Now you can tell me. We don't have to wait to eat."

"See why I thought it was the right moment?" Yanez said, soaking up what remained in the destroyed pot. "It was delicious."

"Talk already, or I'll use the other pistol to blow your brains out and rid myself of your nasty sense of humor."

"Okay, okay, it's not that big a deal. Have you heard of the Paris Commune?"

EXPERTS IN
BUREAUCRATIC . . .

. . .wars are stealthy. They know each office's schedules and know the places where all the capos' secretaries go for cocktails; they distinguish over the phone between a voice of alarm and a voice dominated by the regular use of cocaine; they know the magic words to open computer programs and they know the color of the flames when it's documents that are burning—documents which, not coincidentally, and after years, would otherwise end up in the hands of a senator who wants to go on the six o'clock CBS news.

Experts in bureaucratic wars are bifids and, on occasion, trifids. They practice the language of double tongues assiduously, they lie even if you ask what time it is. They trade favors, they exchange worn-out information wrapped in aluminum foil as if they were precious stones bought in a Soviet tourist shop. They introduce a hint of doubt into any positive statement, letting their voices fall at the end of the sentence to leave a complacent mysterious aftertaste.

Alex was one of those. And he was one of the best. But it wasn't much good while he was in the dark. Before beginning to bite the hands extended to greet him, he should know to whom they belonged.

As he left the SD that Friday and found himself enveloped by the crowd walking up Madison Avenue, his gawky body dressed in a white suit, pale red shirt and a black knotted tie, he moved agilely between the Pakistani hot dog vendors and blacks selling sweatsuits knocked down to five dollars. He was going hunting.

The ideal hunting locales were in Washington, but there wasn't time, he'd have to resign himself to the two lesser options New York offered, the bar at the Palace around five o'clock, when a string quartet accompanied the drinkers of champagne cocktails and The View, the revolving restaurant at the top of the Marriott around nine o'clock at night, just before the show started and the noise made the conversations hard to hear. Between the two he could try the Casablanca Bar on Wall Street. He got lucky at the first. Quinn, moreover, seemed to have been waiting for him.

"I hear you're having an acute attack of paranoia, Alex," said Quinn, confirming Alex's suspicions with just those words. Four calls to Langley, and an hour and a half later the ball was bouncing in New York.

"Go over the score with me, Quinn, and don't start selling me shit. Just tell me who and why."

"I suppose you think you'll get it out of me for free. Alex, you're incorrigible."

Alex stared at his table companion and the latter shuddered. There was something in Alex's attitude that made him a man without friends, with just acquaintances and travel companions, about whom he could never be sure whether they loved him or were so afraid of him they would never spend a day in the country with him, in doubt about whether they'd be lunch companions or servants. Quinn made up his mind and began to talk, just as a gorgeous blonde in a black skirt open to her thigh put a champagne cocktail crowned with an enormous strawberry in front of him.

"Somebody convinced Casey's boys that you're hopelessly insane and that you could turn out to be dangerous to their future. Everyone says it's not so, but your name smells like a cadaver in the board meetings, and they want to fatten up your famous Operation Snow White to ultimately devour you. Before long, people won't touch it with gloves."

"Who?"

"The 'Libyans,' and the DDO. The Libyans want your money to pull out Gadhafi's teeth, and the DDO thinks you're working with Senator Goldwater's group for succession. They say Casey wasn't the only one who had cancer, but the current director too, and that's made everyone extremely nervous."

"And who put this idea in the DDO's head?"

"Until now, I've told you what I know, but if you force me to speculate, I'd say it was Goldwater himself, to turn up the pressure."

"You know what's true and what's not, how can the DDO be so idiotic?"

"These are strange times, Alex," Quinn said, sipping his cocktail and letting himself get caught up in the string quartet's adagio. "Everyone believes what she or he wants, and those who think this is bullshit keep quiet. If they open their mouths someone thinks they're taking sides and will start poking around in their briefcase to screw up their lives. These days in intelligence a sentence in Rambo is worth more than a third-level report. I'm almost convinced that if we want to count for something in this country, we should move to Hollywood. A month ago, it occurred to me to say that Bailey's project on Albania was a joke, that why didn't they give it to Gorba for Christmas. Two days later, someone ordered a review of the investments we'd been making in the Mexican blunders. What do you think?"

"You can't count on anyone anymore, dear. We're more like the KGB every day. But not the current KGB, poor idiots rereading the Amnesty reports on human rights to find out what they can and can't do, the good KGB, the real one, Yezhov's KGB."

"Okay, Alex, we still haven't poisoned each other in the basements of Langley."

"Don't be so sure," Alex said, winking.

LONGORIA HAS A DOG

Longoria told himself: one of two things, either the whole thing was a tremendous, continuing error, or it had been a series of lamentable choices not crowned with success, but indubitably endowed with the best intentions.

That refutation brought about the arrival of a dog to his new life. He'd had a dog in Paris thirty years before, and although the new one was clearly a piece of Mexican trash, the animal reminded him of the long walks through Montmartre and the interminable meetings with the FLN's Algerians in Colombres. The Mexican dog had quickly been baptized Malatesta, and in just two days responded to his name, he must have been so desperate for an identity before his fortuitous encounter with Longoria. The French dog had been named Vocation, for his obsession with smelling everyone's shoes.

With Malatesta behind him, pretending they didn't know each other at all, Longoria crossed one of the little parks behind the maternity pavilion of the hospital and came out around the electrical-mechanical maintenance warehouses, situated very near the red brick wall that bordered the grounds in the back. He suddenly stopped. What was he doing? Why had he come there? He was having serious trouble with his short-term memory; on the other hand, his memories of the past became increasingly sharper, more tangible. A bad sign. Those who live in the past, according to what he'd learned cohabiting with his companions at the asylum, tended to disappear in it, and this was a preliminary and fairly rapid step toward total disappearance.

Perhaps he should heed the advice of his few friends and run away. Run away was just an expression; you can't run away when you don't exist, and formally Longoria in the asylum did not exist.

Two or three false personalities that he had hatched to live in that enormous hospital existed, one of which allowed him to sleep in the home under the name of Leoncio Sánchez. Another made him an outside consultant in the oncology pavilion, a third turned him into a sterile gas supplier. In a microcosm like that of a great hospital, where there was enormous mobility for the patients who came and went as well as for the underpaid workers who left their jobs the moment they could, or that afforded by the daily avalanche of visitors or the changing world of volunteers, outside doctors, interns who spent six months doing their social service, Longoria could preserve an unanonymous anonymity. He could be all over the place without anyone asking what that cranky but still nice old man was doing there. There was always an absurd explanation to give for every question. And the truth is there weren't too many questions asked, because in the ten years he'd been turned into a ghost in the Sanatorio Español he'd only found himself trapped in embarrassing situations a couple of times, one of them for trying to hook up with a fiftyish nun in the midst of a crisis about her vocation.

At any rate, what was he doing there? He hadn't planned to work in his studio this afternoon. He didn't have an appointment or a reason to go into the warehouses, but something useful could always come from an unannounced inspection. Longoria was not the type to squander coincidences. He entered the warehouses and examined the empty workshop where old white coats were flung over workbenches by the operators who had finished the day. At the end of the corridor, passing the door of a bathroom that was out of order due to water leakage from broken pipes, he disappeared behind a metal door that had seemed to be permanently closed. Passing along an unlit corridor, he entered his offices. Longoria had a genius for evil, according to the archaic parameters of Fantomas or Arsène Lupin novels. With a little patience and a long clandestine tradition, he'd launched inside a private hospital a studio for the falsification of documents, including a photocopier, a small Harris printer, a modern model of computerized photocomposition and a working table with all kinds of rubber for the manufacture of stamps, wooden wedges, gauges, lancets, lead molds, all kinds of ink, paper of different textures, grain, density and distinguishing watermarks.

As he tried to remember what had brought him there, Longoria seized the opportunity to use a feather duster on the table and equipment, happily whistling a few chords of *"La Madelon."* Malatesta watched him anxiously.

When had he returned to Paris? Longoria suddenly asked himself, halting his hygienic labor. When had he reinstalled himself in the basement of 67 Rue Victor Hugo? Had he been working on something important and gotten momentarily distracted?

The old man repeatedly hit the palm of his hand against his forehead. In spite of the voices of doom, he knew that the gesture would not kill many more neurons than had already died of natural old age. The dog wagged his restless tail. Longoria contemplated him carefully. It was Malatesta, Mexican dog, distinguished and loyal companion. He was not in Paris.

The blackout his memory had suffered, of which he was fully conscious, made him nervous. He went to a corner of the workshop and took out a bottle of Rioja wine, stolen from a gynecologist's Christmas basket, that he saved for special occasions. His wrinkled hands, full of knots, with bulging blue veins, trembled. They were the hands of an old man. If he had studied them closely he would have known he was not in Paris. There he was only fifty-seven, a young kid. Now, with eighty-three years behind him, he was a respectable adult. His hands, however, had not lost the dexterity needed to take out the cork.

He thought about the last years in Paris, awaiting the death of Franco and a return to Spain that never happened, wrapped up in a thousand plans that failed with the regularity of a Swiss watch, and in the thousand secondary plans to support those plans, which always did come out well and incidentally drove the French police crazy. The poor French police, they were never prepared for the Great Longoria and his magic circus of anarchists with toads and elephants in their hats. Poor *flics,* who after all was said and done he didn't hate too much. What's more, he'd presented them with the country, and they had stuck it up their asses. More still, he had returned the decoration they'd conferred upon him at the end of the war as a hero of the Resistance. What he wanted was for Franco to die so that he could return to Madrid waving red and black flags. Indeed, had Franco died by now, or not?

Longoria lifted his glass and raised it to Malatesta. "To Mexico. To the women I haven't yet met, the banks I haven't yet robbed, the grandchildren I haven't had. To the old comrades, and their bleaching bones."

He emptied his glass in one gulp, grabbed the bottle and

refilled it. The wine overflowed and dribbled onto the table, staining the new series of Mexican passports Longoria was falsifying at his leisure for the Salvadoran boys.

"I drink to the dwarfs, because they see things in their just and humble dimension, from below. I drink to the Seine and to the constructive uses of nitroglycerin. I drink to old friends. May their bones fertilize the cemeteries of our memory."

He drank again. He could be in Paris or Mexico City. He didn't give three shits. As long as he didn't forget the old *compadres,* as long as he remembered exactly on which side of the barricades the good guys lay down, slept and woke up to see the dawn.

He raised the bottle again and said:

"Death to ugly people!" and he drank the whole thing.

S E V E N T Y - T H R E E

SD STOOD FOR . . .

. . . Shit Department, Department of Shit, and shit was exactly what Alex was capable of distributing on an international, national and local level, employing such varied means as DHL, certified mail, the telephone (including collect calls), and the bicycle messenger systems at work in New York. There was only one thing stopping him from initiating a bombardment.

What if they were making him face off against the wrong people? And if Quinn had been the spokesman for an amusing maneuver to force him to shoot his cannons at the wrong targets?

Alex had shut the SD's window, making everyone who wished to enter use the antiquated routes. He was ruminating over the facts Quinn had placed in his hands. Leila studied him without daring to cross to his side of the door while she drank a cup of coffee.

"Okay, enough of the statue routine, I know you're there. I

need to know a few things on the inside. Could you?" Alex said to his secretary without looking at her. "I need to know next semester's budget for covert action in Libya compared with the first semester of this year. I need to know if Julian Smith's daughter is still going out with Cannon's son under instruction from their parents. I need to know whether the DDO was in a good mood or not after the Jackson report. I need to know who started the rumor that Operation Snow White was so wonderful, and two days later, a casualty waiting for a coffin. All that. And tell Eve to come in."

Leila left her coffee on one of the lamp tables of the office and swaggered out. Eve made her appearance almost immediately. Alex was pressing his hands against his temples, trying to control a brutal headache. When he attempted to speak, he couldn't. He gestured for Eve to sit while he caught his breath and the wave of pain subsided.

"Your head, bwana?"

Alex nodded. Eve sat down silently. In two or three minutes, Alex began to speak deliberately.

"What decisions do you need me to make on Snow White? Leave out the ones you can make yourselves."

"Alex, you're annoying, nobody has the complete picture but you. It's hard to walk blindfolded. We're always afraid of making a mistake. We've got several things on hold. The reserve in case the Rolando affair fails. You've seen him, he's diabolically unstable. . . . The exact dates of the conference of intellectuals in Mexico. Sleepy's initial actions. And above all, timing the matter of sowing the seeds. A delay there could be fatal."

"Forget the Rolando thing, I love that guy. He's the only person I've met in recent years who scares me. Bring in Sleepy's calendar, and the sowing business. . . ."

Alex lay back as Eve left the room. Giant drops fell against the window. It was raining in New York. For a moment, Alex wished he were one of those guys on the street peddling umbrellas for three dollars, certain he could outsell everyone. Plus, he wouldn't have this headache.

Eve left two sheets of paper on the chair at Alex's side, silently so as not to disturb his reflections. After a moment, he picked them up. The headache was a result of his lack of style. He had to read more English espionage novels; sooner or later he'd master that cryptic language and slightly simpleton sense of humor, that language of the real spies. He spoke like a Hollywood actor fallen from film to B-level television. That's why his head ached, lack of style.

"Eve, in this office we should swear off coffee and move decisively to tea. It's much healthier. It's the drink of intelligent people."

Eve agreed.

Alex stared at her.

"You don't know how difficult it is to be God, it is so di-a-bol-lic-al-ly demanding, dear," he said, imitating Burton in *Staircase*.

S E V E N T Y - F O U R

JOURNALISTS' STORIES

(G R E G   S P E A K S)

I called Fats from the Colonial Hotel in Zacatecas to tell him I'd been thinking about his grandfather. Katherine had gone out to buy crafts in the market, leaving me a note on the bathroom mirror to meet her for beef jerky in a *lonchería* in front of the hotel.

"For this you wake me up, asshole?" Fats asked. I pictured him smiling.

"I'm in love again, Fats. I'm in love. That's what she says and I believe in these things. . . ."

"Don't fuck around! Is she there? Who is she? Get out of there quick, don't make love with her before consulting your psychiatrist. Practice safe sex. Do you have condoms? Where are you? Are there pharmacies around? Why were you thinking about my grandfather?"

"Because I remembered a story about my grandfather I don't think I ever told you. You're not the only one with a famous grandfather. My mother's father was a famous psychiatrist in New York who once hypnotized Houdini, your hero, Julio. What do you think about that?"

"I knew that somewhere in your remote past you were hiding something, asshole. All these years thinking you were a poor dick gringo I had to take care of throughout the third world and it turns out you're the grandson of the psychiatrist who treated Houdini."

"Don't make me remind you that I taught you how to use the word processor and the remote control for your VCR, you third-world Apache, and furthermore, the doctor didn't treat Houdini, he just hypnotized him one time. Doctor Kellerman."

"And he didn't leave you anything? An autographed photo of Houdini, something you can give for Christmas . . . ?"

"I'm a poor orphan who lost his mother at age three. I don't have anything from before 1955."

"So how do you know about Kellerman?"

"My grandfather was famous. He didn't just hypnotize Houdini, he also corresponded with Howard Fast and Anna Seghers."

"How do you know that?"

"Because Fast told me."

"And how did Fast know that this Kellerman was your grandfather?"

"Because he mentioned his name and I told him that that was my mother's maiden name. . . . Okay, enough, I call to give you some good news and you're giving me a hard time."

"And what is the good news?"

"That it wouldn't be a bad idea to write that famous novel."

"About journalists who . . . ," Fats began, but I had already hung up. It was one thing to give good news over the phone, and another to start working.

A novel about journalists. This year we would die of hunger. To hell with journalism, one year writing a novel about journalists which would probably be a piece of shit and never find a publisher. I had to be going insane. Fats's influence on my life.

I went to the contents of my suitcase, spilled across the middle of the room, mixed with stuff from Katherine's bag, and found a bottle of vitamins. The sun poured through the window, infusing the room with an unreal light. Life itself had become slightly unreal. Love, when it catches you by surprise, does strange things. It starts occupying spaces that had seemed familiar before, it floods into the daily routine, making it marvelously strange, making new things appear on top of the furniture. The same seems different and the differences inundate everything. A novel. Ideas are better than drafts, that's an old law. Drafts are much better than first chapters and the last chapters are always worse than the first. A novel we'd probably never write. Was I getting old? One way or another one gets old. I thought about Kath. Falling in love is a way of getting old. I was getting old. You notice it because the days begin to seem shorter, you become sensitive to the cold, you catch more colds per year. We start to be absurdly obstinate about liking the same things, dreams define themselves rationally as dreams. Nothing seems as though it could suddenly, totally get better.

While I was taking the vitamins with a glass of water, I put on my glasses and started rummaging through Kathy's bag. Among the old jeans and French blouses that had seen better days there was a strip of photographic proofs. From Managua. Kathy appeared in several with Machadito. I hadn't seen him on the last trip. Who had taken the pictures? If I ever wrote the novel, if the novel ever got published, Kathy would take the back-cover photo and Machadito would definitely be a character, albeit secondary.

I put on my last white shirt and left the room still in love. Quevedo had already foreseen this: "It is burning ice, it is frozen fire / it is a painful wound unfelt / it is a good dream, a bad present / it is a short, very tired rest."

S E V E N T Y - F I V E

HOUDINI PLANS TO BURY HIMSELF ALIVE

If I were a Freudian, I would suggest as an explanation that your entire professional career is an attempt to escape the maternal uterus. I am tempted."

"Are you a Freudian, Kellerman?"

"I don't think so, Houdini. Above all, I don't think it matters two hoots since for fifty years you've been attempting escapes from the most dangerous traps, jails and bolts that man has conceived and you have grown. I think that aside from your personal motivations, you, sir, are a parable of liberty, and that's what matters to me. That and that you are not bothered by a headless woman when you dream about a new escape. I would like you to view it this way. The mind is a prison, society is frequently a prisonlike structure, and you have proposed the universal escape."

"Are you an anarchist, Doctor?"

"Aren't you, Houdini? Come on, let's drop the etiquette. Tell me, do you feel calmer since you've begun these sessions?"

"I feel bolder, more euphoric. I think I've lost some of my fears. This week I've begun working on a project that's supremely amusing, it is so thrilling."

"Are you going to expose some fraudulent spiritualist? Strip some famous gypsy of his clients and crystal ball, or perhaps some medium like the one you destroyed in Detroit, revealing the tricks with which the spirits were being 'summoned'? I thought that was an inspired moment when you asked them to tie your arms and legs and from inside the wooden box you made bells ring and made the table tremble, produced the classic touches of 'the beyond.'"

"It was simple, Doctor, it wasn't even difficult to make the false shoe. The audience was amused when I exposed the trick, remember? But no, what I've got in mind is more spectacular. Have you ever heard of the Egyptian fakir Rahman Bey? He bases his spectacle on three kinds of action. The very well-known one where he sticks needles in his chest and cheeks. There's not much mystery to that, it's been proven that if you do it with great speed and in areas where there are no nerve endings, it does not produce great pain; what's more, you can help yourself by anesthetizing the affected areas. Tribal magicians have been performing the games of pain for centuries, including much more complicated and harder to explain things. The second part is a series of acts of traditional fakirism, for example, lying down on a bed of nails or on a series of swords. The trick is in the shape of the blades and how sharp they are, as well as the skin's resilience. That doesn't worry me. But his climactic act is more difficult to explain. He enters trancelike into a zinc coffin with soldered junctions; they then bury him in sand and he remains completely interred. He calls it 'Live Death.' The medical specialists say the amount of air wouldn't allow him to breathe for more than fifteen minutes, but he endures over half an hour. Now he's announcing a live burial in the Hudson Bay, with the coffin under water. I think it's possible to re-create it, Kellerman."

"Houdini, how old are you?"

"I just turned fifty-one."

"And it doesn't strike you that these kinds of challenges are not necessary? You are the undisputed number one, nothing can dim your fame."

"Kellerman, if I die in one of these acts, it will be basically due to God's will and my own stupidity in preparing the act. At this point only one thing really worries me. I don't want to run into my mother's ghost inside the coffin once I find myself buried alive. I have the impression, and don't think I haven't studied the issue, that if one loses control of his nerves and allows distress to overcome him, he is dead. Before they manage to disinter him, the air reserve will have disappeared and he will asphyxiate, a terrible way to die."

"I know a couple of colleagues who've been conducting studies on catatonia; it might be interesting for you to talk with them, Houdini. I also know a doctor in Pennsylvania who has been studying respiratory pneumonia."

"I'd appreciate it, Kellerman, but I'm much more worried about the other problem."

"Let's hypnotize you, Houdini, I think I have the cure for your ills. . . ."

S E V E N T Y - S I X

JOURNALISTS' STORIES

(J U L I O   S P E A K S)

Houdini, the genius, left a notebook that Harry Gibson, future author of *The Shadow,* another of my heroes, later made into two small volumes explaining the great magic and escape acts of the Hungarian master. At this strange stage of life, I had three favorite writers: Bertolt Brecht, Houdini and Ortiz-Cardoso (authors of the *Torbellino* comic strip).

But while the *Torbellino* collection and the complete theatrical works of Brecht were on a bookshelf strategically located in the bathroom, Houdini's works had all but disappeared. Greg's call compelled me to search for the two volumes in the library; they had to be hidden in a back row between the books on disasters and the World War II books.

I am a man of obsessions. I cannot live with a quarrel only half resolved, a lost book, an ambiguity in the middle of my soul, a debt with a dry cleaner. I suppose that's what makes me a good reporter, but also an impossible husband. Elena could never forgive my waking up at four in the morning, turning on all the lights and scattering curses right and left, asking her for *The Forest* by Pommeroy or for the state of our joint checking account. In this case, I didn't care one bit if I had to climb halfway up the bookcase to find the two Houdini volumes. I wanted to see something, something I remembered very well.

The bookcase half emptied out, I found it. Inside Volume II, page forty-five, an escape was highlighted, including a few notes I'd taken when I was practicing. If my memory didn't fail me, it had been an obsession a couple of years ago, when I kept dreaming at all hours that I was arrested. I avenged my nightmare studying Houdini's escape methods. And I had practiced conscientiously. Houdini had called it "The escape from the straitjacket." The straitjacket, the traditional enemy of lunatics, the shameful mark of insanity. Perhaps that's why, of all Houdini's escapes, this one had particularly fascinated me. Liberating the madman from his straitjacket. A complete social paradox.

As everyone knows, a straitjacket is an instrument by which the arms are trapped in sleeves much longer than normal, fastened in the back with clasps. Houdini practiced with professional straitjackets fastened by nurses from an insane asylum. I started at age sixteen with my brother's shirts. Houdini dislocated one of his shoulders, lifted his arm over his head and with formidable elbow work could slip his head under his arms, turning the jacket around and working the clasps with his teeth. It was a matter of talent, skill, practice and years of exercise. I wasn't at all bad.

I looked for my straitjacket in one of the old suitcases in the closet. There it was, surprisingly ironed and gleaming. I took it in my hands and left the apartment. My neighbor, Doña Laura, a retired grade-school teacher and fierce Cárdenas activist, was used to this kind of thing.

"Will you fasten it, Laurita?"

"Ay, Julio, one of these days they're going to see you like this and haul you off to the loony bin."

"Fasten the clasps good and tight, Laurita, no tricks to make it easier for me. . . . Now give me a glass of water and I'll see you in a while."

I began to do breathing and concentration exercises. I should have warmed up my muscles before getting into the jacket, but to hurry it along. . . .

I started with the elbows, loosening the pressure and trying to create space for the maneuver. Just as I was starting to work with my head, the doorbell rang. The mailman. Astonished expression.

"Put the letter in my mouth, pal, and I owe you a tip."

I closed the door with my foot, leaving the mailman with the most flustered face I'd seen in my life. Let him learn the complexities of his customers. I started the elbow work again. My joints cracked.

Half an hour later, liberated from the jacket and covered with sweat from head to toe, I read the letter. The reading left me with an expression similar to the mailman's when he saw me in the straitjacket. "Dear Friend" . . . What craziness was this? "The Foundation for Social Sciences of Southern California in collaboration with Stan Laurel's heirs invite to you participate in the 'Pancho Villa' scholarship competition for journalism, carrying an award of sixty-one thousand dollars." It went on to describe the genesis of the award, a joint deposit made by Stan Laurel and my grandfather, Tomás Fernández, established in '47 but misplaced among Stan's inheritance documents. My grandfather and Stan Laurel founding a journalism award! When had they met? An award called "Pancho Villa"! But the insanity didn't end there, it went on. And the subject was the best part: "for a biography constructed with the most innovative techniques of historical reporting about a contemporary Latin American revolutionary figure, a *caudillo,* who would have followed in the footsteps of the Centaur of the North." The selection committee had sent the offer to 100 outstanding journalists on the American continent, but in my particular case, since I was the grandson of the founder of the fellowship-award, they were doubly pleased to have selected my name along with Greg's based on our "brilliant journalistic work carried out in recent years." We had one month to submit an outline, with a brief description of the character, a proposal of how we would write the report, and a description of the techniques to be used in the narrative setup. Sixty-one thousand dollars! Stan Laurel and my grandfather! They said they would respond twenty-five days after the submission of the outlines.

I grabbed the phone, tripping over the straitjacket thrown on the floor, and asked the long-distance operator to find me the number for the Colonial Hotel in Zacatecas. It took half an hour to reach Greg.

He had to have been doing "strange things" because he answered with a voice straight out of a cave.

"You're not going to believe this."

"I'm sure. I don't believe anything. Call me tomorrow, Fats."

"Did you know my grandfather knew Stan Laurel? Shit, Stan Laurel! Now you can stick your Houdini psychiatrist granddad up your ass."

S E V E N T Y - S E V E N

THE OPERATIVE DWARFS . . .

. . .could not wait. Alex couldn't permit the luxury of letting the bureaucratic wars hold back the schedule of Operation Snow White. Therefore, and rigorously following the chronology of the operative part elaborated by Benjamin and approved by Alex, on the first working day of the year, Grumpy-two entered the Banco Internacional, Branch 37, Las Americas, in Mexico City around twelve-thirty and opened an account both in his own name and in Carlos Machado's in which he deposited twenty-seven million pesos. As it was a joint account in the names of Feliciano Valencia and Machado, he put his signature on file and, claiming that Machado was abroad, he requested that they allow him to send Machado the form for signature. These formalities with the branch manager would allow for his clear identification later.

Two days after this, Grumpy-seven, Caucasian and about thirty-five, with an English accent, rented three rooms in the Hotel Florida in the Condesa neighborhood of Mexico City, under the name of the Bancroft Company. The Florida is a second-rate hotel, fairly hospitable and clean, with relatively cheap prices (if the regular Mexico City inflation hasn't changed it, a double room has to be around eighteen dollars a day). Run by the widow of an Austrian businessman who came to Mexico at the end of the Second World War, it is frequented by the provincial middle class who travel to Mexico City on business. Grumpy-four joined him hours later with three suitcases full of electronic surveillance equipment, which they installed in rooms 22 and 23, and whose controls were left in room 25. After testing the equipment, they removed it with the same care with which they'd installed it and disappeared into the anonymity from which they had come. One of the maids might vaguely remember them.

One day after the culmination of the operation in the Hotel Florida, Grumpy-nine, assuming the identity of George Blair, director of relations with Latin America of the Christie Foundation, headquartered in Carmel, California, had an interview with the organizers of the "Guerrilla Warfare, Partisans and Literature Colloquium," and reiterated the offer of full collaboration in the execution of the event, scheduled for June of '89 in Mexico City. This was not the first contact between the College of Mexico and the Christie Foundation; they'd shared copious correspondence over the last six months. Among the multiple details they'd discussed was the foundation's collaboration in the payment of air travel and hotels for the participants and the copublication of the Congress's reports in the U.S. Blair specified that by the laws of his operation, they were required to have a supervisor over the financial transactions, and that therefore, fifteen days before the beginning of the event, a secretary from the foundation would join the team he was organizing to oversee the problems of travel and accommodations, infrastructure, and the payment of invoices, even though the organizational aspects, the carrying out of phone calls and correspondence, the official receptions and the management of the schedule of debates would continue to be the responsibility of ColMex's coordinators (definitely extremely inefficient).

Blair reviewed the invitation list and the letters of formal acceptance. Basically his mission was to confirm two things, which he did, the existence of correspondence establishing participation in the conference of the Bulgarian journalist Stoyan Vasilev, the writer and Sandinista commander Ernesto Luces, and Nicaragua's vice minister of the Interior, Carlos Machado. But he pretended interest in all the participants and remarked about the presence of four Cuban delegates, an Italian who was said to have sympathized with the Red Brigades despite being sixty-eight years old, and an Uruguayan journalist and founder of the MLN-Tupamaros. Blair took advantage of the trip to go out whoring and as a result of a raucous night in the Hotel Presidente Chapultapec contracted a pernicious urinary tract infection.

While Grumpy-nine was jumping on the mattresses of the Hotel de la Avenida Reforma, Grumpy-five arrived in Mexico City on a night flight from Houston, Texas, and, after spending the night in the Benito Juárez Airport Hotel, he caught an Aeronica flight to Managua on a tourist package called "A Week on the Lake." He spent seven days in Managua carrying out the normal activities of just one more North American, with the exception of one day when he called the office of Carlos Machado and after managing to get past his secretary spoke with the vice minister and passed on a message from his friend Lucy Weiss, editor of the *Monthly Review,* who had worked on the English edition of *Nights of Sun, Days of Moon,* Machado's definitive account of the Nicaraguan revolution. Grumpy-five met briefly with Machado in the cafeteria of the Hotel Intercontinental and, on Lucy's behalf, gave him a book of her poems dedicated to the commander, inside which, marking one of the pages, someone had left a receipt for funds deposited in the Banco Internacional of Mexico City. He also gave Machado a copy of the second English edition of his book, and various long cassettes of country music that Lucy had sent him. The conversation lasted scarcely ten minutes. Grumpy-five introduced himself as a grade-school teacher from Iowa sympathetic to the Nicaraguan Revolution. The commander gave him a Sandinista scarf and asked him to bring Lucy the latest signed album of Carlos Mejía Godoy and the boys from Palacaguina.

Two days later, Rolando M. Limas took part in a very peculiar photo session in the city of Puebla. They photographed him on the streets and in the door of the Hotel Meléndez with a three-year-and-a-few-months-old copy of *Excelsior;* no one noticed the age of the paper except Limas himself and Grumpy-eleven, the photographer. Collaborating in the second part of the session was Grumpy-eight, a model of Guatemalan origin named Domingo Reina from the Lane Agency in San Francisco who had worked for the Agency before.

From the day Grumpy-two entered the bank in Mexico City to the day Grumpy-eleven shot the last photos, coincidentally a special group in the SD called "the little friends of the forest" was at work, falsifying seven letters, two postcards and an autograph. The falsification required making postmarks from the Mexican and Nicaraguan post offices, obtaining the appropriate stationery and envelopes, ink and typewriters, all under the vigilance of a "style director."

Alex watched the operations from a distance, confining himself to briefly verifying their fulfillment without great problems. He was very busy thinking about the internal war.

S E V E N T Y - E I G H T

HOW ABOUT A
BULGARIAN LIKE THIS?
(VI)

In Paris, in early 1961, Stoyan walked with Longoria, holding his arm, under a winter sun that gave little warmth. They began their trek at the foot of the Eiffel Tower and continued for hours circling the Trocadero. In a dozen sentences, they covered their careers since they'd last seen each other at the end of '39 in Toulouse, where Longoria had been practicing his recently acquired skills in the fabrication of passports. Stoyan spoke of Montenegro, of the guerrilla war against the Nazis in the Bulgarian mountains, of his arrest in '49, of the two years directing a company in the Valley of Flowers, near Velingrad, overseeing a TKZS that produced the scent of roses. He spoke of his first assignments as a reporter for the BTA.

Longoria briefly mentioned his adventures in the Resistance, the assassination attempts on Franco and little else. The Spaniard noticed his friend was much thinner, but solid, as if the prison years had tightened his muscles and the skin that covered them. Almost at the beginning of the morning, Stoyan confided his plan. He didn't say "I'm going to do this," but rather "I'd like to do this," in such a way that Longoria perfectly understood that "Tank" Vasilev was very clear about what would consume a good portion of his next years. Vasilev found himself obsessed with the loss of Maria and by his new project, and he couldn't perceive the state of excitement that was agitating Longoria. Months later, upon receiving the news of the Spaniard's death at the hands of two gunmen, Stoyan tried to reconstruct that last conversation with his most loyal friend and could only recall his own words, talking about his plan to publish the black book of the Spanish War to an introverted Longoria who was smoking a lot.

The black book contained the list of the NKVD gunmen who had acted against the Internationals by order of Yezhov and Stalin. A list with names, addresses and data that would allow sending them all to hell one day with a .38 bullet in the temple, subject to the people's judgment, without snares, without rigs, without tricks, without show trials or forced confessions. The book that would bring justice to the communists who died in Spain at the hands of their own party's tyrants, Abel's murderers. It was not a rash decision, a sudden burst of hatred produced years after the fact. It was a logical reflection that had slowly settled in Stoyan Vasilev's head, matured during his five years in prison and two in exile, during his later travels as a journalist, his conversations with survivors, and his stay in Nuremburg as an observer of the Bulgarian delegation during the Nazi war crimes trials. It was a settling of accounts among family. He didn't ask for Longoria's help. The sins to be redeemed were not Longoria's; Stoyan asked just that he lend his voice, that he gather information without saying who it was for, and that he keep some papers Stoyan didn't want on his person in Bulgaria. Saturnino responded that it would be better to make Max and Los Angeles the repositories, as he found himself in a very peculiar position. "In precarious times," he said.

"This is not a romantic lark," Vasilev told him with a tone of anguish in his voice. "You know these things aren't. . . . We owe it to the survivors, and to the future survivors. . . . You know what I found?"

"What you knew you'd find. You already knew it, Stoyan, you knew it in Spain."

"That, but worse."

"What are you saying? I have the impression that it was Lenin's fault for going around inviting Iosif Vissarianovich Dzugashvili to have coffee in London."

"What do you know about what happened to the International Brigades after the world war?" Stoyan suddenly asked him.

"What everyone knows, I guess. I worked with a lot of them during the war here in France. Those from the CP were the height of rampant Stalinism, my friend. They were sentimental Stalinists. They were people. And they had balls. I'm talking about people like Marcel Langer, Fabien, Rol-Tanguy and the guys who filled out the FTP."

"Do you know what happened to the Czechs?"

"London and company. The trials."

"And the Hungarians?"

"I know the history of Rajk. They made him out to be an English agent in order to kill him."

"And the Soviets? You know what happened to Gorev? And Koltzov?"

"They were killed before the war."

"Do you know what Stalin's principal accusation against the Yugoslavs was?"

"That from the beginning of the Spanish War they'd worked for the Nazis. What are you trying to tell me, Stoyan? I've read the papers, the stories run. We did not need a small thawing to figure out what was going on. We all know that Stalin killed more Polish communists and more German communists than Hitler did, and if he couldn't kill more anarchists, socialists and Spanish communists than Franco, it's because we lost the war."

Halfway through the morning the two men slowly descended from the past, without managing to firmly plant their feet in the present. It was as though the Bulgarian needed a voice to confirm that the nightmare was real, and an arm to lead him through Paris.

They went into a small restaurant and Vasilev watched Longoria eat two portions of tripe *à la mode de Caen,* refusing to join him. After dessert, they smoked together in silence.

It was Longoria who spoke of Elisa, but Stoyan didn't follow the conversation. The Spaniard wondered whether he should tell his friend of the hunt for him that was going on. But it was all too complicated. He would have had to tell stories in the history of the fifties. Networks of document falsification, the financing of failed attempts on Franco, strongbox robberies, multimillion-dollar frauds, falsification of treasury bonds, bank IOUs, contacts with the underworld, with the Algerians, with the Portuguese revolutionaries who helped rob a transatlantic ship, with the mafiosos who wanted to use their counterfeiting services and who corrupted many of their friends, with scoundrels and rogues of small and great importance, with men of two or three tongues, two- and three-faced men who in the end did not know who their owners were, nor did they even own themselves. And the dodging of the French police force, in which he had a few friends, like the Commissioner Lévi, whose father had been saved from deportation and death in the Nazi camps thanks to documents falsified by Longoria along with the documentation of 650 other Jews; stories of the persecution by the Spanish secret service, who had a good price on his head. Stories of a world of shadows, of nebulous negotiations, of exchanges and games. In these last years, fortunes had passed through his hands that would have made the Aga Khan shake with envy, yet he drank this third-rate Beaujolais and slept in a cot covered with a bearskin blanket, now frayed, which his friend Jean-Paul had taken as a trophy from room 44 of the Hotel Maurice, headquarters of the German command of greater Paris.

How to tell all this at one time? How to explain to Stoyan why he had counterfeited two hundred million francs' worth of the Monaco casino's chips and what he had done with the money? How to explain that part of the money served to corrupt French customs officials and place a ton of gelignite in Spain, while the other part was taken by one of his incidental collaborators, who was probably now talking about the anti-Franco resistance as he lay in the sun on some tourists' beach in Venezuela? How to explain that for months, it was some kind of insane pleasure of his to retain a gang of kids to throw packets of shit at the Spanish Commercial Legation in Angoulême? Or that he had financed Paco Sabate's personal guerrilla war against Franco? How to set up in one go the stories of marvelous characters, human frauds, cynics, adventurers, opportunists, heroes without a cause, obsessed militants, and men stubborn even in defeat, whose false passports had passed through his hands?

Longoria gave up. He limited himself to showing his Bulgarian friend his fingers, yellowed by the handling of acids, and said:

"I'm content. The state has invented bureaucracy, thousands of papers to complicate your life, to make you prove your name, how much money you owe, how many times you've been in jail, where you work, how many houses you own, whether or not you're the father of your children. . . . Rubbish. I invented falsification. The more papers they need, the more false ones I give them. The best men in Spain carry passports signed by Saturnino Longoria. But I think they're closing in. The stuff with the Algerians puts me in bad odor with the French."

"Be careful with that, Longoria. Why don't you move to another country? Latin America . . . ?"

Stoyan stopped seeing the streets of Paris and found himself looking at a street lined with white houses in Cartagena, Colombia, standing near a wall, drenched by sunlight. Not to be outdone, Longoria constructed in his own memory, from a photograph someone had once sent him, the xylophone playing in the arches in front of the Hotel Diligencias in Veracruz.

"What a couple of characters, dreaming about the tropical sun. Aren't we getting old, Longoria?" said the Bulgarian.

"I'll tell you in twenty years, *compadre,* when I have the proper perspective on the matter," the Spaniard answered.

THE VERSION OF EMILIO SALGARI'S *GOOD-BYE TO MOMPRACEM* CREATED BY STOYAN VASILEV IN THE PLEVEN PRISON

I'm sure they're following us,"
Yanez said.

"The famous eyes on the back of your head haven't lost a bit of their keenness over the years," Sandokan responded.

"They get better with age, as fear increases, little brother," the Portuguese answered.

The two characters, led by a Borneo native, the *Dayak* Kompiang, attempted to open a path among the small crowd crammed into the back alleys of the Chinese merchants' section of Singapore.

In 1873, the city was a racial hotbed that was a synthesis of the entire East Asian world under British rule. Ceremonious Parsi merchants, respected for their lawful use of weights and measures, Chinese men with queues, looking distressed and hurried, Malaysian fishermen offering the fruit of their work at dawn, unemployed Javanese sailors, Bengalese water-carriers, small Portuguese and Spanish merchants, Irish bank employees and Muslim office assistants from West India, a muscular *Dayaks* wearing luxurious pants, driving an English lady on her morning shopping trip.

Our friends passed in front of a mosque, a big British spinning mill and a gaming house whose doors were shut awaiting the night, and they penetrated a back alley with dozens of bazaars of the chinese Middle Kingdom. They went through the second door, beneath a sign in Chinese characters that also had small Cantonese and English letters: "Lu's Justice." The owner, a busy Chinese man dressed in a blue cotton jacket, moved around the assistants and, slithering between the barrels of nails and piles of hammers, drills and saws, approached them.

"Distinguished gentlemen, the humble Lu approaches in person to serve you," he said referring to himself in the third person and snapping his fingers. His employees offered the Tigers a pair of chairs set among the ironmongery and the piles of iron cables, barbed wire and tools of the most diverse origins. An adolescent came at once with a service of steaming tea.

"Your store was recommended to us for the fairness of your prices and the quality of your goods," Yanez said, smiling.

"A friend of ours from faraway lands many years ago, from Macao to be precise, said it. He asked us, indeed, not to fail to remind you of the mutual love you two once shared with the White Rose," Sandokan said.

The Chinese man was bewildered, gentle lines of worry appeared at the sides of his eyes. Then, rapidly, he recovered.

"I suppose that the purchase that the gentlemen are considering will be a large one."

"It's like this, we would like you to furnish the tools we need for an important plantation we're going to establish in Borneo; we'd even like you to take permanent charge of the supplying."

"If the distinguished gentlemen would be good enough to follow me to my offices in the back room, it will be easier for everyone to conclude this deal."

And with those words he led the two Tigers toward the inside of the store. The Dayak Kompiang took his place as guard at the door they'd gone through. Not only had the Tigers of Malaysia gotten into the back part of a Chinese shop, they had penetrated the powerful secret societies, the Singapore tongs, subsidiaries of those existing on the Chinese mainland, fortified by the nationalism engendered among the overseas Chinese after the Opium War, who were cruelly persecuted in every British domain. Secret societies in which hatred toward the Europeans, fraternity among its members and, every once in a while, the less than orthodox interests surrounding their criminal or simply commercial practices created a brotherhood beyond blood among its members, large numbers of whom lived along the northern coasts of the Sea of China throughout all the British and Dutch possessions.

"You are not brothers?" the Chinese asked suddenly, filled with suspicion.

"No, we are not. Or rather, one should say we are because our cause is the same, to liberate Asia from the colonial parasites. Do not fear, Lu, you are talking to Sandokan and Yanez de Gomara, the Tigers of Malaysia."

First confusion, then pride shone in the Chinese's eyes.

"But they said you were . . . Mompracem is practically a legend in these lands. . . ."

"We have just come from a long vacation, brother."

"What can I do for you, distinguished gentlemen?"

"Much more than you think, Lu. We are in search of a man, a Javanese, who is detained here in Singapore by the British. He traveled here on a French sailboat, the *Revenge,* that must have made its port of call in the harbor a year ago, perhaps a little before that. He was accused of robbery and turned over to the British authorities. He's a kid, about twenty-five years old, named Malang. We must find him."

"It will be relatively simple for me, gentlemen. I will get busy on the job at once," the Chinese said, holding his hand out to the two characters.

Sandokan was the first to stretch out his, gently pressing his index finger on the pulse of the Chinese man's wrist, the gesture of fraternal recognition among members of the White Rose tong. Yanez did the same.

A few minutes later, the two Tigers found themselves in the midst of the bustle of the back alleys looking for a place to eat a formidable rijsttafel, which had been highly recommended to them.

"I regret having to inform you that we are being followed, little brother," Yanez said.

"Who is it?"

"I get the feeling there are two of them; one of them is wearing the native Ganges turban, the other is a small Malaysian who can't be more than fifteen years old. Do we have some debt to pay in these lands?"

"It's been six years since the death of the Raja Brooks de

Sarawak and since the East Indies Company went under. Our deeds have long been unheard of so far west of the archipelago, and our old enemies have to have died by now either from boredom or old age. Though you never know, little brother. Our names still invoke fear, and fear invokes hatred and old memories of vengeance. What's more, we can still make certain hearts seethe . . . and doubtless a few Victorian mansions as well. Be careful, Yanez, the Empire does not forgive."

"I think it's a couple of petty thieves. Hold tight to your purse and forget about it," Yanez said. Ignoring Sandokan's gloomy mood and smiling, he went into the small restaurant, where after offering the owner a couple of silver coins they were received as if they owned the Chinese section of Singapore.

It was afternoon by the time they left the restaurant, after having polished off the famous sixty dishes from the "table of rice" that featured dozens of varieties of sauces, *babi ketjap,* spicy *sambal goreng,* meats from monkey brains to baby goat ribs with peanut sauce, moving on to a fish fillet in coconut sauce, seasoned pig's skin, prawns in arrack liqueur, peanut *rudjaks,* all accompanied by plenty of very white, seasoned rice. The meal transpired in almost total silence with the exception of the flattery lavished on the delicacies of Sumatran cuisine by the Portuguese and a brief comment from Sandokan that did not merit a response from his companion because he answered himself.

"And if the Polish countess died in New Caledonia after all? The fever, the climate, exhaustion, a failed attempt to flee, the rifles of a French firing squad. . . . Of course, it doesn't matter, we would still be doing justice to an unlucky love. Our whole life has been filled with this kind of love, little brother."

Upon leaving, Yanez started to yawn and was interrupted by Sandokan.

"I know what you're going to say, that at our age we should take a siesta and meditate about the next steps. You would therefore like to go to Albert Road and look for a small, inviting hotel. . . . I regret having to do the contrary; I don't like the fact that we're being followed one bit, we're going back to the *Vengador* and wait for news from our friend Lu."

"I didn't open my mouth."

"Yes you did, to yawn . . ."

The discussion went no further, because at the mouth of the alley, four Malaysians appeared, their krisses unsheathed.

"Kompiang, cover our backs," the Tiger of Malaysia said quickly. "Me, Yanez!"

The Portuguese did not need his blood brother's call; seeing the Malaysians who were charging them, he took a Colt Baby Dragoon from inside his official navy blue uniform and fired off a shot at the first man's chest. Sandokan had extracted an Unwin pistol-knife from the pocket of his sarong and shot without aiming; the bullet went wild. The surviving attackers, ignoring their fallen comrades, ran toward the Tigers ready for a hand-to-hand fight. Sandokan stopped one of them, ripping the sleeve of his shirt with his knife and pushing him against the wall of a store. Meanwhile, Yanez demolished the second man with another shot from his Colt, though he couldn't stop the man's kris from ripping into his pants, wounding his thigh superficially. The fourth, a one-eyed man with a ferocious look, seeing himself at a disadvantage against the Portuguese's automatic, started to run away.

"Don't shoot, Yanez, he's mine," Sandokan yelled, thinking that his friend was going to end the fight by shooting the man he was facing. Sandokan was making circles with his knife and, in spite of the length of his enemy's kris, kept him pinned to the wall, up against a bamboo drainpipe. The Tiger's face shone with jubilation. The last of the characters who'd attacked them, a very young Malaysian in dirty rags, couldn't take his eyes off the pistol-knife. But Sandokan unleashed a tremendous blow to his head with his left hand and the boy stopped watching the knife and fell as if struck by lightning.

"Kompiang, take him on your shoulder and make for the port at once. Take the dark streets, the alleys. Will you be able to do it? We'll meet in front of the *Vengador*. If somebody asks you, say it's one of your mates who had too much to drink."

"Of course, *tuan,*" said the *Dayak*, carrying out his order right away.

"How are you, Yanez?" Sandokan asked the Portuguese, who was studying one of the fallen, the one he'd reached with the point of his knife, who was writhing in pain from the bullet in his shoulder.

"I shouldn't have eaten so much, I've got a knot in my stomach," answered Yanez de Gomara, the legendary white Tiger of Malaysia.

EIGHTY

THE PROMISED BIOGRAPHY OF CARLOS MACHADO, MACHADITO, WITH EVERYTHING, INCLUDING THE HOLES

He is eating sherbet at the door of a theater and someone says, "Look, that's your dad." He watches the man walk by as if he were no one, as if he didn't exist, as if he were someone else, somebody else's. Years later, in Mexico, he'd become nervous when someone joked: "That one's the son of the milkman." He was the son of a nonexistent milkman. The fugitive milkman, the unknown milkman, like the unknown soldier of the monuments.

He is watching television at a friend's house and he silently watches the empty bayonet caps of the Garand guards bounce up and down and there are hundreds of those assholes attacking a house where one single man is holding them at bay, screwing them with just one M3, and the TV shows that a man is made of balls alone and that one single Sandinista is as good as three tanks, an artillery-armed light aircraft and two companies of the Guard, and even though they kill Julio Buitrago and they don't just kill him, they kill him completely, he's already gone to Paradise forever, and he took us all with him to where he wanted, because if they die this way, for what they believe, for the country they believe is possible, he is the truth and we all fit into him; give me a gun too, to go with Julio to where there is no return.

He is sad and reads other people's poems because he doesn't have the knack for writing them. Poems of love with a pinch of hate, with a pinch of rage, passed from hand to hand, because in Nicaragua you can't publish a book; poems worn by readers who memorized every word by heart and therefore even though the pages were used to clean up children's excrement, the poems would never ever be lost. Poems by Cardenal that say things no one had ever said to him and that he could never say to Yolanda lest he die of awkwardness, but even though you cannot say them, it doesn't take away in the slightest that you feel them.

He is exhausted and just when he thinks he could never be more tired, not one more muscle could hurt, he twists another tendon he didn't previously have, he didn't know was there, and from so much lifting and lowering crates of fruit in the market, for a lousy twelve cordobas, the new tendon reappears and is cramping, sending lazy signals to his head. He is exhausted and he smiles because he is learning biology, the class he failed so miserably in grade school. He swears he will never again eat an orange. He retracts his promise, takes one from his pocket and eats it while every swollen muscle in the world aches, including his own.

He is proud because his semen jolted twenty inches, and there's the stain if anyone doubts it, and those defeated and ashamed in the masturbation competition didn't come close to even fourteen inches measured by scholastic regulation. Proof that one can lift himself from the floor at some sixty years and take life further, and go farther in life and take life much farther, much farther beyond, to the last stars. The last ones, after the final ones.

He is marvelously happy surrounded by kids like him, exactly like him, absolute brothers, intoxicated by their fraternity and drunk with joy because the Front recruited them and now, from that alone, they are better and unique and they will die as no one dies anymore, like in the movies no one makes anymore, of pure and free patriotism, Sandinistas down to their fingernails. Better yet, they won't die and they will win the war to see and love the image that will be there. The Plaza on the day of victory. And then, it might not go as far as that, but that's later.

He is sad because death is a roulette wheel of colors searching for a number and it kills the one next to you without notice, without warning. But he remembers a stanza of a poem by

Rugama, a poem that was not poetry when it said: "May your mother surrender, you son of a whore!" And now they go around making poetry out of those lines, in a nation that won't offer anything more than pure dictatorship, a sick nation, and when it trembles, the dictator's limousine arrives and gathers up the remains to sell them in a surplus market somewhere else in the world.

He is scared to death when he raids a liquor store and a shot flies from his pistol and shatters two bottles of *guaro* and what's more his boss is pissed because a bullet is a bullet and it's not as if there were many, every one costs blood, and what's more a friend sends him out whoring again because he blew two bottles of *guaro* to shit and in the final revolution, those bottles of *guaro* would belong to the people, and you, asshole, go around shooting them to bits. But the fear has passed. I will be back, don't worry.

He is sick and the fever is a different kind of fever, not our fever, and he feels like an Indian infected with smallpox by the Spanish, an idiotic kid trapped by an unexpected whooping cough who can't go out in the sun, can't seize the morning to get sixteen thousand hits off the pitcher on the mound in front of him.

He is eating a pizza on Vedado Street in Havana, Cuba, and he misses the Mexican street tacos that he had just before pizza and a little after salted pretzels on a short walk through the mountains. But of all the things he misses most, it is other people fighting for him.

He is listening to the drums of Monimbo and he knows that when the people rise, others should tremble, and there are three Sandinistas for every thousand rebels. Then he discovers that curious relationship between The Vanguard and the vanguard and The People and the people and the place one holds is just one of many and one wins every day and not because one's leader tells one to, and he teaches three boys smaller than he is to build a barricade. The tanks arrive, the sweaty hands on the Garand rifle and the guard who steps out of the jeep collapses with his stomach perforated and two women applaud the marksmanship from a window and they are almost sent straight to heaven by a shell from the tank. It's important to remember here that the nation is a thing that does not exist, and at best, if it should exist, abruptly revived by indigenous drums and encompassing us all, it is what gives order to our lives. One must also remember all that one learned in that manual of the war between classes, and above all, the gunsight, the bullet in the chamber, is that we are everyone and they are very few, but those sons of bitches are well armed. Almost. We have the drums on our side.

He is furious because in the hideout he's stuck in, someone has pissed on him during the night out of shame, shyness, bad aim, and mostly because he didn't want to turn on the light. With comrades like that, who needs enemies?

He is happy again on the mountain. He taught an old woman to read. There is no ceiling. Freedom belongs to him who stretches out his hand, touches the air, hears the birds, and let them come for us and they'll see, we'll fuck them with our pants down around our knees and off balance. He is happy because the woman whom he taught to read, with her crooked and spiderlike handwriting, wrote the words of Sandino. He is happy because if he could teach a little grandmother how to read in forty-seven days, the totally impossible revolution was totally possible. You have to be blind not to see, illiterate like those before, not to believe.

He is hopelessly in love with a young girl who dissolves him into her smile and melts him inside, and he wastes his pellets of buckshot on early-morning guard duty. They take them away from him and give him advice about how he shouldn't let the cartridges get fucked in the humidity.

He is convinced he's gotten old and it's because he's not standing on his native ground, he's walking through Costa Rica, organizing an arms dispatch which is absolute insanity and which the devil should have organized. He feels old at twenty-two, and then Tomás Borge tells him of Fonseca, he tells him stories after stories of Fonseca, what he saw, what he believed, how he was sure, how he died at war, how he was killed so that he wouldn't still be with us, how he was so convinced. And then he feels diabolically young, and he feels that Fonseca was the father he never had, and sadly has also disappeared, and he discovers that as always, Somoza, the tyrant, is to blame.

He is reading a note he received two months late and he has already read six times and he continues not wanting to understand the words telling him that far from where he is, Paula has been killed. And he'll never understand. Never. Paula is on vacation in other mountains. She'll come back when we move into Managua.

His heart is frozen and, as hard as he tries to explain the sensation to Omar Cabezas, so that one day he can write about it, he does not explain well. Words are practically useless, he says to himself. All the times he tried to explain something and couldn't, all the times he tried to explain what was going on and couldn't. All the times his heart froze and he couldn't make himself understand. If they kill him now he'll take a vacation to the same mountains where Paula is. A man with a frozen heart makes a poor job of revolution, Eduardo Contreras explains a month later in Costa Rica. He decides to postpone his death to the last minute after victory.

He is reading Che and discovers that everything has already been said before and better. He discovers that one's life is worthwhile only if it is lived for everyone.

He is lost in the streets of León, but the Guards are more lost than he is, because they don't know where the guy going backward is going, nor whether they know, even if without knowing, the one who's going forward. He laughs at his thoughts. The revolution unfreezes the heart. Paula is still in the mountains. Please don't let the bullet fail as I sometimes do. Angels have very good aim.

He is looking at the others and sees that they are us.

He is mad with glee as the bells in Estelí chime, and through the streets the red and black flags appear. On the radio, an announcer close to hysteria repeats endlessly that the dictator has taken a map and fled. He chides his boys because they fire bursts into the air. Crazy bastards, we already won, don't go killing angels. Don't go grazing with a .30-caliber Paula, who smiles down on us from the mountaintop, where she always knew the revolution would take victory by surprise.

He is confused and doesn't know how to respond when they name him chief of police in León. He has always had the feeling that in the eternal division of life, he should always be on the side of the thieves. He feels guilty and remembers that in 1962 he snatched a gold lighter through a broken window of a parked car.

He is reading a book a day and that's why he doesn't sleep. He does a lot of other things. A triumphant revolution is the realest shit, the most truly fucked thing he has ever seen. Is there no charitable person who will send him back to guerrilla war?

He is delivering a speech to a litter of pups of the EPs and feels it is someone else talking. Since when does he know so much? When did he learn it? Who the fuck put him behind a microphone in a position of leadership?

He is seated on the bed and is quite happy, because when they arrived with the paper he thought they were kidding him, but no, there on the front page was the photo of a smashed automobile.

The Argentinian comrades had blown up Somoza's ass with an RPG, sending him back to the whore who gave birth to him. Let's see if this time Somoza would learn not to walk the streets, that the streets belong to kids playing ball, not to fucking dictators.

He stands before a mirror and doesn't recognize himself. He is someone else. He hasn't slept. He just finished the manuscript of the book in which he tries to recount what happened. As everything changed, a person changed. He's sure to spend the next ten years revising the manuscript only to end up trashing it, but it doesn't matter. Someone wrote it. It wasn't written by itself. He stands before a mirror and doesn't recognize himself. His name is Carlos, he is a Sandinista commander, he is still alive. He is the same and he is someone else. Time doesn't pass in vain, he says to himself.

E I G H T Y - O N E

ALEX FELT . . .

. . . a premonitory shudder in the bones of his spinal column and instead of attributing it to the New York winter chills, he didn't hesitate to blame the headhunters inside the Agency who wanted to use his scalp as a lampshade.

The information Leila had offered that morning confirmed his suspicions. It was the damned Libyans of the Agency, division UN, the worshipers of the Koran who wanted his head. They spent so much on their obsession with killing Gadhafi that they needed to clean the turf out of budget competition. He opted for alliance and not for an indirect attack. If he started littering the halls of Langley with dead bureaucrats, everyone would lose. He picked up the phone and dialed Virginia.

"Nicholson. Alex. Free line."

"Nicholson," said a voice on the phone.

"I propose a deal for you, boy. You leave Snow White alone and I work for you the entire second semester of eighty-nine. Subordinate to the General facade, ghostwriter."

A brief silence on the other end of the line. Finally the voice said: "Put it in a memo. 'At your petition, and further to our previous discussion, believing you can contribute, you would like to . . .' "

"Done. I'll study geography starting tomorrow."

"Welcome to the Mediterranean, Alex."

"The world's most polluted sea, they say. . . ."

The voice let loose a loud guffaw. Alex hung up. Sons of the great bitch. He'd settle accounts with them soon enough.

"I want to travel to Mexico tonight or tomorrow. I need to see Peter and Pan up close. Are they in Mexico?"

"I'll confirm it in a second, Alex," Leila said, leaving the room.

"No more distractions," Alex said to himself.

EIGHTY-TWO

HOUDINI IN ACTION

On August 5, 1925, Kellerman was one of the expert witnesses, together with several doctors, dozens of reporters, off-duty waiters, maids, employees and gate-crashing spectators who attended Houdini's exhibition at the pool of the Sheraton Hotel.

For effect, Houdini had constructed a galvanized iron coffin six and a half feet long and twenty-two and a half inches wide, the same dimensions the Egyptian fakir had used. Wearing only a pair of black bathing trunks and with a tense face that showed his worry, after allowing the doctors to take his blood pressure and heart rate and measure the normal number of breaths per minute, he began a series of respiratory exercises to fully oxygenate himself.

The coffin was connected to a telephone line and an alarm buzzer outside. Houdini got in. From inside he directed a look of complicity and a sad smile toward Dr. Kellerman. The coffin was sealed, and a small crane deposited it on the bottom of the pool. The official count began. The time was announced every five minutes. An emergency team comprised of lifeguards in gray swimsuits kept watch attentively. Collins, one of Houdini's assistants, was riveted on the buzzer and the phones. Never had a greater silence been heard at the Sheraton pool. Kellerman smoked one cigarette after another, but stopped short of flicking the ashes in the pool, letting them pile up in the pockets of his jacket together with the cigarette butts he put out in the water with a light hiss.

The experts had pointed out that the volume of breathable air in the coffin offered enough oxygen to last approximately twenty minutes. The Egyptian had remained inside for an hour. The minutes passed. At one hour and fifteen minutes, the telephone rang. The crowd stood on its tiptoes. Collins spoke to Houdini for a few moments, then briefed the reporters. He looked worried. Though the coffin was leaking inside, Houdini did not consider himself in danger. The count was called out every thirty seconds. At an hour and a half, Houdini called again from inside the coffin at the bottom of the pool. He asked them to take him out. The coffin was rapidly withdrawn from the pool's floor and opened. Houdini appeared to a thunder of applause. He looked emaciated, his face and body wet, what little hair he had stuck to his cranium, his eyes vacant. He gave off an enormous aura of exhaustion. The thermometer that was inside the coffin showed 100.4 degrees Fahrenheit; that was the highest temperature inside for the hour and a half he'd endured the challenge.

His blood pressure had lowered to 42 from the more than 80 it had been when he entered the water; his pulse on the other hand had increased to 120 from the 84 he had had upon beginning his live burial.

As the applause continued, Houdini gave his first statement to the press:

"There is no trick. If one diminishes corporal movements, respiration stabilizes, anxiety is annulled, oxygen requirements are much lower than in normal situations. Obviously one has to maintain tight control over one's nerves; if anxiety is allowed to dominate, respiration accelerates, the heart rate increases, and if one succumbs to desperation, the air reserve can be exhausted within minutes. I hope this experience can be useful to miners trapped below the earth. As you see, it is not necessary to be a fakir to bury oneself alive."

As the crowd yelled "Houdini," and the murmur began to spread through the halls of the hotel, reaching all those who had not been allowed in the pool area, the escape artist addressed Kellerman.

"A success, Doctor. My mother appeared, but with her head on, everything. She told me: 'I'm taking care of you, son.' This made everything easier."

Houdini and Kellerman grabbed each other's hands in a firm handshake.

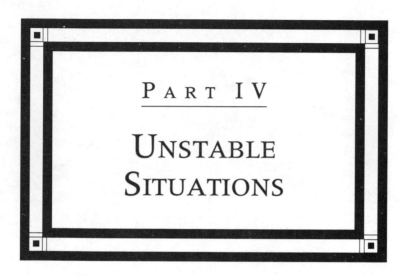

PART IV

UNSTABLE SITUATIONS

MAD DOG ONTIVEROS'S DEALS/GRINGO

Mad Dog Ontiveros enters a cantina on López Street, named for someone as anonymous as one could be with a last name that covered twenty-seven pages in Mexico City's phone directory. He looks cautiously at the faces of the characters hanging around there. He doesn't like familiar faces. He makes good on the saying: "Better to look carefully there than die there." Those with debts are particularly zealous in checking that there are no collectors on their backs.

He orders a double tequila and does not drink it in one swig; today is not a day for drunkenness. It's for recognizance of the terrain, verification of the stability of the borders prior to business. So he savors the tequila. He certainly doesn't pay for it.

He had to have the second one in La Flor de Toluca, a smaller bar with a jukebox that only plays the popular songs of Cuco Sánchez and José Alfredo Jiménez, the majority of them masterfully interpreted by Miguel Aceves Mejía, on Victoria Street, near an electronics establishment. He won't pay for the tequila there either but in exchange he'll drop a hundred pesos to play *"La Cama de Piedra"* and hum along softly through his teeth. A drunk restaurant owner will invite his neighbors to a few rounds with a wad of bills he pulls from his pants. Mad Dog evaluates the potential of the deal. He discards it because he's got bigger things down the road.

He will lay off the tequila, exchanging it for *chocolate con churros* when he sits down with the gringo in a Chinese café on Dolores Street. Big business will require abstinence. He and the gringo know each other so they greet each other with a double *abrazo,* one side, then the other. They are old business acquaintances, the best kind. The kind that don't flip out (at least not frequently) when it's time to get down to business.

"I need two guys whose hands don't tremble, Attorney Ontiveros. Good ones," the gringo will say in English. Ontiveros, who has never gone to law school and who Frenchifies himself at least to someone listening, because he was "Judas in the Kingdom," a judicial cop in the border town of Reynosa, will see the way to move this deal along in his native tongue mixed with that of the North.

"Good, good?" Ontiveros will ask, dunking a *churro* in the *chocolate.*

"Good, even if they're expensive," the gringo will say, who's not deaf and understands.

"Lezama?" Ontiveros will ask, alluding to a mutual acquaintance who worked for the governor of Sinaloa years ago, and even rose to be local chief of police.

"No, I want lesser-known people. Those guys have too many friends, they talk a lot of shit," the gringo will say. He knows Lezama has too many open contacts on the border and talks too much.

"Someone from Los Reyes," Ontiveros will suggest.

"Will you vouch for them?" the gringo will ask, no fool.

"Vouch for, whatever vouch for means," Ontiveros will say, refusing to put his ass on the line for a couple of crazy pricks who shoot first, ask questions later.

"Give me someone else."

"I can get Pecas out of jail for a night, lend him to you, you use him and return him."

The gringo will consider the option seriously. A murderer in for fifty years at the Eastern Prison is not a bad idea. He hesitates. Pecas is perhaps a little taller and blonder than Machadito. Ontiveros will follow the gringo's thoughts and read the doubt in his eyes. He'll offer an alternative:

"El Renco. That's it. Am I right?"

The gringo will agree practically without thinking about it. "Is he around?"

"I heard he was in Puebla doing a deal, but he's around now, I saw him yesterday."

"Okay, El Renco, and keep Pecas in reserve just in case," the gringo will say, closing the deal.

"You're set with one?"

"For now, yes."

Both of them will remain there thinking about the hit man from Oaxaca. Neither will say a word about what they both remembered. Ontiveros will ask for $2,000 for the mediation, the gringo will offer a million and a half pesos in advance and a couple more million if it comes out well. Breadcrumbs. The two must have been quite aware that in this case they were trading favors, not deals.

Now it's about finding something out. The bigger deal. That's why Mad Dog's a bride, not a bridesmaid. Because he knows (and he never read it in Marshall McLuhan) that information is of value on the market.

"Will you speak to him for me? I want him available the first few days of June."

"How much should I offer?"

"Five million. And here's a good deal for you. Have you heard of Oidmo, a Japanese importer, located on Alvaro Obregón 110 on the first floor, manager of a Los Angeles Nisei store named Aoyama? Half is plastic from Hong Kong, the rest is coke."

For that, the Mexican cop would have been off the hook and, proving that he is not stupid, would have taken careful note of the date. And calculating at once how much he could make off the crook in what the accountant could enter as protection.

"We'll split it fifty-fifty," the cop will offer.

"We're friends," the gringo will say. "I'm happy with twenty-five."

After that, nothing less than a farewell bear hug, the moment when the gringo will slip his envelope in the pocket of Ontiveros's bag. Then goodbye and we don't know each other until next time.

That, for appearances, because Ontiveros, alias Mad Dog, on his way out of the Chinese café, very probably will point to the gringo with a tilt of his jaw and have two underprivileged guys from his group trail him night and day on shifts. Because friends we are, but there's work to do. . . .

JOURNALISTS' STORIES

(G R E G   S P E A K S)

Magic Johnson hid the ball from Hansen and slipped below the backboard, gently depositing it in the basket. I clapped furiously, to Julio's consternation, because after having gone to all the trouble in the world to find a friend with cablevision, Julio was watching the Boston Celtics succumb to the Los Angeles Lakers.

Fats says his basketball tastes are more fringe than mine. I am a fan of a team of black players, he is a fan of a team with three whites in a sport where there are increasingly fewer.

Larry Bird sank a three-pointer and Fats threw me to the floor with a slap on my back.

"Did you see that, asshole, they're still alive."

"Deceased, brother, that's the rattle of death, even though they can still move a little."

As if to prove me wrong, Robert Parish stole the ball from Cooper and, with two dribbles and a jump, he practically broke the hoop, leaving the backboard vibrating.

"I suspect you're going to have to switch to Pepsi Light. I'm going to vomit just from watching you drink that. . . . Pepsi Light, and without rum, ugh," Fats said, beaming. I distanced myself a few inches, he was not going to give me another hand slap.

We had bet that the loser had to give up alcohol for one month, and I began to doubt the supreme confidence with which I'd made the bet, though at that moment Kareem Abdul-Jabbar, who'd been particularly erratic in the whole first quarter, managed to score a marvelous skyhook, leaving the Celtics staring at the hoop, stupefied.

"Look at that, they're like *mensos,*" I said, using the Spanish word for idiots.

I loved the word *menso,* it had a very special sonority. Of the ton of Mexicanisms introduced into my life, the insults, bland and harsh, the most interesting in my new personal dictionary were without doubt: *mensos, babosos, pendejos, mamones, mamadores, mascapitos, culeros, mandilones, nopales, putetes, tarados, ojetes.*

We had made a pact to leave our strange business aside during the game, and until now we'd managed to do so. Basketball was a very serious thing, much more serious than other trivial affairs. I held to the maxim that human tribes divide themselves into nationalists and thieves, primitive Christians and raging Calvinists, Muslims and neo-Stalinists, Sandinistas and Jews, Gadhafi fanatics and Lakers fans. I belonged to the latter. It struck me as politically much safer; it produced less disenchantment than traditional doctrines. In theory. Until now, when, after a spectacular drive, they seemed to be losing the game's rhythm. Cooper missed a three-pointer from ten yards away, Kareem lost the rebound and the Celtics were on a brilliant counterattack, sparks flying in battle, culminating in a layup by Bird, who, after flying around over the hoop, swooped down, giving them two more points. Fats howled like a wolf. I started to think about the thankless possibilities of Pepsi Light and almost had a coughing attack.

The NBC announcer, no doubt some white guy from the East Coast, said: "Bird makes things happen." The camera lingered on the criminal face of Robert Parish, and Ainge had just stolen the ball and cleanly sunk a three-pointer. The future was becoming frankly revolting.

At the end of the third quarter, the Lakers were losing 87 to 83. Fats took two beers from his friend's refrigerator and left an IOU for 100 pesos in their place. That's what I loved about Fats, he was always prepared to make amends for abuses, his own and others'.

"What do you think?" he asked, taking advantage of the commercial breaks.

We had already spoken some about the matter. It didn't sound bad. Absurd, yes, but not bad.

"We'd have to make a list of possible candidates. . . . According to the ground rules, it has to be someone alive. My Mexican contemporary history is not in good shape, but I don't see anyone quite right."

"Me neither, I'm more inclined to go with a Nicaraguan or a Cuban."

"Omar Cabezas would be good but he's already writing stories. What do you think about Borge? Too well known, right? Machadito would be good. I like Henry Ruiz."

"And a Venezuelan? Douglas Bravo, for instance."

"I know very little about that."

"A Chilean? Pascal Allende. . . ."

"It'd cost us a fortune to get down that far. Plus there are the secrecy problems. If you ask me, I'd say a Nic."

"Okay then, a Nic," Fats said and he turned up the volume on the TV.

In ten seconds, Magic Johnson threw a sixteen-yard pass to Green and the Lakers sank two points. I rubbed my hands together.

E I G H T Y - F I V E

MAX'S PHOTO ALBUM

For the benefit of his own memory, the man born in New York, Max Kerrigan Lewis, known during his acting career in Hollywood as Max Lewis and back to Kerrigan in the final years of his life in Los Angeles, had arranged his existence in a photo album. He had arranged it in such a way that when he died, the album would wind up in the garage sale of some distant relative and would fall into the hands of someone intelligent enough to decipher the story, and therefore the sense of history, the reasons and the dishonesty of life.

He, Max, would not have been able to decipher the meaning of Max Lewis's life, but he knew it was there, hidden in the album of photos and clippings, in that apparently chaotic structure of elements in disarray.

The album began with a glorious nude shot of Max, showing

his sex to the onlookers, at the age of four and a half months. A chubby, bald baby with dimples in his cheeks.

It continued with a photograph of his International Brigades card, which had hung for years in the New York Lincoln Brigade veterans' office. Then three pages of rose petals covered in cellophane so that they wouldn't dissolve into rose dust upon contact. What a great title for a song, "Rose Dust," with Max Lewis on the piano. Too bad Max didn't play piano and the song would never be composed.

Several pages of photos of a teenager dressed as a cowboy followed. In 1926, for a young Irish boy from Brooklyn, three pages of cowboy photos were the least he could concede to his own craziness.

Max had entered films as a solitary cowboy, through the back door of the MGM studios in 1934. His first role was as a good pirate in *Treasure Island,* in which Wallace Beery played a brilliant Long John Silver, as drunk as the character himself. The album extensively documented the event.

Two pages of press clippings followed on the founding of the industry's photographers' union, in which Max had been very active, though in fact he was a mere apprentice to a camera assistant.

If we believe that photographs don't lie, we find in the first pages of the album a portrait of a smiling youth, eating ice cream on the corner of Hollywood and Vine, that seems to say Max had reached the mid-1930s disposed to prove himself a man without limits. He acted, he was an assistant to a photographer, he wrote (though his first three screenplays never got beyond the first step), and he believed the world of film was a space where borders were stretched, where impossible stories were told, where the mythical and pure side of the North American conscience unfolded. It was much better to work in dreams than in nightmares, he told himself.

The album also contained the crumpled *Playbill* featuring his adaptation of Upton Sinclair's *The Bronze Check,* paper napkins with lipstick prints, a hard and yellowed press clipping from the *Hollywood Reporter.*

Memory albums are quick. A viewer should know that to capture the life, one should turn the pages slowly, observing each detail, allowing the necessary time to compress the life. Otherwise, the succession of pictures and clips seems to be just a collection of unconnected acts, without vitality.

Max carefully tended to that peculiar detail. He included every possible sample, every testimony, even if it seemed insignificant: a grocery receipt from the 1930s, the corner of a gnawed handkerchief, the page of a telephone book.

There's a ton of signed Laurel and Hardy photographs. They bore witness to his contributions as the Bengalese lancer and handsome gypsy in *Bonnie Scotland* and *The Bohemian Girl,* and Max finally reappeared as a cowboy in an MGM production in early '36 called *The Robin Hood of El Dorado* directed by William Wellman. Though at that time that may not have signified triumph.

The photos from Spain broke away from the epic. He'd chosen blurry Polaroids, anodyne group shots, friends in uniform sharing a jug of red wine. Max roaming the Plaza Mayor of Madrid, or staring dumbfounded before the lions in the Plaza de la Cibeles or the Puerta de Alcalá. There were pictures of Stoyan and Longoria, pictures of the three pals in a trench outside the Casa de Campo. Too much glory, too much emotion for the photos to do them justice. They were humble photos of guys who were passing through destiny luckily. There were photos of the Scottish poet McDonald, walking over the ruins of a bombarded house in Barcelona, and photos of Stoyan conversing with an Italian deserter after the Battle of Guadalajara.

Later in the album the postcards with daisies began to appear. And in the middle of them, a photo of a young boy, dressed in a black striped suit on a street in Paris, Laurent, a companion, a friend, a platonic lover with whom to heal the Spanish wounds, as he, a young photographer, made him discover Paris through the viewfinder during the months before the war exploded and he decided to return to the States.

It was Max's fault that the relationship had been platonic. No doubt about it. And the Parisian photo summed up some of the desolation of incomplete loves. Had Max been in love with Laurent? The photo was there, forever, to try to help him answer the question.

There was extensive proof in the album of how upon his return to the States, Max regained his place in the industry, working, curiously, in Sherlock Holmes movies, the series starring Basil Rathbone and Nigel Bruce. Max was not just coscreenwriter but also got a cameo as a cop in some of the movies. Max enjoyed those years and the photos have the festive tone of a world that seems inviolable in the midst of another world, which was crumbling. Rathbone, Bruce and Max looking at a Greek parchment. Max with Sherlock Holmes's immortal pipe, Max with the puppet who did the gorilla of Sumatra, Max with the special effects man, both of them surrounded by black widow spiders, Max decked out as a cowboy drinking coffee with Sterling Hayden dressed as a London bobby. Max testing the gallows of the London executioner with his neck.

The document that follows in the album seems like the continuation of the previous photograph. It is the paper that turns Max down for the service upon his reentry to the United States during the war. The assessment of "premature antifascist" now seems like a joke. Max doesn't want to forget. He'd first crumpled it up in an attack of fury, but then he'd ironed it out so as to leave the testimony in his album.

There are two years missing. Then a war told with photographs. Not an actor's story, but the story of a witness. With Hemingway in London taking photos of the exhausted Spitfire pilots during the Battle of Britain for *Life* magazine. Insurgent Paris. A passport photo falsified by Longoria in that absurd failed attempt to flee to the Bulgarian mountains and join the patriots.

More gaps in the album. It would seem as though Max's story was a stammering return to normalcy which never ended up being normal. Hollywood reappears, but with less glamor now. Photos of reunions, a new friendship and, if the eyes of the actor holding Max by the arm don't lie, a new platonic love.

There's a curious nude shot of Carole Lombard, never circulated publicly and not even included in the actress's personal photo collection. It was taken by Max during a shoot when, as she spoke of tennis and Gogol novels, Carole undressed to change her clothes. She wasn't wearing underwear. Noticing Max's confusion, the woman looked at him with a faint smile and said: "I wouldn't have done it if I thought it would bother you." Max took the picture unexpectedly. She smiles elegantly.

And suddenly the album is lively again, the photos tell a social history in minute detail. Max the character blurs with Max the photographer. The trial of the Hollywood Ten, Bogart speaking into the microphone of a radio station. The mobilization of the cinematographers' community faced with the aggression of the witch hunters. Howard Fast testifying before the Senate subcommittee. Max seated at the bar of the Ritz in New York having a drink with Dalton Trumbo, both with the fatigued faces of defeat;

one day later Trumbo would be jailed. A UPI photo in which Max is seen being arrested by two stout uniformed police trying to beat up Sterling Hayden.

There is one page with nothing but the prison lending library card. Absurd photos follow, having to do with survival stories mixed with receipts, newspaper clippings that recount the times when he was a traveling knife salesman in Oklahoma, a ghostwriter for soap operas, signed with a pseudonym, and, covering just half the page, photographs of children.

The return to the industry, after thirteen years of exile, shows Max collaborating in the wardrobe selection for *Spartacus*. There's no sense of victory, just return, concentrated professional work. The tears, if there were any, remain hidden in photographs not taken.

Max refrained from including photos from the year of his black depression. There is no proof of his insanity. Just a few photographs of a supermarket cash register showing him with a face more drawn than usual, his chin slightly fallen. There is not one photo of the hospital where he was shut away.

Invitations to the past twenty-five Oscar ceremonies are in the album. In the last ten years, the invitations are accompanied by press photos: photos of Max shaking Kubrick's hand. Photos of Max chastely kissing Jane Fonda. Photos of Max with Oliver Stone (he didn't just vote for him as best director for *Platoon,* he also played a small role as a drunk gringo in *Salvador*).

There was much glory, along with many ashes, and not just in the metaphorical sense of the word.

There are strange photos covering the end of the seventies and early eighties, photos of a solitary Max paddling a canoe down some river in the Northeast, photos of a graying Max reading the Gnostic Gospels. Photos of an extroverted and happy Max in front of the psychiatric ward of the Mount Sinai Sanitarium, sticking his tongue out.

Toward the end of the album there are photos of the house in East Hollywood, bought with the money inherited from his Uncle Seamus, his mother's brother, the origins of which he preferred not to know. There are pictures of the two-story house of ocher wood that looks like the village church in *The Villains of Yuma* (and the similarity was not entirely accidental), where he lived on the top floor and rented the ground floor to an esoteric bookstore. The happy owner does not appear in the photos. In just one, you might be able to make out a shadow near a light that could be Max himself reading a book. If that's the case, he can't recall who might have taken it. He's lived alone so long.

The last photos stuck in the album showed his sporadic reappearances in Hollywood, this time as a set designer for 1930s gangster movies. He had several memorable keepsakes. He had selected the little boy's car filmed standing by the staircase in *The Untouchables,* and the ideas for the wardrobes of the teenagers in *Once Upon a Time in America* were his.

Pictures of the house, food coupons for the grocery store, memories converted into the nostalgic papers of the Hollywood myth filled the final pages of the album, along with dates with Malraux and Scott Fitzgerald.

That had ended up being Max Lewis, a Scott Fitzgerald character trapped in other people's dreams. A homosexual who never was, a radical converted into a passive ruin, a sad man, solitary and old.

Sadness was the price or the prize for solitude. He wasn't sure the album managed to express that other story.

E I G H T Y - S I X

FOR ALEX, MEXICO CITY . . .

. . . was the ideal city-setting for Operation Snow White. First, it was the world's biggest city, with its twenty million inhabitants crammed into an enormous valley surrounded by volcanoes, invisible due to the pollution. Second, it was a sufficiently complex city that a good player could obtain and keep resources in reserve. Third, every time Alex flew into Benito Juárez Airport, he felt a pair of metaphorical vultures flying over his back, utterly Mexican buzzards; he wasn't sure whether this was due to his peculiar ability to attract birds of prey or to the innate virtues of the city. Whatever it was, he understood the sensation as a premonition of good luck.

Benjamin and Grumpy-six were waiting for him in a rental car. As they traveled through the viaduct toward the center of the city, Benjamin brought him up to date on the progress of his subdwarfs.

"I've got the murderer. I've got his double living like a prince in a hotel in Acapulco. I've got the woman accredited by the organizers. I've got the press campaign ready, in case we need it. My part is running like a watch."

"It's not your part I'm worried about," Alex said.

"Then what's worrying you?" Benjamin asked.

The soundproof car ran through the viaduct like a ghost. Alex hesitated to answer.

"That it won't rain that day. I've imagined it raining. I've imagined the entire operation on a rainy day."

Benjamin wiped the sweat running down his forehead.

E I G H T Y - S E V E N

HOW ABOUT A BULGARIAN LIKE THIS? (VII)

Stoyan had a vague recollection of what had happened between the withdrawal of the International Brigade from Spain, that famous procession in Barcelona, and the beginning of the war. He remembered the place of confinement behind the barbed-wire entanglements in France, near Bordeaux, the flight, Paris and the two failed attempts to enter Bulgaria, the final link with the IC and his trip to the USSR, the guillotine ambiance permeating Moscow, the decision to return to Bulgaria and the indications of contradictory political attitudes in his party about the conflict going on worldwide.

The war was an interimperialistic war and therefore the objective of the Bulgarian communists was to press for the signing of a pact between Bulgaria and the USSR similar to the existing pact between the Soviets and Germany, simultaneously maintaining the industrial sector's offensive against Bogdan Filov's fascist party and the monarchy. Stoyan said yes, comrade, but the war begun in Spain against the Nazis had to continue; if the Internationals didn't understand it, he did. He accepted the orders so that he could return to the Balkans. He traveled to Prague, followed by an accidental stay in Yugoslavia during the Montenegro Insurrection. His memory played a good trick on him, blurring the interim of caution in which he lived between the two wars. The friends who disappeared in friendly territory, the rumors, the widespread expectation of a purge, the infernal comedy of the newspaper stories according to which, as acts of magic, the great red generals like Tukhachevsky and Berzin became German spies and disappeared into the blaze, the Polish CP was dissolved, the Molotov–Von Ribbentrop pact was signed. Now history reconstructed the nightmare, but with the soothing distance needed if one is to go back and recognize that insanity. He had been a wanderer who for the first time in his life didn't know which side he was on, who his people were, who the enemy was, now endowed with a thousand new and perplexing faces. He took the news of the German invasion of the USSR with a sigh of relief in a tiny hotel in Prague, where he found himself stranded after having lost contact with his liaisons for three weeks.

If one could choose the roads on which one must travel knowing where they lead, history would be much simpler. In the summer of '41, Stoyan wasn't even choosing routes. He followed the path of least resistance and thus found himself in Dubrovnik, intending to cross Montenegro and Northern Macedonia, then cross by foot into Bulgaria. He traveled with two suitcases stolen in a Paris station, full of the paraphernalia of magic tricks, and under the pseudonym of Lencho, Bulgarian magician, who'd lived in South America for many years and now was returning to his country, his memory filled with color sketches of parrots. His passport didn't say that, but he wasn't overly worried. What magician had his artistic name stamped on his passport? Indeed, the passport, he thought he remembered years later, was a marvelous work, falsified by Longoria in Barcelona using the passport of a dead comrade.

Passports? How did he feel forty years later? Did he love or hate them? They'd saved his life more than once. Passport, definition: "bound booklet concealing one's true identity from those who read it, and serving to cross borders." Well then, he was the proprietor of a magician's personality who knew no magic tricks and held a passport of a friend who had died near a rice plantation in El Jarama and who had no political background. He also had exotic stamps Longoria had invented, confident that no European customs official would know that next to the authentic Mexican eagle on a cactus, or the little crossed Venezuelan flags, that wonderful red ink stamp that said "Veranda. Southern border" was false.

Such was Stoyan's state when he took a nose-dive into the Montenegro Insurrection. He remembered the story more precisely than others, perhaps because it had been so absurd, so irrational, so brilliant, so mad, that he had determined to himself, in those August days of '41 preceding the uprising, to keep it alive in a corner of his memory of the past.

It all started in Montenegro, in Podgorica, when he bumped into Djilas, whom he'd known in Spain. It was not a good place to run into a comrade. The city was full of blackshirts and armed Italian policemen. The Yugoslavian communist told him the ground was heating up, and he showed him a newspaper article about the nationalist assembly of the day before, in which they'd declared Montenegro an independent state, in the form of a constitutional monarchy tied to the Italian fascist monarchy.

Stoyan fell into the maelstrom. Without knowing how (perhaps time had blurred the intermediary steps) he remembered fighting with the Yugoslavian patriots against the police garrisons on July 13th. He also remembered the arrested Italian soldiers asking for cigarettes. The insurrection was swifter than its protagonists. On the eighteenth there was combat in Berane, where a revolutionary government had been created. The Italian armed police defended it behind barricades in the police quarters. The Fascists, an entire corps of the eleventh army, advanced toward Albania. When did I get involved in that? Stoyan Vasilev, revolutionary without a nation, disguised as a magician, asked himself. The Spanish lesson, however, was clear. All that one had was a common sky beneath which one could easily die. The Insurrection had triumphed, but the Italian military superiority was imposed a moment later. The guerrillas, the soldiers and the subofficials of the Yugoslavian army retreated into the mountains. Stoyan sensed that that would end in a bloodbath, that the uprising had been premature, and he exchanged his submachine gun for two revolvers before taking off for Bulgaria.

Maybe it was the surprising end, the initial years of fascism on a worldwide scale. And if he had to die, he wanted it to happen on the cobbled streets of Sofia, at the end of the summer. He was in time to fulfill his destiny. Destiny, as far as Stoyan knew, was inescapable. Something from which one could for a time take a short vacation, duck into a hotel for a few days making love with a woman, but that in the end would reappear around a bend in the road. He took great care that his two revolvers had ample ammunition. He would use it all before dying.

E I G H T Y - E I G H T

ALEX DEMANDED REALITY FROM UNREALITY . . .

. . .and from his two consultants, and to them it seemed an amusing but apparently impossible challenge.

"Let me explain it to you, Alex, to see if we've understood it right. You made us study some guy's biography and now you want to know his motivations for doing something he didn't do. Right?"

"I'll ask the question another way, Ellison. What's in this guy's biography that would make him abandon the revolution for money, a lot of money? And without patently betraying it, become corrupt and abandon ship, line his pockets with money and flee, escape to, let's say, the Bahamas, with a yacht and the twelve little

Playboy bunnies of eighty-eight, a majordomo and a villa in the hills of Nassau?"

"It's not in what you gave us. What do you think?" Dr. Ballard meditated, addressing Dr. Ellison. "To me, it seems a very clear case. The revolution gave fatherhood to this man. He is full of debts to this entelechy that the revolutionaries call revolution, moral, emotional, very profound debts."

"With the dead girlfriend, for example," Ellison said.

Alex signaled Leila to bring the tea service. He looked out the window distractedly. Now it was snowing. It was relatively absurd. Hours before, he'd been under the merciless sun of Mexico City, in the dryness of the ozone-contaminated environment. They talked about the humid heat in Managua, and here it was snowing. He was increasingly convinced that incomprehension was a climate problem. How the hell could two Harvard doctors understand Machado?

"Let's see, Doctors, I need your help. Suppose we add two pages to the biography I submitted with events we've only just learned and that inform us that this man has entered into a drug trafficking operation and has made millions with it. How would you explain this change psychologically?"

"We couldn't," the doctor said, looking to her colleague for confirmation.

"I'm sorry, Alex, no one can construct a personality over so many years and then destroy it. It's too much work for every one of us to make by ourselves. There would have to have been profound changes in this man's life, in his current surroundings, his relationships, his information, for him to leap into a void like that. It's almost an act of magic. With what you've given us on his past, I'd say there's not even a two percent chance that he'd turn drug trafficker."

"What the fuck are you two? Sympathetic to the fucking Sandinistas?"

"Alex, I think you're losing your perspective. I've worked for the Agency since seventy-three," said Dr. Ballard.

"What are his weaknesses?" Alex asked, changing his focus. "Which leg of the Carlos Machado table wobbles?"

"I suppose his need for affection," answered Dr. Ballard.

"I believe it's his feeling of inferiority before figures of greater intellectual development. Not even more intelligent, but surrounded by more cultural glamor. That's where his origin wells up, the son of a maid, unknown father, mediocre schooling, scholarships, abandoned studies. But even if you read the book he wrote, you'll see that his personality has not jelled badly, he's not totally disgusted with himself; or in other words his permanent disgust is his motor, and does not turn him against himself destructively nor does it lash out at others.

"I believe he has emotional deficiencies, but money can't resolve them. He would have to be convinced that money is a shortcut to getting affection. I don't believe he'd be taken in by such elementary bait. He knows money can't buy power or strength, it's not a synonym for success."

"Is there lunacy to his behavior, something to indicate some temporary disturbance, a neurosis hidden somewhere, something like that?"

"Alex, you've seen what we've seen," Dr. Ballard said, accepting the tea that Leila brought in at that moment. "It seems to me that at times he has acted outside the normal parameters, that story when he went into the police station with two grenades without firing pins, when he made them surrender or he'd blow them up and himself, too . . . , but that's not at all unusual in war, I believe it should be seen as the logic of the leader of a group of kids who doesn't want to lead his men to death, and who finds a desperate solution by which he could easily die, but which would save lives among his men, something like that. The guy has a strange kind of courage, deluded in fits and starts. There aren't many of these acts, but they occur every once in a while throughout his military history."

"There are some elements of profound sadness, depression sprinkled around, but they don't strike me as beyond what's normal," said Dr. Ellison.

Alex contemplated the possibility of murdering the two psychiatrists, dousing them with a gallon of gasoline and a lit match. If these two country bumpkins didn't find a motive for Machado's alleged acts, the entire base of the operation would falter, it would have the fragile glass legs of unbelievability.

He tried again:

"Means and ends, what's there? Jesuit thought. What are the chances he's engaged in dealing drugs to obtain money for others? I don't know, for . . ."

"Against the wishes of his companions of the Sandinista persuasion?" Dr. Ballard asked, making a gesture of surprise. But at least this time she didn't say no immediately, and sat there thinking.

"It would have to be a very strong motive for him to act behind the backs of his colleagues. He is a man who maintains profound ties of loyalty with the people who surround him," Dr. Ellison said.

Alex tried to formulate the hypothesis for him, but he didn't like it one bit, it forced him to further complicate the situation by including the Salvadorans.

"Let's suppose that when the Sandinistas decided to suspend the open shipments of arms to the Salvadoran guerrillas, Machado was against it. Let's say he interpreted it as an act of weakness, an absurd concession to international pressures. He knows how difficult it was to attain arms during the fighting period against Somoza, he knows how at times the lack of a decent rifle cost them lives, made them have to retreat, leaving the region unprotected before the repression. Suppose then that he didn't mind making dirty deals if, with the money from those deals, he could supply the Salvadorans with arms. Would it work?"

"I haven't seen anything in the material that would lead us to hypothesize his opposition to the Sandinista move."

"There's nothing. If that discussion took place in the heart of the Sandinista elite, where it should have, it was not a public discussion and there are no leaks on the matter. The bulk of the information work we did was distorted to try to demonstrate that the Sandinistas were getting arms into El Salvador via the Gulf of Fonseca. No one was interested in proving that they'd stopped doing so, at a time when intelligence material, which around here they eat for breakfast, was forced to find motives to maintain support for the Contras."

"I don't know, it doesn't ring true," said Dr. Ballard.

"What is the guy's attitude toward drug addiction? There's no information on that. Perhaps it's a problem he never saw in the social circles in which he moved and is therefore unreal to him, absurd, just as the Mexicans viewed our prohibition laws in the 1930s; or as we viewed obligatory Catholic matrimony in Spain fifteen years ago. Something incomprehensible and therefore unfettered with morals, just a simple issue of loyalty."

"I don't know, Alex, I'd have to think about it more, but I'd give it a twenty percent shot at the start. Are you prepared to operate with something so unlikely?" Dr. Ellison asked.

"I agree with him," Dr. Ballard said before they asked her.

"If you don't give me anything better, I don't know what alternative I have."

E I G H T Y - N I N E

JOURNALISTS' STORIES

(J U L I O   S P E A K S)

Okay, I practice the culture of gestures, I am of a generation that came of age with the culture's pleasure in symbolic acts, the challenges of appearances, the destruction of formal rules. What could you do, I'd grown up with Sartre rejecting the Nobel and García-Márquez accepting it in a windbreaker. That's why I invited Elena to lunch in Basque Center, in Madero Six. It was a restaurant where I could handily defeat my ex-wife. The menu of the day was moderate, but even so, I could leave Elena dumbfounded as I devoured the food, I could place her in front of the repertoire for vandals and listen to her complain that she couldn't eat so much, how could someone swallow all that, that I was fatter every day.

I rubbed my hands together. What would it be: Fish stew or cream of corn, paella or *fabada* or tuna empanada, *chamorros* with sherry or chicken casserole or *cuete mechado* or filet of sole, desserts and all for nine thousand pesos, four dollars at the day's exchange rate.

While I waited for her, on the top floor full of plants and with very high ceilings, I downed a couple of tequilas, "to whet my appetite." Elena would come late, conforming to the unwritten rules of the role she'd assigned herself. And she'd say something like:

"I'm dying of hunger today, I could eat it all. I could eat more than you, little fatty," Elena said, altering my script.

"We'll see if it's true," I grumbled. Elena was wearing a white halter dress, the kind that leaves the naked shoulders bare like the beginning of a riddle.

"You order."

I stuck my head in the menu that I knew by heart. I knew Elena was watching me.

"I think I have a good theory of why we separated," she said.

"The first or second time?"

"The second, I don't really remember the first. . . . I believe it was because I didn't read your articles and you didn't read my essays. I believe that's the fundamental reason."

"I can add another half dozen, like for example when you decided sex limited intellectual activity and we spent a month of abstinence, or when you decided that *you* were getting fat and you put *both of us* on a diet of carrots and lemon, or when you declared war on the landlord and started throwing flowerpots at his window."

"What do you conclude from that?" Elena asked with a broad smile.

I didn't want to reach conclusions, I didn't want to reach anything. I was a poor, miserable reporter who at breakfast no longer believed in tomorrow's worldwide revolution and who was absolutely in love with a woman he could not live with.

Fortunately the two fish stews arrived.

"Did you read it all?" Elena asked between spoonfuls.

"Everything. It's very clear that you cannot finish your degree in anthropology."

"Why?"

"Because they don't understand you. I loved your thesis proposals. Two of them border on genius; the one about the invisibles and the one on Neanderthal Marxism captivated me."

"Fats, you're not lying?" I shook my head. My mother had told me repeatedly until she wore me down never to speak with my mouth full. "I adore you!"

"Marry me," I said, unable to avoid it, and I spilled half the soup on my pants.

"Again?"

"Are you seeing someone?"

Elena hesitated. Bad. She finished her soup in four vertiginous spoonfuls and lit a cigarette. Bad.

"And you?"

"Alone, as in loneliness."

"Are you making the offer seriously?"

"No," I said quickly. Then I corrected, "Yes," then I corrected again, "Maybe."

"I see a guy from time to time who's a retired knife-thrower," she told me.

I choked on my soup. But I couldn't blame her, Elena used to do that when we were married, now it was different. She gave me a couple of slaps on the back and made me lift my arms toward the sky.

"It's not very serious, Fats. . . . Raise your arms, and don't try to breathe yet. Now, little by little."

By mutual implicit agreement, we left the subject until dessert; it could be dangerous to digestion.

The *fabada* was good.

"I have one of those stories you love, and it might be the opportunity to get my stupid thesis. If I don't get it by December, they chase me off the grounds."

"I'm all eyes."

"All ears."

"That too."

"Suppose there's a high-ranking CIA official who's retiring. He wants to hide away in Cuernavaca. And he's prepared to talk. Not in detail, because you know, the law of state secrets thing . . . , but he'll talk generally, citing examples, even though not very clear ones. He's prepared to talk about what he knows best. . . . About disinformation. Twenty years of disinformation stories, this fine gentleman is an archive. And he's prepared to be interviewed in depth, as many times as I want, comparing materials, discussing my focus. Bad conscience, guilty conscience I suppose."

"What's his name?"

"I don't know yet, but he knows about Africa, Latin America, AIDS, drug trafficking, TV, Nicaragua. . . ."

"How'd you get hold of this?"

"A friend with a master's in political science who coincidentally was connected to a friend."

"Are you sure they weren't looking for you?" I asked her. I didn't believe in coincidences, or chance. About not believing—I didn't believe in luck, or fortune, or random fate, or lucky stars. It was professional wisdom acquired over years in hotel rooms, office waiting rooms, jungles, and newspaper editorial offices.

"No, I haven't even said yes. I wanted to consult with you first. I also wanted help. Especially after the first series of interviews."

I devoted myself to the *chamorro al jerez*. Elena began to show signs of gastronomic exhaustion. She touched my hand. There was no electricity, but I do remember. The skin has a memory more deceiving than the memory of the mind.

"And why is your friend the knife-thrower retired? Why doesn't he rejoin the trade, increasing his chances of an accident? Why doesn't he go back to the circus and on opening day, you give him two uncorked bottles of *maderito*?"

"We're all getting a little cynical lately," Elena said.

"Some more than others," I answered.

"Will you help me?"

"After next week, because we're going to do something with Carlos Machado, who's going to be at a conference here this week, at a seminar at the College of Mexico."

"Do you still stick your pants in the closet to cool?" Elena suddenly asked.

"And you, do you suck the point of the pens when you're writing, and then walk around with a purple tongue?"

Elena laughed. Again, I asked, "Do you want to get married again?"

"Maybe," Elena said enigmatically. Then she smiled at me a little.

N I N E T Y

LONGORIA ABANDONS
THE REFUGE

On his ride to the airport on the subway, Saturnino Longoria was contemplating a sentence he'd read in the memoirs of his old and now deceased comrade, Julio

García Oliver: "With the years, the memory dissipates but continues to be slightly present. What makes things unforgettable is solitude."

Thinking about the past did not keep him from observing his fellow passengers. It had been several years since he'd left the sanctuary of the Sanatorio Español, and he almost didn't recognize the city outside. That was why he preferred the subway. The tunnels, the transfer connections, the platforms, were all an extension of his caves and hiding places in the gardens and buildings of the old hospital. The people were not more rushed than usual and did not seem different, the subway was clean. How many years had passed since he'd last ridden? Longoria looked at himself in the glass of one of the pneumatic doors: scarce white hair, almost yellowish, combed back, a ridiculous striped suit with a red bow tie over a white shirt that barely covered his bones. The best: the crafty look over his mustache and aquiline nose. He had stolen the suit from one of the recently deceased, a well-worn suit, stashed together with a heap of other clothes, masculine and feminine, in a room for the disabled in the tuberculosis pavilion. They had to be used for something. He made a gesture of weariness. The city up above him might not have changed excessively, but he kept getting older.

A young office worker misinterpreted his gesture of exhaustion and tried to give him his seat. Longoria looked at him with repulsion.

"You see me as so very old, kid?" he said.

The amiable bureaucrat buried his head in the paper to avoid a quarrel. But Longoria didn't forgive him.

"Whenever you want it, we'll have a race, or see who can row faster, or who can lift more weight."

"Stupid, worn-out runt," the office worker said.

"You can also ask your mother about my skills in bed."

Longoria was saved from a row because he found himself at the airport stop, and before the violence was unleashed he jumped agilely onto the platform and disappeared into the crowd.

The airport's international departures area was congested as usual. Flights from the United States crossed with the weekly from Lima and a Lufthansa flight to Hamburg. Longoria approached the gate, dodging distant relatives, and showed the service policeman a correspondent's credential from the London *Times* in the name of Harpo Marx. The photograph was not very new, four or five years old, but the pass was from the same time. They waved him on to baggage claim and customs. He climbed the stairs to passport control. He made out Stoyan from a distance, and waved to him. Once the Bulgarian had crossed the immigration gate, they embraced in the middle of the stairs. They didn't speak for a long time. Stoyan patted Longoria's skinny cheeks and Longoria punched him softly in the stomach.

"Asshole. I thought you were dead, Longoria, dammit. I felt guilty for not having convinced you to leave Paris the last time we saw each other. And suddenly the letter arrived."

"I ended up heeding your advice. When I got hit with two bullets, I realized it was serious, friend. . . . We don't have much time, the conference people must be waiting for you outside. What hotel are you staying in?"

"El Florida."

"Tonight at nine-thirty, go out for a walk after dinner and turn right, I'll meet you."

"What's up, is something wrong?"

"No, I simply don't exist, my fine Bulgarian. An old man's obsessions," Longoria said, shaking Vasilev's hand with both of his. Then he turned and bounced down the stairs.

Longoria was right. At the exit, two friendly scholarship students from the College of Mexico met Stoyan with a cart and rushed to relieve him of his bags. Drinking an Orange Crush in one of the smaller stores, Longoria watched him pass by.

Suddenly his greenish eyes saw something else. From a distance, someone was watching his friend and the two students accompanying him. A gringo in a corduroy sport suit with elbow patches and sunglasses. Stoyan was being followed. Longoria's historic intuition couldn't be fooled. What the hell was this? As the gringo walked toward the exit following Stoyan, Saturnino put a tail on the tail. If they wanted to create problems for the Bulgarian, they hadn't counted on Saturnino Longoria's skills, at this point in his life half-man/half-ghost, but always capable of kicking the enemy in the balls, no matter who the enemy was.

The old man almost screwed up the whole thing by forgetting to pay for his drink.

A GREAT STAGE . . .

. . . was made from elements that shouldn't be in that place. The golden dream of an interior decorator was to always be able to put something unexpected in the corner of a room. In one of his baroque raptures, Alex thought the Mexican stage was still impoverished. Reality tended to be more absurdly complex, and by falsely reconstructing it, he made it rather logical. If it continued like this, the Dream of Snow White would seem like a bad play watched through the eyes of some intelligent observer. Alex worked for posterity, and that being the case he needed everything to have a magical touch, even if no one appreciated it for the next twenty years. Twenty years, cosmic dust. In other words, he needed to improve the stage, make it a little more sophisticated, more complex, add a few touches of Kafkian unreality, even though he was sure that Mexico City would provide its own.

The best stages were composed of things that in ordinary life didn't go together: a boat full of Haitian refugees, a lunch at the St. Francis for dishwasher sales executives, a retired German sailor who killed old ladies in the Callao. How could he tie together such marvelous ingredients?

Operation Dream of Snow White wasn't so bad. Here he had a Sandinista commander, an astonishing Bulgarian, a Mexican drug dealer, some journalists, an Australian prostitute, a Congress of partisan writers, a murder. . . . He needed a Spanish Catholic bishop, an Aztec archaeological treasure, a photograph of gay models, things like that.

The beauty of it all was managing to weave it all together in a braid that would move through time and space.

He had never had something as beautiful as Snow White in his hands. A masterpiece is recognized the moment you can smell it, even when it's cooking in a place so devoid of smells as the kitchen of one's thoughts.

He pulled the chain and contemplated the water flowing in the toilet. He carefully buttoned his pants and then his vest and crossed the office looking for a pad of paper and evading Leila, who wanted to give him a telex.

What had he said?

An Aztec treasure, a Spanish Catholic bishop, a picture of gay models. . . . What else?

"Alex, do you want to go over the territory of the journalists?" Eve asked.

"Do you have it with you? Bring it in. Even if we did it poorly, there's not much we can correct at this point," Alex said, falling back into his chair and lighting a cigarette.

"We could reinforce, but I'm afraid of saturation, we'd make the whole thing very transparent. . . . First the rumor was sown among the North American correspondents in Mexico who cover Central America that we had a mole inside Sandinismo, the product of blackmail. The sowing provoked smiles. We let it trickle out to five guys. They haven't published one line, three of them asked questions. The rumor has to have run quite a bit. Let's suppose not enough yet. Simon and Fernández are not in close contact with the trade, they're more lone wolves. It might not have reached them. At any rate, as agreed, if they don't get it and don't use it, someone else will use it later. . . ."

"Fine, stay calm. Nothing else. If you force it, the affair will collapse," Alex said.

"Second, we've been pressing the story of the Pancho Villa award for a month. We sent invitations to every journalist who writes testimonial books, so the affair has an iron-clad cover. We tapped Fernández's phone and he called Simon immediately after getting his letter. The story is perfect: Stan Laurel, the Mexican's grandfather, the whole thing. . . . It's so absurd it rings absolutely true."

"It is true. It's just buried out there somewhere."

"How did you uncover it, Alex? Just tell me that and you'll make my whole afternoon."

"I was a lawyer once and my highest honor was to work on Stan Laurel's will."

"That's a lie."

"Of course it is."

Eve's crossed eyes got worse. Suddenly it seemed as though she was simultaneously looking at a picture of Salvador Allende murdered in his office in La Moneda and an old Greek newspaper clipping, hanging in the door jamb. To dissemble, she poured herself some tea. These things could happen if you looked closely at the SD's walls, the eyes found two objects at once. As she returned, stirring with a little plastic spoon, she completed the information.

"An approach was made to Fernández's ex-wife, I'm not exactly sure of the results. Grumpy-six did it. You've got his report on your desk."

"Anything else? Is Sleepy still missing? Won't it be too much? It's always the same story. Too much or not enough. Too much will push them away, too little won't captivate them."

"We could stop Sleepy, there's still time."

"Don't even think about it, he's got to play two cards, not just one. But I don't want him to enter the stage until they're lapping up the bait. . . ."

Alex reclined in his chair and half-closed his eyes. His last observation was fairly cryptic to Eve:

"When you can't enter by the front door, it's not a bad idea to go in through the kitchen."

He put on a thick sheepskin jacket and went out to the street.

Midtown Manhattan was covered by a cloak of sleet. The mist descended, coating the tops of the skyscrapers. He stopped at Lexington and Fifty-third Street to contemplate an enormous blue building disappearing. No one realized they could be watching the end of the world. The Chrysler Building vanished under the mist, it was slowly losing its stories in the darkness, disappearing. Nobody realized that one day it could all end like this, a God, until now unknown, eliminating the skyscrapers with a giant eraser, story by story, until He reached ground level.

Alex crossed to the side of the Marine Midland Bank just a few steps from his office entrance and raised the collar of his jacket. At that point he was assaulted by a horde of flyer distributors: introductions to a "European Body Wrap," described as one of the Belles Artes, offering eight free minutes on a vibrating table which equaled hours of traditional exercise. Coupons for video cameras from "The Four Guys." A computer center that offered to pay your cab ride with a purchase of fifty dollars if you kept the receipt and presented the flyer. Roy Rogers coupons with vouchers for one dollar with the purchase of four hamburgers. Pink flyers from AAA Finger Nail, hailing the wonders of therapeutic programs for nail-biters. Offers for your own "personal consultant on psychic matters," Mrs. Donna, who was able to confront bad luck and the sorrows of love. Madison Square Garden schedules, and material on Dora Lyn, the spiritualist from the Deep South who promised to resolve the problems of those who could not save money or had strange illnesses.

Alex took them all and saved them in his pockets. They might have been more than flyers; perhaps together with the buildings vanishing in the fog the flyers held secret keys, messages from beyond, and maybe the offer of a Kung Pau chicken at Lam Ying, a Chinese restaurant on Fifty-ninth Street, concealed a date with the future. Perhaps the coupon for three bottles of shampoo with the purchase of two that Village Cutters offered. . . . But if that was the case, he would have known. For now, no one had warned him. Just in case, he did not throw the little colored papers in the trash can on the corner.

JOURNALISTS' STORIES

(G R E G   S P E A K S)

For the Aztec powers, the masters and lords of the Anáhuac Valley, Teotihuacán was a place to be feared. The dreadful strength of the earlier peoples' vanished gods, the legend of royal cultures, showed in the pyramids that challenged the sky. The immensity of the city-temple terrorized the upstart warriors. Aztecs from far and near Teotihuacán eyed it only from a distance.

It seems that fear is a contagious, cultural sensation, because years later the Spaniards demolished the statue of the god crowning the Sun Pyramid, leaving it a maimed and solitary heap of stone. A priest and a captain took turns directing the operations.

Early in the morning, we'd traveled some eighteen miles on the freeway that separated Mexico City from the ruins of Teotihuacán, an open city, protected only by hills, just as it was fifteen centuries ago.

Years ago, I caught the back tire of my motorcycle in a streetcar track. It was in San Francisco, and those tracks were out of service, but some incompetent city worker had forgotten to give the order to remove them. It was raining and the ground was wet, with a light patina of water. Attempting to steer the motorcycle out of the track and failing, I forced the handlebars on the second try and the bike skidded out of the track. I did what my instinct and the manuals advised—let go of the bike and fell off—while the machine was flying at a modest forty miles an hour. My wounds were slight with the exception of a completely dislocated wrist bone (the X rays showed something that looked like the trigger guard of a shotgun). A minor operation and a month in a cast and wristband were sufficient, but when it rains or when I'm the victim of an athletic binge, like trying to do twenty push-ups, when I make love more than twice in one night on top of my partner, or when I go up a pyramid of thousands of steps and have to use my hands to help me climb, the pain returns. That miraculous cures exist is a lie. Injuries to the bones and to the heart share the craziness of permanence, they are as enduring as you are.

Fats had his problem with excessive smoking and I had mine with my wrist. In the end, we reached the summit of the Sun Pyramid, protesting. Armando hadn't yet arrived.

"You know what they say about Galicians, brother?" Julio asked me.

"What?"

"That if you find them on a staircase, you never know if they're going up or down. The same theory should apply to pyramids and Armando."

From the top of the Sun Pyramid, you could contemplate the dead city, reorganized for the tourist trade. The sun shone straight down, burning the few neurons we had left after the ascent. I was entranced by the geometry of the dead buildings: the Moon Pyramid, the Roadway of the Dead, the Citadel, the Temple of Quetzalcoatl. I'd once read in a manual of the Museum of Anthropology that one could not continue to speak of Teotihuacán the city, but rather of Teotihuacán cultures and cities. It was not one, but several, built one on top of the other. Glory over ruins, greatness over burial ground. In its final years, the city had even suffered sackings and a fire, around the year 700. The temples had been burned, the statue of the Goddess of Water of the Moon Pyramid carried off, her jade heart torn out. There are no symbolic gestures, there are revenges that at times destroy stone hearts as a way of burning the hearts of humans.

"You, from a country with no history, how do you feel? Eh, little gringo?" Julio fired his jab at me.

"Don't start pretending to be pre-Hispanic. If a couple of Teotihuácanos grab us up here alone, we'll both be cooking in the same bonfire. They don't give a shit if I'm a Jew from Manhattan adapted to the palm trees of Los Angeles or you're a rat from Mexico City of Spanish immigrant origin. We're both fucked."

"It's not that. It's the air of greatness. It's the Mexicans' turn for a return to glory. If we're going to make a country, it's got to be by mixing the ruins of this with the ruins of Mexico City."

"I'll lend you Hollywood Boulevard to add to it and you'll make yourself a beautiful country."

Julio kept thinking about it, the idea didn't entirely bother him. We had traveled through too much countryside, crossed too many borders to take customs and borders, barbed-wire fences and passports seriously.

Armando's face appeared on the eastern side of the pyramid. He was not disheveled, the ascent of the pyramid had not moved one hair on his head, there wasn't a drop of sweat on his face. I started to think he was a tropical robot. A kind of RmanD2, known in these parts as an "Arturito." An "Armandito," an improved model.

"Gentlemen . . . ," he said. I waited for him to pull a complete cocktail service from the pocket of his white linen suit, including lemon rinds, salt to crystallize the glasses, mint sprigs, martini olives. He didn't.

"Armandin, my son," answered Fats, specialist in putting everyone in his or her place. "How is that you make us climb a goddamn pyramid . . . ?"

Armando shook off a nonexistent bit of dust and contemplated the countryside burned by the sun.

"It's very beautiful, isn't it? And what's more, quite discreet. No witnesses."

Fats took out his cigarettes and sat down on the base of the altar destroyed by the Aztecs and Spaniards. A novel deity in the Teotihuacán book of saints: "Fats, smiling journalist," item in the catalog of 1657.

"Are you going to tell us something without beating around the bush or have we come to play Chinese spies?"

Armando gave him one of his best smiles from the Lon Chaney repertoire. He took out a pack of filterless Montecristos. Fats threw his Delicado to the ground without the slightest respect for the Teotihuacán ancients and accepted one. I joined the nicotine ride.

"Someone told me there is a mole in the Sandinista elite," Armando said. "A big mole, a complete pipeline, and that the CIA may take advantage of it, use it, you know, something like that. I don't know."

"And what's with us? Who wants what from us?" I asked, distrusting all information that seems to be free, although I loved Armando's indirect style, his incapacity for transparency.

"I don't have proof, just rumors."

"That's enough for the Sandinistas, a good rumor is enough for them to put up their antennae," Fats said with a smile. If Armando wanted something from us, we were going to make him sweat a little.

"The thing is I don't dare pass it on, because if it's bad, it could be a trick to sow distrust," Armando responded without looking at us. "Shit to poison the air."

"You like it?" I asked Julio.

"Not one bit," Fats answered.

"Gentlemen, how many times in your lives have you hit the lottery?" Armando said.

"Wait a minute, I got it," I said to Julio. "Someone wants us to investigate and they give us the lead because they know we're serious reporters, and that we won't take the apples from the fridge until we're absolutely sure they're ripe."

"No, it's more than that, this is about someone we know," Fats responded while Armando dicked around, observing the stone landscape. "Someone we know. . . ."

"Come on, Armando, I'm not as interested in the story you want to tell us as the one you don't want to tell us. Who wants us to dig in as investigators? Who wants us to verify that there's a mole inside Sandinismo? We'll put it very simply: who do you work for?" I asked.

"It has to be something exotic," Fats said, not looking at me. "Something almost paranormal. His employers have to be exotic: Los Angelenos, Yugoslavs, UCLA, a Buddhist sect, circus owners, the Portuguese secret service, the sons of Torrijos. . . ."

"I like that one," I answered.

"You know the worst? That with the exception of the latter, you're right about everything. The man is Carlos Machado," Armando said very seriously.

"Machadito, a mole?" Fats asked.

"No te jode!" I said, using an expression I'd learned in Madrid's airport. It says "Don't fuck me over," but it could mean almost anything, according to the circumstances.

N I N E T Y - T H R E E

THE VERSION OF EMILIO SALGARI'S *GOOD-BYE TO MOMPRACEM* CREATED BY STOYAN VASILEV IN THE PLEVEN PRISON

When the Tigers boarded the *Vengador,* the situation couldn't have been more desolate. The guards had been reduced to half, and up on deck several men were doubled up with nausea. Kelly, the Irish doctor, had the infirmary and the halls that led to it packed with unconscious, convulsing men.

"A poisoning, Sandokan. Someone poisoned our food, and I can't identify it. I don't know how to combat it."

"What are the symptoms?" Yanez asked.

"Very high fever, vomiting, convulsions, tremendous stomach pains."

"It could be the juice of that poisoned fruit, upas," Sandokan said softly to Yanez.

"Has anyone died?"

"Not yet," the doctor answered with a gloomy face.

"Let's wait until the dose has been reduced. Treat them with coconut milk and keep them cool," Yanez said.

Yanez pulled a silver-plated amphora from his back pocket, opened it and took a long swallow. Sandokan looked at him strangely. "Do you have some symptoms, little brother?"

"No, it's madeira. I'm simply preparing myself for what's ahead. If we go up on deck, it won't be long before we see the danger in some strange form. How many healthy men are left, Kelly?"

"No more than twenty, and I've got the majority of them busy here doing nursing work."

After instructing the Irish doctor to use their own cabins as an extension of the infirmary, the two Tigers went on deck. The *Vengador* was a steel-armored steam frigate that displaced close to four thousand tons and was armed with fourteen twelve-inch cannons. Constructed for the Tigers by important intermediaries in the shipyards of Hamburg, it was indubitably the most powerful ship that plowed the seas of the Northern Pacific at that time.

"Kim, who is at the helm?" Yanez asked the young Hindu. He was less than fifteen years old, but had an impressive physique and a face of great vivacity, furrowed by a tremendous scar that made it asymmetric.

"Second Lieutenant Mendosa."

"Tell him to prepare to leave port. I prefer to confront this situation on the open sea."

"Look," Sandokan suddenly said, pointing to a series of small boats approaching the starboard side of the *Vengador*. Apparently they were wretchedly small canoes and barks that carried various merchandise. In Singapore, any moderately important steamship in the bay near land would often be besieged by these commercial barges, offering regional foods to the sailors as a change from the ship's unvarying provisions; fruit and roasted turtles, monkey brains, fresh vegetables; but also pieces of imitation jewelry, knives, clothes, suits. This time, however, with night already falling, it seemed unlikely that these were their intentions, even though they approached with all kinds of lights and lighted braziers and signal lanterns.

"Kim, grapeshot in the two cannons on the forecastle, you on one of them, leave the other to me. Tell Kompiang to bring a box of grenades and a half dozen rifles on deck."

"Sambliong!" Sandokan yelled, helping Yanez in the preparations.

The old Malaysian came at once. His extremely long beard was completely white and his mouth was missing several teeth.

"Take charge of the machine guns."

"At once, Tiger," he said, showing a fierce smile.

"If they come with ill intentions, they'll soon see that we're a hard nut to crack, little brother," Sandokan said, his blood coursing violently through his veins, rejuvenating him for an instant.

"Tiger," Kim yelled from the bow. "There's a boat coming, all lit up."

"Grapeshot ten yards in front of the boats, I don't want them coming any closer," Sandokan said.

As if they'd been waiting for his order, the two small cannons on the quarterdeck fired, guided by the trained marksmanship of Sambliong and Yanez himself. The impact raised a great wave of water a few yards in front of the approaching boats.

"White flag on the lit-up barge," Kim yelled again.

Yanez approached his blood brother coming down in two jumps from the quarterdeck.

"Careful, the shots must have alerted the British naval patrol. The last thing we need at this point is a couple of tightfisted nosy British snobs meddling with the *Vengador.*"

Sandokan agreed.

"Let them come on, but if one of the other boats approaches, open fire. Turong, machine-gunner on deck! Dammit! If they want to see our blood, we'll paint the forecastle with theirs."

Meanwhile, Yanez waited for the brightly illuminated barge to gather the ropes thrown from the *Vengador.*

"Good evening, gentlemen. To what do we owe this nocturnal visit?" the Portuguese asked, leaning over the edge.

"The astronomer, Mijail Vasilev, desires an exchange of words with the captain of the ship," answered the elaborately dressed Malaysian steward.

"Tell him he may come up," Yanez answered, and gestured to Kim, who was at his side, to offer a ladder.

Sandokan had taken his place next to the Portuguese and both of them offered a hand to the strange personage who appeared at the rail. He wore an unfamiliar military uniform of dark gray cloth and gold-plated buttons, his exposed head was crowned by an enormous tuft of white hair, and a fine aquiline nose protruded from his face.

"For a man without a country, it is the highest honor to meet you, gentlemen," said the new arrival in imperfect English.

"We still don't know if we should think the same, but we prefer to assume so," Yanez said sarcastically.

"I come to offer you my services. Mijail Vasilev, native of the Balkans, serving the fight for liberty, astronomer without a telescope, magnificent marksman, champion of saber-handling at the Academy of Sandhurst, unlikely sailor and unrepentant bachelor."

"Sir, the canoes and other small boats are still approaching," Kim said into Sandokan's ear.

Noticing the Tigers' uneasiness, Vasilev clarified: "I have nothing to do with those boats, sirs."

As he spoke, there was the sound of two shots. One of the Tigers who was on guard astern collapsed with a bullet wound in his chest.

"Careful, they're trying to come alongside," Sandokan yelled.

And so it was, one of the small launches had managed to come close enough to the *Vengador* to throw boarding lines and attempt to come in close. The dozen Malaysians on deck reacted rapidly, cutting the lines with their boarding hatchets.

"Fire! They've initiated hostilities," Yanez screamed.

"Astronomer, we'll continue our conversation in a few minutes," Sandokan said, removing a pair of Colt revolvers from his red silk belt.

"On my boat, there is a man you have been looking for, Malang, and two friends of mine from the lands of Indochina who can offer you invaluable services."

Yanez carefully studied the Bulgarian. What he saw gave him sufficient confidence, and he agreed, "Have them come aboard."

Meanwhile, the chaos had spread. Sambliong fired one of the artillery pieces almost point-blank, inundating one of the launches with grapeshot and dismasting it; but dozens of others were dangerously nearing the ship. A rain of fire fell over the deck.

"They're hurling chunks of burning coal."

Yanez took one of the machine guns in his hands and started to fire at the occupants of a small boat twenty yards from the *Vengador*. The ancient cannons and two or three small ones from the boats responded. The noise was deafening. From the stern, half a dozen Chinese armed with machetes fell upon Sandokan and some of his Tigers. Covering the body of his leader, old man Mirim-Lili took a tremendous slash on his forehead. Three of the Chinese invaders fell to Sandokan's revolvers, but the fourth lunged toward the Tiger of Malaysia and fell rolling with him on deck.

Mijail Vasilev, appearing together with his companions, stopped the other two assailants with his saber, allowing Sandokan to catch his breath.

Yanez, meanwhile, wreaked havoc on the small boats, using the agile artillery piece on the forecastle for the purpose.

"Go at them, they're nothing without the element of surprise," the Portuguese yelled, inciting the dozen Tigers of Malaysia. Sambliong had managed to position a second machine gun and fired with sure aim at one of the boats from which the attackers were attempting to board. Soon the surviving boats began to retreat, several of them damaged by the *Vengador*'s artillery and one in flames. "Sambliong, order Sir McDermont to bring the engines up to full speed. We're leaving at once," the Tiger said, jumping over the corpse of the Chinese collapsed at his feet, as if in homage to the fearful power of the old pirate.

MAD DOG'S
DEALS / COKE

The cop will enter Aoyama's office, eluding a secretary and a chief of production until he encounters the insurmountable barrier of the boss's assistant's desk. Faced with the impossibility of verbal persuasion, he will opt for direct action and, taking a .45 pistol with the eagle and serpent of the national shield over a wide-brimmed hat engraved on the butt, the cop will give him a tremendous push, shattering two of the assistant's teeth and knocking him down bleeding over a large container of distilled water for the cooling system.

Ontiveros will thus guarantee a spectacular entry into the office of the Japanese, just one more guy to him, without distinction as to race. And after seeing him and verifying that his natural yellow has become even more so, and that fear appears in the wrinkles of his forehead, destroying the myth of the imperturbable Oriental devoted to the plastic industry and the trafficking of cocaine, he will say:

"I'll be blunt, man, I want thirty-five percent of everything or you suck my cock right here."

"Police?" The Japanese man asks, conscious that this guy could be a lunatic just out of the Mexico City metro, bringing with him the acceleration and the inertia of the pushing and shoving.

"You stupid, man? As I'm going to cost you a lot, you can call me by my real name, which almost nobody knows. But I tell it to you with affection so that you use it with affection: Leandro, Le-an-dro," Mad Dog will say, and then will feel obliged to explain: "Commander of the Special Force of the Federal Judicial

Police, Leandro Ontiveros, to serve God and you in that order."

The matter, however, will not be as simple as it might have seemed at first, because Mr. Aoyama already splits his profits with other federal officers of the narcotics force and even has a gringo from the DEA in Los Angeles on a fixed salary with bimonthly checks. That, on the one hand.

On the other, the boss's assistant, spitting blood, will enter the office with a shotgun and will stick it in the gut of Mad Dog who, after repeating several times "motherfucker," will think that business in Mexico City is getting worse every day.

The Japanese, who until a moment ago didn't speak Spanish, will reveal himself as a Japanese native of Mazatlán, Sinaloa, a city with an ocean view and replete with tropical palm trees where the drug dealers occasionally race cars on the dike. He will say to the cop:

"Leandro is a faggot's name."

"If it wasn't before, it is now," Commander Ontiveros answers, setting a precedent in the new relationship and mentally lowering his split from thirty-five to twelve percent, that if he's lucky.

"Close the door, Marcial, we're going to chat with this gentleman," the Jap will then say.

Then the phone will ring and the diligent Japanese will pick it up, only to hear a deep voice (in reality the voice of one of Ontiveros's sisters-in-law who works part-time as a prostitute in the eastern truck drivers' center):

"Either you tell your associate to drop the rifle or we bring up the others with the M1 and we heat up the present you're planning to give your bride, you stupid Jap."

Ontiveros will dramatize the affair slightly, prompting:

"Pass me the phone, I'll speak to the boys, they're not going to get nervous," and thinking he could raise the split to twenty-five percent of which he'd have to give two percent to his sister-in-law, strategically located in the telephone booth on the corner with binoculars (pure science of modern police investigation), because if she doesn't talk, the operation is fucked.

The Japanese will hand him the phone and the assistant will close the door. Ontiveros says into the apparatus:

"Everything's under control, R10," (which is the name of a

Renault model no longer manufactured in Mexico, but which sounds very technical, very ad hoc).

And he will say to the Japanese: "So, Leandro is a faggot's name?" Because introducing oneself is the best way to initiate a deal.

NINETY-FIVE

HOW ABOUT A BULGARIAN LIKE THIS? (VIII)

Stoyan hated Turks. This was an irrational attitude that went far beyond all the ancestral, racial and historical hatred that Bulgarians feel toward Turks. It was a peculiar and concrete hatred resulting from a railway accident, a switched suitcase and the reinstitution of the vice of smoking, dormant during the period of guerrilla war. He concluded from the affair that the Turks had attempted to kill him.

The affair began in Prague in 1947.

He woke up in a small hospital with his head in bandages. He remembered reading Miguel Hernández's poems in Spanish on the train as it approached Prague. The nurses were speaking in Czech. He divined a train accident. He was bandaged and naked. The room empty right now, two other beds abandoned, one of them still had soiled, bloodstained sheets. A dog howled in the night. At dawn he stood up and looked for his suitcase. It had disappeared; in its stead a new papier-mâché suitcase was at the foot of his bed. He placed it on top of the sink and opened it. It was full of Turkish cigarettes. Some two hundred boxes. The next day he traded fifty of them with the hospital administrator for some gray slacks, a white shirt (originally belonging to some dead person) and a few crowns. They removed his bandages. He had a new scar along his hairline, a straight scar almost three inches long. He strolled out; he was in the Mala Strana, the city's old quarter. His mission was to interview two English reporters who were prepared to tell what they knew about the operations organized by the MI5 against Bulgaria from the Greek border. The appointment was on a Tuesday, in the afternoon, in the middle of the Charles V Bridge; the Englishmen and he wore red scarves. Stoyan didn't know what period he was living in. A vendor selling used books from a cart told him it was Tuesday. The Bulgarian opened one of his packs of Turkish cigarettes and started smoking.

That April day of 1947 he walked through Mala Strana smoking, enjoying the constant details that made every house a new surprise. A trellis, a green-painted wooden door, a frieze on the wall, a ducal shield over the door of a fire station. He walked down to the river looking for something to eat, but the Church of St. Vitus stopped him. The church, after St. Vitus, to whom the Spanish attributed the evil of uncontrollable motion, would have been much better baptized as the Church of St. Parkinson, now that we can look ahead to years that will be free from idolatry. Inside, he discovered a mural by Alfonse Mucha. Art nouveau in a cathedral, perfect. Just appropriate. He ran into a group of young soldiers. They had youthful acne. The aged faces of eighteen-year-old adolescents. The war had aged everything. He ate boiled potatoes and meatballs.

He arrived at the meeting point on the bridge without a red scarf, but with a silk handkerchief of the same color tied around his neck. In exchange for his disappeared cigarettes, the Turkish tobacco smuggler now had a suitcase that held a Spanish volume of poems by Miguel Hernández, a black suit with worn-out elbows and a red scarf. Stoyan wasn't sure who'd won.

The seagulls flew up from the islands left by the river at a very low tide. They glided over the bridge, shitting on the strange statues of warriors and medieval saints. He liked King Charles, the king who had founded the university, but the cold stone saints and the warriors, with gold detail, deserved the seagulls' salute. He stood momentarily absorbed by the sound of the water and the distant music of a strolling organ-grinder, the whispered conversations of lovers, the discussion of two old men reading a paper. The water of the Vltava River constituted a changing landscape, in motion, replete with blues and grays stained by the froth that ended on the banks and the brilliant green of the trees touched by the breath of spring.

The Englishmen arrived punctually. They seemed like two elegant officers and gentlemen of the RAF on vacation. Their red scarves waved in tandem, blown by the breeze that came from the Vtlava. Hours later, in a hotel room, one of them would take out a .38 with a silencer from his coffee-colored brown jacket and fire at Stoyan, missing, because he had been expecting it. The Bulgarian would break the Brit's head with a paperweight and leave the room, walking with the dead man's pistol in the waist of the dead man's pants that he had just inherited. He would leave the second Englishman to grapple with the problem of explaining to the Czechoslovakian police why he had a half-naked cadaver in his room.

Thirty years later, they would extract a piece of Stoyan Vasilev's lung due to a benign tumor and, though the operation fixed the problem, the Bulgarian would spend several months of convalescence fearing that the tumor would regenerate. Over all that time, he convinced himself that it was the Turks' fault. That the illness had been hatched in Prague thirty years earlier due to those damned 150 packs of Turkish cigarettes he'd smoked.

N I N E T Y - S I X

ALEX LOVED . . .

. . .the Latin American Department of the Agency in the same corrupt and condescending way Kipling loved the British clubs of New Delhi: that corner of the CIA seemed like a refuge of old sahibs, human bodyshops of old colonial automobiles overcome by nostalgia for the sweat that stained the armpits of the shirts south of the Rio Grande. In mid-April, Alex found himself obliged to leave New York and take a drive to Langley, to talk to the DO and his assistant a bit, as little as possible, about Operation Snow White. They received him drinking Tabs and coffee, which by its smell must have been Colombian, with cold milk.

Just as there is a culture of the memory, there is also a culture of all that is forgotten. Better said, there are rules to preserve innocence. Contrary to what any normal human being might think, the more you rose on the Agency's zigzag chain of command, the more they knew and the less they wanted to know. Oh no, none of the dirty details, please. Alex didn't quite know what Bradley and the poliomyelitic doctor Nelson wanted to know. Rather, Alex wasn't exactly sure what they didn't want to know. Nor did he particularly want to say anything. He didn't like these guys as an audience, he preferred them as a static museum. He greeted them with a nod and Rutherford, who entered the office a couple of times under the pretext of stealing some sugar for his coffee to see whether he could pick up a little information, or Simmons, the legendary adviser to the Argentines, whose seven years of work had been fucked by the Falkland Islands, appeared in the hall with voluminous files stuffed under his arm and pizza stains on his shirt.

Two years before Alex had had a long conversation with Bradley, which gave birth to the "Doctor Stanley" project. A good point in Alex's official career. The outline of the project had been entirely his: they had asked him for a smokescreen over the history of the relations between the Agency and the Bolivian coke-dollar generals. Alex had responded with a strange plan: he wrote two books aided by a group of ghost editors and by the Agency's own data banks. The first one, titled "The CIA and the Bolivian Generals," signed by Astrid Glover, narrated with a wealth of details, many of them not known before, the tormented love-hate relationship between the Agency and the Bolivian generals. It proved the CIA's intervention in the successive military coups of the last ten years in La Paz, the generals' relations with drug trafficking and the support the Agency had given in several operations in which arms traffic, intelligence work and cocaine distribution were mixed. It was a frankly interesting book, so much so that it almost reached number fifteen on *The Village Voice*'s best-seller list.

Six months later, Lucille Barnes, a second nom de plume hatched in the kitchen of Alex's inferno, edited *The Paranoia of Disinformation,* an excellent sociological analysis on the paranoid mentality of journalistic work, which encounters conspiracies and secret treaties everywhere it looks. The seventh chapter was dedicated to Glover's book, and that, using the errors that Alex himself had sown throughout the previous text surrounded by coherent information, destroyed the work on Bolivia. Any moderately interested reader accepted, after reading the two texts, that the CIA had had little to do with the coke-dollar generals, if not nothing, though they might well have had a lot to do with other things.

"Alex, good to see you around the house," Bradley said. About forty years old with a prognathous jawbone, Bradley considered the happiest times of his life the afternoons just before Christmas, when he spent time with his three daughters, trimming the tree and laying out the gifts in front of the chimney; he had once broken out with nervous herpes on his left arm when he was station chief in Guatemala and had ordered the assassination of two Jesuit priests in El Quiche.

"Passing by," Alex said, showing a broad smile.

"I hear Snow White is worse than one of those manuals that Peter is going around handing out to bring you up to date on communication. That you've broken your own record," Dr. Nelson said, hobbling over to the chair where Alex sat and gripping his arm.

Alex kept smiling. It seemed like the end of a movie that was congealing in the last scene.

"What I like best about your operations, Alex, is that I don't understand anything. . . . And then they turn out well. You must have turned into the devil," Bradley said, sipping his coffee.

"They say that if you had to take the mental health exam that all new recruits take, they'd lock you away forever in a mental hospital in Alexandria," Dr. Nelson said, squeezing his arm tighter.

"I have a few notes I'm going to read to you. In the end, I just want a yes or no answer," Bradley said. He took a small notebook and read calmly:

"Operation Dream of Snow White has for its objective: to create a profound crisis in the Sandinista elite. Affect the relationships among the commanders, foster friction between them and the Sandinista base, revive the old tendencies that divided Sandinismo, affect their relationship of trust on the popular level, politically neutralize some of them, affect their credibility on a worldwide level, morally discredit them. The central target of the Operation is Machado, vice minister of the interior."

He paused. Alex, who had not given up his smile, said: "Yes."

Bradley continued: "It is about, and I am quoting you, Alex, consolidating the following in international public opinion: (a) Machado is a drug trafficker and has a fortune hidden in Mexico, he has used Sandinista resources and materials to do so. (b) Luaces finds out and Machado kills him. (c) The news leaks to Tomás Borge, who conceals it because Machado is one of the GPPS. (d) It is possible that there are other Sandinista officers implicated in the operation. In sum, and in terms of international public opinion, Sandinismo is a cave full of rats with drug dealers, murderers and harborers."

"Yes," Alex said.

"And how the hell are you going to do it? You don't have a point of departure. There's nothing to base your story on," Dr. Nelson declared.

Alex smiled and remained silent.

"The foundation of the entire story is that journalists don't believe in coincidences, and you are fabricating a million," Bradley said. "Everything is based on 'involuntary vehicles.' Isn't that what you call them?"

"Yes," Alex said.

"And you trust a group of radicals, leftist journalists, a former Dajnavna Sigurnost Bulgarian agent for an operation worth six hundred fifty-four thousand dollars?"

"That's right," Alex said.

"I don't like this, Alex. It will be a miracle if it works."

"Have they been throwing something on the trees?" Alex asked after a few moments of silence. "You don't hear the birds."

"Dr. Nelson has been eating them, Alex," Bradley said, ending the conversation.

Alex left the room with his hands crossed behind his back; he had to catch a flight to Mexico City. Good, they weren't going to thwart him; better yet, they weren't going to attempt to collaborate in ruining everything. They'd even said that the thing would fail and the conversation had no doubt been taped, thereby absolving them of responsibility. And furthermore, what Dr. Nelson was doing to the birds was fucking them, not eating them.

HOW ABOUT A
BULGARIAN LIKE THIS?
(IX)

In the Pleven jail, the days were longer than the nights, Stoyan supposed. He was guessing because he never saw the sun from his cell. Maria would be ten years old, nine, twenty-five, and he had never been able to give her a doll, never taken her to her first dance, he'd never been able to tell her stories on stormy nights, he'd never been a father to his lost daughter.

That's why he rewrote *The Count of Monte Cristo,* and *Winnetou's Revenge,* and *Good-bye to Mompracem;* that's why, and because locking himself in with Karl May, with Dumas and Salgari, was revenge against the inherently boring lectures of Bulganin's reports and Malenkov's pedagogical texts. That's why, and because even though they were monitoring his dreams, it didn't serve them at all. Because he dreamed of tropical islands, with mangrove swamps in which you could hear the tigers roar, with plains where the buffalo still grazed, where a silver rifle was a man's most precious possession, along with his horse.

Through a window painted on the cell wall with charcoal, he contemplated the world. At times, seeing the Eiffel Tower or the suburbs of Madrid, or the muddy waters of the Adriatic, he wondered whether he had become a deserter of the worldwide revolution, one of those who no longer wanted to open the door of the new world and make it spin on a different axis; one of those who no longer believed in the possibility of profound change in the rules of the human game. He told himself no. That others had been the ones to abandon ship, others had passed to the enemy's side, not he. Others, for example, the people who kept him imprisoned.

The days passed. Stoyan had no idea what was happening outside. He tried to sense the changes in the world situation through the subtle mood swings of the guards. He tried to infer that an offer of a new cup to replace an old broken one signified an uprising in the working-class neighborhoods of Berlin or an open letter from Bertolt Brecht, or an agrarian crisis in the Soviet five-year plan. The offer of an old newspaper for hygienic purposes could mean the death of Yezhov or a slip in favor for Beria. The paper itself was a fountain of information when read between the lines.

In those years, he thought a lot about Fucik, and those words he wrote in jail stating that the Nazis could make mincemeat of his body, but they would never have access to his ideas, to his soul. During those years, Stoyan was never alone. Perhaps that's how he defeated his captors. Accompanied by Edmund Dantès, the Count of Monte Cristo, old Shatterhand and Winnetou and Yanez and Sandokan. His company and perseverance made him invincible. The dictators were mortal, man's stubbornness was not. Nonetheless, he kept good notes on the blood debts created between the persecuted and the persecutors.

Not only did Stoyan Vasilev have a blind faith in adventure novels, he also had a certain confidence in the kindness of time become history.

MAD DOG'S
DEALS / SUICIDE PACT

Commander Ontiveros placed the Japanese man's hand near the pistol, just to the side of his own hand, and although the rigor mortis was setting in on the big asshole, he pressed his finger on the trigger, firing a shot at the ceiling. Two burned cartridges, right. One in the temple and the second, of course, at the ceiling, "everything just right," all set. The Japanese was almost smiling, almost thanking Mad Dog for the favor of making it a suicide and not a murder. A much better story for the grandchildren. "My granddad, in accordance with the Bushido code, shot himself in the mouth when they found out he was smuggling coke." And in verse, no less. These stupid guys, so kamikaze. The other asshole, the partner, got a shot in the forehead, it looked like a third eye planted equidistant from the other two, making a Bermuda Triangle. Mad Dog must have looked at them closely, almost affectionately, like someone contemplating a fine work of art in print. Drum-roll! A suicide pact!

"Drumroll my ass," he would say to himself later, once the euphoria of having thundered the pair of faggots wore off. How much money can you make off a dead man? Taking their wallets, pennies from their pant pockets, and even a credit card, negotiable with an irregular agent, a godmother who worked for him reselling televisions bought with stolen credit cards. Nothing. Pure shit. He could sell the corpses to the competition, sell them the favor, but they wouldn't give much, because the Japanese and his mate had been entering the market with the timidity of Ukrainian dancers. Pure bullshit, then. He had to recognize that he'd killed out of stupidity, exclusively out of stupidity, out of getting heated up.

The shot had escaped him in the midst of discussion in the hotel room where they met him.

Mad Dog Ontiveros would go off in a different direction to make amends for his stupidity. He would go over the coke deposits and see whether he could shop them around, or if it would better suit him to "discover" it—the photographer from *La Prensa* would photograph him among a pile of little sacks and he could thus make it through the month. One third for the photograph, the rest for the business. No, he was too fair with the nation, he could have passed for a good functionary. A quarter for the picture of the "discovery," the rest for business. That's it, none of that "my flag is raised on the mast . . ."

The dead men were smiling at him. Those stupid corpses, so nice, he would say to himself that afternoon.

JOURNALISTS' STORIES

(J U L I O   S P E A K S)

Carlos Machado opened the hotel room door and embraced Greg. I looked at him twice. He was the same. With so many things coming apart in the middle of the road, only intuition is left to do away with your doubts.

"We have a lot to talk to you about, Carlos," said Greg, who also seemed to believe in intuition, though perhaps less than I did. Go figure.

"The best thing is the revolution," Machado said. "The second best is to have friends. Or they're equal, brother, because without one, you can't do the other, so."

We sat on the carpet and a bottle of *Flor de caña* immediately appeared. The room seemed to come straight out of one of the battlefronts. Someone had been reading magazines on the floor and the bathroom had been too small to hang the recently washed socks. Machado carried with him this sense of disaster. He could turn a room at the Ritz into a mountain encampment.

"You look like you've been working a lot. Greg looks Mexican and you look like a gringo, Julito."

"They say you're in trouble," Greg said, not beating around the bush.

Machadito looked at us carefully, first one then the other. Then he took our glasses of rum on ice from our hands and put them out of our reach on the night table.

"Seriously? Really? You look like somebody turned you around and you didn't believe him, but it's left you in a stew."

Bloody hell, if this continued, we'd never be able to play poker again. Everyone could guess what we were thinking. Our faces had become transparent. Bad for a reporter. Greg and I were going to have to practice in front of a mirror with a picture of Buster Keaton.

"There are rumors out there," I began.

"Out there? Where?" Machado quickly responded.

"They say there's a mole in the Sandinista elite, that the CIA has him fucked on some drug thing and that's how he toppled. They say you've got problems. They say the commanders are fighting among themselves," Greg said, summarizing and always the professional, not revealing his sources.

"Motherfucker, a pipeline of deceit, the snitches in this world," Machado said, his only response; then he took the offensive. "And you bought it?"

"The vice ministers answer, the journalists ask questions," I told him.

"But we're more than that, we're friends. Or not anymore?" Machadito was screwing us.

"So it is, *compadre.* Because we are friends, we came and we ask questions, clearly, with no double edges."

"Go ahead, then. No double edges. Who's the mole? Who's the source? Which commanders are squabbling among us? What problems do we have?"

"You're the mole, the CIA caught you doing something and they've got you blackmailed."

"That's what they're saying?" he asked.

"That's what they're saying," I answered, swallowing my saliva.

"Good to know. Now I've got to know why they're saying it.

It's nothing but slander. Give me two days to turn these stories around. That's all, two days. Because you don't believe I'm the mole."

"If you're a mole, we're Chinese," I told him. Greg agreed very ceremoniously; then he pulled up the corners of his eyes with his fingers and tautened his face. Shit, he really looked Chinese. Machado laughed.

"If something comes up that can go to press, you'll have it first, a twenty-four-hour advantage. I owe it to you."

"I like hearing that from you, Mister Vice Minister," Greg said. I sighed audibly.

"If you don't give me back my rum, Carlito, we're not telling you the other story, the good one, the true one," I said.

Machado walked to the night table and returned our glasses. "So there's more, eh?" he asked.

"We want to write your story, Commander."

"Don't bullshit me, brother. If you two are serious journalists, you only interview Nobel prize winners and Oscar-winning actresses, ministers and up. . . ."

"So you see, asshole," Greg said with a Mexican accent.

ABDUCTION

As she fixed a false eyelash in the mirror of the elevator, Eve felt a finger pressing into her stomach.

"This is a kidnapping, you cross-eyed old dumbshit," the dwarf said.

Eve, who did not speak Spanish, looked down and contemplated a dwarf trying to pierce her navel with a sharp fingernail. She wasn't biased, but if she was going to enter into relations on an elevator, it was not going to be with a dwarf's finger and not by way of the navel. What, they didn't teach Sex Ed in South America?

"By God, you better raise your hands," the dwarf insisted in Spanish.

Eve tried to pull a revolver from her purse, but she had nothing but cosmetics and a small notebook. She tried to remember where she'd put her small revolver. Meanwhile, Marcelino the dwarf pulled out a monumental (at least for his size) .45 and aimed at the place where his finger had been seconds before. He stuck his other hand under Eve's skirt. The woman looked at him in surprise. The things that went on in Manhattan elevators: Spanish-speaking rapist dwarves. The only thing missing was for him to whip out a guitar to liven up the affair. The dwarf's hand ascended to the elastic of Eve's bikini and began playing with it.

"If you don't raise your hands, fatty, I'm going to take off your underwear," Marcelino said.

"What are you going to do when we reach the lobby?" Eve asked in English.

"Continue on to the basement, little girl," the dwarf said in English, imitating Edward G. Robinson's accent. Hearing that, Eve realized this was serious. The dwarf, in turn, seeing the transformation in the woman's attitude, thought about the changes one could accomplish with the magic of languages. St. Berlitz watches over.

Benigno was ready, pistol in hand in the basement. The dwarf led Eve to the car, pushing her buttocks with the little hand up Alex's assistant's skirt.

"My boss is going to bury you two hundred yards below the Hudson," Eve said.

"Your boss knows you're with us, he loaned you out for a long party, two nights at least, girl," the dwarf answered.

"What's she saying?" Benigno asked.

"That she likes dark, big guys like you, but prefers small guys with balls like me. And she also said she likes maraca players."

"And when did she say all that?" Benigno asked, suspiciously.

"In the elevator."

Eve, who had understood the international word "maracas," thought they were going to serenade her after all.

Without removing his hand from inside her skirt, the dwarf led her to the backseat of a Japanese car and got in beside her. Eve tried to free herself from the little hand before sitting but the dwarf

adjusted it just right to keep his hand under the skirt, now in front.
When Eve tried to protest, the dwarf showed her the black hole of
the pistol. If the woman tried to move, he was going to uproot half
the tuft of her pubic hair in one shot.

"Did you leave the kidnapper's note?" Benigno asked.

"In an envelope in the office mailbox of those assholes," the
dwarf answered. Benigno started the car.

ONE HUNDRED ONE

THE VERSION OF EMILIO SALGARI'S *GOOD-BYE TO MOMPRACEM* CREATED BY STOYAN VASILEV IN THE PLEVEN PRISON

Old tigers perhaps, but not
toothless, Yanez thought as the *Vengador* plowed the open sea
toward the islands of Sunda. Raja Brooks, the Englishman's dog,
had died five years ago, the Sultan of Jahore had disappeared
consumed by venereal diseases, Cowie the Scotsman had vanished
in the mangrove swamps of the Philippines, even the East Indies
Company had gone on to a better life six years before. But the
Tigers were alive.

"How old are you, Sandokan?"

"Don't remind me, little brother. Are you trying to ruin the
sunset?"

Exactly. A garnet sun set the waters of the Indian Ocean
alight, staining the blue of the sea with a deep red. They had sailed

due east for the last eighteen hours with the crew still depleted by the strange disease, and the rest of them exhausted.

Yanez gave a faint yawn.

"I think it's time to have a talk with our strange Bulgarian," Sandokan said. "Indeed, where is his native land?"

"It's a small country in the Balkans with coasts along the Black Sea; one that's been in Turkish hands."

Responding to the nonexistent call, Mijail Vasilev appeared on deck, accompanied by a young Javanese whom the Tigers had hardly noticed during the skirmish the night before. Perhaps that's why they observed him closely instead of casting their eyes on the Bulgarian astronomer. He was a twenty-five-year-old boy with an olive complexion and a confident stride. Under a red turban, a face of fine features and shrewd eyes appeared. On the left side of his chin was a small scar.

"Thank you, gentlemen, I am alive thanks to my friend Vasilev and your hospitality," Malang said immediately, stretching out his hand.

"We have come very far to find you, little friend," Yanez answered. "The pleasure is absolutely ours. A bottle in the ocean saved us from retreat, call it 'spiritual.' "

Sandokan snorted, remembering the alleged 'spiritual' retreat, and shook the boy's outstretched hand.

"Fine, now, you owe us an explanation," Yanez said. "How did you find out we were looking for you? What is your relationship to Vasilev? How did you escape the Sirim jail? I understand you were imprisoned there, is that right?"

"We'll trade the answers for the story of the bottle," Mijail Vasilev answered. "I'm sure it is just as interesting as ours."

"Sambliong, bring a table on deck and a basket with chicken, cold cuts and some bottles of wine," Yanez ordered. "A good story is told in style."

He then turned to watch the sun disappearing in the ocean and lit a Manila cigar after wetting it with his saliva.

ALEX OBSERVED THE GROUNDS . . .

. . . like a stage decorator contemplating his work on opening day. He was seated in the back of the small auditorium, enjoying a laboriously manufactured anonymity. Thermally X-rayed, the assistants would have acquired warm and cool tones. His were the blues, the secretary of the Christie Foundation, a black woman busily circulating through the aisles, Grumpy-ten, the Australian reporter who generously revealed her thighs in the third row, Sleepy, farther away, near the exit to the lobby, smoking. The Sandinistas were in red, one of them at the table waiting his turn to participate, seated next to an Italian writer; and out there in the second row, his favorite Bulgarian, a little old perhaps, perhaps not as absorbed as Alex needed. A little farther back, he made out the journalists Greg Simon and Julio Fernández; curiously, next to the latter sat Elena Jordan. Had Alex accidentally propitiated a matrimonial reconciliation? That would be excellent, worthy of the best soap opera. How silly, he reflected, to be watching the story's characters as if they were armies. Actors on the same set, each imprisoned by a role. In the Alexian universe, there could be slipups, moments of insanity or rancor, obsessions, but there would always be, in Alex's opinion, the return to calmness, the impartial perception of the game and the elements in dispute, the very British sensation of fair game in the best context of a gentleman's sport. Even the worst pig has a heart. Without listening to the words spoken into the microphone (a writer of Angolan stories was speaking, a kindly mulatto trying to explain to his colleagues the difficulty of being a writer in an illiterate world), Alex watched Machado carefully. The small commander listened attentively, drank in every word. From the beginning of the conference, he had adopted the role of eager student, and took notes in a notebook, asked the other writers circumspect questions in the halls, exchanged books.

Alex perceived the murmur of the simultaneous translations whizzing through the earphones and tried to give it a musical line. He looked at his watch. He looked up and saw that Sharon Williams, the Australian reporter, had switched seats to be next to Carlos Machado. Good, he said to himself.

A friendly hand touched his back, shaking him from his role as play director. Benjamin was behind him. He wasn't supposed to be there. A grotesque grin distorted Alex's face. It started at his mouth and culminated in his eyes.

"There's a special jet waiting for you at the airport, they want to see you at Langley within five hours, boss," Benjamin said.

"Do you know what's happening?"

"Have you heard of a Cuban general named Ochoa?"

"One of the guys they've got in Angola?"

"I think so."

"And what about him?"

"I don't have the slightest idea."

ONE MORE OF ELENA JORDAN'S MANY REJECTED THESIS PROPOSALS

$\mathbf{G}$od, wishing to play a practical joke on Mexico, in the late 1970s revived Guillermo Prieto, poet and marvelous social critic, renowned liberal (see Carlos J. Sierra, "Guillermo Prieto," Mexican Journalists Club, 1962) and Secretary of the Treasury in one of Benito Juárez's administrations who died destitute, of whom it was said that even as Minister and custodian of the nation's treasury, he did not have the money to buy the buttons that fell off his overcoat.

God, in His macabre omnipotence and wanting to endow the joke with all His dramatic consistency, got him an incognito job in the financial auditor's department of Channel 13 TV.

Prieto, author of such memorable phrases as: "Woe is he who seeks state service as an opportunity for loot," was drinking an Orange Crush in the cafeteria his first day on the job. He was attempting to keep his long white beard out of the ketchup on the foul hamburger he was eating, when he heard a conversation that made his venerable ears perk up.

Someone was talking about three grand pianos that had mysteriously disappeared the week before. Don Guillermo, who was having trouble locating himself in the ways and uses of the language of the second half of the twentieth century, did not, on the other hand, have problems conceiving the inherent difficulties in the theft of three grand pianos, considering their size, the constant police vigilance exercised at the TV station's doors and the necessity that some fairly large vehicle would have had to participate in the operation. So he took note of the matter in his notebook with the black marbled covers, and promised himself to investigate it.

After the first week of work, the notebook gathered other notations on similar matters, for example, a sentence overheard from the subdirector of production which Don Guillermo promised himself he'd study carefully: "Jeepers, jeepers, finder's keepers," the precise meaning of which he couldn't quite capture, but the general meaning of which he had little doubt about. He had a few other cryptic notations in his notebook about the Persian rug mystery. It seemed that for the setting of a Western-style soap opera on an open-country set specially constructed on the back lot, they'd bought a sixty-five-yard-long Persian rug, costing several million pesos. The Persian rug, of course, disappeared seconds after having appeared. This posed an additional mystery, as well as a good question: Why did they want a Persian rug on a country soap opera? Even better, or at least just as good, was how the rug had entered the station in the carpet company truck at 5:15 and left the station at 5:32, setting a precedent of uncommon efficiency in decentralized public companies.

Don Guillermo's notebook also had notes about the existence of triple payrolls in the news department, two of them illegal, on which one of the station head's nephews and his chauffeur, the girlfriend of one of the night program directors, and a cousin of the news director were listed as newsroom employees, though no one had ever seen them around the place.

In the midst of this strange information, the gathering of which had taken up a good part of his working hours, Don Guillermo had also found time to interest himself in the interpretation of one of the channel's directors who had inquired into the whereabouts of some "master," seemingly not knowing he referred to the general control room; or obtaining information about a few memorable cocaine-induced sessions (a fine powder, according to Don Guillermo—similar to the talcum powders so popular as a remedy for chafing during his era—which the children's program animators insisted on stuffing up their noses).

And so on.

The current work attempts to follow a course similar to the investigations of Don Guillermo, obviously with him as a character, and analyze the Judge Advocate's court (see copy dated April 1986, opinions of the General Control of the Federation of June 16, 1985, and April 16, 1986) and the public denunciations (see *Proceso,* April 23, 1984, *La Jornada,* December 6, 1986, *Uno Más Uno,* December 5, 6 and 9, 1984) that the administrative management of state-run Mexican television over the last six years made in the years between '82 and '86, in light of the moral thinking of nineteenth-century national liberalism.

It would be something like reviving H. G. Wells, obviously in *The War of the Worlds* (there are no ulterior cultural motives in the citation). A confrontation of morals, notions of public service, absolutely different practices in state management and of which we could mention (see Journal of Congressional sessions, April 1987, the participation of the PRI delegates, Langorica and Ríos Smith) that the second ones are said to be, paradoxically, heirs to the first.

The thesis will provide a couple of supplements dedicated to quotations by the functionaries who regulated the life of public TV during those years, particularly mentioning the eminent high officeholders of the nation who served as an umbrella for the plunder.

Elena Jordan, Mexico City

P.S. 1. Attached is a detailed biography and a provisional chapter outline.

P.S. 2. Given the repeated rejection of proposals the applicant has received in the past months, I would be interested in the jury's specifying, in case of further rejection, whether it is for methodological reasons or out of solidarity with the corrupt practices of the station mentioned in the proposal. Thank you in advance for the explanation. E.J.

HOW ABOUT A
BULGARIAN LIKE THIS?
(X)

W hen Stoyan was able to do
what he really wanted, someone thought he was too old to do it.
Stoyan proved he wasn't. He hustled more than anyone. He arrived before the story and told it better than most. He made dozens
of new friends. He improved his Spanish and enriched it, picking
up Argentinean words here and there *(medias* instead of *calcetines,
bombachas* for *bragas)*, Chilean words *(pucha)*, Cuban *(acere*, he
said to the DPA telegraph operator), Mexican (six ways to say
testicles: *tompiates, talayates, guevos, los merascas, la bolsa* and
macetas), and Bolivian words. The current generation of Latin
American revolutionaries loved that Bulgarian, who did not seem
European, serious or mysterious, who did not like neckties, who
had a romantic past (bloody hell, he'd been in the International
Brigades in Spain and a guerrilla soldier in the Balkans) and who
shared the carefree attitude, the jokes, and the idea of the revolution as a passionate devotion, the moral adventure, as well as
knowledge about the shot cadence of the Garand 0 or the M1.

In '61, he was in Havana with Che, but in '65 he'd been in the
Venezuelan mountains with El Bachiller interviewing Americo
Martín, and was photographed drinking wine with the MIR commander Miguel Enríquez. They said he'd been an intimate friend
of Raul Sendic and that when he flew KLM or Air France, he
painted Tupamaro stars on the bathroom walls. He had interviewed César Montes in Guatemala and some said he served as a

messenger. He was the suitable type to invite to drink maté and you didn't have to explain how to make it. One could ask the Bulgarian to sit down and listen to an ancient record of *carnavilitos* from the old country. He had an enviable collection of Mexican *bandanas,* one of which was given to him in the Lecumberri Prison by Demetrio Vallejo, and he knew by heart many of Roque Dalton's unpublished poems, because he'd heard them recited from a notebook by Roque himself in Prague.

Vasilev, the "Bulgarian Grandpa," believed as everyone does that this was the time of the furnace and he wouldn't see more than the light. He was thus witness to victory and defeat, more of the latter. He recognized the cadavers of friends, he tried to get interviews in jails that were denied him, he followed the trail of the exiled, he watched as the smoke columns rose black and plumed from the presidential palace of La Moneda and contemplated with his eyes wide open the attempt of the last ELN men to attack the Latakia barracks when the army had risen against Torres in La Paz. He was essentially a witness, and that means he told many stories, heard many more, kept many secrets that were turning into anecdotes to remember in time; he wrote dozens of articles, took millions of photos, hardly any worth collecting.

Just when it seemed that defeat would be the common theme of the great wave, and that he would be one of the many journalists testifying to a time of death without destiny, the end of his story came about, altering the whole thing.

Stoyan got to Managua in time to enter with the Sandinista columns. He was seventy-two when he traveled by jeep with Machadito, who was twenty-four upon reaching Somoza's bunker.

There is a photo taken by the Mexican journalist Pedro Valtierra in which Stoyan Vasilev and Carlos Machado, arm in arm, atop a tank, are screaming to each other at the top of their lungs, yelling to be heard over the shrieks of jubilation of the people turned out in the streets. You can't tell which of the two's mouth is wider open.

They walked through the bunker together. Stoyan stopped to contemplate the remnants of the dismantled tyranny: old boots, women's lingerie hung over a curtain rod and drying in the bathroom, a telephone off the hook, bullet cases, a television with a broken screen, a toilet perforated by one last bullet, the deserted plastic rings of a six-pack of beer, some Japanese slippers, military fatigues abandoned in the fight. . . .

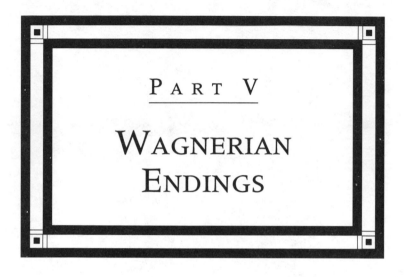

PART V

WAGNERIAN
ENDINGS

THE INVISIBLES OF
FORTY-SIXTH STREET

Just when did the Baja Californi-
ans arrive on Forty-sixth Street? At what point did the subtle
invasion occur? Who was first? Blurred, dancing silhouettes, hazy
soft presences under the protection of skyscrapers. Invisible skyscrapers.

Alvarito was the first to arrive. He got a job in Blimpie's, a
fast-food restaurant, taking out the garbage and washing metal
trays. He did not speak English and made himself understood to
the manager, a Turk, by gestures and at times with the help of one
of the delivery boys, who was Salvadoran. Shy, silent, absolutely
convinced that if he wandered fifteen yards from his job he would
lose it and never find another one. For the first weeks, to protect
himself from the enormousness of the city full of incomprehensible
signs, ungraspable languages and signals made by others, he slept
on the street, in a wasteland reserved for parking a short distance
from the restaurant. For a few dollars, he'd arranged for the
Peruvian night watchman to let him sleep from midnight to five
a.m. under an old Porsche that had been there for months, its
owners on safari in Africa. That's how the first one arrived and the
last one left.

On Mondays and Tuesdays when a Pakistani replaced his

Peruvian acquaintance in the parking lot, Alvarito slept standing up, on the corner, under the rain and neon lights. He wasn't alone for long. In a slow pilgrimage, the others began to appear: Gustavo, Alegrías, Fermin, El Cochi. They became the jacks-of-all-trades of the five restaurants serving fast food and breakfast to the offices in the area: the Hotel Wentworth restaurant, open only from seven to eleven, a Roy Rogers on the corner of Fifth Avenue, the Lim, which delivered breakfasts to the offices, and Harry's, which had the best salad bar selection.

Little by little, the invisibles invaded the street. Their melodic Spanish began to dominate the ordering, the cries, the information: where to put the garbage and when to take it out; where to get cardboard boxes, where to put the bottles of soda and juice, how to prop the door ajar so that it didn't totally close and drive away the customers but so that the wind couldn't blow it open, flooding the basement with rain.

Around five they disappeared again. Now they lived in Brooklyn in a seven-by-twenty-foot room, their bedding on the floor, where they had access to the bathroom at the end of the hall. They commuted by subway. A daily trip going, a daily trip returning. Same stops. Down on Sixth and Forty-eighth. They always carried long sharp kitchen knives under their jackets. They'd learned to live with them. Potential enemies could sense the knives hidden against the chests of the silent invisibles.

They had become even more invisible. No one looked at them, no one saw them. If you asked the retired dance teacher, the Panamanian who worked in a record store on Sixth, the young black library assistant working to pay his way through NYU journalism school, they could answer in all honesty that they'd never seen them. All the invisibles, however, wore the same jacket, undefinable, interchangeable, orangeish nylon, with the Atlanta Braves logo.

Forsaken, inconstant, immune to the rains and the terrible and surprising snow, silent, inscrutable, the five invisibles had a lot of time in their respective isolations to figure out what was going on around them. Treated like furniture, pieces of machinery, disconnected from all reality by language, they had access to other people's stories that they were able to make out or guess. The invisibles knew who smoked marijuana, and why the wife of the Portuguese shopkeeper selling leather bags was cuckolding her husband with the Korean manager at the hotel reception desk;

they knew that the Florida juice distributors gave a better discount to Pete from Blimpie than to the rest of the competitors, and they knew exactly what kind of music each of the regulars liked on that long block between Fifth Avenue and the Avenue of the Americas. In a certain way, with their kitchen knives carefully sharpened every day, carried in a leather holster strapped around the neck and stuck to the chest, they were guardian angels and keepers of order.

On rare occasions, though, they abandoned their silent clouds to touch the bread of the mortals. No one had called upon them to intervene yet. Theirs was a mission of observation, isolated, cautious, seemingly temporary, until they could leave the strange and damned city and return south. They might never return, in which case they would have to reconsider their swift pace through the lives of others; perhaps they would stay in New York (was that the name of this city?) forever. But to plan for eternity, to stay forever, they would have to get wives, make tribe. And although this was not cause for worry during the initial months for those five small-statured men, those swarthy men with very black and bristly hair, decked out in brilliant orange jackets, invisible to the rest of the city, after the sixth month they began to fixate on women. They were looking for the same thing they could offer: a tribe, a clan to protect them from inclement weather, attacks, illegal labor, loneliness and unemployment. It could have been those three Puerto Rican saleswomen at Mart's, an electronics store in the middle of the block, if it weren't that the Puerto Rican electronic girls were in social ascent in a society that measures its waves of new citizens by their proximity to the unreal center of a circle of integration, an objective that could be expressed by the idiotic face of a WASP appearing on a television ad buying fire insurance at the center. At that point, the electronic girls were on the eighth interior circle and the invisibles on the twelfth at best. Nothing there.

It was Alegrías who discovered six gorgeous Pakistani teenagers who worked in a clandestine dressmaking workshop in the middle of the block. But Alvaro also found their zealous parents. They couldn't get close enough to the women even to make signals from a distance.

That was the state of the invisibles when Fermin and El Cochi saw La Gringa eating a breakfast of scrambled eggs and bacon. Both were absolutely captivated. Love at very first sight, they declared when they told each other of the apparition of the woman who glanced at them. They remained totally in love with her, and by extension (conversations, information, descriptions exchanged) spread it to the others.

That could have been the beginning of an impossible love, but it was a good love.

ONE   HUNDRED   SIX

ALEX NEVER GOT
TO . . .

. . . Langley. Dr. Nelson, a gentle woman who awakened all the lost compassion in the world with her poliomyelitis, had gotten a message to him. She was waiting, smiling, in the VIP cafeteria of the Pan Am terminal at JFK. Smiling. Piranhas had that same amorous grin on their mouths just before breakfast.

"Alex, I have good news," she said without inviting him to sit down. "Read this. The return flight to Mexico leaves in ten minutes. Louis will accompany you," she said, pointing to a Texan with rabbit teeth who looked at him with a smile similar to that of his patroness.

"You made me come for this? In the middle of an operation? In the final phase? This is going to cost you your head, Virginia," Alex said, calling her by her first name for the first time.

"You're simply going to adore me when you read that file . . . ," Dr. Nelson said, pointing to the yellow ringed binder with about fifty pages. Alex took it in his hands and weighed it.

"What is it?"

"We bought a Mexican diplomatic report obtained through an editorial leak in *Granma,* the Cuban Communist Party's organ. As you read it, don't forget the source of the information. It's slanted. A story about which we had previous, but insufficient knowledge, and which was in the freezer waiting its turn. Now it is something like your ticket to glory with Snow White. When you finish reading it, hand it over to Louis, he'll take care of everything. Carry on with Snow White; even if the operation is not complete, let it advance. It's the best time. That," she said, again pointing to the file, "is something that will publicly burst next week. There remains just one thing: to consider the timing. The DDO thinks it might be too much to tie Snow White to that. I believe the opposite. The decision is yours. . . . Think about it, saturation of the media and those things. Give me your assessment via Louis. A simple yes or no."

"What about the marriages?" Alex asked.

"Exactly the same. A yes or a no. . . ."

Alex turned his back on her. As he stored the file in his briefcase, he felt the Texan come to his side.

"Incidentally, they asked me to advise you of something lateral. Yesterday a dwarf kidnapped your assistant. For God's sakes, Alex, the things that go in on your cave. You are the only one of us who would triumph in the movies, the rest of us are so, so boring."

"Don't worry, Doctor, that would be for reasons of passion. My secretaries have always had trouble with dwarfs."

O N E   H U N D R E D   S E V E N

JOURNALISTS' STORIES

(G R E G   S P E A K S)

Armando handed me the photo and waited for my reaction. I had none. I studied the two subjects photographed on the streets of a Mexican city (Morelia? Querétaro? Puebla?) I raised my eyes and looked at my old acquaintance, Armando. Perhaps unwittingly we had always placed him on the wrong side. Maybe he worked for the English MI5, or the French services. It wasn't hard to imagine Armando speaking in a Sorbonne French.

"Who is the other one?" he asked.

"What city are they in?" I asked.

"Puebla, if you study the photo carefully you can see the date of the newspaper in the other man's hand. . . . Who is the man, Mr. Simon?"

"I have no idea, but it doesn't matter, Armando, because you're going to tell me, aren't you?"

Fats had gone over to a vending machine that sold coffee and chocolate, taking advantage of one of the breaks in the conference. Armando had chosen that instant to appear, taking out the photo from inside a book. I tried to decipher the title of the volume. If it was Spengler's *The Decline of the West,* Armando worked for the German services; if it was the *History of the French Revolution,* by Michelet, Armando worked for the French; if it was Jane Fonda's method for losing weight, Armando worked for the CIA.

It was *Where the Air Is Clear* by Carlos Fuentes. Who the hell did Armando work for? The Mexican government?

"This is about Rolando M. Limas."

"You, who are all-knowing, Armando, tell me. What were this Señor Limas and the Commander Machado discussing when the photo was taken?"

"The weather, Mr. Simon. They are talking about Puebla's climate, how it's gotten worse recently and is dryer every year. . . . You can keep the photo forever as long as you don't say you got it from me."

Armando turned around. I no longer saw his vest embossed with flowers and birds. I turned my eyes back to the photo. Machadito hadn't come out very well, he was slightly bent over, but his gaze seemed to be riveted on the Mexican drug trafficker. Not *a* drug trafficker, the best, the biggest, the quintessential drug trafficker.

"Wasn't that Armando, *compadre*? What the fuck was he doing around here?" Fats asked, balancing the coffees.

"A picture. He came to bring us this picture. Fats, what the hell is happening here? What the fuck is going on here?"

THE OCHOA FILE/THE
FILE ALEX READ ON THE
PLANE

Alex opened the binder, noted
that the first page of the original report was missing, and read:

- In March of '89, Fidel Castro asked the Ministry of the
  Interior to open an investigation into the possible collusion
  of Cuban officials in drug trafficking activities. His petition
  was based on information from "Colombian friends" who
  were gathering information on their own local drug dealers,
  and in the depositions of two drug dealers detained in
  Miami there was a certain international echo. Fidel
  requested specifically that they establish beyond doubt the
  existence of a "Cuban connection" and the involvement of
  people from the Ministry of the Interior.
- A few days later and in the course of the investigation,
  Counterintelligence detected radio signals crossing between
  Cuba, the U.S. and Colombia. Analyzing the material, they
  arrived at the conclusion that indeed they were executing
  drug trafficking operations using Cuba as a step in
  transports between Colombia and Miami. The signals
  were detected from the last days of March until the 24th of
  April. The intelligence operation managed to precisely
  locate the region of emissions, in the outskirts of Havana,
  near the Almendares River, but did not advance further,
  because the emissions ceased for no apparent reason before
  the operation reached its culmination.

- On the 27th of April, an evaluation meeting was held, attended by the directors of the Ministry of the Interior. Among many others and not having anything to do directly with the detection of the radio signals, Colonel Antonio La Guardia, chief of the MC Group (commercial antiblockade operations), attended the meeting.
- For over a year the DEA kept a thick "Cuban" file. It was based on some recordings made in Panama between one of their cover agents and a Cuban military captain who had offered the DEA man the opportunity to use Cuba as a step. The Cuban insinuated that he had official support for these operations. The second element was the confessions of Reinaldo and Rubén Ruiz, cocaine traffickers of Cuban origin detained in Miami, whose interviews with the district attorney's office gave an account of the use of Cuban military installations (specifically, a military airport in Varadero) in 1987, as a step between Colombia and the United States. Among the depositions given by the detained drug dealers there was information that caused doubt as to their soundness, like the one that claimed they had access to the cigars Fidel smoked (Fidel had quit smoking two years prior to 1987). The Cubans will subsequently have access to this information and will suppose furthermore that the CIA has more information, but is reserving it for either a blackmail operation or a rigged accusation.
- Parallel and unconnected to the aforementioned, the FAR's Department of Counterintelligence had initiated an investigation against the division general and chief of the Cuban mission in Angola, Arnaldo Ochoa. The origin of the investigation had been a series of reports on scandalous military behavior (note: the general had, in Cuban parameters, an almost untouchable past: soldier in the revolution, in the invasion of Las Villas with Camilo Cienfuegos, assignments in Venezuela during Che's era, chief of combat troops in Ethiopia, a mentioned candidate for the direction of the Cuban Army in the west). There had been scandalous parties, womanizing, smuggled goods, financial tricks outside Angolan law. This investigation led Raul Castro to call Ochoa to a semiprivate meeting (the 29th of May), which Generals Abelardo Colome and Ulises

del Toro also attended, where they denounced his behavior. Ochoa granted importance to the affair, but apparently did not satisfy his superiors, because the investigation continued.

- Raul Castro called Ochoa to another meeting, this time private (June 2nd). He was not promoted. It is already obvious, at that point, that he will not be named chief of the western military in Cuba. The investigation continues to accumulate elements and directs itself toward Ochoa's assistant, Captain Jorge Martínez Valdés, and toward Colonel Rodríguez Estupinan, the general's aide-de-camp in Angola.

- The investigation has already revealed a series of connections implicating Ochoa and his two assistants in dirty business, corruption, the smuggling of ivory and diamonds, the sale of military stores like sugar and fish flour, relations with prostitutes whom they brought into combat zones; monumental parties and orgies where they "blew the house down," gifts made to subordinates to create a good atmosphere. Fraudulent deals against the Popular Sandinista Army and the Republic of Angola have surfaced in which Ochoa acted as an intermediary in the purchase of arms and kept a portion of the proceeds. The accusations center around Diocles Torralbas, minister of transportation, Brigadier General Patricio La Guardia, representative of the Angolan Ministry of the Interior, who had served as a contact in various deals, and his brother, Tony La Guardia, MININT colonel, in charge of the famous MC section (he first directed the CIMEX Corporation, and later the Z Group). Note: these two later characters also have an outstanding career in the revolution from its early years (they come from the Revolution Governing Body) to the present day. Tony was an officer of the Special Troops and Patricio was in Chile during the overthrow of Allende.

- General Abelardo Colome interviews the La Guardia brothers May 30th and June 2nd. Patricio is deported to Havana away from his assignment in Angola, and Tony has been dismissed as the director of the MC Group. In the second interview, they are interrogated about their relations with Ochoa and the contraband business in

Angola. They try to cover up. The crux of their argument is that bartering operations frequently develop in the terrain to obtain provisions destined for the Cuban Army during operations.

- In conversations with Raul, the existence of a foreign bank account in Ochoa's name is discovered. ("Do you have a foreign bank account?" "Ah, yes, a few little funds." "But how many do you have?" "Nothing, just peanuts.")
- Sunday, the 11th of June, a meeting is held in which Fidel, Raul and several high officials of MINFAR, including General Leopoldo Cintra, who is at that time in charge of the mission in Angola and who brings new elements to the investigation, participate. They decide to arrest those implicated after evaluating the possible repercussions on public opinion and the requisite international campaigns.
- June 12, 1989, Division General Arnaldo Ochoa, Captain Jorge Martínez, the La Guardia brothers—Brigadier General Patricio and MININT Colonel Tony—Colonel Rodríguez Estupinan and the minister of transportation, Diocles Torralba, are arrested. News of the arrests does not leak out of the country.
- A few hours later, documents appearing in the house of Captain Martínez reveal the first signs that this is more serious than they thought. Connections are discovered between Martínez and foreign Colombian characters, a false passport. . . .
- On the night of the 13th, the investigation proceeds toward the MC Group, formerly Department Z of the MININT, which is devoted to commercial operations to break the blockade and which was until a few days ago headed by Tony La Guardia. Implications are discovered that a group of officials were involved in multiple illegal dealings and, more important, the keys to a network of drug trafficking organizations from the Ministry of the Interior begin to appear.
- On the 15th, Section Chief Captain Amado Patrón, Section Chief of Naval Operations and Lieutenant Colonel Alexis Lago, First Lieutenant José Luis Piñeda, Captain Leonel Estevez, Major Gabriel Prendes, and Officers Antonio Sánchez, Rosa Maria Abierno, Miguel Ruiz Poo and Eduardo Díaz Izquierdo (treasurer of the group from

which half a million dollars was seized) are arrested. A total
of one million dollars and a quarter million Cuban pesos is
confiscated from the group. One of them, Patrón, owns
eleven cars; all of them own collectible weapons and
electronic equipment. This must be evaluated in the context
of normal Cuban conditions of material shortages.

- The investigation reveals that Ochoa and his subordinate
  Martínez have been in contact with North American
  mafiosos and people from the Medellín cartel to use Cuba
  as a middle step in narcotics trafficking operations.
  Specifically, since mid-1986, Martínez, speaking for Ochoa,
  has maintained relations with the Colombians through
  contacts realized in Panama with an Italian–North
  American, Frank Morfa, who proposed that Martínez
  participate in money-laundering operations and be in
  contact with Fabel Pareja, a man from the Medellín cartel.
  This latter suggested he travel to Colombia and says he will
  get him a Colombian passport so that he can speak directly
  with Pablo Escobar. Ochoa green-lights the action. The
  conversations deal with potential trafficking operations
  that would use Cuba as the intermediate step (he offers
  them $1,200 for every kilo transported) and the possibility
  of setting up a laboratory somewhere in Africa. Ochoa
  doesn't have the infrastructure and turns to Tony La
  Guardia and his group for support. None of this is stated
  explicitly.
- Ochoa does not know that Tony La Guardia's group has
  been executing successful drug operations for the last two
  years on its own, using connections with exiled Cuban
  boatmen, Mexican drug dealers and indirect contacts with
  Colombia. For this group, Ochoa's intervention serves only
  as reinforcement. This group's first operation dates back to
  April of '87. A Colombian plane landed in the military
  section of the Varadero airport (controlled by the MC
  Group) and unloaded 400 kilos of pure cocaine in IBM
  computer boxes. From there, a month later, it is forwarded
  in speedboats to Miami. This is followed by a marijuana
  operation. In May, a second coke operation with the same
  mechanisms and two more at the end of the year; 500 kilos
  are moved. Two more in 1988 and eight in 1989. In several
  of them a new technique is used: phosphorescent packets of

the drug are dropped from a plane into the sea, in the waters north of the Varadero, and speedboats then gather them up. The group has executed a total of nineteen traffic operations, fifteen of which were successful. They have moved six tons of coke and received $3 million for their collaboration. The MC team has provided clandestine houses for the Miami boatmen, has offered military bases to land the airplanes, has frequently brought Colombian, North American and Mexican drug dealers to Cuba and has lent the infrastructure, boats, warehouses; all this using the cover with other forces within the Ministry of the Interior so that its department's normal operations included obtaining goods subject to the blockade (specialized technical parts, tobacco smuggling operations with the United States, stores for the pharmaceutical industry and hospitals).

- Two hundred million dollars show up in Ochoa's bank account in Panama.
- How can the corruption of fourteen officers of the armed forces and the Ministry of the Interior be explained? The versions by the accused and rumors indicate that irresponsible money management, the temptation to make deals, the development of privileges among sectors of the bureaucracy created an atmosphere of "anything goes." It is possible that some of the implicated got involved in the operations thinking they were authorized operations and that the funds obtained in this way would help them obtain currency to fortify other operations in which they were involved, but the trading of dirty money corrupted everything it touched. It is extremely difficult to evaluate the origins of this behavior.
- It has been decided in Cuba to make these stories public and therefore bring those implicated to justice. On the 14th of June, *Granma* published a short article reporting Ochoa's arrest, which has unleashed all kinds of rumors. It will publish a good part of this information (the material they have received to elaborate it is the base of this report) on Friday, June 16th. One thinks of the possibility that this is the beginning of a broader anticorruption campaign.
- Cuba has categorically denied its implication in drug trafficking; all this information, therefore, signifies a hard

knock to the revolution, the consequences of which are today impossible to evaluate. One would have to add, among many other things, a change in the Cuban attitude faced with the economic repercussions of perestroika that are interpreted on the island as debilitating to morale and stimulating to the return of capitalism. The responsibilities of those in high posts in the Ministry of the Interior are not clear, but indubitably and at least they will be accused of negligence, if not something more serious.

- The implications of the Mexican drug dealers in the operation are quite secondary. It seems that they participated in the proposition solely to create a land entry network in the United States, but the conversations came to naught.
- One would have to. . . .

There it ended. Alex glanced at the date of the report he'd just read. It was dated the fifteenth of June by the Bradley office. Today was the sixteenth; the story was being made public. From the arrest of the accused to the publication, less than one month had passed. He had to make a decision with regard to Snow White.

O N E   H U N D R E D   N I N E

MAD DOG'S DEALS/TAXI

I don't want a fixed-fare taxi, I want a taxi, asshole."

"Another one?" Mad Dog's contact asks him, scratching an annoying, sudden nervous itch that has just set in. "But you've already got six, pal."

Mad Dog Ontiveros is not the sort to allow himself to be intimidated by such crushing logic, and will say to the jerk, very nicely:

"That is one of the five thousand things that should mean shit to you, simpleton," after which he smiles amorously at his contact, whom he has already sufficiently frightened.

"Okay, then. Now what do I do?"

"You exchange it for me, pal," Mad Dog says, taking out a silver-plated toothpick and cleaning his incisors.

"Don't fuck with me, Commander Ontiveros, how am I going to change a stolen fixed-fare taxi for a new taxi?"

"That's your problem, pal. That's your stupid problem. Don't look at me," Mad Dog will say, turning his back and walking slowly toward the garage exit. Upon reaching his parking spot, the Commander Ontiveros does a sort of Spanish heel-tapping dance, a brief version, no need to exaggerate it. Then he will get into his red Mustang with Tabasco plates and will take it down Tacubaya Avenue listening to José Alfredo Jiménez songs on the stereo, the lyrics of which he doesn't quite know, though he thinks he does. He therefore sings them halfway, changing phrases here and there like someone changing socks. In Sanborn's Restaurant, a colleague, El Mierdas, will be waiting, with whom he has a few dealings. Ontiveros looks at him from afar, leaning on the bar, hovering over a *café con leche,* and speculates:

"Now I can guess why your snout is always dirty, from so much licking the boss's balls," he says, coming in. And then orders *chocolate con doñas.*

"The boss wants us to grab the stupid canary birds. Now, right away, this morning. He says they're fucking him over and over again and that he's got to hit the papers hard so that the lawyer doesn't fuck with him," El Mierdas says.

"What an asshole. Weren't they his own friends?"

"It's okay with him."

"And just the two of us are going alone?" Ontiveros asks, sopping up his chocolate. "It's an operation for at least an entire group, with a frigging tank and everything."

"The boss said you owe him one, Ontiveros, that you shouldn't be a dick, that we're going alone, we machine them and then once we've got them neutralized, he sends us the stupid truckload of grenadiers to do the bragging. What's more, he wants bullets, a shitload of bullets. And if we behave well, he sends us a helicopter," El Mierdas says to the guy, who was not cheered even by the bit about the helicopter. He was practically already on his way to taking out a life insurance policy in the name of his mother, a fine woman who, when forced to abandon the prostitute business due to old age, started a small used-clothing store on La Merced.

Ontiveros is rendered pensive in mid-bite. He hasn't gotten where he is easily, not without thinking a little. The chocolate drips down the corners of his mouth.

"How many agents have died this month in the line of duty, Mierdas?"

"Not one, pal. As long as you don't count Librado, who died of cirrhosis, even though he had a slash in his arm when they buried him."

"This guy is an asshole," Ontiveros says, referring to his boss in a loud voice, realizing that he and El Mierdas not only have to fuck with the canary birds, but they are also behind on this month's death quota for the special investigators, instituted for the press to show that the humble servants of the public also kick the bucket.

"What the fuck?"

"He tells us to throw ourselves at the canaries, and he's definitely already told the canary guys that you and I are going after them for some deal of our own. No one gives a fuck if they reshape our asses with bullets, asshole."

"Can you lend me some money?"

"I'll lend you the flowers for your funeral and a stick to stick up your ass to make your cadaver nice and straight," Ontiveros says, clearing up the incident and thinking about how to get out of the affair.

JOURNALISTS' STORIES

(J U L I O   S P E A K S)

When you're fucking, you're fucking. And when you're not fucking, you rub your prick furiously against the refrigerator door or against a brick wall. It had been a good while since I'd gotten hot, and Elena aroused my hormones, she made them dance the conga, charge the Light Brigade, do the antediluvian twist, in a bad way. Fortunately, the forgotten ones (as Buñuel would say) and Julio Fernández, who have not had sexual relations in a good while, have the marvelous remedy of onanism.

The art of St. Onan has a host of virtues. Among them is the ability to throw yourself retrospectively at Brigitte Bardot, when she was not yet old and broken by unfortunately tight girdles. And so on. It allows you to lock a first-rate catalog in your head and choose among Kim Novak, before Kirk Douglas arrives, and fat Susan, who worked in a pie shop near the high school and who when cutting avocado leaned over the counter, exposing her breasts; between the second from left in the third row of the Tropicana *mulata* chorus and Fanny Cano in a 1960 slapstick movie. And so on. A great selection in the catalog—eclectic. And one didn't have to explain one's very particular sexual tastes to anyone.

One did not have to explain to any psychiatrist why one puts one's pants in the fridge (for one's pecker to feel nice and cold in the mornings, obviously). Or why at thirteen one went to his aunt and uncle's house to beat off, in the absence of his uncle and the nearness of his aunt.

I was in one of those intimate relations with Sophia Loren (1952), under St. Onan's aura, when the phone rang for the second time. I tried to maintain my concentration, especially on the focal point—the prodigious oscillations of the woman's ass—when the telephone, acting as the Vatican's censor, rang again.

It was Elena.

"I've got what you need, Fats."

"There's no doubt about that," I said to myself, holding up my shaft to come in my hands.

"I know everything about Rolando M. Limas."

O N E   H U N D R E D   E L E V E N

THE VERSION OF EMILIO SALGARI'S *GOOD-BYE TO MOMPRACEM* CREATED BY STOYAN VASILEV IN THE PLEVEN PRISON

They were on their second glass of champagne, the seagulls announced the closeness of firm land, the clear sky presaged calm.

"This is your last chance to tell us who sent you," the white man said to his frightened prisoner, who was chained to the ship's bridge in front of him.

"Let's not waste time, throw him to the sharks," suggested the impressive Malaysian who accompanied him.

The young prisoner, whom they'd captured during a duel on a street in Singapore two days before, trembled like bamboo cane in a storm.

"No, sirs. But you have to protect me if I confess."

"You don't need to worry about a thing. From this moment on you are under the protection of the Tigers of Malaysia."

The boy contemplated the two richly adorned men. The old Malaysian, in a white linen suit, crowned by a half turban with a pink pearl occupying the place of honor, and his European companion, dressed in a simple white shirt, heavy twill pants and an embroidered Mexican sombrero practically hanging over his eyebrows to shade him from the inclement sun. Another European and a Javanese were just a few steps behind them; judging from their attitude, perhaps their guests.

"It is Mirim, king of the beggars. He has promised us a kingdom of gold to be shared by all if we return with your head."

"And what could a Singapore prince of beggars want from us?" Yanez de Gomara, the terrifying White Tiger, asked his blood brother, Sandokan, because this was about his head.

"Describe this Mirim, boy."

"He is a one-eyed man, about fifty years old. He's not Malaysian like I am. They say he was born in Bengal and that before becoming the king of our city's slums, he was a terrible pirate in the junks of Stal Inchu."

Sandokan was about to utter a loud curse when he was interrupted by the old man, Sambliong: "A strange object is approaching, Tiger," he said into the deposed Maharaja's ear.

"I'll be with you in a second," the Tiger of Malaysia said to his guests as he retired from the table. Yanez followed him.

"What's going on?" the Portuguese asked.

"Something's approaching."

"On the starboard side?"

"No," the Malaysian responded.

Yanez studied the horizon from east to west. The ocean shimmered in its immense solitude.

"On our tail, perhaps?"

"No, White Tiger, it's coming from the sky."

Yanez lifted his gaze to the sky incredulously and discovered, less than one nautical mile away, a balloon made of red and blue panels, the odious colors of the Union Jack, with a large golden dragon painted in the center, extending its wings and belching out its blazing breath. The globe flew some eighty-five yards above the sea, impelled by a gentle east-to-west breeze. It was, without doubt, a beautiful spectacle, but it terrified the Malaysian sailors, who'd never before seen one.

"Tell them it's a Chinese kite, that they needn't worry, a big kite, with men inside. There's no magic to it," the Portuguese said to Sambliong, who left instantly to carry out his task.

"What do you think?" Sandokan asked his white brother. The guests, the young Malang and the strange Balkan, had come up to them and together they watched the globe, which slowly approached the ship on a parallel course.

"Call to action stations, Yanez, I don't trust anything. For several days now only strange things happen to us," Sandokan said.

Yanez signaled to Parang to sound the boat's bells. The crew mobilized at once, uncovering the cannons and machine-gunners.

Sandokan's decision had been extraordinarily timely, because at that moment, small hand grenades began to drop from the balloon, exploding just a few yards away from the *Vengador*.

O N E   H U N D R E D   T W E L V E

LONGORIA GOES INTO ACTION

Saturnino Longoria carefully observed the boss of "the other guys." He was an astonishingly thin man, with abundant very white hair and a poorly shaven face, a character who looked like a country-music singer after a stint in the hospital for alcoholic rehabilitation.

When the black man with the look of an assassin approached "the other guys' boss" from behind to whisper something, Saturnino confirmed his first impression from the initial two days of the conference. The guy was controlling something, he was the boss of that nebulous something. That guy was the organizer of the guys who were trailing his friend, Stoyan. The rest of "the other guys," he had discovered, numbered about half a dozen. Something serious was under way: the black man, definitely, the gringo in the leather jacket who had followed Stoyan from the airport, the blond reporter in the first rows speaking with an Italian delegate. . . .

The boss of "the other guys" stood up. Longoria waited a prudent time and slipped out the side exit of the auditorium.

Malatesta the dog was waiting for him, prowling through the troughs in front of the College of Mexico. A vagabond dog, blind obedience suited him perfectly. Wherever Longoria left him, he could sooner or later be found. A discreet dog, unlike many, he contained his bark, he did not have excessive parties and he identified clearly with his master. Longoria gave him the cookies he'd stolen from the conference, little cinnamon cookies served with the coffee and tea in the back of the auditorium. Malatesta gobbled them down in one bite while his partner attentively observed the boss of "the other guys" get into a car with a chauffeur and disappear toward the Periferico.

Longoria watched Malatesta finish off the reserve of cookies and began to elaborate a small scenario: What nationality were they? Who did they work for? Were they armed? What did they want? Could they be emissaries of the deep past that Stoyan was disinterring?

He lit the butt of a Canadian Gitane that he'd recovered from one of the ashtrays; the best thing about international conferences was that they offered international leftovers to organized pariahs. The polluted air of Ajusco blew through Saturnino Longoria's sparse hair and made Malatesta, a tropical dog, ill adapted to the cold and rain, shudder and then vigorously wag his tail. Longoria needed money and infrastructure. The rest was child's play, as one of his cousins used to say, the phrase buried until that moment in the most distant memories.

THE INVISIBLES LOSE TO
NEWFOUND LOVE

The whole thing could have been impossible love from afar, but it was good love.

Soon, in the Brooklyn room where they slept and engaged in nocturnal battles with the cockroaches and black ants, the invisibles spoke only of the blond goddess who had smiled at Fermin and El Cochi. The golden woman whom Alvarito had seen from afar. The woman with the perfect legs whom Alegrías had seen in the late afternoon, not covering her face or head even though it was raining. The woman whom Gustavo had followed to a nearby office building. The woman who had brushed Alvaro's hand when he brought her a coffee.

The woman was cross-eyed, but that minor defect had no importance. Indeed, the slight squint made her gaze more intense, stranger, more desirable.

But cross-eyed or not, had the woman at some point really seen them? There was no doubt that they had brought her coffee, two sugars, one spoon of cream, but had she seen them? Had she noticed one of their faces? Had she seen the fixed gaze crowning one of the electric-orange jackets?

Alvaro swore that that was the least important thing. If she agreed to live with the five of them at once, they would feed her, bathe her and . . .

El Alegrías was the one to carefully investigate the strange situation. He was emptying the trash cans from the basement of the Madison Avenue building, an extra task for which he got two dollars a day, when he saw a nasty-looking compatriot with a .38 in his hand guarding the elevator doors. Hugging the filthy basement walls, El Alegrías disappeared into an almost completely dark area between two black Cadillacs. He took off his jacket and bundled it up under one of the cars. Then he waited for the guy to do whatever he'd come to do so that he could calmly go on with his work.

The doors of the elevator opened and the invisible discovered to his surprise that a dwarf emerged, pushing, his little hand under her skirt, the woman they all adored.

She spoke in English and the dwarf answered in the same language as they walked toward an emerald-green compact car.

"What's she saying?" the skinny Mexican asked.

"That she likes swarthy, big guys like you, but prefers small ones with balls like me. And she also likes guys who play the maracas," the dwarf answered.

They then got into the car and the conversation became inaudible. The woman did not seem very scared, she did not tremble demonstrably. El Alegrías was on the point of vanishing out of pure love.

Hearing the car motor start up, El Alegrías seized the opportunity to get out of his hiding place and run up the parking lot ramp. The car would have to make a complete circle around the basement to leave. The afternoon light almost blinded the invisible, and without thinking about the terrible consequences his actions could have, he hailed a taxi and in Spanish said:

"A green car is leaving right now from right there, follow it and don't lose it," and just as he was going to draw his knife from its sheath to lend emphasis to his request, a voice answered him in Spanish with a Sinaloan accent:

"Of course, *compadre*."

THE NIGHT OF MARCH 23RD . . .

. . . Alex was lying down on one of the twin beds of room 210 watching a pair of television monitors. The rest of the operative group of Benjamin's Grumpies ran the controls of three recorders and a telephone around him. The monitor on the right displayed the unattractive scene of an empty hotel hall. The monitor on the left showed a room similar to the one occupied by the North American group with an unmade bed. Stoyan Vasilev, the old Bulgarian journalist, had just entered the room and dropped a bundle of books on his twin bed. Television from the silent movie era, Alex said to himself as he smoked a cigarette. Vasilev started to undress on his way to the bathroom, leaving the camera's range. Looking at himself in the mirror above the dresser, Alex flicked his cigarette ashes furiously. A second cigarette butt smoldered in the ashtray. The room was hot. Grumpy-four had taken off his shirt and was dancing around the room in his undershirt looking for a glass to hold the two ice cubes he carried in his hands. Grumpy-seven worked a crossword puzzle in an old copy of the Sunday section of the L.A. *Times,* and Benjamin read the Mexican edition of *Playboy.* At 9:37 the telephone rang. Alex answered.

"The subject is with the Australian woman in a hotel in the city center. The conditions have been met," said Grumpy-three.

"Thank you," Alex responded. He hung up and looked toward the monitor; he studied the Bulgarian's empty room. Vasilev was still showering. Alex lit another cigarette. Later, addressing Benjamin, he said:

"Heads up. We're waiting."

His gaze was nailed to the monitor of the Bulgarian's room, while behind him the others in the room finalized the details.

"Is Orlando in the room?"

"He's got the TV on. I can hear it," Grumpy-four said.

"We should have risked monitoring the Nicaraguan's room," Benjamin said.

"No. If they found out, the entire operation would fall apart. Why are you worried? We saw him go into the room on the hall monitor; he's alone. Over the microphone of the room next door, we hear the TV. What are you worried about, Ben?" Alex asked.

"Nothing," Benjamin said.

Alex watched the monitor in Stoyan's room as the Bulgarian returned to the bedroom wrapped in a towel and reading a magazine.

"We can proceed," he said.

Benjamin walked to the little room adjoining the suite, knotting his tie with a nervous gesture. He signaled with his hand toward Grumpy-eight, the Guatemalan Domingo Reina, who was reclining in a chair, clearly dozing.

"Roll the tape," Alex ordered Grumpy-seven, who was in the main room.

Grumpy activated the device and in Stoyan Vasilev's room a discussion began to be heard that seemed to come from the room next door. Alex put on the earphones to listen and compare the sound to Stoyan's reactions.

At first the Bulgarian, absorbed in his magazine, seemed not to hear the noise that supposedly came from the room to his left.

"Let's go," Alex muttered. "Aren't you curious anymore? Have you gotten old? Are you deaf?"

Shit, what if the Bulgarian really was deaf? Or hard of hearing? That was something unforeseen.

"Turn up the volume a little, without exaggerating," Alex ordered Grumpy-seven. The eyes of all present were nailed to the monitor offering images of the Bulgarian reading the international section of *Proceso*. Stoyan moved toward the minibar and opened it, took out a soft drink and a tiny bottle of rum and made himself a stingy Cuba libre. Suddenly he seemed to react to the screams heard through the wall of the room next door.

"That's it," Alex mumbled. "That's it. Let's go, let's go."

Vasilev put on his glasses. Alex thought: to improve his hearing, that's it. He needs to see well to hear better.

"Snow White attacks," he ordered in a voice devoid of the hostility that emanated from the conversation on the other side.

After checking the barrel, Benjamin handed a pistol to Domingo Reina.

"The hall?" Benjamin asked over a walkie-talkie.

"Clear," answered a voice distorted by the apparatus.

Benjamin stared at Alex. It was the definitive moment of the operation.

"Let's go. Rattle the Mexican from his cave," Alex ordered.

"Snow White," Benjamin said into the walkie-talkie.

The image of Grumpy-eight, emerging from the door of the suite, appeared on the hall monitor. He was diminished by the camera, with a pistol stuck in the back of the waist of his pants. It was like a game of spies, a waltz in a Vienna court, in a grand salon that reflected and multiplied the dancers. At the other extreme of the hallway, the Mexican gunman appeared. He was blindfolded. The Guatemalan Grumpy-eight put the gun in his hands and led him like a blind man's guide to the door. Alex almost could have sworn he'd heard the man gently knock twice with his knuckles.

"Zero in the Bulgarian's room."

Grumpy-seven lowered the volume of the tape Stoyan was hearing to zero. Alex tried to divide his gaze between the door that should be opening and the Bulgarian's reaction to the end of the argument, but he didn't manage more than an alternating cross-eyed stare.

Now everything depended on the timing, the absence of accidental interference of onlookers and busybodies, and on coincidence just once disappearing, evaporating those short forty seconds when Alex needed to be unobstructed. That's the way it had to be, playing against all possible coincidences, to put together the assassination.

There was no slow motion on the monitor, but Alex seemed to feel that everything had lost its normal rhythmic speed, that Grumpy-eight had removed the blindfold from the face of the assassin slowly and moved aside, waiting for the door to open. Alex knew that only when the double shots occurred would reality return.

And it's because there is no possible reality in games like these, until blood runs, until Snow White has its first death, Alex said to himself.

JOURNALISTS' STORIES

(G R E G   S P E A K S)

Everyone in the world would like to be something different from what they are," Kath said to me, "but only because they haven't experienced the other."

Later she laughed at how she'd unwittingly complicated an idea that had once been simple. We were taking pictures of kids in the streets of the city's center. She took them. I tried to understand them, figure out what she was looking for in every angle, why she sometimes turned them around so much, distanced herself, waited for the smile or the gesture that I didn't see. Photographic magic. The sun was out, a mild sun with little warmth. We spent half an hour in Palma following at a distance a ten-year-old kid who sold plastic spiders hanging from a tiny thread.

Fats sometimes spoke of these working kids. He didn't do it in the schmaltzy way I'd heard from other Latin American friends; nor did he speak of them as numbers in the hands of a statistics professor, nor did he pretend to practice demagogy about the affair. He usually made another kind of observation. I tried to reconstruct it for Kath.

"Fats says Mexicans are losing their best generation since the end of the Mexican Revolution. That all these kids who work, who have to work because of the economic crisis, are the best, the most intelligent, the nicest Mexicans, but they work eight, ten, twelve hours a day, from five, eight, ten years old on. They don't study, they don't have time to play. They are brilliant, agile, swift, the street has made them so. But the street has limits. They are like little adults who cannot be and will never be able to be different. They are the best, but they're not going to be able to be the best. Do you understand me?" I said. I realized I couldn't express an idea clearly either, even though before I put it into words it had seemed extremely clear.

Kath snapped the camera. I never figured out what she was shooting. And she pursued her idea. It seemed that she would somehow synthesize Fats's version of the children of Mexico City with her story. Make one of the two.

"Sometimes I dream I'm a teenager from Zacatecas who dreams about being a teenager from Oklahoma who dreams about being a teenager from Zacatecas. You know what I mean?"

"Yes, but what does that have to do with the kids you're photographing and Fats's kids?"

"Nothing," Kath said, sticking her tongue out at me (which drove me crazy, I had to be passing through the adolescent stage of my being in love). "But you'll see, when you see the pictures. I never was very good at explaining things."

I looked at my watch. It was almost one-thirty. I tapped Kathy; Fats would be biting his nails.

No. Fats was eating a chocolate ice cream cone in the Fountain of Frogs and contemplating the recently cleaned streetlamps on Bolívar Street. Curiously, he didn't ask us where we were going to eat, but rather cut to the issue at once. The only problem was that it was a strange issue which only he understood and whose question only he could answer.

"Who is Valencia? The account opened at the bank. . . . Valencia is a guy who opened a bank account with our friend Carlos Machado at the Banco Internacional. The account exists. Several million pesos. Who is Valencia? What is that account for?"

"What are you talking about?" I asked.

Kath had meanwhile moved away, partly to avoid Fats's effusions and partly following her curiosity, photographing the porphyritic streetlamps.

"Elena is telling me stories about Limas on the phone, I hang up, I go back to the bathroom to finish my business and read a Graham Greene novel and the phone rings again. And they hang up. And again. And again on the third time, I tell them I'm going to remember their whore of a mother, and some guy with a Cuban accent says: 'Valencia, Banco Internacional, Branch Thirty-seven, Machado.' And hangs up. A guy that sounds nervous."

"With a Cuban accent?"

"That's right. And I go and make eyes with the subdirector of the bank and check it out. Machadito has a joint account with that

Valencia, here in Mexico City. I ask. They don't remember Machadito, this Valencia is a Chicano, a chubby little guy always in dark glasses. So now what?"

Even though we reporters are supposed to have brilliant instincts, and we're supposed to think better on our feet than sitting down, I stopped Fats's words with a gesture.

"Me gringo slow, think better with Tecate beer."

"And what about me?" Fats asked.

"Tecate beer also for the Mexican friend."

Kath smiled at us from a distance and snapped a photo.

O N E   H U N D R E D   S I X T E E N

ALEX, WHO WAS
WATCHING . . .

. . .the monitor, couldn't believe what he was seeing. Where had the waiter come from? A disguised waiter? Elegantly dressed in a white bolero jacket and tie with a black knot, he was like the Creature from the Black Lagoon or a cousin of the comic strip character The Daredevil. But there he was.

Reviewing the videotape repeatedly, over the subsequent few days, time and again evoked the same sensation in Alex. It was an elegant mask, a disguise, like El Zorro's or the Lone Ranger, but the mask did not make the prehistoric long-barreled Colt .45 that he carried in one of his hands less visible, while in the other hand he carried a tray with a bottle of wine and three glasses.

The absence of sound contributed to the air of unreality which the acts that took place in that hallway created: masked, gun-carrying waiter suddenly appears and smiles. Smiles? The hired Mexican killer who is waiting for the Sandinista to appear in the door will not notice the new presence until it is too late. Instead, Grumpy-eight, Reina the Guatemalan, will notice him and will start to back away down the hall. The door will open and the confused, half-shaven face (the soap drips down the right side of his jaw) of Luaces the Sandinista appears, but the only shot that will be heard clearly, and this, yes, breaking the soundlessness of the videotape, will not be fired by the hired killer. Instead, he'll receive the bullet. A fatal impact in the center of his back that will hurl him, pistol still in hand, into the arms of the Sandinista, who, not lacking reflexes, and with the experience gained from years of dodging the shots of the Somoza Guardia, will fall to the floor and half-close the door to his room. The waiter will smile again and carelessly hide the pistol in his waistband, trying not to hurt himself with the barrel, and Grumpy-eight, who is there by virtue of his uncanny resemblance to Commander Carlos Machado, will back down the hallway, almost tripping over the old Bulgarian.

"God," Alex will say in English, since everyone in the world knows what it means. And he won't know whether he said it to call upon a greater force which had miraculously completely screwed up the fundamental phase of Operation Snow White, or simply to use an interjection that came to him from his infancy.

O N E H U N D R E D S E V E N T E E N

MAD DOG'S
BUSINESS / THE CANARY
BIRDS

Pull up your underwear, Señora. Aren't you ashamed?" Mad Dog Ontiveros said, climbing through the window. The woman looked at him with surprise, not as much surprise as she should have, given the face of an unrepentant rapist that Commander Ontiveros usually and now more than ever displayed: his eyes were fixed on the pubic matte of the roundish fifty-year-old lady who was trying on some emerald-green Playtex underwear in the bathroom of her house and who, by pulling them up to only half-mast, was subject to the phrase: bodily misshapen.

"Ontiveros, my life, so good, now that you caught me like this, it's best we take advantage, no?" she said, revealing an intimate relationship woven throughout the years, and she started to strip off her lime-green brassiere, which contained two monumental cross-eyed breasts (one looked one way and the other another).

"I come with a plan of action," Judas said, lifting his leg over the edge of the window, taking care not to injure one of his balls on the metal frame.

"Oh, how sweet," said the woman named Dora (Dora the mamadora, Mama-Dora, Aspira-Dora, or Solita Dorita, what she gives she does not take away).

She shook her breasts to the rhythm of a nonexistent mambo number eight by Perez Prado, but with the wild notes of his masterpiece, and the obstruction of the underwear halfway up her thighs, made her trip, falling into the cop who had only just recovered from the entry through the window and gasped.

"Bless my soul," Ontiveros will say, tardily returned to ritual Catholicism, and will stick a .45 in Dorita's mouth that will take out two teeth and will make her faint in the arms of the man, sliding her innocent chest down the man's body and drooling a little blood on his shirt.

Ontiveros, ever practical, will rapidly discard the idea of throwing himself on the fainted citizen, in spite of the fact that he usually wants it in similar circumstances, and, taking advantage of the fact that he already has the gun in his hand, he kicks in the door of the bathroom and enters firing at the room where he suspects he will find the canary birds, only to discover that inside there is nothing but a TV reporting to a nonexistent audience that Luis Manuel Pelayo has died.

"I've already screwed up," Ontiveros says quietly. And so it is. So it will be from here on, because everything is turning out, if not badly, at least strangely.

The shots make prolonged echoes in his deafened ears, as if they continued to rebound off the walls and fly from one end of the room to another full of smoke with no one but Ontiveros himself, who wherever he looks cannot find anything to aim at and send to the next world. And that will be why his long professional experience inspires a profound intuition to look under the bed, where he will discover the oldest canary, already shot several times, with a very sluggish grin that would be a smile, and Ontiveros will drag him out by his shoeless little foot, the asshole didn't even have a sock, and confirm what is quite evident, that the guy was cold and is cold and now they will charge him with the death. And then Ontiveros, who has found himself in many similar predicaments, turns around and sees his loyal friend and companion the inseparable El Mierdas aiming at him where his back would have been with the face of an asshole, slothful and treacherous, now menacing his front. The two are shooting at the same time but El Mierdas will be less accurate and an easier target and Ontiveros will put a hole in the guts of his prize. A black hole, nice and round, almost perfect, out of which blood gushes in a fine stream.

Ontiveros approaches his friend sprawled out on the floor and says dryly:

"Because you're lazy, asshole. Who served as your guarantor to help you buy a condominium in Naples?"

El Mierdas, whose name is Enrique Castillo on paper, but who forgot it long ago, over the last ten years, when they started calling him El Mierdas away from his mama and a child he's half forgotten, will make a grief-stricken gesture, which Ontiveros will confuse with pain and, inflamed by the ungrateful treason, will not wait for a response and will stick the butt of the gun in his colleague's snout, taking out three teeth, and, as if to justify himself, will deliver himself of one more piece of rhetoric:

"And who loved you like a brother?"

"I forgot, pal," El Mierdas will say, sitting on the floor and crying like a grandmother in a Mexican movie, partly out of the pain of the bullet in his stomach and the rest out of guilt, "a gringo called you at the office, he told me to tell you, *ay*, that he was, *ay*, looking for you, for you to call him urgently."

Ontiveros took note of the message and with difficulty left through the bathroom window through which he'd entered. The patrol car sirens of his Mexico City colleagues sounded. They were coming to finish off fucking with him, and would find themselves with an altered script.

"KILL HIM . . .

. . . ," Alex said, watching the monitor, transfixed as the waiter disappeared down the hall and Grumpy-eight ran toward the other end, at the same moment Stoyan Vasilev, the Bulgarian, was opening the door of his room and saw Machadito who was not Machadito fleeing, just as foreseen by Snow White, only the dead man was not the dead man and something strange, something unusual had slipped into the middle of Alex's game, to corrupt it, to destroy the perfect puzzle that had taken him eight months to construct. And it's certain, coincidence had been the key to the crisis in an operation based on the fact that journalists don't believe in coincidences, and Alex had fabricated sixteen of them, only for a coincidence—a coincidence, a true and uncommon coincidence (God! A disguised waiter)—to appear at the last moment in the middle of the work and break the delicate, scenic equilibrium.

"Kill him," Alex ordered, pointing to the figure that had disappeared from the monitor.

Benjamin, frenetic, opened a briefcase and took out two small revolvers with silencers; he handed one to Grumpy-three and put the other behind his back and both practically ran out of the room.

"Fold up camp. Let's go," Alex ordered his assistants. Alex, however, remained immobile, while around him a feverish activity was unleashed as the Grumpies made cables and recorders, electrical connectors and monitors, disappear inside their suitcases.

Alex grabbed his head between his hands and reconstructed for the tenth time what he'd seen. Then he started laughing. Was he laughing at the coincidence?

JOURNALISTS' STORIES

(J U L I O   S P E A K S)

At the entrance to the Nicara-
guan Embassy in Las Lomas, there was an agglomeration of journalists, radio reporters with recorders and mobile television teams
with their portable cameras over their shoulders. The smell of
news. So many times. . . .

Making his way to the doors was old hat to Greg, sliding his
body into the crowd, putting on a Pulitzer prize face when anyone
tried to detain him. With the air of an intellectual who had a minor
chance at the Nobel, he peered over his glasses at the subjects who
tried to stop him. I let him go and stayed a few meters away,
smoking a cigarette, leaning against a post. Stoic Mexican journalist takes the affair calmly. Greg returned empty-handed after a
while.

"Commander Machado is not granting interviews. The embassy will offer a press communiqué in a few minutes. . . . I
couldn't get further than that. I sent Machadito a note reminding
him of the phone in his house."

The morning had entered my life very rapidly. A voice on the
radio spouting incoherencies about an assassination of a Mexican
gunman in Machadito's hotel; the questions. . . . The subway trip
to the hotel, the diplomatic disappearance of the Sandinistas, who
had been called to their embassy; the gates lined with Mexican
police, who seemed to be already on their third morning coffee.

"Scrambled eggs and ham with plenty of Mexican salsa," I
proposed to my associate, the gringo who apparently could endure
the dawn better than I.

"This is why I like being a weekly and monthly magazine
reporter, being freelance, not being on staff, not having an editor-

in-chief. If I don't have anything intelligent to say, I don't say it. I don't have to set about inventing an article, like our colleagues do today," Greg said, taking out his filtered Delicados and starting to walk toward the fixed-fare taxis coming down Palmas.

He couldn't have been more right. There is nothing more harmful in a man's life than having to pretend he is intelligent in the morning.

ONE HUNDRED TWENTY

HOW ABOUT A BULGARIAN LIKE THIS? (XI)

Stoyan Vasilev knew that a man dressed in a black leather jacket with a red scarf around his neck had been killed with one shot to the chest in the middle of the hall, barely three yards from his door. He did not have the slightest idea who that man could have been, he'd never seen him before, not in the hotel or at the conference. He also knew that when he opened the door he had seen a small man in a black T-shirt whom he could have sworn was Machado, fleeing down the end of the hall.

He knew that Machado and Luaces were sharing room 223 next to his. He had been in the room with Machado yesterday having a glass of aged rum. He knew that a few minutes before the assassination—a single shot—the two Sandinistas had been violently arguing. The thin walls between the rooms had made it almost impossible for someone to avoid hearing something like that. One of them had been accusing the other of something to do with drugs. They had spoken in rapid Spanish and much of it had escaped Stoyan. But there was no doubt that his hotel neighbors had been exchanging strong words.

He had seen the Mexican police taking pictures of the corpse, roaming through the halls, asking questions. He himself had been briefly interrogated, but after answering the first two questions in Bulgarian, they'd left him alone. After a long life full of educational experiences, he wasn't going to start collaborating with the Mexican police now.

He knew all this, but he couldn't quite understand it (and for a man of action, and even though Stoyan was eighty-two years old, he continued to be so); not understanding and therefore not knowing how to act was the worst of all possible situations.

Stoyan was treating his bewilderment with a Cuba libre when, fortunately, Longoria, dressed as a waiter, appeared at his half-open door.

"Room service, Señor, here are the sandwiches you ordered," he said as he lifted a finger to his lips begging silence and then took Stoyan's hand and led him into the bathroom.

The Bulgarian watched him, smiling. He loved conspiracies, and Saturnino seemed like a conspirator out of the most archaic past, with the manners of the Scarlet Pimpernel and the look of Bela Lugosi.

Longoria was turning on the water faucets of the shower and sink, and turning the background music all the way up and plugging in the electric shaver.

"What's going on, Saturnino?" the Bulgarian asked, but Longoria was clearly incapable of listening.

"The corpse was one of 'theirs,' " the old Spaniard said enigmatically, and then with a proud smile he added, "I cooled him off."

Stoyan kept quiet. Whoever Longoria's "they" were, they were part of the legion of demons who, for the last seventy years, had been on the other side of the barricade. How had the Stalinist dogs figured out his intelligence games? Did they know enough to want to kill him? What did Machado have to do with this whole story?

"I have to take Malatesta out to piss, I've got him locked up in a closet downstairs. Then I'll tell you. . . . Okay, okay, I don't know what the hell I'm going to tell you because I can't figure it out, I must be losing my faculties," Longoria said, leaving the bathroom.

Stoyan was left even more confused. Who was Malatesta? An old anarchist, of course. But why did Longoria have to take him out to piss? He finished his Cuba libre in one swallow and decided he too would move to action. He'd never played good roles as an observer. He put on his shabby black wool coat, stuck his passport in one pocket and a fork that had come with the untouched sandwiches Longoria had brought in another. . . . He'd been in tougher battles with worse weapons.

O N E   H U N D R E D   T W E N T Y - O N E

"COULD YOU TELL ME WHAT . . .

. . . happened?" Alex asked.
Benjamin stared at him and then said:
"How would you like me to tell you?"
"In the most concise way possible. The most transparent way. Without our software, without interpretations."
They were having a few tequilas in the El Mirador bar, on top of the Torre Latinoamericana, the needle encrusted in the sky of Mexico City. They were already on their third round. A gentle, pleasant afternoon. Looking west, they could see a dark cloud moving toward them.
"There was a shooting in front of the room of the Nicaraguan government functionary who was staying in Mexico."
"A shooting?"
"A shooting of just one shot. . . . A Mexican, about forty years old, named Leonel Posada, alias El Renco, with a long and shady police record, died in front of the room. With a history of drug trafficking, prostitution, murder. A guy not worth a lot, well . . . according to their logic; according to ours a wasted character. Nobody's going to cry, and we're not even signing his life insurance. Journalists like death."
"And then," Alex asked.
"Well, that's it, nothing else."

"And who killed him?"

"You saw the same tape I did. What's more, we saw it together. What's more, I still can't believe it. It's quite unreal, quite absurd, it's like a Spielberg movie. You're sure it wasn't a setup of yours?"

"A waiter dressed up like El Zorro killed him."

"No, just a mask."

"But only you, your Grumpies and I know that."

"In other words, no one knows. Because we are not a public source, we do not exist."

"And what did the Bulgarian see?" Alex asked.

Benjamin began to feel uncomfortable. The backs of his hands prickled, the collar of his white shirt was choking him. Alex never confided, never offered extra information, never argued with his associates. He simply dictated conferences, asked questions the answers to which he knew, and informed the world of the divine intentions.

"He saw . . . someone who looked like Machado run down the hall . . . ," Benjamin whispered. Now he knew where Alex was going.

"Exactly. The Bulgarian saw Machado run down a hall where there was a dead Mexican ex-assassin. And he didn't see anything else because the waiter had vanished."

With a gesture he ordered another round of tequilas.

"Snow White never dies, Ben. We have a kingdom of immortal snow in our hands," he said as a corollary. Waving down the waiter, he asked for the check.

It wouldn't cost him too much to become a regular in the place. He liked that view of the city trapped by clouds of pollution and storm, seen from above, diminutive men and cars and trees. His provisional offices were six floors below. They weren't very big, nor did they have exotic access like the SD offices in Manhattan, but for now they were sufficient for an operation on the verge of disaster. Alex smiled at his attack of pessimism.

Benjamin doubted for an instant whether he should mention what was running through his head; finally he plucked up the courage:

"Alex, there remains one small detail, I don't know if you'll be able to, but I can't sleep without knowing who the waiter dressed as the Lone Ranger is and who he works for. More than anything who he works for. And whether his masters are meddling with Snow White, or the whole thing is a coincidence."

"How good of you to remind me. That's the assignment for your Grumpies; verify it. I suppose that now it's you who won't be able to sleep. For me it really doesn't matter that much, but I'd like to know no later than tomorrow."

ONE HUNDRED TWENTY-TWO

JOURNALISTS' STORIES

(GREG SPEAKS)

There is a song by G. Brown on *Havana Moon,* a Santana record, that repeats the phrase in a country rhythm, "And they all went to Mexico," their friends went, their pals went, even their dogs went. I suppose that is part of the conjunction of two of the healthiest North American traditions: taking to the road (thank you, Woody Guthrie, Kerouac, Wyatt Earp, Bob Dylan, John Dos Passos, Calamity Jane, Spiderman, John Garfield, Ernest Hemingway) and crossing the border in search of the South (thank you, John Reed, Indiana Jones, James Taylor, Clint Eastwood, John Huston, Babe Ruth, Carleton Beals, Mike Gold, Burt Lancaster).

I suppose I'd gone south one time or another over the last few years, driven by those two national motivations. But it wasn't easy to go south. Every piece of knowledge brings a dose of guilt, equal in weight and importance to whoever acquires it. To be a U.S.-citizen-born-gringo in Latin America is a pastime for the unconscious, economic gangsters, commercial missionaries, radicals on the verge of jubilation, freaks, dreamers or crusaders. They all furnish the continent south of the border with their own demons. They travel with their ghosts. Then there are the others, us dreamers, those who believe there are no borders or countries, just landscapes and songs sometimes sung in unknown languages. Of all the monsters who travel south, we are the most dangerous because we believe we don't have the original sin that has to be forgiven; because we rationally think that we are not excessively different, that we can coexist with the natives on fair terms: You give to me, I give to you, you smile at me, I smile at you, even though at night we have nightmares in which half-naked, starving children, the live Latin American ghosts, point their fingers at us.

Going south is, as Malcolm Lowry and Joseph Conrad and Ambrose Bierce knew, a descent into hell itself. Leaving the deceptive North American Paradise, the true hell, the demons attack, they attempt to escape from the skin and gush forth. One knows it when traveling south, one knows the Martians who play Ping-Pong inside our heads. And in the end, one is grateful that it is so and not any other way. Anyone who doesn't have hells will be content to die kneeling in front of a television in a place as ludicrous as Indianapolis.

Okay, I was here. And if I sometimes didn't understand things, the natives didn't seem to understand a whole lot either; at least in this absurd story, from what could be deduced from reading the papers. I said so to Fats. He answered that when he was brushing his teeth, he did not have time for racist North American shit. He said it more or less like this:

"shing teeth, North 'mer'can racish shit."

"A good dose of rationalism would not be so bad for us, little brother Fats," I said to rattle the Hegelian demons. "For example, make sense of the little we know. . . . First: rumors permeate the scene that the CIA has a mole inside Sandinismo. Second: they tell us about the bloody awful connections of our friend beyond suspicion, Machado: relations with a very popular drug dealer, a strange bank account. . . . Third: they kill the extremely famous El Renco outside the door of his room. . . . And was this guy famous before he died or are they following the Mexican tradition by which only cadavers can be famous? Fourth: the embassy shuts its doors on us. . . . Add it up."

"I'm adding," Julio Fernández said, coming out of the bathroom and putting on a Sting T-shirt.

"What do you get?"

"I don't know."

"Yes, you know," I said, lighting my penultimate filtered Delicado.

"Okay, I get that Machado is mixed up in something dirty and the CIA found him in it and they're out there squeezing him. . . . That's what I get."

"But you and I spoke with Carlos and we didn't sense that, right?"

Fats walked over to the window and opened it. The dense, smoky air of his apartment was swept away by an icy breeze.

"Bloody hell, it's cold," said Fats, who whenever muddled sailed the oceans of the obvious.

"No, we felt that it couldn't be Machado. Now then, you are the less rational of the two of us so you have to reach the conclusions. . . . Pass the cigarettes."

Fats disappeared down the hall and returned without the cigarettes but with two cans of Tecate beer.

"You really think Machadito could be mixed up in a ton of shit?" Fats asked me with a sad face. "I can't believe it."

"So it seems. But that's not what we're talking about," I said, looking him in the eyes, as I rarely had to do, because Fats had never misled me. "What we're talking about, and neither you nor I is saying it, is if we pull together a story and Machadito is full of shit, are we going to write it?"

"I think so, *compadre.*"

"That's what I think too."

"We're a couple of whores, so loyal to journalistic truth and all that shit. We're capable of drilling a hole in the Nics as long as we get the truth. Fuck truth," Fats said, falling into a chair without spilling a drop of the foam that crowned his can of Tecate.

"No, don't bullshit me. We're going to write it because if we don't write it, we'll never be able to write anything else. Because, either you tell it all or you tell nothing, *compadre.*"

"Don't speak to me in English, I'm distracted," Julio said.

"Well, if we're going to write, we've got to start confirming exactly what's going on."

"No, if in addition to having to swim in the shit, we're going to have to work. Bloody hell."

"Add."

"Why the hell would Machado have money in Mexico and be seen with a drug trafficker?" Fats asked.

I thought about trips to the South. At one time I had wanted to be a sports journalist, live in Le Mans, speak French, take a Turkish wife who would make me strong coffee three times a day. The telephone rang.

"Fernández," Fats answered laconically. He was silent for an instant as he listened; he covered the mouthpiece with his hand and said:

"Armando wants to tell us a story; you in the mood to hear it?"

ALEX TOOK THE PHONE . . .

. . .that Grumpy-five handed him. She was an ex-schoolteacher who'd gone on vacation to Managua and was currently set up as his secretary in the SD offices in the Latin American Tower. Alex said simply:

"Smith here. Who may I ask is calling and what can I do for you?"

"Everything is fucked, right, Mr. Smith?" Rolando M. Limas answered on the other end of the wire. The telephone line was full of grumblings and strange sounds. They said that after the earthquake, rats had been eating the telephone cables of Mexico City. Fine, let them enjoy. Mutant rats, full of absurd conversations like this one.

"Snow White lives, Señor Perez."

"No, my friend, I give up. For this we have the fine tradition of buying insurance. This is why my friends kept me blindfolded up there in New York. I called only to say goodbye and to tell you that you better not go looking for me out there, that it turned out bad, period. We'll lend you a hand on the next one, and, Alexito, we still love you out there the same as always, not more, not less."

From his window, Alex contemplated a green blot that had to be Chapultepec Forest. It must have been raining over there. Every once in a while, lightning flashed.

"Señor Perez. If you abandon the deal, your insurance will be canceled."

"All of it, pal?"

"All of it, Señor Perez, the company's insurance on your car, the travel insurance, the comprehensive insurance."

"If we break relations, your insurance will be canceled too. And here in Mexico City, that is a problem for a gringo company, my good man. Gringos don't get along well in this city, this city is bastardized, it devours them, the sewers swallow them, it sprays them with water that isn't boiled. They get drunk like idiots in Garibaldi. . . . No, a million things."

"I suspect that this city is not good for border people either, Señor Perez. They don't like them here, they seem strange, quasi-abnormal."

"Fine, I'll leave it at that, I hope it's easy for you," Rolando M. Limas said, hanging up. The line went dead. Alex remained contemplating the phone for a few moments. Then he gestured to Grumpy-three, who sat at a desk near the bathroom door. A forty-year-old in a suit, with graying temples and very thick myopic glasses.

"Can your contact in the police force do anything for us, the one who found the corpse?"

"They say he's the best, Alex."

"Put him behind Limas, I want Limas dead as soon as possible. Really dead. After shooting him, have him put a mirror down his throat to make sure he's not breathing."

Grumpy-three stared at Alex. The thing Alex liked least about this Mexican operation, besides the food, was that he never knew whether his boss's boss, the boss of bosses, was serious or not.

"What time does Sleepy have his appointment with the reporters?" Alex asked his temporary secretary.

"Right about now, more or less in minutes, boss."

"Over there, in that forest?" he asked, pointing at Chapultepec.

"Yes, sir," the secretary answered, looking at him. "It would be impossible to cancel it. . . ."

Alex did not return the look; he was very busy figuring out whether the lightning was striking Chapultepec Forest, imagining whether the lightning was tearing up the trunks of the Mexican coniferous trees planted there by order of a Spanish viceroy who didn't even like trees and who yearned to return to the barren countryside of his Castilian plains. Alex would have to start studying Mexican history if he was going to stay in these offices.

THE VERSION OF EMILIO SALGARI'S *GOOD-BYE TO MOMPRACEM* CREATED BY STOYAN VASILEV IN THE PLEVEN PRISON

The third nitroglycerin bomb hit the *Vengador* near the ship's forecastle, shaking the bridge and killing one of the artillerymen. The malignant balloon, in all its colorful beauty in the radiant afternoon, descended in search of the cruiser, whose stacks belched out dense clouds of black smoke, evidence of the terrible power contained in its boilers.

"Shoot it, Yanez," Sandokan yelled.

"Impossible, little brother, it's still too high," the Portuguese answered, but readying, nonetheless, one of the blazing machine guns that had been installed on the forecastle.

Another bomb hurled from the globe shook the vessel as if a gigantic hand pounded the ocean.

Yanez then began shooting bullet after bullet from the machine gun, taking advantage of the balloon's slight descent due to a gust of wind. He saw the impacts of his shots hit the basket, and even clearly saw one of the wounded fall from the globe into the ocean. The Portuguese's dexterity allowed him to adjust the shot immediately, aided by one of the Tigers of Malaysia who held the tripod of the machine gun. At that moment, hell broke loose on the

Vengador as one of the nitroglycerin bombs flung from its mysterious enemy's globe hit the main deck.

The last thing Yanez saw was a sky filled with seagulls with a monstrous column of smoke ascending. . . .

O N E   H U N D R E D   T W E N T Y - F I V E

HOW ABOUT A
BULGARIAN LIKE THIS?
(XII)

Stoyan Vasilev appreciated the Mexican heat. That may have been why he slowed the pace of his walk, and not, as Longoria said, because he was having an arthritis attack. The heat hit his head and warmed his hair; the rays of the sun illuminated his hands and gave them life, a sensation that spread through his body, sank into his bones and rose through his skeleton. The sun, as a native Peruvian in Lima had once said, warmed the bones, that was its purpose. What's more, the sun was the great evoker of memories, the great reconstructor of nostalgia, the ideal creator of dreams. The sun transported him to other stories, some of them strange like these, others simpler, basic duels between journalists and power. The sun reminded him of the flat-roofed terrace of the University of La Paz in Bolivia, a normal, mild day; Stoyan had been smoking when he saw a tank advance toward the building.

He wanted to explain to Longoria what it was like to live inside a head populated by ghosts, but the Spaniard, who insisted on rushing him and made him cross the streets near La Alameda at full speed, did not sympathize.

"And what do you think I've got in my head, birds?" Longoria said. "Novelists say we elderly turn senile due to arteriosclerosis. They don't know squat. I have to live with a Neapolitan who sold me a false lottery ticket and with a Parisian cop I stabbed to death. One gets old from revisiting his or her deaths and insanities, hell. . . . Keep moving, old man."

Stoyan admired and revered the Latin American Tower. A building that size in a city of terrible earthquakes had an abundant dose of magic. That may be why he looked at it with distrust when half a dozen blocks away Longoria pointed it out with his clawlike finger as the object and refuge of "those guys."

"Let's go in. I'll show them to you. Let's see if you recognize someone or you can get half an idea of who they are."

Stoyan agreed. It wasn't about disproving his *compadre,* who'd become irascible with the passing of time, as far as he could tell. It was a risk of survival.

They took the elevator to the thirty-third floor and accidentally got out at an importer's office. Longoria took the initiative and quickly found the service stairwell. They started down the stairs. The Spaniard had set the style: lost in the entrance of the building, innocent in the walk around the thirty-third floor, stealthy in their descent down the steps.

In front of the service elevator door, Stoyan, who'd been leading the way, discovered a familiar figure waiting there. The door opened and the man started to go in.

Stoyan had only one way of knowing, certifying. He took out the fork which he'd stored the night before in the pocket of his wool coat and as the elevator door was closing he leaped forward, stabbing it into the hand of the guy he'd seen fleeing down the hall, the man who was and was not his friend Machadito. The man let out a bloodcurdling howl, feeling his hand, the one with which he'd pressed the button for the thirty-second floor, pierced by something sharp. The door shut.

Stoyan saw the commotion he'd created and prudently backed up a few steps. The scream had attracted a few onlookers.

"Why the hell did you stick a fork in that guy's hand?" Longoria asked, staring at the closed elevator door.

"That was the guy I saw in the hall, that's Machadito, a friend of mine, Carlos Machado, the Sandinista, but it's not. I wanted to leave a mark on him, a scar on his hand, if it's not him, they were trying to confuse me. . . ."

"I don't understand a thing, *compadre.* You're getting more

Bulgarian all the time," Longoria said, and with almost no transition, when the door opened, in the best Doc Holliday and Billy the Kid gunman traditions, he arched his back and took from his belt his monumental long-barreled Colt.

Stoyan had not lost the historic reflexes that had kept him alive into his eighties and jumped aside out of the line of fire, hurling himself against the door of a Jalisco alcohol company, lamenting the loss of his only fork.

The shots were already ringing, mixed with screams, when Stoyan returned to the hallway armed with two bronze paperweights. People had thrown themselves to the floor. Longoria was defending his position behind a dismantled metal desk which someone had fortunately placed in the hall. The Spaniard's .45 barrel peered over a crate. On the other end of the hall, a black man cautiously peered from behind one of the office doors and fired every once in a while at Longoria, making metal splinters of the desk-trench. Spectators by no choice of their own were strewn across the floor, trying to eat the carpet; half a dozen innocent victims avoided raising their protruding heads even one inch from the floor.

Stoyan analyzed the situation in less than a second and, with his bronze paperweights and all, turned back into the office of the Jalisco tequilamen and crossed it like a lightning flash, in search of an interior door leading to other offices or a window to pass through. He got nothing but a flustered look from a secretary, who, if bilingual, had lost even her mother tongue when Stoyan asked in Greek how to get out of there without using the door. He corrected himself immediately, switching to Spanish, but still obtained no more response than an anguished look that begged for compassion. Things were not going well enough for him to comply, so the Bulgarian searched for more throwable objects. A couple more shots, two-caliber, the bark of the black man's .38 and the dry thunderclap of Longoria's .45 made him rush, tripping over a desk as he carried under his arms a bottle of Flash Tequila (its name illustrative of its ulterior motives).

"When the fire starts, back up toward the stairwell," he said to Longoria, placing all his trust in the tequilamen's not lying about the degree of purity, uncorking, wetting his handkerchief and making the first recorded tequila Molotov.

One, two . . . and the sudden blaze appeared near the black man with the .38 revolver. Stoyan jumped behind the curtain of fire and made his way to the door of the service stairs. Gasping, Longoria appeared at his side.

"The things that happen in this life, *compadre*! Reality is becoming more and more Bulgarian."

Stoyan didn't bother answering and started down the stairs in leaps. Feeling as if his heart had disappeared. He was consoled thinking that Longoria's must have been floating in limbo too.

O N E   H U N D R E D   T W E N T Y - S I X

JOURNALISTS' STORIES

(J U L I O   S P E A K S)

A branch of the Periferico ring crosses Chapultepec Park near Los Pinos, the presidential mansion. The forest is wet there due to the rain and army trucks can be seen in abundance; the president's guards have their quarters a few meters away. There are elevated yellow bridges placed at intervals over the speedway for pedestrians. In the middle of the bridge some two hundred yards in front of Los Pinos, Armando was waiting for us, leaning on the handrail, watching the cars pass and slipping a nostalgic look toward the trees every once in a while.

"Are those seagulls? No, they can't be, there's no sea around here. They must be doves," he said upon seeing us arrive, referring to the pale birds which occasionally emerged from between the Mexican coniferous trees and the pines.

"In Mexico City, they are buzzards, Armando," I answered in keeping with my black mood.

"It's hard, isn't it?" Armando asked with a sad look.

"Don't make us cry, Armando," Greg said, lighting a cigarette he protected from the rain, sheltering it with his hand. "This story is making me lose everything; sense of humor, capacity to enjoy the melodrama, love for Japanese movie spies. . . . If you've got something to tell us, tell it already. If we're going to play guessing games, find yourself someone else."

I looked at the trees, trying to hide my smile. Greg acting like a tough guy was a poor imitation of Humphrey Bogart. If Armando had seen *The Harder They Fall,* we were doomed.

"We thought we had to tell the story about Machado. . . ."

"Who thought so?"

"We did."

"Who is we?" Greg asked again. If he was going to carry the weight of the interview, I was grateful, I wasn't in the mood to play intelligence games. I was reserving myself to throw Armando a rabbit punch if he wasn't careful.

Armando made a gesture with his hand in the air. A vague gesture in which the "we" dissolved into the midst of the humidity and the cars passing on the Periferico.

"We thought the story had to be told. At least we had to pull the string and see what happened."

"And what was the story?" Greg asked.

"Well, at this point you must know substantially more than I do. Machado, his relations with Rolando M. Limas, his joint bank account with that Valencia in Mexico, those things. . . ."

"And now? Because that's what you thought before, no? What do you think now?"

"I realize that I started out trying to push you into the story. That is no longer my intention."

"Come on, Armando, enough circles, this is like a skating rink," I said.

"Machado does not want the money for himself. Machado wanted the money to buy arms for the Salvadoran army. After the Nicaraguan provisions sent through the Gulf of Fonseca were interrupted, Machado thought he couldn't just let that happen, that he had to continue supporting them and he sought out resources from other areas. . . . At first we thought he was amassing a personal fortune, now we know it wasn't for himself. He wanted to aid the Salvadorans with arms and he found the money where it always is, in the drug trade. He did a couple of favors and got the money. . . ."

"And now what do you want from us?"

"Tactical silence, I suppose. . . . If I were you. . . ."

"But you're not, Armando. . . . I'd like to know a few things," I said. Now it was my turn. "You say Machado has been trafficking drugs. You say Machado is beholden to the CIA because they discovered him in the affair and they're blackmailing him. . . ."

"I didn't say anything about the CIA, and if I said it I was wrong. And besides, I didn't say anything," Armando said, who never said anything about anything. He pulled a cigar from his pocket and lit it.

"It's a story that's already over," he said. "It's not going anywhere. What are you going to do?"

"We're going to win the Pulitzer with it," Greg said very seriously.

"We're going to write it and we're going to keep it and then for years we're going to send you copies of it. . . . If you give us your address," I said.

Armando looked at us sadly, he handed me a folded newspaper, he turned around and started to walk toward the other end of the bridge.

As Armando disappeared among the trees, Greg looked at me. He didn't look at Armando walking away, he looked at me. I contemplated the last drops of water dripping off the leaves. A little puddle had formed around my feet. The rain dampened the paper in my hand. I opened it and read the headline: "Scandal in Cuba. Army Personnel Implicated in Drug Trafficking."

One Hundred Twenty - Seven

THE INVISIBLES FIND THE
LOVE OF THEIR LIFE

Whatshall I play for you, my love?" said the dwarf. "I can play anything from gentle tropical rhythms to Gershwin's *Rhapsody in Blue,* with nothing but my maracas, my queen."

Eve didn't pay him much attention, and remained absorbed in the television. Benigno had fallen asleep on the other bed and was snoring. The dwarf insisted:

"I would do it for pleasure, not out of obligation. . . . It would be fun. We could also do something more sexual. Something like I tie the maracas to your breasts and we make them dance one on top of the other."

They'd spent two days suffocating in the New York summer heat in an unair-conditioned motel room. Benigno and the dwarf had opted for underwear and walked around the room in their boxers. Eve, after thinking about it for a while, had followed the example and swaggered around in nothing but a frankly scanty, bone-colored bra which was starting to show signs of wear and a pair of lilac panties. At night they used the twin beds and she slept on the rug between both beds, handcuffed to the dwarf's ankle.

Topics of conversation had been exhausted in the first few hours and ever since they simply repeated with increasingly more isolation and less variation: "Why are you keeping me here? You don't know Alex, he's not going to give this the slightest importance. . . ."

Benigno was starting to tire and looked at the telephone more and more anxiously, waiting for the magical call from the boss that would end their confinement. More and more often he offered to do the shopping and he lingered in the grocery store longer than necessary.

The dwarf was not in a hurry, he liked the cross-eyed woman, he liked New York television's forty-two channels, which the motel's cable left at his disposal, he even liked the city he imagined out there, whose smells and sounds did not penetrate the double-paned windows.

"Two cold Pepsis for table five, Benigno!" the dwarf barked, managing to wake the taciturn bodyguard, who looked at him balefully.

"Can I take a shower? Why can't I take a shower?" Eve asked.

"My sweet," answered the dwarf, "because there's a window in the bathroom. If you let me sit on the basin, my friend Benigno and I see no problem whatsoever. Right, my black man?"

Benigno turned over in the bed, putting his back to them.

Eve tossed her short disheveled hair and gestured acceptance.

"Let's go, shorty, anything's better than another day of sweat."

The dwarf clapped his hands joyfully.

Eve started undressing on the way, not waiting to get into the tub. Marcelino the dwarf began to sweat at the unexpected show.

The noise from the shower kept Marcelino from hearing the invisibles enter the room, or Benigno's warbles when one of the boys placed the blade of his knife against his neck. So when a hand pressed against his shoulder, Marcelino tried to shake it off, since it distracted him from the furtive vision of Eve's body behind the shower curtain, and only when the supposedly friendly hand was substituted by a sharp onion knife did he realize something strange was happening.

Eve got out of the shower and was surprised not to find the dwarf there. She walked into the room and was profoundly disconcerted upon seeing her kidnappers tied down to the floor and five boys outfitted in orange jackets with enormous kitchen knives in their hands, contemplating her adoringly.

The words were stuck in her throat. She aimed a smile at the boys. They returned it timidly.

The evil spell was broken, the invisibles had just become visible.

O N E   H U N D R E D   T W E N T Y - E I G H T

HOW ABOUT A
BULGARIAN LIKE THIS?
(XIII)

Stoyan wondered at times how Maria had disappeared. He had even tried writing on the flimsy paper of his memory various versions of an occurrence he never saw and would never be able to reconstruct with the least bit of precision. In one of them . . .

Maria, an eight-year-old girl with blond braids, hears the terrifying screeching of the Stukas as they swoop down out of the sky to drop their bombs. She is frightened and crying.

In another one, Stoyan Vasilev, who finds himself in the Kostrovo line of riflemen, in the mountains, simply receives a sweaty letter handled by dozens of loyal and loving mail-carriers who have risked their lives so that he and others like him will know that someone awaits them. In the letter, his wife (who was his wife then?) tells him that they have had a girl, that the girl is named Maria. Stoyan is afraid to imagine his daughter. It is a bad time to fall in love with ghosts.

In another version, Vasilev arrives at his small house, little more than a shepherd's hut near the Greek border. He has been pursuing a group of Greek smugglers who work for the Donovan boys and occasionally sent explosives to Bulgaria. A few hours ago, he killed one, shot him in the back with a rifle that had telescopic sights. He doesn't regret it in the slightest.

The goat that normally grazes near the entrance to the cabin is not there. Inside the cabin, he has a camp bed and a bucket of water. Now a girl is washing her hands in the bucket. She plays with the water, moving her tiny hand like a boat among the waves that disappear. Stoyan asks her her name. She answers in Greek, "Maria." He decides to adopt her. She is without a doubt a lost girl. The lost girl who has been waiting all these years.

Longoria appeared at a distance with a couple of postcards in his hand.

"What an imbecile, *compadre,* look, I bought two. It's the tradition. . . ."

But it is not Maria, it is Saturnino, his friend. Stoyan is sitting on a stone tiled bench outside the back garden of the maternity pavilion, in Longoria's sacred territory. He lets the sun warm his white hair, his tawny mane.

"Who were they, Saturnino? Weren't they the Stalinists who are protecting the guys I have on my list? It couldn't be them, they looked like North Americans. They wanted to tarnish Machado."

"But the one with the fork-pierced hand wasn't Machado. Machado showed up on TV with normal hands," Longoria said.

"I suspect that you really screwed them over, Saturnino," the Bulgarian summarized. "It's good and hot here, this place of yours is really nice. How did you get an entire hospital for yourself?"

"I bought these two postcards. You like them?" the Spaniard asked without responding to his friend's questions. Who cared who the "they" were this time? "They" were always out there, destroying countries, inventing borders, plotting complicated schemes understood only among themselves. Throwing water in the wine and filling the papers with shit.

Malatesta came up behind the old Spaniard at a happy trot. Stoyan patted him and the dog paid him back by licking his hand.

"We are a couple of little old men taking sun in the garden of a sprawling hospital," the Bulgarian said. "Do you realize I sound more and more like the character in that movie we saw in Madrid. . . . *Scarlet Pimpernel.*"

"I sound more and more like an imbecile. I guess with age you get the urge to talk about all the things you've been putting up with the rest of your life. And when you kept quiet, you were more intelligent, or at least it seemed that way," Stoyan said.

"But you've got fantastic reflexes, *compadre,*" Longoria told him. "Look how you didn't hesitate. Who taught you how to wield a fork like that, like the sword of El Consario Negro?"

"Life, *compadre.*"

MAD DOG
ONTIVEROS / UNHAPPY
ENDING

The gringo had said sharply to Mad Dog Ontiveros: "How much for a man's head?" And he had answered, "A big asshole or a little asshole?" The gringo's silence had spoken wise words and Commander Ontiveros, not to underestimate, asked for five million pesos, dedicated five minutes to trying to get three and ended up agreeing on two million, three hundred.

After the deal, the gringo said: "Rolando M. Limas," and that was when Commander Ontiveros, who couldn't quite recover from the fraud his boss had pulled on him with the story of the canary birds, no longer saw it so calmly or as such a bargain. He could have killed himself, because even though Limas was a big dick on the border and here in Mexico City you got less for everything; even so, Limas was a pretty big dick. But a deal's a deal and after having informed his employers by phone that his dear companion, El Mierdas, had kicked the bucket and that in the fulfillment of duty one of the canary birds was already dead, and then playing deaf under the pretext of kidney colic, Ontiveros left, headed for nowhere, like somebody who says he's just going out into the city streets when it's getting dark.

Prostitutes hang out with prostitutes . . . , so Ontiveros reasoned, tracing the friends he and Limas might have in common, and letting the word spread that he had a contract on that old man for half a million dollars. Whether or not Limas picked up the rumor, Ontiveros never found out, but someone out there did him the favor and sent him to the back room of the Casablanca bar, where M. Limas was doing a few small deals with the owners of a plastic factory gone bankrupt, who now thought that since honest industry had left them bankrupt, God might revive them.

Ontiveros will see him from a distance, he'll recognize him more by his fame than by his appearance, and to confirm it he only has to let out a scream to see whether the other one responds to the call and thereby confirms it:

"Yo, Limas."

But Rolando M. Limas will know that the yell is ill-intentioned and will take out an automatic from under the cowboy hat lying on a table at his side and will fire the shot at practically the same time Commander Ontiveros empties half his chamber.

The plastic factory people will fly out. Rolando M. Limas will die without speaking a word. An awful way to go for someone who sang so many popular songs in his life, and Ontiveros will roll across the floor with a hole in his lung, dying, furious over his lack of professionalism.

And what bothers you most, what really bothers you, Mad Dog, if you had the time to think about it, is that some son of a bitch is going to give you a stupid posthumous prize for going around so lazily dying in the line of duty, and that he will give it to your idiot of a sister.

Journalists' Stories

(G R E G   S P E A K S)

A good story with four hands is written in three phases: first, ordering the information; second, giving it an initial structure, inserting the supporting arguments, choosing the guiding thread, selecting the testimonial quotations that support it, situating the contexts; third, editing by turn, cross-correcting. A bad story with four hands is written the same way. Fats was wearing a T-shirt, a sign that he had taken the matter seriously. I read the notes taken out of the typewriter for the third time. I put my preconceptions aside and tried to clear my vision. It didn't work. I was completely baffled.

Julio walked over to the record player and put on a country album very softly. I appreciated the favor, he did not like country music. I didn't either, but somehow I thought I should. We had never spoken of this.

"Is something missing?"

"Coherence is missing. If we decide to publish this we're going to burn Machado in green firewood. If we have decided information above all else, first the facts and then friendships and judgments, the least we can do is tie the story down on all four corners."

"Deep down I have no desire whatsoever to write this. I guess that's part of why I'm not capable of tying the facts together."

"Don't get upset, Fats. The facts aren't adding up because things are missing. From this corner of Mexico City, Greg Simon, the voice of pragmatic experience will not be contaminated by emotions."

"Read me that piece of shit, *compadre,* and don't get wrapped up in yourself."

"Get me a ham sandwich and I'll read whatever you want."
Obligingly, Julio went to the refrigerator.

"Serrano ham, tomato, avocado, Chihuahua cheese, three drops of oil, salt but not too much."

I agreed, nodding. He couldn't see me, he had his back to me, but it didn't matter. We had a long history of shared sandwiches. Aside from that, did we have a long history of writing? Yes, we did; too many coincidences in a row make a certainty. Here there had been an excess of fortuitous encounters. I did not believe in coincidences.

"A Sandinista, with a notable prior career during and after the revolution, is tied to one of the Mexican drug czars. There are photos that confirm it, we've seen them. . . . Rumors spread that the CIA has a mole inside the Sandinista elite, someone they caught with his hands in someone else's pocket, and they're blackmailing him with that. . . . They tell us that Machado had relations with the Mexican drug dealers to make deals and buy arms for the Salvadoran army, after the Sandinista shipments ceased. . . . Machado has a joint bank account with a Chicano named Valencia. . . . A Mexican gunman dies in front of the door of his hotel room. . . . All facts up to there, now your questions, then mine: What deals did Machado have with the drug dealers? What did he give them in exchange for the money? Did he give them a base in Nicaragua? Why did the CIA want Machado if they'd already discovered him? Wasn't the scandal better? Who does Armando work for, that initially he wanted us to throw Carlos out on his head and later wanted us to shut up? Could the bank account be a Sandinista affair? Who the hell was the gunman who died in the hotel? What . . ."

Fats was coming out with the sandwiches on a plate and another one in his hand that he was eating, when the telephone stopped him, cutting my enumeration in half. . . . He listened carefully for a few seconds.

"Thank you, my queen," he said, hanging up, and then he told me: "Elena says they just announced on the radio that Rolando M. Limas died in a shootout in a cabaret. A duel with a police officer. Both died, a few hours ago. . . ."

"Bloody hell, what is this?"

I took the plate with my sandwich. It was raining. I leaned out the window to see the storm. It's always raining in Mexico City, and when it's not raining, you feel as if it's about to rain.

"Someone is cutting off the loose ends. Who? Machado himself? The Nics? Your compatriots?" Fats asked.

The doorbell rang. With my glasses in my hand I went to the door. Carlos Machado, dressed in an ill-fitting gray suit, no tie and dripping water from every corner, smiled at me.

"They told me at the Embassy you were looking for me, boys. Do you have a towel, Fats?"

Fats handed him his half-bitten sandwich and without altering his Bogart-like expression walked down the hall. Machado took a bite of the sandwich. I hesitated an instant; I concealed my confusion searching for a lighter to light a cigarette that I couldn't taste at all; then I handed him the page I was reading.

"Read this, Commander, then talk to me."

"Thanks, Greg."

Machado sat down on the floor, on a cushion that Fats had bought in Laos, nibbling at someone else's sandwich. Julio appeared with a towel.

"You gave him my notes?" I nodded. "That's what I was going to suggest," he said to me. We stood there looking at the Sandinista.

"I didn't kill that kid, I was with the Australian journalist in her hotel. But I think that if this is a setup, she'll deny it. Will you believe me?"

Fats didn't answer, I grumbled something unintelligible.

"Son of a bitch. This CIA stuff makes me laugh. The bank account stuff. . . . I have never in my life seen it, but if you lend me the number, we'll empty it and teach those assholes to open a bank account in my name."

He raised his eyes and looked at me. "I don't know anything. I don't know Limas, I've never seen him. Do you have the photo where they say I'm with him?"

Fats walked over to the file cabinet, took out the photo and handed it to him.

"Shit! That's me," Machado said. "But I don't remember. Where is it? And April sixth? I was in Mexico, but I don't remember the gentleman."

"It's in Puebla."

"Gosh, even if it's me, I wasn't in Puebla that day."

"And the stuff about the arms to the Salvadorans?"

"Don't fuck around. If we could have given them arms, we would have, but you can already see where this thing is going." He made a gesture as if wanting to explain the absurd complexity of the international situation.

"What color was the Australian's pubic hair?" Fats asked.

"Dark bone," Machado said, apologizing for himself. "What shit, what a first-class setup they're pulling on me. . . ."

He returned the photo to Fats and attacked the sandwich.

"And now what, *compadre*?" Fats asked me. "Do we believe this guy?"

"What the hell do I know?" I answered, looking at the Sandinista commander of mythic proportions, who, without letting go of his Serrano ham sandwich, was drying his head with the towel.

"It's okay then," Carlos Machado said, smiling at us, revealing the crumbs of the sandwich between his teeth.

"Do you want another one?" Fats asked.

And even if there were a novel in this, it was a novel Fats and I would never write. A wonderful novel written with four hands that would never be written, with an uncertain ending, whose core would be about information and the journalistic ethic, and the stories one knows but doesn't know, and a city where it rains incessantly, waiting for a catastrophe and a Sandinista commander eating a second Serrano ham sandwich with such a happy face he couldn't possibly be a CIA agent.

O N E   H U N D R E D   T H I R T Y - O N E

ALEX ORDERED A
DOUBLE VODKA WITH
A . . .

. . .lemon twist as soon as he sat down in the wide seat of the airplane cabin. The only reason to travel first class was to leave no space between boarding and the first sip.

Part of Snow White was failing, the most important part. It was vanishing as if it were a paranoid Walt Disney dream. They might be able to recover fragments, debris from the disaster. He was going to have to make a lot of explanations. He was going to have to revise all his theories on coincidence. He was going to have to work as a slave in the Libya section for six months.

Alex ordered his second double vodka and through the window contemplated the lighted magic carpet extending below for scores of square miles. Yellow and green lines, intricate designs that started off geometrical and ended up abstract, the red sparkle of the avenues illuminated with magnesium and tungsten, the mercurial whiteness, the glow born of seven million television sets turned on, half a million cars circulating with their headlights opening the darkness, three hundred thousand light posts, street-lamps, open refrigerators, night-table lights, even several million candles. What a city, a great scene, a Bosch painting subjected to the electric chair. He swore to himself he would never again get involved in Mexican operations, this country was annoyingly unpredictable.

He knew he wouldn't keep his promise. Promises about Mexican things were created to be broken: they are something you make to forget later, like juvenile passions, which when gone back over make the whole affair more amusing.

He ordered a third vodka and began designing a new operation. He would call it: "Electric Blanket." A small homage to corrupt Mexico City.

THE MAKING OF A DRUG
TRAFFICKER'S LEGEND
(IV)

Ever since you disappeared, Rolando, nothing is the same. Some jerk is even going around calling the Río Bravo the Rio Grande and nobody corrects him. We all walk around deaf. Out there in Nogales, a couple of assholes removed some asshole's guts with their knives, but neither of them dared to eat the dead jerk's liver, as they say you once did. Now you don't deprive them of sleep, with the sleep you never indulged in on the boulevards of Hermosillo and now they even grow pot in the flowerpots of the La Raya municipal presidents.

They say you were so invisible you almost disappeared, and that's why you fled to a leper colony in Mexico City where they treat people who are losing bits of themselves, but you chose the wrong city, pal. In that city you die just breathing in the failures, in that city even assholes die, those who must be worth something if they came from the North, now they're from here, and you, asshole, take the road the other way, going back from where they go, returning. This is why you're only half, this is why you're fading away and you're now incomplete, from going around smelling that air that kills and you walk around out there wearing a blue raincoat which if you take off, later, later, we'll see that you're missing an entire side. You're only half.

Others say none of that, that it's all baloney. That you died to show them how. But now they've already forgotten. A duel in the sun with two .45s in the middle of the street. The broadest you could find, a stupid central road thirty yards wide. They say it was a dogfight, in the sweet afternoon, with marimba music and the sound of fantasy horns, three hundred cockroaches playing "Camelia the Texan" afterward, once the echoes of the shots had died down; jukeboxes beating to the rhythm of the smoke that rose from the long barrels of the .45s. And neither you nor the other asshole stuck around to see it, to blow it away.

That's what they say, but there's no one left to believe it, because lately they even lie poorly around here. Not even the fucking rumors have the same taste as the ones before. They say you didn't even make it to the funeral. Food for the dogs. Mexico City's rain dissolved you.

That's why, knowing that this rain doesn't get you wet but kills you, we no longer wait for you. We waited but now we stopped waiting. Or rather, now you're gone, asshole. And here, it's out of sight out of mind. But they say you come back on weekends, on a chartered plane to Tijuana, for no reason but to remember, to recall how it feels when they put new red carpets under your feet and when they light your Camel cigarettes with twenty-dollar bills. That's why, if you really do come back.

And if you don't come back. . . .

We the last assholes, the biggest shits, the worst bastards, will stay here taking care of the border for you, as if it were our daughter, our saintly mother, watching that nobody crosses the line and leaves us without a job.

We, the biggest dicks, the biggest assholes, the biggest asses, kiss your shadow, Rolando M. Limas.

Marcelino the dwarf, Tijuana
December 2001

DAISIES

Max opened the door of his East Hollywood home and the mailman, without looking at him, handed him a postcard.

The old photographer walked to the room where the television was on. He studied the postcard front and back, not letting the game show he was watching distract him.

On one side, palm trees, beaches and the tropics. But the postcard had been sent from Mexico City. Where the hell were the palm trees, sand and tropical sun in Mexico City? He smiled, thinking about the trick his old companions had tried to play on him. Stoyan's writing was less steady than usual, the leaves of his daisy trembled. Saturnino's was still the daisy of a man who'd never cultivated flowers. "These are strange times. We're thinking of you," said the note accompanying the flowers. Max put it aside, on the arm of the chair.

He slowly swallowed a sip of the ginger ale and bourbon he was drinking. He fixed his eyes on the TV screen, but no longer saw the images across it. He dozed off thinking of palm trees, tropical sun, seagulls softly gliding over an overwhelming blue sea. Seagulls over a large field of daisies.

CONFIDENTIAL REPORT

. . . that this jury recommends the acceptance of the thesis proposal entitled "The Paths of Disinformation," in application for a graduate degree in social anthropology by the candidate Elena Jordan, omitting further evaluation, by virtue of the problems listed in the history of this document, in particular, subparagraph b (seventeen previously rejected proposals) and r (the penal lawsuit against the authorities of the school of which the aforementioned has given notice).

Yours faithfully,
Dr. Mario Limón
Copilco, June 1989

FIFTEEN DAYS LATER IN CUERNAVACA

The sun hit the white walls of the front patio where a small stone fountain spurted up a thin stream of water. A maid dressed in a white apron led the two reporters to the back of the house. The fat Mexican sported a thick beard; the small North American was weighed down by an enormous telephoto camera.

Greg Simon and Julio Fernández exchanged a couple of conspiratorial looks. They hadn't seen any kind of security. There was no bodyguard; not even an electronic alarm system. Crossing an enormous room, they came out to a porch in the back overlooking the swimming pool. The house seemed to be in the process of reoccupation: a few paintings on the floor, furniture still covered with sheets, a huge unopened chest in the middle of the room. The smell of stewing chicken soup emanated from the kitchen. Elena was sitting on the porch wearing a T-shirt that Fats recognized as his over her bikini; the tape recorder was on. The North American was not in sight. The journalists tried to adapt themselves to the change from the sun's brilliance on the white walls to the semi-darkness of the porch.

"Fats, you came after all! And you brought Greg!" Elena said, standing up to draw them to the table. In the shade, a North American of an undefinable age, somewhere between the low fifties and low sixties, very white long hair, a bony face with a jutting jawbone and bristly cheeks from three days of not shaving and a slightly erratic stare from powerful blue eyes, observed the two recent arrivals.

After the introductions, the old North American, whom Elena introduced as Brandon Smith and who had a firm handshake, continued looking at the two journalists. Greg held his gaze.

"You are very popular in certain circles. In the Agency, for example, you are read with great interest."

"Unfortunately, we cannot read everything the Agency writes about us," Fats said. Greg aimed the telephoto lens, the North American made a face, but even so, remembering Katherine's wise lessons, Greg snapped the shot.

"I guess no one can read everything the Agency writes. It's a great paper-producing, computer disk-filling machine," he said, recovering from the minor incident.

As the retired CIA agent played insignificant verbal games with Fats, Greg studied him closely. He saw the same thing Elena saw in him. The man had the fascination of Conrad's self-destructive and morbid characters and Peter O'Toole's decadence in that movie where he played a film director. He was a guy with a sickly aura, a snake-charmer.

"I understand that Elena is interviewing you about stories the Agency has not yet made public, issues of disinformation, Mr. Smith," Greg ventured.

The old gringo nodded.

"And how long ago did you retire?" Julio asked.

"A couple of years ago, after Colby died, I prudently waited a few months and. . . ."

Some sixty-five feet away, in a corner of the pool, over a garden, a dwarf played the maracas to a cross-eyed buxom gringa wearing a bikini three sizes too small. Julio thought he heard the rhythm of *"Mama Iñes."*

"Okay, we'll retire," Fats said. He did not want to lose the day. Elena dissolved into gratitude and, after making a formal date for the next day, stuffed her notebooks, books and tape recorder into her enormous beach bag. They left the house led by the same wooden-faced maid.

"That was Fernández and Simon?" the cross-eyed woman asked once they'd left.

"That's right, Eve," Alex answered, tearing at his hair. "They don't seem like much, do they? The funny thing is that, like me, they don't believe in coincidences. . . . You can make people like that dance to the sound of your own orchestra."

Julio hesitated at the hall door.

"Where are we going to find a taxi?"

"Let's go eat *carnitas,*" Greg suggested.

"You've got to hear what he told me today, an insane story about Nicaragua. . . . You really would have laughed, he alone is giving me my thesis," Elena said, waving her cassette.

"Do you like the guy?" Julio Fernández asked his colleague, Greg Simon.

"Not a bit, but that's what this is about, right? I couldn't like an imperialist, retired from disinformation."

An old shiny white Cadillac appeared on the cobblestone road in the middle of the laurels and stopped in front of them.

"Can I take you somewhere?" Armando asked. He was dressed in a gorgeous white suit and a floral-printed vest.

THE VERSION OF EMILIO SALGARI'S *GOOD-BYE TO MOMPRACEM* CREATED BY STOYAN VASILEV IN THE PLEVEN PRISON

They found themselves in a strange underground cell, a kind of pit dug into the rock. About thirty feet up, tropical vegetation hung over the ledges. Yanez shook his head several times and stood up. They'd left him his cigarettes and his gun. What had happened to the *Vengador*?

"Come on, about time, little brother. Give me a cigarette, I didn't want to ask you before so as not to wake you," Sandokan said.

"Where are we?"

"I don't know. But every once in a while a man up there dressed like a beggar appears and sends down a basket of food."

As if by an incantation of Sandokan's words, at the mouth of the pit thirty feet overhead, a series of torches appeared.

"You're finally awake, it took you a long time, perhaps too long," said the unmistakable voice of their enemy, Stal Inchu. "I wanted to come say goodbye to you. . . ."

The torches illuminated the old Chinese man's face smiling at them for an instant. The sound of locks and chains could be heard.

Sandokan shot at the opening of the ceiling that was mechanically closing, but his old friend had retreated in time. The bullet must have injured one of the torch-bearers, because before the last sign of light disappeared behind the crack, they heard a dull scream.

"One less wretch," said the Tiger.

Yanez parsimoniously lit his pipe. Sandokan was hitting the walls of the small underground cell where they were imprisoned with his kris, trying to find some fissure, some hole in the impenetrable stones.

"Now what's going to happen, little brother?" the Tiger asked.

"I suppose they'll take advantage of the high tide of the river to flood this small cell and drown us. Have you noticed some of our predecessors' bones blanching in that corner?"

"They could also throw down a basket full of cobras or some local variety of poisonous snakes," Sandokan said, smiling.

"Or drop a couple of orangutans in heat . . . or inundate this small pit with burning fig leaves for their toxic vapors to carry us to the worst possible death."

"They could do something even worse," Sandokan said. "They could forget about us forever. They could leave us here for years, dozens of years, until even our bones would be unrecognizable. Until even our friends wouldn't remember us. They could condemn us to oblivion."

"No, they couldn't, they hate us too much," Yanez answered with a smile.

Sandokan stopped searching for a nonexistent hole in the rocks with his double-edged kris and fell to the floor.

"Can you see me?" Yanez asked.

"No, little brother, where are you? Wait, now I can, I can make out the embers of your pipe."

"You know what?" said the Portuguese, his voice perhaps a little more hoarse than usual. "Sometimes I think they'll never do it. . . . They'll never be able to kill us, and if they somehow did, no one would believe them. Because others would then dream they were us."

"So many times they've said we were dead, little brother, what's one more time, even if this time it's true," Sandokan answered.

For a moment, all that was heard in the underground cell was Yanez's laughter, drowning out the sound of the water that entered by hidden pipes, and the hissing of the poisonous snakes, and the orangutans' grunts and the crackle of the burning, envenomed fig leaves emitting their malignant fire.

"Now I know how we're going to get out of here," the Portuguese suddenly said.

"How?" asked the Tiger of Malaysia, with a lilt of hope in his voice.

"Stubbornness. You'll see, little brother," Yanez said, and his teeth shone in the darkness in a diabolical, affectionate, brotherly and fraternal smile. . . .

Mexico City, April '86–November '89